P9-CNI-182

Received On:

OCT 3 1 2015

Ballard Branch

NO LONGER PROPERTY OF
SEATTLE PUBLIC LIBRARY

ALSO BY KAREN OLSSON

Waterloo

ALL THE
HOUSES

ALL THE
HOUSES

KAREN
OLSSON

FARRAR, STRAUS AND GIROUX   NEW YORK

Farrar, Straus and Giroux
18 West 18th Street, New York 10011

Copyright © 2015 by Karen Olsson
All rights reserved
Printed in the United States of America
First edition, 2015

Library of Congress Cataloging-in-Publication Data
Olsson, Karen, 1972– author.
    All the houses : a novel / Karen Olsson. — First edition.
        pages   cm
    ISBN 978-0-374-28132-8 (hardback) — ISBN 978-0-374-71419-2 (e-book)
    1. Families—Washington (D.C.)—Fiction.   2. Domestic fiction.   3. Political
fiction.   I. Title.

PS3615.L755 A79 2015
813'.6—dc23

                                                               2015023333

Designed by Abby Kagan

Our books may be purchased in bulk for promotional, educational, or business
use. Please contact your local bookseller or the Macmillan Corporate and
Premium Sales Department at 1-800-221-7945, extension 5442, or by e-mail
at MacmillanSpecialMarkets@macmillan.com.

www.fsgbooks.com
www.twitter.com/fsgbooks • www.facebook.com/fsgbooks

1   3   5   7   9   10   8   6   4   2

This is a work of imagination that draws from the historical record.
Some details of the Iran-Contra Affair have been altered,
and although certain characters are based on real people,
here they exist in an invented world.

TO MY FAMILY

I have been here in the city for more than twenty years already. Can you even imagine what that means? I have spent each season here twenty times . . . The trees have been growing here for twenty years, how small should a person become under them. And all these nights, you know, in all the houses.

—FRANZ KAFKA

PART ONE

PART ONE

For a few years my father was known. I mean his name was known, in Washington. It floated in the swirl of names around the Reagan White House: not a big name, not a Weinberger or a Deaver, a Casey, a Meese, but one that surfaced every so often in print, toward the end of a piece in *The Post*. At other times his name was hidden, that is to say he was quoted anonymously, as a source within the administration. A source orbiting close to the sun. He worked for the State Department as a deputy assistant secretary and briefly for something called the Office of Programs Review and then joined the National Security Council staff, where he remained through the spring of 1987. So he was known to the people that knew people.

I remember certain signs of his authority, the deference of other dads, for instance, who asked for his opinions while their daughters, my friends, fidgeted and tugged at their sleeves. I remember the tan-colored telephone in his study that we weren't allowed to touch, which I now know to have been a secure communications device, and then there was the fact that he was so rarely home, and tied up on that sacred line when he was home.

Still, I wouldn't call him a "Washington insider." He never had the social chops for that—no clubby inclinations, no instinct for placing himself at the center of the story. He didn't want to be there, that's my hunch, if only a hunch, since back then I was a girl, and I thought he was important in the way that kids think their dads are important. He was the dad, the smartest man in the world, who left before dawn every morning for his big-deal job (something I felt pride about but hardly understood) and who was more significant to us, my sisters and me, for having built all our wooden beds himself, for snaking the drains when they were clogged, imposing the punishments when we strayed, paddling us down the rivers of Maryland and Virginia in rented canoes, and taking us out for dinner at the Magic Pan or the American Café. And now that I am—I still hesitate to say this—an adult, it's not the peak of his government career but the abrupt ending that I remember most vividly.

One Saturday morning in December 1986, two men showed up on our porch. I happened to be in the front room, prone on the sofa, when I saw them through the window: a couple of men wearing overcoats. I'd been waiting for my older sister because it was basketball season, and on those winter Saturdays we were due at the school gym at 10:00 a.m. sharp. She often made us late to practice, though, and then the two of us had to run extra sprints, a.k.a. suicides. So beforehand, I would lie on the sofa and attempt a kind of ESP summons, trying to will her downstairs by repeating her name in my head, over and over, until the sounds forced their way out of my mouth and I would shout: *Court-ney!*

That morning I kept quiet. I answered the door. The taller of the two men had a briefcase, his bare red fingers curled around the handle, and the shorter one was carrying flattened file boxes under one arm. They said nothing at first, as though each were waiting for the other to begin, or maybe they expected me to speak up. I didn't say "Yes" or "Can I help you" but just waited. I already knew them to be adversaries. Then one of them, the taller one, asked for my dad by name, and what struck me as strange was not that I'd suddenly found myself acting out a scene from TV (the one in which detectives knock on a door, and the door is answered by a woman or a kid)—no, that wasn't strange, since some part of me still believed that life would eventually take the shape it took on television. What was strange to me was how young the men seemed, younger than my teachers, much younger than my parents.

It was a long time ago, but I do believe that these things I recall are more or less true. A sourness in my stomach. The way my socks slouched around my high-tops. How I found my father after I went to get him: lying on the kitchen floor with his head inside the sink cabinet, surrounded by the spray bottles and desiccated sponges he'd taken out of there. He grunted as he fiddled with the pipes. I told him some men had come to see him, and when he pulled himself out of the cabinet, he had a small wrench in his mouth. (He *was* always trying to fix something, whether or not he was fixing the sink on that particular day.)

At practice we ran and ran and ran. When we got back, Dad was still in his study, and the men were still in there with him. Our mom had taken a quiche from the freezer, as though these visitors were friends who would join us for brunch once they'd finished whatever they were doing, and I remember how angry she was after Courtney and I, gobbling up whatever we could find, ate more than half of that quiche. Still frozen in the middle. To Mom, the fact that we hadn't heated it up or used forks made things worse. And even then, even as she was asking us how come we had to go and stuff absolutely everything down our craws, the house was so quiet, all fogged up with a silence that her words, or the sounds of the faucet or the refrigerator door, wound their way through without dispersing.

Courtney started up the stairs, and I trailed after her, and just as she reached the second-floor landing, the taller of the visitors came out of the study. For a second or two we all froze: this man (who, I could see now that he'd taken off his coat and rolled up his sleeves, had fleshy arms) and the two of us in our sweatshirts and shorts and damp socks. As if he were one sort of deer and we were another. Courtney tossed out a "hi," like a challenge. From behind I saw her stand up straighter, and when she started walking again, it was the walk of a girl who knows she's being watched. The man looked, then caught himself looking, coughed out a "hello" and turned toward the hall bathroom. Courtney bolted up the next flight of stairs, to her bedroom on the third floor, and I slipped into mine on the second.

Maggie came in and sat down next to my bed. She asked whether Dad would be arrested. I said the men had probably come to the wrong house, though by then they'd been there for more than three hours. She lay down on the rug and arranged my lip gloss and chapstick tubes into a geometrical design while I turned the pages of a magazine I had already read.

Up in her room, Courtney turned on her stereo, and I could hear the muffled extremes of a song, a pulsing bass joined by the off-and-on babble of a synthesizer's high notes. I guessed that she'd climbed out onto the roof to smoke, something she did even when our parents were home, daring them to go up there and catch her at it. They never did. Wanting to catch her myself, I opened the window for a whiff of the cigarette. Then we heard slow, heavy footsteps descending the stairs, and we hurried into our parents' room, which overlooked the street, to watch as the men carried their file boxes, now filled with the contents of Dad's desk, to a gray sedan.

And did I really see one of our neighbors, Mrs. Morse, watching from her doorway? That might be an embellishment, some stock image that I converted to memory. The day that the FBI agents came and seized Dad's files, I had no idea who they were, what was happening. Even after they left, we weren't told. Although the idea that parents should communicate openly with their children was on the rise in 1986—we were supposed to have heart-to-heart talks about drugs and sex and feelings—our mom and dad didn't really go in for all that. Drugs and sex were not mentioned, never mind matters of the heart. We were more of a head-to-head family. I used to see this as a failure, the failure to speak honestly and candidly. In my twenties I decided it was my parents' great flaw, though I've since come to recognize that (surprise!) I'm much more like them than I once believed.

What do I really remember from that day, what would I state for the record? We were all in different parts of the house when they came. I was lying on the sofa. Even before the men rang the doorbell, I sensed a shift in the light, or the tone, or the key. A yellowness. They stayed for a long, long time.

And suicides: hurtling forward and back, forward and back, on jelly legs, from one line on the court to another, slapping the floor with our hands. My sister was fast that day. I chased her, flailing, never catching up until the very end, when we stumbled right out of the gym and through the lobby and out the door, drawing icy blades of air into our lungs. As I ran, parts of songs would spin in my head, one bleeding into the next, *you and me, my part time lover,* and *la di da di we like to party* and then, when everything else had been wrung out, a bit from the *Black Beauty* record we'd listened to on our plastic turntable when we were younger. After each chapter had come a sung chorus about the poor horse's plight: *Black Beauty! In the wind and the rain!* We used to tear around the house singing that.

A few days after my thirty-fourth birthday, in October 2004, my dad had emergency surgery. He went to the hospital with chest pains and was discharged the following week with a huge scar on his torso and a vein from his leg sewn into his heart. He was sixty-three at the time. I relied on Courtney and later Dad himself for reports by phone and e-mail about his recovery, reports that only renewed my anxieties, that only marked the beginning of the wait for the next useless report. There came a spell of cool, windy nights when I'd be in my Pasadena apartment, watching but not really watching the TV campaign coverage, and on the screen would be John Kerry's long mug jawing away, as outside the wind shushed the city with all its own failed campaigns, its canyons full of taillights, and Kerry would remind me of my dad, in a way that was hard to put my finger on, since there was little physical resemblance. It could've been that both of them had been forged by Washington into unnatural versions of themselves, not that I knew what the natural version of Kerry would've been, not that I knew in my dad's case either. Or maybe it was just that both had been kicked in the balls when they weren't expecting it—even though they should've expected it, Kerry should've known they'd come after him with their steel-toed boots on, that they'd hit him with every last thing they could dream up, Swift Boat and all, just as my dad should've known he was getting in over his head back in '85 and '86.

My parents had long since divorced, and my father now lived by himself, which I'd fretted about in an abstract way before then, but after his surgery it was like I'd had an extra thing installed in my own heart, a black vein full of worry. "I'll just come now," I told Dad over the phone. "I'll get a flight tomorrow."

"You don't need to do that. The doctors said I'm doing well. They're transferring me to rehab in a couple days."

"Have you talked to Mom?"

"She called. She was already planning to be in town next week, so she'll stop by, I think."

"I'll come next week too. You're just going to be sitting in that rehab place."

"No reason you should have to sit there too. Why don't you come at Thanksgiving? I'll buy you a ticket."

"I'll buy it. You don't have to buy it."

"Just e-mail me some dates."

I couldn't tell how he was doing. I tried to ask him, for example, whether he was in pain, and he would answer by listing the medications he was taking. Vicodin, Lovenox, Plavix: oddly menacing names all built from the same kit. "I'll have to get one of those geriatric tackle boxes for all this junk," he said. He would make jokes about how he was an old man now, but I suspected it was true, the surgery had marked the close of middle age for him, and now here was the next (the last) act. Although he said he was fine, his voice was thin and evasive.

I would tell him the same thing, that I was fine, but in fact I'd had a tough year. My boyfriend and I had broken up, I'd briefly dated another man who revealed himself to be an awful and disgusting person, and then I promptly dropped into a depression like it was a hole in the sidewalk. I began to dread leaving the apartment. I would stare out the window at the sunburned man on the

corner, who would arrange fruit in upturned straw hats of the same
kind he wore on his head, jumbo strawberries and pineapples so
sweet you could practically smell them from my bedroom. He sold
these marvels for not very much money at all, the prices marked
in childish handwriting on pieces of cardboard. As summer wore
on, I'd spent more and more of the day in bed, watching C-SPAN.
I looked forward to the speeches of Senator Byrd the way other
homebound women might look forward to *Guiding Light* or *Oprah*,
and I sent long e-mails to my sisters complaining about Congress
and the Bush administration and Karl Rove and so on. How boring it was to be depressed! And in this case, the boringness of my
depression somehow got all muddled with the boringness of our
nation's capital. I had bad ideas about how to jazz things up. I'd
been trying, fitfully, to make the switch from production crew
person to writer, and to that end I'd found myself a manager named
Phil Franklin. He would call, and I would float notions for movies,
say, a film in which malevolent robots from Dallas take over the
White House. Or a television series called *Appropriations*, about
short, ugly male lobbyists and their hot wives.

Phil was a decent but impatient man who had prominent ears
that he was self-conscious about and that he would try to hide by
wearing one of those snap-brimmed tweed caps—which only made
him look goofier, since the L.A. weather for the most part wasn't
tweed-cap weather. And anyway the ears stuck out from under the
cap. This futile cap nevertheless seemed right for him, as Phil was
theoretically capable of listening but was always half-covering his
ears, generating too much interference to listen for very long. I
couldn't make it through a sentence without hearing him start to
type on the other end of the line. Granted, the quality of my pitches
might have had something to do with it. We had agreed on a brand,
the Helen Atherton brand, a quirky-funny-girl brand, not compatible with robot political thrillers. "People don't go to Sur La Table
to get their oil changed," Phil told me, and I couldn't decide whether
he was being sexist or just unhelpful. "They go there for kitchen
shit," he said.

The real problem, though, was that my whole sensibility had not aged well. In my twenties, everything had been funny, everything had been absurd. Back then, "quirky" had positive connotations. But some time after my thirtieth birthday, I started to feel as though I were parodying myself when I tried to be amusing, and besides, I wasn't as quick as I'd been, or as up-to-date. My timing was off. My jokes became barbs. I felt like this somewhat desperate single woman who was trying too hard. Not a summer month went by that I didn't spend a thousand dollars going to somebody else's wedding. Occasionally I would call one of my sisters in tears, and I would talk about leaving Los Angeles, because it was the only way I could think to change my life. "Maybe I should just move," I'd say.

There was a time when they would encourage me to hang in there, but lately they were more likely to offer suggestions of where to move, such as Missoula, Montana. That came from Maggie, who must've had some fantasy about Missoula. And Courtney hinted that D.C. was a different place now than it had been when we were growing up. I might like it if I gave it a chance.

Hell to the no, I thought when she said it. Ever since I was a teenager I'd made my own special thorn out of Washington and its faults. The segregation, the small-mindedness, the wonks. The "Where do you work?" The acronyms in response. The weight of institutions and of so much self-inflation. The blazers, the pearl necklaces, the bow ties, the stuffed shirts, the eager-beaver bullshitters. The rules and regulations. The righteous nonprofits. The low, drab buildings and the alphabet streets, the statuary, the Potomac, the traffic circles, the Metro, the Tourmobiles, Wisconsin Avenue, Mazza Gallerie! My lame hometown, that is to say the soft, white, northwestern portion of the city where I grew up. Throughout high school and college all the futures I imagined for myself unfurled themselves elsewhere, anywhere else, Rome, Missoula, Mongolia, the moon, if only because I thought nothing good would ever happen to me in Washington, D.C. Nothing bad either. Nothing at all.

And yet. From time to time I would feel a tug and know that I was leashed to the city, leashed in some way I didn't understand or like. Some might call that tug a homing instinct, but is there actually such a thing in humans? And if so, is it really that we want to go back to the place we came from, or is that wish just a proxy for the desire to go back in time, to return to childhood? All I can say is that as I grew older my contempt for the city loosened, it was like a lid that I could lift up, and underneath it was this lousy longing to go there. A part of me did want to return home, the home that was still, in spite of my having lived in other places for fifteen years, Washington, D.C. All I needed was a reason, and when my father had surgery I knew that I would go back and help him while he healed.

I didn't leave immediately. I figured that I might stay in D.C. through the holidays, and so I had to make arrangements for a long absence. Then there was the fact that by moving there, even temporarily, I'd be doing precisely what Courtney had been telling me I needed to do. I'm not proud of it, but because my older sister had instructed me to go, I delayed going. We had these ridiculous conversations. I would ask her, "When should I come?"

"It's really up to you," she would say.

"Won't he need someone at the house with him? I could just come. I'm kind of between things anyway."

"If you want to—"

"Well, I'm saying, if he needs somebody—"

"If you're asking me whether he'll manage without you, the answer is yes. If you're asking me whether you should come see Dad who just had heart surgery—"

"He told me to wait until Thanksgiving."

"Of course he would say that."

"I'm trying to figure out the best time and how long to come for. If now's the best time—"

"I can't tell you what to do."

The rehab place where my father had been sent was called the Renaissance Center. Naturally I pictured the staff prancing about in doublets and breeches, gnawing on big turkey legs. I couldn't get Dad to tell me much about what it was actually like there. I would ask him questions you might ask a child. What did he eat for lunch? Had he made any friends? Never had he been more opaque to me. I couldn't muster much to say, but I hated to hang up the phone and think of him returned to his wheeled bed, the emphysemic who shared the room, the TV. I asked Maggie, Do you think he's depressed? I would be, she said.

On the day I finally left L.A., the sun was wearingly sharp, and the bougainvillea had metastasized, and suddenly I felt sure of my decision. I was going to Washington! It did occur to me that I was going not just to help my dad and maybe not even primarily to help my dad. Westward ho, that had been me in my twenties (pun intended), but now the winds were all blowing the other direction, to the east. In the nation's capital, I would practice restraint. I would wear small gold earrings and date men who wore blazers. I would read the front section of the newspaper in its entirety. I would live like an East Coast city-dweller, without a car. These were the sorts of ideas that accompanied me to the District of Columbia, ideas of an entire new life I would lead, for a month or two at least. And! (I told myself) I would work on a Washington screenplay I'd started a few years earlier, neglected but not forgotten. I would reinvigorate it with on-site research. With boots on the ground!

Suddenly my boots—ankle boots—were on the ground. I had boarded an airplane, a red-eye, and instead of sleeping dropped eighteen bucks on three flagonets of Jack Daniels, which, I told myself, would be the last of my drinking for some time. It was a more serious city, Washington, and I intended to approach it soberly. And there I was, a woman in an out-of-season and out-of-style denim miniskirt stepping off a plane at Dulles, tipsy, stricken, already asking myself *What have I done? What have I done?*—already sensing the walls on every side of me encroaching, and the curved roof above my head about to come crashing down.

And there they were to greet me. All the Washington fathers. The terminal was full of them. I mean the men of Northwest and the near suburbs, men of the jogging paths, of the offices and lacrosse game sidelines, in their parkas and loafers. Analysts, economists, attorneys, administrators, lobbyists, consultants, chiefs of staff. A tribe of which my own father was a senior member, by age if not by rank. He'd insisted on taking a cab out to meet my flight, he said it would be fine, he had nothing better to do, and after following a stream of groggy Angelenos to the baggage claim I found him waiting there to claim me, my lanky, hapless father, smiling so brightly it made me want to look away. Baggage, oh yes. His broad face had a way of letting on more than he knew he was letting on, and no airplane cocktail was shield enough: my heart jumped up, the teenager in me shoved it back down, and I shut my eyes for a second, beholding there the reddish blooms of a detonating headache. I reminded that teenager to love him as I opened my arms, and we squeezed each other quickly.

He looked better than I'd feared he might. I'd worried that he would be stooped and drained and sallow. The person before me had the same pinkish skin he'd always had, and he was standing up straight, though he did seem diminished, he'd lost some muscle, I thought, and he took small, careful steps, moving with a guardedness that I also saw reflected in his eyes. Still he tried to lift my suitcase off the carousel, which was such a typical thing for him to do that I almost let him.

"I got it, Dad," I said, cutting in front of him. I started toward the doors, toward ground transportation. He stopped me with the "Helen!" he'd been barking at me my whole life, the pronunciation of my name that means "stop." He pointed the other way. "I brought the car," he said.

"I thought you weren't allowed to drive yet."

"Do you know how much a cab costs, all the way out here and back?"

"You can afford it."

"It's just driving. It's not like I went for a jog. They said four weeks, it's been three . . ." He flapped one of his arms out to the side, as if to dispense with the remaining days.

"You shouldn't have done it," I said, with a sharpness that sprang out of me, unbidden. He was already taking slow, pawing steps in the direction of the parking lots. Once, I'd followed those same legs around the hardware store, only they'd been so much larger then, his stride gigantic. I insisted I would drive.

It was almost November, and Virginia was nonsensically beautiful, the trees draped in their fall finery, and I wanted badly to smoke, though I hadn't had a cigarette in years, or months at least, months that felt like years. Signs for Langley, McLean. New buildings dotted the road, dark gray boxes with mirrored windows. At LAX I'd seen at least a dozen uniformed military personnel, tramping around the terminal in their desert camouflage, buying *People*, eating frozen yogurt, and as we passed the mirrored buildings that, my dad had explained the last time I came home, were full of homeland security contractors, I thought of those soldiers whom I'd watched with curiosity and fleeting shame.

Whenever I came back to D.C. to visit, which I did once or twice a year, I found I didn't explicitly remember how to get to most places, I couldn't have given directions to anyone else, yet if you put me behind the wheel of a car I could generally find my way. Somewhere inside my brain was a subconscious map of the city (or certain parts of it), along with who knows how many other Washington imprints. Out of the corner of my eye I saw how tightly Dad was gripping the door handle, as though he were expecting me to crash any minute, and meanwhile I was on the verge of a different kind of crash. A distress signal trilled from within. My head was starting to hurt, which must've been the whiskey's fault, or mostly the whiskey's fault.

remember a weekend afternoon when we sat at the kitchen table, Dad and I, with a big black cassette recorder between us, its heads spinning. My seventh-grade English teacher had given the class an assignment to interview an adult about his or her life and write a report, and I'd picked him. I asked questions like: What was your favorite subject in school? What were some trips you went on when you were a kid? Who were your friends? He put his elbows on the table and answered carefully but not directly, circling around the question until he landed on something that mattered to him, a story he thought was worth telling. That was the first time I heard him talk about Gerald Sayles, his favorite professor in college. He also told me about the time he and a roommate drove all the way to Guatemala, which was incredible to me, not merely that they drove there but that it was possible to drive to Guatemala at all. It was this trip, he said, that had been his introduction to Central America. I called my paper "The Biography of My Dad." Three pages, hand-written, double-spaced. It had seemed to me far more grown-up and significant than any school assignment I'd ever completed before. And I remember how the Dad I interviewed seemed distinct from the Dad I knew, my first perception (muddy, prepubescent, wordless) of the difference between people as we come to know them and people as the subjects of the stories they tell about themselves, which are not about the lives we see them living but about their most cherished departures from regular life.

As an adult I had tried, off and on, to write a screenplay about Dad and the scandal that waylaid him. It was the form I was most familiar with, and its demands—the tight structure, the periodic reversals—helped me to fill in the gaps. (Better to invent than to ask him directly. He never brought up the scandal, and neither did we.) In the draft I wrote, the government official "George Swansinger" blows the whistle on his boss, a well-intentioned but compromised national security advisor, with the help of a brassy female reporter. I never finished that script. The story I'd come up with wasn't anything like what had happened in fact, and when I complained to other people that I was stuck, they invariably (if gently) questioned whether there was really a need, at the dawn of the twenty-first century, for an Iran-Contra movie of any kind. I had those same doubts myself, and eventually I set the project aside. I couldn't get the tone right. It had toggled between satire and thriller, as though my only options were to ridicule Washington or to inject it with false drama.

My dad's real name is Timothy George Atherton.

He had a small part in that whole mess, enough of a part that he was questioned by investigators and later summoned before the congressional joint committees, and for more than two years the threat of prosecution hung over him. But he was a peripheral figure, even in a scandal crowded with obscure people. Some of them were made famous by it—not him. After he testified, during the second month of hearings, the article in *The Washington Post* was cursory, with no accompanying photograph. The record of his testimony takes up only nineteen pages in the official proceedings, and there's not much in those pages. He's one more source for a committee already drowning in data, a committee impatient to move on. None of the honorable members (Cohen, Rudman, Hamilton et al.) imply that he himself was at fault; they hardly even bother to posture, for Dad wasn't going to make the nightly news, although in his own life, this was the closest he ever came to Washington notoriety.

Page A16, lower left. "Singlaub, others, offer details on Contra funds." He was one of the "others." To this day I don't know whether to think of him as a coconspirator or a complicit bystander or just someone who was in the wrong place at the wrong time.

He still lived in the house that had been our house, the house on Albemarle Street that he and my mother bought when Courtney was one and Mom was pregnant with me. After they split up, she'd wanted to sell, but he paid her for half and preserved it, a little museum of our family-no-longer. The interior had been rehabbed from time to time—furniture had been rearranged or replaced or divvied up, rooms repainted, a wall between the kitchen and family room knocked down—but the changes had been gradual, so that it felt like the same house it had always been, though a little smaller and emptier every time. It was the house my parents had brought me home to, when I was just a wailing bald thing in a thin blanket, and the house I had left behind when I left, long-haired and pimply, for college, and the house that awaited every time I came back to visit. Not the largest or the most elegant house on the street, but a stalwart painted-brick three-story house with black shutters and squared-off columns on either side of the porch. And do they have a technical term for the kind of memory that flared during the walk I took from the driveway, along the path by the shrubbery and up the porch stairs? I mean the series of trivial recognitions—there is the concrete step, there are the porch planks, there is the brass doorknob, there is my outline in the storm door—that sum to something greater than the parts, an "Ah!" of wistfulness and dread.

Dad took advantage of my little trance and grabbed my suitcase, then started to heft it inside. I reached for it, and at first he didn't want to let go.

"I can lift a damn suitcase," he muttered, but he let me take it from him. He opened the front door and I hauled it straight up to the second floor and parked it just outside my old bedroom. I heard someone whisper "Fuck, fuck, fuck"—it was me saying it. Then I went back downstairs, still winded (no, I was not in the best shape) and suddenly at a loss for how I would occupy myself for even one day in D.C., even the half a day that was left.

The house was too cluttered and too empty. When she'd moved out, Mom had taken some of the furniture but not the boxes of videos, the board games, the paint-spattered screwdrivers, and Dad instead of getting rid of the stuff had hunkered down. Everywhere I looked I saw artifacts of our lost civilization, pot holders we'd made at summer camp, bicentennial coasters printed with excerpts from the Declaration of Independence, old headphones, a cracked lazy Susan that Dad had recently dug out and superglued. He was the museum's custodian—he kept it all up.

I tried to tell Dad about the soldiers in the airport, but what was my point? I didn't know.

"It's good that they let them board first," he said. "Do you want coffee?" I'm all right, I told him. "A beer?" It was not quite noon. I said no. He was still wearing his jacket, and he took his phone from one of the pockets. Slowly he pressed some buttons, which seemed too small for his big fingers, and then brought the device to his face. "Hi there," he said. "Helen's here."

Whenever I came to town he took great pleasure in informing the other members of our family that I'd arrived. It was Courtney he'd called, and I knew that after the call ended he'd likewise inform me about whatever task my sister was completing at work, probably a transparent excuse she'd used to get off the phone—"she's doing her expenses." Both our parents would tell my sisters and me these kinds of basic facts about the other two, as though telling us about people we didn't know well. In fact we knew one another so much better than our parents knew us that it was almost unfair, and at times it even seemed to me that when my dad reported my presence in D.C. to Courtney, or when he told me about her work, he was unconsciously asking us to give him something in return, some of our deeper knowledge. But we would never betray it, no matter how mad we sometimes were at one another, for it wasn't even something we could express in the language he spoke.

That night we went out to dinner with Courtney and Hugo. They swung by the house, and we took their car to the restaurant. Hugo, ceding the passenger seat to Dad, joined me in back—my brother-in-law and I were the kids in this group, and not just because of where we were sitting. I heard my sister and father cut in and out, their voices mingling with the radio's voices.

My sister got louder and asked, as though refuting a point he'd just made, "But how've you been feeling?" He said he was feeling well, thank you, and she asked whether he'd been taking all his pills. She said that I should double-check that he was taking them. "Helen, do you know where his pill box is?"

I pretended not to hear, scanning the Connecticut Avenue awnings for new additions. Every second or third time I came home, a new bistro or bakery would have popped up, replacing an older bistro or bakery, or else rising up from the ashes of some defunct repair shop, one of the businesses that used to exist around there, shops where the owner fixed lamps or vacuum cleaners, or would sell you one he'd already fixed. Now it was mostly upscale food. People threw broken lamps and vacuums in the garbage.

"Helen?"

Courtney had tied a soft, expensive-looking scarf around her neck, and her hair, falling over the folds of the scarf, looked expensive too. Her hips seemed wider than last time I'd seen her, I noticed after we got out of the car, and they shifted mechanically as she walked, like big wooden gears. I wondered whether she was having an affair. Recently on the phone she'd mentioned a man she worked with, mentioned him more than once, for no other reason than to relate some opinion or anecdote he'd shared with her. So I was looking for signs, a telltale glossiness, a coiled spring in her step.

She did strike me as chattier than usual. As we entered the restaurant she was cataloging for my benefit the chef's lineage, listing all the places he'd worked before this one, and at the same time she was surveying the dining room for people she knew, until at last she lit on a middle-aged couple—but no, I realized as she waved to them, they were my own age, only dressed like older people. They were precociously stodgy, but also perky, in that Washington way. It wasn't like L.A. lacked for ambitious preeners, but this city had its own brand of them, I thought, people who glowed with purpose and intramural knowledge, glowed with wonkish visibility itself, as though they were headed to or had just come from a guest spot on a political talk show. We sat down, and Courtney told me their names and the place where each one worked, which might have been law firms or consulting firms or some other kind of firms, who the hell knew.

My sister herself was the deputy director of an environmental nonprofit. Her job was to raise money from wealthy people and foundations, the same thing our mother had done for much of her career. The work didn't really suit Courtney, in that she hated to ask people for anything, but she hoped eventually to become executive director, if not there then someplace else.

"What do you guys usually get here?" I asked Hugo.

"It's all very good."

"Not all of it—remember that time the risotto wasn't hot?" Courtney said.

"Oh yes. You sent it back to the kitchen." Hugo was from Mexico City originally, and his English was more careful than a native speaker's.

"This man would never send anything back. He thinks it's rude. But I mean, it was not hot."

Dad's face, as he listened to her, seemed to become broader and livelier, full of an appreciation she'd never had to earn.

"Risotto's not supposed to be piping hot, is it?" I asked.

"Of course it's supposed to be hot."

"I just feel like I've had it when it's not all that hot."

"It was, like, cold. They took it off the bill."

I made the mistake, once we'd ordered, of asking Dad whether he was still thinking about voting for Kerry. He had been a Republican all his life, but he couldn't stand George W. Bush, in part because he thought the war in Iraq had been a terrible mistake, yet his aversion ran deeper than that. Something more fundamental offended him, the president's whole persona rubbed my father the wrong way, and after a few glasses of wine he would make overblown declarations like, "We've lost our moral standing in the world!" As if the United States' moral standing—whatever that even meant—had been untainted until Bush took office. He meanwhile joked that I had become a "Hollywood liberal." I think he really did believe that I'd come by my political leanings in California, that I'd more or less tossed them into a cart along with a bag of avocados and some flip-flops. The truth was that I'd been much more idealistic as a teenager, if fuzzily and quietly: it was when I'd last lived in the same house with Dad that I'd actually been the ardent lefty he thought I was now. Since then, we'd both inched toward the center. Earlier that year Dad had said he wouldn't vote for Bush again, and I let myself hope that he represented an entire tribe of disaffected Republicans, one that might tilt the election toward Kerry. But now he drew back and pinched his lower lip before he spoke.

"I don't trust John Kerry," he said, as though he knew the man personally. "He strikes me as a panderer."

"Oh please," Courtney said. "They're all panderers."

"Some more than others."

"So you're going to vote for Bush?" she asked.

"I may leave it blank."

"Blank?" She scoffed. She looked down at her lap and read a message on her BlackBerry that made her smile.

"What is it?" I asked her.

"Oh," she said, "work." Then she started complaining about their realtor. She and Hugo had sold their Adams Morgan condo and bought a house in Spring Valley (which was incredible to me, Spring Valley!) and it had all been very hectic and fast and stressful and thank god it was over, but now she was having déjà vu because she'd been trying to contact the realtor—she needed a forwarding address for the previous owner's mail—and she hadn't been able to get through to Bonita Pope. That was the realtor's name. It had been like that ever since the house went under contract, she said. All the subsequent back-and-forth had taken place over voice mail, a series of demands left after the beep.

"Once they've got you on the hook, that's it," she said.

"So you're moved in, that's amazing," I said.

"The whole time we were closing, we would call and call and nothing."

"But she left you messages."

"She knows our schedules. She knows when to call so that she doesn't have to talk to us."

"I can't wait to see it," I lied.

"She did leave us a nice gift," Hugo said. "It was a pie."

In the middle of the meal, Courtney excused herself, and I said I'd go with her. Although we're not those women that need or even like companionship in the bathroom, I wanted to see her away from Dad and Hugo. I was hoping for something, I'm not sure what. She walked ahead of me into the ladies' room, and we each entered a stall and then were silent.

"Dad seems like he's doing okay," I said.

"Yeah," she said, but her tone condemned me. My sister could tell me she liked my shirt and I could hear in her compliment that she thought the whole way I lived my life was incorrect.

"What do you mean?"

She sighed, which I took to mean the usual thing, i.e., that she, the only sister living in D.C., understood something that I didn't. She bore the burden of our dad, or so she'd convinced herself, no matter that she was married and worked long hours and so it wasn't as though she saw him all that often. She *knew*, and Maggie and I didn't know. I waited for more of an answer, but none came. I heard a series of tiny clicks, the sound of her fiddling with her mobile device.

Back home, in my childhood bedroom, I unpacked my clothes, clothes that looked all wrong now that I was in D.C. Too much yellow and turquoise, too much cotton jersey. Polka dots. Summery, girly things I couldn't wear there. I unpacked and then puttered, the way I always did in that room, which wasn't exactly my old room any longer—my mother had made it her office after I left for college, and so gone were the beanbag chair and the striped wallpaper, gone the glow-in-the-dark ceiling constellations, gone the taped-up photos of the cast of *The Outsiders*. But still it was my old room, sticky with old-roomness, with the residue of having lived in it from ages five to eighteen. It hypnotized me, and I did what I always did when I came back to it, which was to start opening drawers and pulling books off the shelf and rummaging in the closet, looking for scraps of my younger selves.

In other words I put off going to sleep. I never knew what my childhood bed had in store for me, because sometimes it was the most comfortable and comforting of beds, the standard by which all other beds invariably fell short, and at other times it was like there was a wormhole in the mattress—I never knew when some flood of teenage sorrow would shoot through it and overwhelm me, and I would wind up sobbing.

I picked up a picture from the bookshelf, a framed photograph with a label below it, in metallic script: *Girls Varsity Basketball 1986–87*. It was from my sophomore year, the one season that Courtney and I played on the same team together. Twelve girls wearing game uniforms, in the gym, lined up at midcourt. Six of us kneeled in front and the other six stood behind, flanked by our coach on the left and the assistant coach on the right. I stared at my grainy, remote face and then at Courtney's, remembering her then, how good a player she'd been and how confident, right up until near the end of the season. Then she'd changed, in part because she hit the adolescent skids: she was even arrested, a couple of months after that picture was taken. It was as though some switch had flipped. A light went out inside her head, or a darkness was activated.

In the photo her smile was clean and wide. We were so young! That was my gee-whiz reaction, looking at that picture. Teenagers! The eighties! Holy shit!

My first days at home with Dad, it became clear that if he needed any genuine help, he wasn't about to tell me what kind of help that might be. He was moving around more cautiously than usual, but he could manage just about everything himself, or so he insisted, and I even caught sight of him one afternoon, in his bedroom, doing exercises with some small purple hand weights that must've belonged to, then been abandoned by, one of my sisters or maybe our mom. He did let me take him to a doctor's appointment. Other than that the most useful thing I could figure out to do for him was to make lunch or dinner. A low-fat, low-salt cookbook had come into his possession, and I followed one lackluster recipe after another, most of which involved blended-up vegetables, so that the food might as well have been baby food, and though Dad and I would try to improve the situation with eleventh-hour transfusions of butter or soy sauce, usually it was too late to salvage the baked chicken, the pureed squash, the pasta with peas.

What he wanted me to help with were his projects around the house, and here I dragged my feet, because these had always struck me as make-work. He had this Protestant itch he had to scratch. Not only that, he'd been a part of that tier in Washington that

defined people by their occupations; he'd been, for many years, as
dedicated to his work as anyone; and once out of that world, missing its pace, he jerry-rigged his own treadmill. He liked to be constantly running errands and doing chores and making needless
improvements. One afternoon he asked me to go out to the shed
with him, a long narrow shed he'd put up himself years ago, where
as it turned out he was having a hard time unscrewing a plastic hose
hanger from the wall. His reason for removing the hanger was that
he'd bought a little wheeled cart for the hose instead, a summer
remainder, half off. The final screw was jammed in tight, the head
rusted, and he wanted me to brace the hanger as he worked the
drill. I didn't think it needed to be braced, but he'd grown frustrated and in his frustration needed me to be working too.

After a series of long exhales and G-rated oaths, he told me, "I
had a talk with Judge O'Neill the other night." Kit O'Neill was a
retired appellate court judge who lived down the block. Some
nights he would walk over with a bottle of Evan Williams and
wobble home after they'd drunk the better part of it—when Dad
said they'd had a talk, that's what he meant. "His son-in-law just
started law school, and he's thirty-six. Come to find out, there are
a lot of second-career attorneys these days."

I pretended that I hadn't understood him. "This is Ruthie's
husband?"

"I bet that someone with your experience in the entertainment
world—"

"I don't think I want to be a lawyer."

Actually I had considered it, like I'd considered so many things,
pouring myself a glass of wine and then sitting down with my laptop and clicking away at one web link after another, studying the
sites of various law schools, picturing my life as an entertainment
lawyer, that is to say the suits I would wear and the house I would
own. When I was younger it had seemed more important to be
interesting than rich, and law school hadn't had the slightest
allure, but the older I got, the more the idea of financial security
overshadowed whatever notions of self-actualizing I'd once had—I

could no longer even recall why I'd thought that becoming a screen-writer would help me be myself. What would help me be myself, I now thought, was money, and there was something pleasing about the notion that Dad had tipsily imagined me as a lawyer, just as I'd done.

And yet, even if it wasn't too late in principle, it was too late for me. I would not go to law school. Surely he knew that.

I used to get these e-mails from him, often time-stamped midnight or 1:00 a.m.

Helen:

The other day I ran into Roger and Ann Sullivan at Safeway. They are well. Geordie (their son) is living in New Jersey and has a job working for Bell Labs. They said he is always happy to connect with old D.C. pals and tell them about potential opportunities with the company.

You should consider opening an IRA (Individual Retirement Account) since you aren't invested in a 401k. I've attached some information.

Love, Dad

"I just thought it could be an option worth exploring," he said. He'd taken his eyes off the drill, and it was starting to carve out the center of the screw head. I pointed at it and said, "Stop, stop."

"All right," he said. "I think I know what I'm doing."

"Sorry."

"Have you talked to your mother lately?"

"Not since I left L.A. Why?"

"No reason." He patted the hanger. "You try holding it over on this side and I'll try from that side."

At last the screw came loose. I took a step back and the hanger came with me. "There we go," he said.

"So who've you been spending time with these days? Anybody besides the judge?" I asked.

"Spending time?"

"Do you still get together with the Osborns?"

"They have a place in Florida now, so they're gone all winter."

"You see Courtney, I guess."

He'd taken the hanger out of my hands, and carefully, as though it were something he intended to save, he set it down just outside the shed door. "She's very busy, as you know. And I've been busy myself. I mean I was, before the surgery."

"With teaching?"

My dad's postscandal career had been uneventful. Right afterward there'd been a scary stretch when he'd been out of work, but then he'd joined a big telecommunications company, as public affairs director. He'd been paid very well, though he never liked the job. On the side he'd taught night classes in government and policy at American University. This he loved. Many of his students were immigrants, for whom he undertook to explain the ways of our nation. A few years earlier he'd retired from the day job, and now the classes were it.

"I've also been preparing for—I've been invited to speak on a panel in several weeks. I'm preparing for that."

"What about?"

I assumed it would be related to the telecommunications industry, his area of reluctant expertise, and so I was surprised when he told me the name, a long-winded name, something about Bush's national security policy in historical context. It was at the S—— Club, he said.

"Who's sponsoring it?"

"It's a group affiliated with Hopkins. I hope you'll be able to come."

"I wouldn't miss it," I said, though something in his voice made me nervous. And was he blushing? It might've been that the cold air had reddened his cheeks. A lean gray cat had snuck into the yard, and now it padded into the shed with its tail high and hooked. "Oh hello," Dad said. We watched it for a moment, and then he added, "Too bad Maggie isn't here." There was this idea in the family that my younger sister was a cat lover, because as a kid she had followed the neighbors' cats around, though as an adult she had never owned a cat. "If Maggie were here she would bring you some milk," he told the cat. "Wouldn't you like that?" The animal completed its tour of the shed and slipped back out again. We followed in time to see it climb the back fence. It walked along the top and then disappeared.

Ours wasn't a huge yard, but it did have a pool, a rectangular one with flagstone around it. The pool had been drained for winter and covered with a sheet of green vinyl pulled taut with springs. A grid of nylon straps ran across the cover, like coordinates for locating points in the hole underneath.

Mostly how I remember that first week or two in Washington is as a series of nights, long nights in a quiet house, during which it gradually became apparent that while I had come home, supposedly, to help my father, he believed that I was the one who needed assistance. We quickly arrived at a mutual-aid stalemate. Neither of us had a clue as to how to help the other. Neither of us knew how to talk to the other: that much had been true my whole life, but only recently had I detected in myself an old, flattened-out hope, a dulled dream that we would somehow, someday be more fluent. I'd carried that hope for such a long time but hadn't named it, and even now that I recognized its existence, it was only a vector, pointing to an outcome I couldn't see or even envision.

I did little during those two weeks but was often exhausted by the evening. I'd been taking an antidepressant that had put an air pocket between me and the sadness that had paralyzed me over the summer, so that instead of feeling bad I felt neutral, even while having some of the same thoughts that had gone along with the erstwhile bad feelings. Over the summer I'd often woken up at 3:00 or 4:00 a.m. and thought, *What the hell am I doing with my life? What*

am I supposed to be doing? Is it too late for me? Now I slept through the
night, and when those questions came to me, intermittently during
the day, I just let them go by. Sometimes it was like I was watching
the movie of my life and wondering why they hadn't cut out some
of the slow parts. I don't mean that I was entirely passive, only that
there were days when I wished I could speed things up, and I couldn't.

I did still intend to rewrite my old screenplay, or reinvent it,
and so I tried to read (secretly, in my room) a long account of the
Iran-Contra Affair that I'd bought in Los Angeles. The book was a
thick, oversize paperback, exhaustive, exhausting, which I would
leave splayed facedown on the floor as I dozed off, so that its bind-
ing became a register of my naps, each one logged by a new crack in
the spine. What I did stay awake for, I couldn't wrap my head around.
To me, it was a suggestive but ultimately indigestible scandal. I'd
read other Iran-Contra books, or sections of them at least, but for
all the facts I'd taken in, if someone had asked me to explain the
whole thing I could barely have managed a summary.

Here's what I could say. The main players were a few bureau-
crats and a gang of freelance old hands, drawn to the rush of coun-
terrevolution and back-channel deals. Their foes were communists
and hostage takers, not to mention certain State Department guys
with their thumbs up their asses, not to mention the U.S. Congress.
They had encryption devices for sending secret messages back and
forth. They had secure telephones. They met with middlemen and
mercenaries in foreign cities. They kept cash in a safe. They gave
themselves false names. They got carried away with it all, and they
almost got away with it all.

Some aliases: Mr. Goode. Mr. East. Steelhammer. Max Gomez.
The Courier. Blood and Guts.

Compartmentation, that was one rule. The big box, the one that
investigators would later pry open, contained smaller boxes, which
in turn contained smaller ones. You knew only what you needed
to know, the contents of your compartment.

The men in their tiny boxes wrote memos in coded language.
They caught flights down to Miami or Tegucigalpa and glad-handed

commanders who asked for more bullets, *por favor!* During the three or four hours of sleep they allowed themselves each night, they dreamed of sorties over the jungle, of walking across hot tightropes, of cats circling. They awoke in a room in the Old Executive Office Building with three video terminals and three phones and a window overlooking a neglected courtyard. A warning bell, connected to one of the terminals, rang all day long.

Who were they? These men, or most of them, had served in Vietnam. They were in government now but not of it, no sir, they still set store by clearly defined missions and chains of command, not by the vagaries of politics. Or that was one way of putting it. Another thing you could say was that they would do almost anything to keep from abandoning other men, other fighters, the way they themselves had been all but ditched over there and then had been forced to ditch the Vietnamese in turn. Another was that they were desperate to please a genial but distant father figure, their commander in chief.

As their children must have wished to please them. To the extent the men led private lives, they led them largely in absentia. They whispered drowsy goodbyes in the early morning, called home from the office to wish the kids good night, drove the station wagon to church on Sunday. Now and again the histories of the affair will allude to families in Chevy Chase or Falls Church—for instance, there's a moment when Oliver North (a.k.a. Steelhammer, a.k.a. Blood and Guts) and a Justice Department lawyer chat about their daughters' love of horseback riding. A different set of books, the biographies and memoirs, lay out the domestic basics: where these men grew up, how they met their wives, when their children were born. More than once the reader encounters a flashback scene, circa 1970, in which the father-to-be, at his desk, learns that his wife is in labor and must speed to reach the hospital in time. The sections of black-and-white photographs, while dominated by pictures of men in the company of other men, serve up a few family snapshots too: baby pictures, Mr. and Mrs. X walking down the aisle on their wedding day, Mrs. X with their young children, and then, much later, Mr. and Mrs. X leaving the congressional hearings together, marching hand in hand past the reporters.

These photos are the ones I stare at, trying to stare them into life. My unofficial investigation would seek to discover what they said to each other and what they didn't say, the husbands and wives and fathers and children. My own final report on the matter would detail what they were able to let go of, eventually, and what continued to rankle or haunt, what they bore for years and years, after everyone else had forgotten almost everything, after their disgrace became a footnote.

One way in which the affair is remembered, for those people who remember it at all, is as a bunch of sound and fury: for all the drama, the hearings, the prosecutions, in the end nobody suffered serious consequences, at least not officially. Nobody went to prison, and those few who were convicted were later pardoned by the first President Bush. The main figures in the scandal had gone on to well-paying jobs in the private sector, and Oliver North had almost been elected a U.S. senator!

As for my father, it was true that on paper he'd done fine. But there was more to it than that.

In the evenings, Dad and I came and went, passing on the stairs or watching the news on the small television in the kitchen. Sooner or later he would go mess around with the computer. He might come to the kitchen and fix himself a drink—he liked a martini with plenty of ice—which he would take back to the study with him and sip slowly as it turned to boozy water. Or he might forget it there on the counter, and I would find it and bring it to him in his office on the second floor, where he didn't always bother to turn on the light. He'd be sitting in the dark in his captain's chair with a clog in his throat, making clogged throat noises as he checked on his stocks. A line graph on the screen in front of him.

He'd taken to playing music from his computer. With the exception of one or two Linda Ronstadt records from the eighties, Dad had kept himself ignorant of popular music after about 1975, but he liked female singers from his youth and young adulthood, a woman singing gospel or country or R&B. *Something's got a hold on me. Why am I treated so bad? Move on up a little higher! I'm too far gone.* Some of the songs were upbeat, but many more were slow and sad, so that the overall mood flowing from his study was a sad one, the same computer that plotted his stock portfolio also wailing over lost loves. It was as though he had a designated mourner in his PC.

Twice I heard him making a phone call after 10:00 p.m.—who could he be calling at that hour? I didn't know. Was he okay? Was he not okay? He seemed to me a little lonely, a little slowed by his surgery, otherwise his usual self, his usual impenetrable self.

"You know what I think would be a good TV show? A political show with regular people, instead of the professional talking heads," he was saying. I'd been cooking dinner, and he'd been keeping me company in the kitchen, drinking a beer he'd poured into a glass, both of us half-watching the news. "You'd have whatever issues that week, say it's the farm bill, and so you get a farmer and let's say a barber from out in farm country, maybe some other people who are affected economically. They could analyze it from their perspective. From inside the barber shop, even."

"Like, Sunday-morning reality TV." I was skeptical.

"The entire show could happen in barber shops. Every week a different one," he said.

"Sure."

"I think people would watch that."

"You want me to set up some meetings for you, Dad?"

"I could see a C-SPAN or even a CNN—"

He stopped short. He'd knocked his beer over but didn't bother to right the glass or wipe up the puddle on the counter. He stared at the TV. On the screen, a man near his age was being interviewed about a book he'd written. I looked back at Dad, who hadn't budged.

His eyes were bulging and his face was going red.

Oh, I thought, *oh god*. I rushed over to him.

He was trying to talk but nothing came out. I reached out my hand in the direction of his arm.

"I'll call 911," I said.

At last he said, "No! No, no . . ."

He shook his head and pointed at the TV. The man's name, it said at the bottom of the screen, was James Singletary, and his book was *A Call to Honor*. "I used to work with that—that weasel," he said. He coughed ostentatiously, like he was trying to cough a weasel up whole.

"At Intelcom? Who is he?" The name sounded familiar to me, but it was that kind of name.

"He was at the White House. Piece of work."

"Oh right. He quit pretty recently, didn't he?" I remembered: another defector from the Bush administration, now peddling a memoir of his time on the inside.

"He was also there before. He was on the NSC staff when I was."

NEW BOOK CRITICAL OF ADMINISTRATION, said the scroll at the bottom of the screen, CALLS PRESIDENT BUSH "A WEAK CONSERVATIVE."

"And?"

Dad changed the channel, then wiped up his spilled beer with paper towels.

"What was his deal? He was a hard-liner?" I pressed.

"Oh sure. They used to call him Red Menace. In his mind there were communists plotting to take over Mexico and the public school system and the Methodist church. But that was the least of it."

"What else?"

"He was always a self-promoter. I see that hasn't changed. And he was a liar. He lied. That book of his is full of lies, I guarantee you. You wouldn't believe some of the . . ." He stopped, walked over to the trash can, and threw out the soggy paper towels.

"What?"

"Forget it," he said. "Forget it."

He didn't forget Singletary, though, I knew it by how cranky and gruff he was all through dinner, he hardly ate anything, and afterward he trod heavily on the stairs, shouldering some invisible beast. And I was left with a strange and unnerving afterimage, a trace of the way his face had changed when he'd spotted his old colleague, hardening into a mask of anger that I had at first taken for something worse than that. It lingered, this wisp of what I'd seen, like the ghost that used to hover on the screen after you turned off a television. That angry mask, as I called it to mind, transformed from a rigid and superficial expression to something molten, as if I'd had a peek inside of a private furnace. As if I'd looked where I shouldn't have been looking. At the same time I couldn't keep from second-guessing Dad, from wondering whether his denunciation of Singletary had been motivated by something other than outrage. Or more than just outrage. Could it have been envy? Envy, that is, of a former colleague who had managed to hang on to his status and was now on TV touting his memoir, while Dad taught at American University as an adjunct.

Later that night I heard him talking loudly, in his bedroom. "Damn it!" he was saying. "Damn it!" I thought he was on the phone, but then I heard him say, "Damn it, Tim!" He was cursing to himself, possibly cursing himself.

A day or two after that he invited me to come to the campus with him, to see the place where he now worked. With his adjunct professorship came a shared office in the political science building, and Dad would go there most mornings, to prepare for the panel, he said. I don't know what he meant by that exactly. My guess is that he read news articles online and chatted with his officemate, a Dr. Mohammad.

I hadn't been to that campus since high school, when I'd gone to the library a few times to do research for papers, though often as not the book I'd gone looking for was missing or had pages torn out of it. The office was small and cramped. Dr. Mohammad was out.

On Dad's desk, in the same cheap frames, sat the photos that had logged years on much larger desks elsewhere, at government buildings and later at Intelcom, vacation pictures of my sisters and me, beach-brown and bug-bit, tummies pouting between the panels of our little-girl bikinis, teeth missing from our sky-wide grins.

"This is not bad," I said, a poor diplomat. But then he took me to a café in the student activities building, and as we walked there I felt better about it all. I loved to stroll alongside my father. There was something about the fresh air and the movement that took him out of himself, or rather lit up the part of him that had majored in history, and he would grow expansive, free-associating, deciding for whatever reason to tell me about the wisdom of a decision Eisenhower had made or to dredge up some little-known facts about Whittaker Chambers. His stride was strong, and in his wool overcoat and crimson scarf he drew interrogative looks—not from undergraduates but from people my age and older, trying to figure out whether he was somebody they ought to recognize.

After lunch he was quieter than usual, and when we reached the benches in front of the library he said he wanted to stop for a moment. It was cold out, and we shivered under our coats. I asked him whether he was all right. He didn't answer, nor did he sit. He said, "There's something I want to give you. It would be best that you take it." He withdrew an envelope from his coat pocket and I shrank away from it. "Dad—" I began and then stopped. It was as though this entire outing had been an excuse to give me a check, as though there were some reason he couldn't do it at the house.

If I'd said there were strings attached, he would've denied it. He would've said he just wanted to help. But that meant: to help me help myself. I could prep for the LSAT, I could apply for an internship, I could ease myself into a reputable life like a good solid car my dad had bought me, I could drive it off the lot and cruise toward retirement.

I was in fact unsettled, and had I any reason to think that a check from my father would settle me, I would've snatched it out of his hand. Or I might've taken it if I'd thought that taking it would rid him of his worries. Was it because I myself felt uneasy that I saw in my father so much discontent? But I had evidence. In the place where we'd eaten, he'd barked at the cashier because they'd run out of lemon meringue pie; he'd bemoaned that his preferred style of shoe had been discontinued by the manufacturer; and then he'd criticized the war in Iraq in the same aggrieved tone, as if all three things had come from the same source, some central kitchen of disappointment.

The reason to accept Dad's money was not that I had no savings, though it was true that I had no savings. It was not that I should've used it to subsidize a career switch, to try to hail-mary myself into whatever legitimate profession might've sheltered me, much as that would've eased his mind and maybe my own. It was that he wished for me to accept the money. Taking it would have pleased him. I didn't let him give it to me, though. I didn't even look to see the amount written on it. I'm pretty sure that if he'd been in my position, he wouldn't have taken it either.

D id I ever tell you about the time Dad took me with him to a meeting at the White House?" Courtney had asked me once, a long time ago. It was my first year out of college, when I lived in San Francisco. She'd come to stay at my little apartment on Dolores Street. We'd watched a videotape and afterward lay on the dusty rug and spoke as much to the ceiling as to each other.

"It would've been when he was working at the State Department. I think I was, like, six or seven. It was a Saturday. Mom had gone away for the weekend to see Grandma or something, and Dad had to go to a meeting."

"I have no memory of this."

"Dad brought us all over to the Behrendorfs', you and me and Maggie. He was going to leave us there while he went to his meeting. I *hated* it there, though, you had Sarah Behrendorf to play with, but I knew I was going to get stuck watching Maggie. And that house always weirded me out, it smelled weird and remember Mrs. Behrendorf, how you could always see her nipples through her shirts?

"I begged him to take me along, until finally he said that he would. That's when I found out that he was going to the White House. I was psyched. I couldn't wait to tell my friends. I remember walking in—everyone always says how the White House seems smaller than they thought it would be, but to me, as a kid, it was not small. It was a castle, and everything I saw, I thought must be the best possible way for that thing to be, like a mirror—I remember a mirror with a gilt frame, thinking that must be the best kind of mirror there is. There was this room where I was supposed to wait for Dad while he went into his meeting, it had a desk and a sofa, and the sofa was upholstered in the same fabric as the curtains. I thought, that's what fancy is, it's having a sofa and curtains that match. Dad sat me down on the sofa and said I had to keep quiet. He was using that Dad voice, you know, *Courtney, this is a very important meeting. Do not make any noise.*

"This room, it was a little office or something, was connected by a glass door to where Dad was having his meeting, but there were curtains over the glass, so you couldn't see what was on the other side. I sat on the sofa for a while. I didn't have anything to do. Then I saw this pink eraser on the desk, and I went and got that. I played with it on the floor, I don't know what I was doing, whatever a bored kid does with an eraser.

"It wound up under the sofa, I guess it rolled there, so I had to get it. I lay down on my stomach and tried to reach. It was dark under there, I couldn't see much, so I was just feeling around with my hand. Then I heard this *pop!* At first I didn't feel anything and then I did. It was a mousetrap. It closed on my hand. Right at the base of my thumb.

"I didn't know what to do. I opened my mouth and then I remembered what Dad had told me. Don't make a sound. So I didn't. I got myself back up to sitting. That metal bar was pressed into my thumb, I remember the skin bulging around it. I tried to pull it off, but that hurt even more, so I just sat there, and tears were running down my face, and I was wiping snot on my sleeve, but I was quiet the whole time. I don't know how long I waited there like that. It could've been five minutes or it could've been an hour.

"Finally Dad comes out to check on me and when he sees me he freaks out. Freaks out. I've never seen him look that way, like,

I don't even know how to describe the look on his face. 'Oh Jesus, Jesus,' he was saying. He got the mousetrap off, and then my hand started to hurt even more, and he picked me up and I think I might have peed on myself. He carried me out, he carried me all the way back to the car, and I mean that must have been hard, I was a decent size, and he was—well, definitely upset. I know we went to the emergency room, but I don't remember that much about that part, except I think I was bummed when I didn't get a cast. It turned out nothing was broken. I had a huge bruise, was all."

"I can't believe I didn't know that," I'd said to her when she was done.

"You were only five."

But it wasn't that I couldn't remember it, it was that I'd never heard the story retold. In my family we hardly ever recalled our past to one another. We compartmentalized.

"That's so crazy."

So crazy but so Courtney: the wanting to go where our dad went, the wanting to please him, the tremendous will she had, the tolerance for pain. After she told me, I switched off the TV and went to pour myself a glass of water, bothered in a way that I didn't understand. I suppose it bothered me that I'd never heard that story before, but then I turned around and never spoke of it again.

left my father at the AU campus and went to a movie, and afterward I walked past a bookstore and saw James Singletary's memoir stacked in the window display, *A Call to Honor A Call to Honor A Call to Honor A Call to Honor.* Between piles of books, a placard announced that the author would soon do a signing there at the store. Singletary's photograph was at the bottom of the sign, his wrinkled face like a face etched on money, weighty and remote. Or it was trying to be such a face. He had a small mouth and a large forehead, and though you couldn't see his arms I imagined that they were folded across his chest. He looked every bit the hard-liner. While I couldn't say for sure based on that one image, it seemed that even his skin had a hard quality, like old rubber.

It started to rain, and I went inside. During the short journey from the store entrance to the shelf of new releases, I started to concoct a fantasy in which I would attend the Singletary book-signing and ask piercing questions on Dad's behalf, questions that exposed the author as full of shit. A revenge fantasy, even though I didn't know what it was I'd be seeking retribution for: I would get back at this man I'd never met for various unspecified lies from twenty years ago? It was a desire that had less to do with Singletary than with a certain impression I had of Dad's career. For my father hadn't been utterly disgraced, he'd led a perfectly decent life, and still there was something I wanted to avenge. Some kernel of shame that he and maybe our whole family had never managed to disgorge: Who was responsible? Maybe this crusty would-be pundit? Once I had the actual book in hand, the specific fantasy of debunking him at his book-signing faded, for what did I know, compared to the admiral, the columnist, the CEO whose accolades appeared on the back of the dust jacket?

The darkness outside made the store a bright shelter, and people twisted and sidled to pass one another in the narrow aisles between the shelves, readers floating in and out of worlds. A Leonard Cohen album played softly in the background. I scanned the book's chapter titles, oblique and portentous. *Saigon 1973. Phoenix Rising. Morning in Central America.* The cost was $24.95. Then I saw someone I knew, or had once known.

I didn't even see him so much as I intuited him viscerally. An intuition of a fancy coat and the shaved back of his neck. It had been years, but his name dropped into my brain like a raider from the clouds, like a Meal Ready to Eat, even though the names of people I'd met more recently so often escaped me. Rob Golden, golden boy. At seventeen he'd been a heartthrob and well aware of it. My father and his stepfather had been friends, and so we knew him that way too. He'd gone out with Courtney for a little while, and I'd been jealous but also anointed, cool by association.

To say he was the same, what does that mean? That he was the same person? That he had the same effect on me? A river I stepped in again, maybe. Or a pile of shit—I would argue that you actually can step in the same pile of shit twice.

Having been around each other so long ago, it was as if we'd known each other intimately, though that was in no way the case. I'd had a crush on him, and my sister had dated him, so he'd been very present in my life for a minute or two, but I hadn't been a part of his life at all. As though that crush had just been in remission for two decades and now had returned, I had trouble saying his name. I gurgled it—"Rob?"

And then he turned around.

"Helen?" he said, and I was all too flattered, that he remembered my name after so many years. That he'd even known it to begin with. He'd been considered gorgeous, though it was more his energy and the twinkly leer in his eyes than his features, which were slightly skewed, as though someone had come along and tried to adjust something and done a poor job of it. And he had a heavy face; it would've been no surprise to find he'd grown fat since high school. In fact his body was lean as a runner's. Other than the shadow of a beard that covered his fleshy jaw, he looked exactly as he had, down to the clothes, which were the designer versions of what he might have worn in high school, high-end jeans and sneakers.

He asked whether I lived in D.C. and told me he'd only just come back there himself. I pretended to know less than I did about him, for the truth was that news of Rob had continued to circulate, just as it had in high school, when his activities—fucking a girl in the darkroom, casual drug sales—had been widely noted. Later, instead of courting detention (or worse) he did work in far-flung countries, Bosnia for one, and in the Green Zone he'd been some kind of consultant, and now he was back here, doing something else weighty and unclear.

Your hair is short, he said. As if the only thing I'd accomplished in the meantime, while he was intervening around the globe, was to get a haircut.

Yeah, I said. I was in L.A. but now I'm here, I said. There was no way to explain all that had led up to this shorter haircut, all the styles and colors preceding, the layers, the products. I had this impulse to apologize for it, for my hair, that is, because of the way he was looking at it and at me with his head atilt. I've never been able to acknowledge attraction as such, not until a person is actually kissing me (and sometimes not even then), and so I couldn't have said for sure whether the tilt of his head and the steadiness of his

stare expressed sexual interest or mere curiosity. I only knew that
I myself felt all the old tingling and that it was uncomfortable.
Even when he asked for my number, I told myself he was just being
polite.

My parents used to throw pool parties. All through the late spring
and summer they heaved these outdoor occasions into precarious
existence, inviting a handful of people over for a "casual" afternoon
party and then straining from Friday evening until Saturday afternoon to ready the house and yard and bar. Up until the last minute
they would go on desperate hunts for a missing chair cushion or
count the number of good towels. The narrow strip of flowerbed had
to be weeded, the pool vacuumed, leaves and dead insects (and once,
a drowned rat) removed from the drain baskets. My mother would
make curried chicken salad and walnut brownies. My father would
undertake last-minute runs for more gin, lemons, ice.

There had been summer vacations when my sisters and I never
had dry hair during the daytime, when we were continually div-
ing into the pool, lifting ourselves back onto the flagstone, racing
in and out of the house, trailing little puddles behind us. But then
Courtney started high school, and she would "lie out" for hours,
trying to tan herself, which was slow going in muggy D.C. Not
me: I burned before I tanned, and I'd become self-conscious about
how I looked in a bathing suit. Even when I went in the pool I would
wear an enormous T-shirt, which billowed around me in the water,
trapping spheres of air. The T-shirt said *RELAX* in big black letters, but in the pool that message was distorted into something
splotchy and sinister. After I hoisted myself out of the water, I would
wring out the bottom of the T-shirt and then pull the wet cotton
away from my body to keep it from clinging. Once Dad had started
to ask why on earth I was wearing clothes in the pool, but Mom
had shushed him.

I'd just finished eighth grade, and my father was everything at
once: the dad of my childhood, who knew all there was to know,

who could fix anything, and the clueless dad of my teenage years, who understood nothing, and the elusive dad who was seldom home. I would seek his attention, but on the rare occasion I actually won it I wanted only to shuck it off again.

The first time I spoke to Rob was at one of those parties. Dad's friend Dick Mitchell had brought along his infamous stepson. Rob was older than I was, but friends of Courtney's talked about him and sometimes bought pot from him, or so I'd overheard them say. The common understanding was that he had slept with a teacher. In person, he was dimpled and cocky in a way that maybe only a teenage male in a letter jacket can manage without coming across as a pure numbskull. He had black hair and eyes so intense that I would think of them as green until I studied him again and found that they were brown.

Because of his reputation I was fascinated. Trying not to look while he moseyed along the pool's edge and sized up the water. Trying not to look when he pulled one-handed at his red T-shirt and then lifted it—and yet I did see the patches of brown hair under his arms and the strip that began below his navel and ran on downward. A smirk bided its time on his face, illuminated from below by the reflections off the pool.

Underneath my own large shirt, there was not much difference between me at fourteen and me at eleven, aside from the fact that I was a couple of inches taller. I imagined that I had made an impression on him, though, that he was secretly intrigued by my androgynous style, that if I were to duck inside the house he might follow—though my idea of what would happen next was indistinct. (There was a television commercial in which a woman would take off a baseball cap and toss her head so that her hair swooped in slow motion around her face. In my dream life I did the same, despite the fact that my own hair wouldn't swoop at any speed.) I was able to partially sell myself on notions that some boys did like me, *in secret*, and maybe if I hadn't had an older sister I could have insulated myself with those notions, kept up a belief that I was *secretly very attractive*, but the fact was that without leaving the house I could easily observe the way boys, sometimes the very same boys, treated certain other girls. It wasn't the way they treated me.

Rob nodded at my hat. "Are you an Orioles fan?"

I shrugged. "We went to a game. I got a hat there."

"I used to play baseball."

"Why'd you stop?"

"The coach had it out for me. I was more serious about wrestling anyway."

Was Jodi Dentoff at that party too? My parents' friend Jodi, who was a reporter for *The Post*, would show up in her giant sunglasses, wearing a sarong tied over her black one-piece. A tiny woman, she would sink into a chair with a Bartles & Jaymes and pronounce her contentment—"Oh Eileen, I feel like I'm in the *Bahamas*, not Washington." But she would've left our number with someone, and as soon as the PIO or Deputy Assistant So-and-so called, she'd dash inside and take a seat on the stairs with the phone cradled against her neck, a notepad balanced on her petite knees.

Courtney strolled outside in a terry-cloth cover-up, and as soon as she appeared, Rob had no more use for me. I remember him cannonballing into the pool right near where she was standing, and her hopping back as though the splash might singe her. "Don't be a jerk!" she called when he came like a seal to the surface. "Don't be a jerk!" he echoed in falsetto. She rolled her eyes. They didn't speak beyond that, but it was obvious that everything they did was for the other's benefit. And when she went back inside, he waited maybe a minute or two before asking where the bathroom was. That was almost a year before they actually started dating, but there you have the humid onset.

I held on to the edge of the pool and kicked, gradually increasing the force of my kicks to see how much of a wake I could generate, and forgot the party, briefly, until my mother told me I was splashing too much. I climbed out of the pool and volunteered to go inside and get more ice.

Rob and Courtney weren't on the first floor. I thumped my way up the stairs. Her room was empty, and I thumped back down, then went down some more. Our basement was cold and grubby, with exposed, foil-wrapped pipes above and cracked concrete below, only barely a "finished" basement: dirt seemed to seep in from the edges of the walls, from beneath the floor, from behind the flimsy blackened doors. There was a laundry room and next to that a furnace room, into which I had only dared to peek sidelong, and that only once or twice, for it seemed to be the place where the house blended back into the ground. Beyond those two doors, in an open area, boxes were stacked against one wall, an old Ping-Pong table folded up against another. Always I had the sensation that I was not as alone down there as I might have wished, that animal life lurked nearby, pawing at the walls, sliding through cracks.

I'd descended with bated breath, expecting I might see something scandalous, my sister pushed up against the wall by a shirtless, hairy boy. But that wasn't happening. They had found a crate of my parents' old records and were kneeling next to each other, looking through it and giggling at the likes of the Kingston Trio.

"I found you guys," I announced.

"Here we are," Courtney said.

I was still soggy, my sister oiled. Without being too obvious, I tried to determine whether the two of them were discreetly touching each other in any way.

"It's getting wiggy out there," I said. "They're all just like eating chicken salad with their hands and shit."

"Yeah right," Courtney said.

"What are you guys doing?"

"Rob wanted to look at these records."

"He was just like, 'Hey, do your parents have any records in the basement?'" I was too timid to address him directly.

"Pretty much," Courtney said.

"Do you guys want to play Ping-Pong?"

I thought I saw a flicker of interest in Rob's face, but Courtney said no.

"I think there's some rum in one of these boxes," I said.

"Barf," Courtney said.

"Too bad we don't have a record player down here," I said. "Or should I say, a hi-fi. We could get down to some Harry Belafonte."

"So did you come down here to do laundry?"

"Day-O!"

"Why are you talking so loud?"

"What is that one you have?" I asked, suddenly desperate to hear Rob say something.

"Bill Haley and the Comets."

"Shweet."

"So your parents don't listen to these?" Rob asked.

"Did they ever listen to them?" Courtney said. She had freed her hair from its elastic, and when she bent over the crate it fell against Rob's brown arms. Naturally it seemed then as though music would always matter to us and that our parents' silly LPs couldn't ever have mattered as much to them.

"At crazy, crazy parties," I said with a hiccup. Rob laughed, and I tried to laugh at myself.

"Let's go back up," Courtney said to Rob.

"Okay," I said.

"I wasn't talking to you."

"I'm supposed to stay down here?"

"You can do whatever you want to do."

I folded my arms and waited for them to go upstairs, thinking up witty things to say later, and then I sat down by myself with the crate and began to look through the same records I'd looked through many times before. I unfolded the table and for a while I served Ping-Pong balls to no one. Then I went upstairs and found Maggie in her room, and we played board games for what seemed like hours, until everyone went home.

I'll cut to the chase, or lack thereof. Just a few days after I bumped into Rob in the bookstore, I slept with him. The lead-up was more like a summons than a date. I remember that night as if he'd seized me by the arm and dragged me from one place to another, because that was the kind of pull he had, all instinct and snap decisions and that flashing quality to his eyes, a simulacrum of delight. He alluded to his time over there, and "there" meant one place and then another, the heat, the bartering, the cats and dogs, the deserts. He didn't bring up his stepfather's death, and naturally I didn't either, but I was aware of it, this thing that had happened sixteen years earlier. Dick Mitchell had shot himself late one night in his garage.

After our drinks I made to leave, but he took my hand and said, "You can't." "Are you wanting to get me drunk?" I asked, already drunk. "I want you in your element," he said. When he invited me back to his apartment I did drunkenly convince myself that we were going there to watch television.

Was it against the rules, to go for a drink with someone your sister had briefly dated in high school? We didn't talk about Courtney.

His hair was shorn close to his head and his grin was waggish; he was gliding behind me, guiding me, *après vous, s'il vous plaît.* The power of an overcoat and a scarf: picture your ninth-grade crush now wealthy, or wealthy enough, youthful silliness retained but with a sophisticated veneer over it all, the illusion at least of giddy invulnerability.

Suffusing his apartment was a coziness I didn't immediately recognize as purchased, part and parcel with the catalog furniture, everything beige or gray or crimson. There was bamboo in a glass vase with polished stones at the bottom. There were ivory pillar candles that had never been lit. He moved around the apartment, shoeless, quick, as I stood there waiting to see what would come next. I had stepped away from myself, not knowing what my own reactions might be.

The whole thing had the feel of a ritual, like some ceremonial bath for which I was a distillate tossed into the water, both necessary and beside the point. In his practiced way he brought the drinks, he brushed my arm with his fingers. We shared a cigarette at the window. An acrid blue kiss: I went limp.

And then we burrowed into our bare selves. He was exact in his wants, pushing at my shoulder, lifting up my ass, pinching my nipple, frisking my chest with his sleek head. Here was a person in a cage and trying to find a key, drilling inside me to see whether I had one, as I sank into water, deep, deeper, then surfaced to hear him ask did I want this, and this, and this. I gasped. He paused, waited, straddled me, waited. Yes please: I hung the words from my throat. He went slowly, whispering the things everyone whispers, watching for what he already knew I didn't have, and then one-two-three-four-five. Afterward, I heard him put music on and saw that the sheets were pin-striped like a suit.

We slept far apart. I say slept. I listened to the rain, walked out into it, realized I'd forgotten my shoes, and woke back up and started all over again. The night leaned its weight on me. It went on and on. I was sore and sour, and it kept raining, so that dawn never really came. The sky traded its inky tarp for a drab gray uniform. I dozed again, and when I opened my eyes he was tucking in his shirt, headed out. It's okay, he said, take your time. The door will lock behind you. He reached for my hair and set a piece of it in place, then cocked his head and backed away and made a conducting motion with his finger. "You've got my number," he said. Did I? The heavy door swung closed in slow stages, years passing before I heard it latch.

Without him the apartment was cool and deflated, but I wasn't inclined to leave. I would've liked to belong there. I investigated the place, though Rob's weren't the sort of secrets you pulled out of a drawer. Laundry bills, takeout menus, ticket stubs, those were what I found. Soon I was bored with snooping and got dressed.

Once I was out on the street all the judgment I'd managed to stave off the night before, the misgivings, came swashing up and then disappeared again. (Hardly for the first time—I am all too prone to delayed reactions, that is to say that I experience things as they happen more or less neutrally and then later develop feelings about them.) I realized that it was Thursday, that Dad was probably at home wondering where I was, and that I was still in the thrall of the night before, the night now leaking all over the morning.

When I was a kid the news was full of hostage takings and faraway bombings, so that I can remember lying in bed, turning over in my head the problem of whether to "negotiate with terrorists," which the president had declared we would not do. I would imagine some member of my family, usually Maggie, taken hostage on a hijacked airplane, and picture myself arguing with her captors, heroically winning her freedom with the sheer force of my logic ("You are bad people!" etc.). During the same period of time, as Americans were continually reminded of our vulnerability, the talking heads would debate what it meant to be a superpower, which I recall even though I had no special childhood interest in international affairs. There was the question of *whether America was willing to act like a superpower.* Our nation was failing to do its superpower duties, some people said. And after the Iran-Contra schemes were made public, the same critics would paint them as a consequence of our weakness: because the nation was too divided, too hamstrung to act boldly, a small group had been pushed to take matters into their own hands.

I never really knew what that meant—what proper superpower behavior was supposed to be—but now, as a person who has in her

own life consistently failed to act in any way like a superpower, I
can relate to the wish for megapotency, the desire for bold strokes.
I grasp more fully why middle-aged men living in the Virginia
suburbs would've been so taken with anti-communist guerrillas in
Africa or Central America.

Maybe some of Rob Golden's draw, for me, had come from a
similar place. I'm not saying he was any kind of revolutionary, much
less a superpower, but his assurance was compelling in itself, even
if he had worked for Halliburton in Iraq. Even Halliburton had not
eliminated the adolescent mystique.

He didn't call, though, and I resisted the urge to contact him.
Instead I called Maggie in New York and started to tell her the whole
story. Or not quite the whole story: I left out his name.

"Who is this guy?"

"He's like this D.C. player, he's done all this stuff, like he
worked on reconstruction in Iraq, and—"

"That's going really well, I hear."

"I know, but still—"

"He's a big swinging dick."

"Well, medium-size."

"Are you going to see him again?"

"I doubt it. Maybe. He hasn't called."

"Was it nice? Did you have a nice time with him?"

"Did I have a nice time with him?" I repeated slowly.

I wasn't sure. It was late and I was lying on the bed with a cord-
less phone, and all I wanted was for Maggie to tell me that I would
see him again. I could picture her in her little apartment in Red
Hook, tidying up as she talked to me, putting her takeout contain-
ers into a flimsy white plastic bag and knotting the handles before
she wedged the bag into her small trash can. She taught English
literature at Hunter College and was strapped with some large
number of classes per semester (was it four? five?) so that she was
always overwhelmed with papers to grade, and it took her at least
an hour to get to work and to come back to the apartment she
could barely afford, and yet she'd become one of those people who

claimed that they could not possibly live anywhere other than New York City, as though there were something debased about the idea of having a yard or driving to the supermarket or not working ten hours a day, and even though every time I visited New York it seemed to have been even further infiltrated by the customs and retail chains that prevailed in the rest of the United States, even as it gradually turned into a much more expensive version of the same city everybody lived in now, my sister never stopped believing that in any other place she would wither away and eventually die of boredom and/or *mal du pays*.

"What did you think of him?" she asked.

"I don't know. I mean, there was something there, but it's not like he was that curious about me. He mostly talked about himself."

"So typical."

Maggie had been single for a while, and lately when I asked her whether there were any prospects, she would say no, not really. I've just been working so hard, she would tell me. And I would try to tell her not to spend her whole life working, but I knew she believed that I didn't understand her life and what she had to do to get by. She was right, I didn't understand it. She started to tell me about a student who thought he knew more than her—there was always at least one—and then she said that maybe he did. "Or not that he knows more than I do, exactly, but in a practical sense he's probably smarter, he can spend his whole day reading and thinking, with his unspoiled, twenty-year-old brain. He doesn't have to grade papers or deal with department e-mails. What I know, what I used to know, it's buried under so much junk at this point."

"That's not true."

"It is. I think I kind of have a crush on him. I can't even look at him because I'm afraid that I do. If he ever comes to my office hours I'll probably jump out the window."

"Maybe you're just not around enough guys."

"Well yeah, I mean it's all twenty-year-olds, or the fossils who teach in the department. Courtney thinks I should try Internet dating again."

"She's always saying that," I said. "She says that to me. It's because she never actually did it herself, so she doesn't get how soul-destroying that online shit is."

"I just feel like there's this cultural hypocrisy in play when it comes to marriage and family, you know? Like when we were younger we weren't even supposed to be looking for love. I mean I did go out with Marco for a few years, but I knew he wasn't, like, a life partner. I remember the one or two friends I had who obsessed about finding husbands—I thought that was so dumb. I wanted to be serious. You were supposed to be serious about your life, and that meant figuring out your career. But then you hit your thirties and if you haven't found the guy, you start to sense that people are looking at you in a certain way, wondering what's wrong with you? And so now I'm supposed to make a project out of that, looking for a marriageable man? I already built my life the way it is, I don't have time to be on some heavy-duty manhunt, and anyway it's New York City, which is like a smorgasbord of women where all the single men can just pig out all day long. They don't even want to get married."

This sounded revisionist to me—or at least not true to my memory of my own past. For most of my twenties I'd wanted to hang out with men and to sleep with some of them, and twice as a result of those activities I'd fallen in love and stayed with one person for a while, but until recently the notion of "settling down" had been off-putting, and I put it off. I did suspect that I was at a disadvantage compared to the people who'd come around to the concept sooner, but that was my own fault, not the result of cultural forces.

I didn't say any of that. "You'll find someone," I told Maggie, and I meant it: underneath her harried professor guise, she was the sweetest person in our family, the one who'd played nurse to her dolls and doted on animals and been friends in school with a bunch of gentle, giggly, artistic girls who hugged one another a lot. It had surprised me when she decided on academia—I'd seen her as a doctor or a therapist, tending to people in some way. She was also the prettiest one of us, I'd always thought, although Courtney was more photogenic.

"Yeah," she said, in no way encouraged.

"You will. You're great." That only made things worse, of course. It was one of those phone calls that faded into weightless assurances and unspoken disappointment. She said she'd see me soon, at Dad's panel. He'd mentioned it to her multiple times. He seems really excited about it, she said. Yes he does, I said.

Dad had a cable modem, and so to check my e-mail I had to bring my laptop to his study and connect it, or else use his machine. I was, post-Rob, checking all too often for a message from him, one that didn't appear, and still I would go back again and again for my sugar-drip. Just checking! In my spare time, i.e., the intervals between e-mail checks, I would often read in my room, where I'd hidden *A Call to Honor* under the bed as though it were something dirty. If only: the book could've benefited from a little obscenity, a little salt at least. In fact it was just another dry political memoir, a self-serving recap of James Singletary's employment history, full of meetings, crises, encounters with important people, abstractions. Other than the occasional mention of his wife, there were no relationships to speak of besides relationships of power, in other words what you might expect from one of those Washington men who believed that the warp and woof of their own lives mattered less than their ideas about foreign policy, who hadn't exactly kept track of their own lives for that matter.

I had no way of knowing whether the book was full of lies, as Dad had said it would be. Certainly it was self-serving: Singletary seemed to hold all the right opinions, while those around him were misinformed, weak-kneed, blind, naive, dumb. He was absolutely free of self-doubt, on the page at least. More than once he made a point of saying that if he'd had to do X or Y over again, he would do it in just the same way he'd done it the first time. None of it felt real, none of it felt at all *felt*.

Most of the book was devoted to an insider's take on the Bush White House, circa 2001–2003, but in the first few chapters Singletary recounted his prior career. He'd been on the National Security Council staff in the eighties, specializing in Latin America. That would've put him in regular contact with my dad, who'd worked there too and had expended much of his time and energy on conflicts to the south of us.

When I say Dad had a role in Iran-Contra, that's what I'm talking about, really just the Contra side of the hyphenate. The U.S.-backed fight against the leftist government in Nicaragua. How many people even remember it? If you were alive and watching the news at the time, maybe this rings a bell: circa 1984, Congress blocked military aid to the Contra rebels, and after that a small clique of people did an end-run around the ban by creating a privately funded, secret supply system. And so followed the whole fever dream: you had the Contras, bunches of ragtag, bantam boys with indigenous faces down in the jungle, continuing their fight against the Sandinistas, while in the fun-house mirror of our own country another sort of unlikely brigade—this one composed of midlevel officials, soldiers of fortune, and blue-rinsed wealthy widows—went on providing them with their aftermarket weapons and secondhand camouflage.

My dad was pulled into it because of Dick Mitchell—even as a teenager I'd inferred as much. Dad had followed his buddy into the murk and had suppressed his own better judgment along the way. I don't mean to suggest that Dad resisted doing what he did, just that it began with his friend. Mitchell the schemer, the political savant, the flirt, Mitchell the alpha to his beta. They'd first met when my dad was a Cornell undergraduate and Mitchell was a teaching assistant. I suspect that Dad would've seen through him and fallen under his sway all the same. He had that kind of charisma. I think this, I know this, I feel sure of it despite having very little hard evidence. I'm just drawing from my adolescent perceptions, from seeing them interact at family parties. (Later I would read Mitchell's testimony before the congressional subcommittees, not that it included any information about his friendship with my father.)

Dad, for his part, never talked about Mitchell now. Aside from the outburst that Singletary's TV appearance had triggered, I couldn't think of the last time he'd brought up his White House years at all. And so I was looking for a way in, a trapdoor to Dad's past. I wanted more from *A Call to Honor* than it could've possibly contained—that is to say, when I picked up the book I think I'd subconsciously hoped to discover the story of Mitchell in it, if not the story of Mitchell and Dad. Some clue, at least.

But naturally I didn't find anything like that.

Singletary had written: "After September 11, confusion prevailed inside and out of the White House." And: "Regrettably, there were those in favor of what I would call a run-and-hide approach." And: "Every administration has to make tough choices." And on and on. Still, those clichéd pages had opened something up for me, a box full of questions not answered. While my days were still loose and undirected on the surface, I began to feel that I had come home for a purpose, albeit a purpose that wasn't clear to me.

One afternoon while Dad was out, I checked my e-mail and then stayed at his desk, succumbing to screen daze. I scanned the headlines and did some clicking, downloaded the class schedule of a yoga studio in Dupont Circle, then closed the browser and started hunting around for the download.

I opened a file on the desktop with an opaque name (DL061504 .doc) and found not a list of yoga classes but a letter that Dad had written, earlier in the year, to Senator Richard Lugar. *VIA FAX* it said at the top. He had a habit of communicating by fax. The only letters I'd ever sent by fax had to do with changing my car insurance or terminating a health club membership, but my father used his fax machine to send notes to people he didn't care to call on the phone. I guessed that these were people, like Senator Richard Lugar, who wouldn't have been likely to take his call, and that Dad might've been hoping that they would nonetheless be moved, because of the wisdom contained in the fax, to want to talk to him. But then again I have a way of making him sound needier than maybe he was. For all I know, he didn't give a fig whether they talked to him or not.

Dear Senator Lugar, began the fax, *I enjoyed our conversation last night at the National Press Club.* The document went on to suggest a foreign policy agenda for Bush's second term in office, with a series of bullet-point proposals (Scale Back Our Military Commitments, Reopen a Dialogue with Iran, and so on) followed by short explanations. I had no problem with the proposals, which seemed reasonable enough, but the fact that my dad had written the letter, and presumably faxed it to the senator's office, where it lay, no doubt, in a bin of other unread faxes—I wished he hadn't done it. I preferred to view Dad as someone who'd gone into more or less permanent exile and who possessed, if nothing else, an exile's dignity, better that than a pitiable faxer.

I looked in the fax machine itself, which had in its tray of already-sent pages a couple dozen invitations to the panel he'd told me about, personal invitations he'd faxed to people I doubt he knew, at best barely knew. They were members of the present-day national security establishment (administration officials, congressmen) and of the city's old guard more generally. *Dear X, Because of our shared concern about the progress of American intervention in the Middle East, I am writing to invite you to a panel discussion . . .* All that time he spent in the study, I'd thought he was just checking his stock portfolio. Come to find out it was this.

I began to feel irritated by all the Northwest Washington nabobs who wouldn't answer his faxes or attend the panel, who would sweep him aside. I thought about James Singletary, who was clearly no smarter than my dad, only more arrogant, and yet there he was on TV, pushing his ponderous book, the capstone to his dully distinguished career.

Too late, I realized Dad had come home. He walked in on me. His faxes were still in my lap. He saw them there and his face cramped up.

"Sorry," I mumbled, "I was just looking for a fax I sent."

"I see. Carry on," he said. He turned to go.

"You can stay. I'm pretty much finished in here."

"Did you find it?"

"The fax? I think I must've thrown it out."

I heard what sounded like heavy equipment outside, a bulldozer on the move.

"Do you have the number you sent it to? The machine will tell us whether it went through or not," he said.

"That's okay. I bet it went through."

"You can just press the up arrow button, and it'll tell you the last ten numbers it dialed, and if you want a report—"

"It's okay, Dad."

I was depriving him of something he wanted, which was to take refuge in the subject of the machine and its capabilities. He found that kind of talk easeful, and I did too, since it was simple enough to listen to him explain things and so color in the silence. Here I don't mean the silence of things not said, of elephants in the room, but the silence of people at some remove from whatever it is they might've said in an alternative, talking universe, the silence of family who after decades of elision and evasion know each other both too well and hardly at all. Who sit like well-trained dogs on either side of a nonexistent fence and regard each other with a trampled-on, mute curiosity.

It was then that a suggestion arrived in my head and slid out of my mouth. Had he ever thought about writing a memoir, I asked him. He could write about his time in government, lay out his views, and (though I didn't say it explicitly) surely he could outdo the likes of *A Call to Honor*. He could write something real—whatever that meant, I was suddenly convinced he could do it.

I was surprised to hear that he had, in fact, considered it. "I was working on a proposal," he said. He mentioned the name of a lawyer and deal maker in town, and even I knew who this man was, somebody who brokered book contracts for ex-presidents. "I met him once, and we chatted for a bit. I thought I could send it to him, see what he says."

This seemed as unpromising to me as all his faxes. "And did you?"

"I started it a few times and then—"

"I could help you with it," I said.

"Well. It's a question of what I remember, my getting that down on paper."

"You'd be the one writing it, but I could interview you. Or you could record yourself talking about what you remember, and I could take a stab at writing it up." Offering to serve as Dad's assistant was a terrible idea, but I went on. "Or we could start with an outline."

"I don't think so."

"Or I could just send you some questions. I could e-mail them to you."

"No, no. Thank you, but no."

"Okay. I just thought I could—"

"I don't think so. No."

"Okay."

I suppose it had been fanciful of me, downright obtuse to think that I could barge my way through a locked door. Yet even his out-and-out refusal didn't deter me. Just the opposite. I believed I could still convince him. I indulged this vision in which my dad was a weird, wounded king and I the knight come to heal him. No matter that the king had shuffled off to the kitchen for a beer, that the knight was now checking her e-mail yet again, now looking at clothes online.

Later that evening I was still thinking about the book I could help my dad write, which in my mind had turned into something important for my father to do, something "good for him," as if remembering and writing were unalloyed virtues. And, I thought, what if he could write a halfway-decent Washington memoir, one that wasn't dead on the page, a real book? Wouldn't that be something?

I found him in the family room, sitting in front of the TV, and I asked him, abruptly, whether he remembered the time he took Courtney to the White House and her hand had got caught in a mousetrap. It was the wrong place to begin. He frowned.

"Her wrist, I think it was."

"How awful. You must've been freaked out."

"Freaked out?"

"What did you tell Mom?"

His hand went toward his shirt pocket, reaching for the pipe he'd stopped smoking years ago, then traveled up to the side of his neck. My father had always been lean, but because age had softened his body, it now seemed at odds with itself, skinny here, fleshy there. Although he still jogged, still took his shell out on the Potomac, a small gut had appeared on his frame, like a jellyfish on a pier.

"I don't recall," he said.

"She must've been surprised."

"I could ask you some questions too," he said. "How about I ask you some questions."

"I'm not accusing you, Dad. I just wanted to hear your version. Never mind. It's no big deal."

"Your mother thought it was a pretty big deal at the time."

Until then, I'd considered Courtney's mousetrap story to be a story, nothing more. I hadn't seen it as implicating him. I hadn't considered him negligent. "I'm sure Mom was upset, but it's not like it was your fault. You didn't know she had a mousetrap on her hand. You couldn't have—"

"I don't want to discuss it!"

"Sorry."

He contemplated the screen.

"What is this?" I asked. "A movie?"

He continued to watch or at least look in the direction of the TV as he said, "I could ask you where you were the other night. I could ask you that."

"I was out."

"I gathered as much."

"With a friend. I had a little too much to drink and so I crashed at their place." Even as I said it I was asking myself why I had to lie about it, or at least bend the truth. What was the point? Why *their* instead of *his*? "I'm sorry I didn't let you know, it was so late by the time I realized I wasn't coming home—"

"So is that what you do, you 'crash'?"

"That's what I did."

He sat there as though there were a heavy cloud right above him, pushing down.

"Next time I'll call," I said.

"Or how about next time, just come home?"

"I'm an adult, Dad!" I was too loud.

"Behave like one, then. Have some dignity."

"Oh please. *Please*—"

How had this happened? It had come on so suddenly. My throat had gone tight, and I could feel myself canceling my own claim to adulthood and becoming exactly the sixteen-year-old he imagined was standing there. I wanted to yell like a teenager, *It's my life! It's none of your business!*

"Are you going to just . . . just sleepwalk your way through life?" he asked.

"I can if I want."

"Don't be pathetic."

"*I'm* pathetic?"

I'd just been parroting him, but even so I'd hit a tender spot, I saw it in his eyes in the instant before we both looked away.

What was I doing? I remembered something, an important principle that I'd flouted when I moved back: I couldn't live with my dad, in the same house, not for long. I told him with a controlled quiver that I was going to bed and then I did.

can picture Dick Mitchell's rangy legs lying on the rubber slats of one of our poolside loungers, his white polo shirt hanging from the side of the chair. His forehead was broad and lined by old troubles, but he obscured those with bangs and carried himself easily, even elegantly. He had the bearing of a man in an old movie. Yet at one of those summer parties he showed up in Jams, the flamboyant surfer shorts: a gag, but he pulled it off. I remember hearing his deep voice as it traveled across the yard. I also remember the way he would kiss my mother on the cheek and then squeeze her hand while he told her how great she looked. He came over regularly, and he was present (though not wearing Jams) for the unlikeliest of my parents' parties, the one to which they invited the Saudi ambassador's right-hand man. According to my father's later testimony at the joint committee hearings, it was Dick Mitchell who'd met this man at a reception and then told my father about him. The party might well have been Mitchell's idea.

(*From the testimony of Timothy Atherton, June 24, 1987*)

   . . . MR. COHEN. And did you tell the national security advisor about your contact with Mr. Abdullah?

MR. ATHERTON. Abdulaziz, sir. I believe that I mentioned it to Mr. McFarlane, yes.

MR. COHEN. And what did he say?

MR. ATHERTON. He said it sounded like a good person to know.

MR. COHEN. Anything else?

MR. ATHERTON. I offered to arrange a meeting between them. Mr. Abdulaziz had expressed an interest in that. But he was otherwise occupied at the time—

MR. COHEN. By "he" you mean Mr. McFarlane?

MR. ATHERTON. Yes, Mr. McFarlane. He didn't feel, you know, that he could fit it into his schedule.

MR. COHEN. So you decided to pursue this "contact" on your own hook.

MR. ATHERTON. Basically, yes, I did.

MR. COHEN. And did you inform Mr. McFarlane that you were doing that?

MR. ATHERTON. I don't believe I did. No.

MR. COHEN. This was your own operation.

MR. ATHERTON. I don't know that I would call it an operation, Senator.

MR. COHEN. What would you call it?

MR. ATHERTON. Making connections.

MR. COHEN. And Mr. Mitchell was helping you make connections.

MR. ATHERTON. (pause)

In the conversation that my parents might've had before the party, Mom would have been anxious to get things right. What was she supposed to say to them? What would they eat?

Just don't get a ham, he told her. No pork.

Of course I'm not going to get a ham. I wouldn't get a ham.

No BLTs. No cocktail franks.

No Spam?

No Spam.

They were talking in the kitchen as she put brownies on a plate and he turned pages of the newspaper.

But how do we greet them? Are they allowed to shake hands? she asked.

Why wouldn't they be?

If they consider us unclean or something.

He picked up an ice cube that had fallen on the floor and tossed it into the sink.

You don't normally shake hands with our guests, do you?

If I don't know them I do, she said. Am I supposed to kiss them? And what about Boris? I thought they didn't like dogs.

They don't?

I read it someplace, she said.

Put him in the basement.

He won't last down there.

Then after they get here we can tie him up out front.

Are they going to swim? Are they bringing their bathing suits?

I doubt it, he said.

It was the same summer that Dick Mitchell and his wife brought Rob over, but this was a different party, and Dick and Martha came without him. They had shown up first, Dick talking loudly and steering Martha around with his hand at the middle of her back.

Just as my parents were beginning to fret that their special guests weren't coming, the Abdulaziz family arrived in a chauffeured black sedan and filed up the steps in order of seniority: Mr. Abdulaziz, his wife, an older girl, a boy, and a younger girl. The man had a funny mustache—all mustaches were funny to me when I was that age—yet I could see that he was handsome, like an Arab Tom Selleck. His plump wife wore a shimmery silk tunic over white pants, and gold earrings and bangles that sparkled when she moved. The older daughter seemed a little older than me, Courtney's age, and she had a sullen face, weighted by thick eyebrows. I noticed her jeans were the very light-wash Guess! jeans I'd coveted, which our mother had declared too expensive. When she was introduced by her father—my daughter Jamila—she said nothing and did not smile. Only the two younger ones, who'd worn their bathing suits under their shorts and T-shirts, seemed glad to have come.

Dick and Martha tried to give their lounge chairs to the newcomers. My father vigorously shook everyone's hands, even the children's little hands. Then Jamila and her mother sat down on the edge of one of the loungers, while Mr. Abdulaziz remained near Dad and the little kids peeled off their clothes and jumped in the pool. Three heavy souls and two light, bouncing ones. Jamila asked my mother, "Is there anything to drink?"

"Would you like a lemonade?"

"Yes," Jamila answered. Then she went over to the table where Mom had put the food and picked out a brownie.

Maggie had joined the two kids in the pool, and they were playing Marco Polo, then doing handstands and flips, while the adults watched. I was sitting at the pool with my feet in the water, but then my mother told me to "go be polite to our guests," which meant I was supposed to talk to Jamila, who was now by herself with the brownie and the lemonade. "Where's Courtney?" I asked, but Mom didn't answer.

I struggled with my assignment. "I love chocolate, don't you?" I asked Jamila after I'd joined her.

"Yes."

"Where do you go to school?"

"The Islamic Academy," Jamila said. "It's in Alexandria."

"I think we played you once in basketball. You can't wear shorts, right?"

Jamila nodded. "Our sports teams are really bad. Though not as bad as they would be if I played on them."

"You don't play anything?"

"I play the flute."

"I took piano, but I never practiced."

"Oh."

We turned to watch our siblings in the pool. "Do you like to swim?" I asked.

"I'm not really into it."

"I'm sorry."

"Don't be," she said indifferently.

"Where are you guys from?"

"My father is from Saudi Arabia and my mother is from Egypt. I grew up all over, different countries. For my first year of high school I went to boarding school, but I got kicked out."

"Kicked out?" I was impressed.

Jamila nodded. "Switzerland—it was fucking freezing cold every day and everyone was mean. I didn't want to leave my room. So I didn't, I didn't leave the room except to go to the bathroom or get food. Honestly I think that place would have been happy to keep taking my father's money if I'd just gone to class, like, once in a while? And agreed to see the school psychologist, which I refused to do anymore after I talked to him one time. He was this perv from Austria. It was classic."

"Wow."

"I was failing everything."

"Did you have a TV in your room?"

"I wish. I listened to music, mostly."

"What kind of music do you like?"

"Hardcore."

"Cool."

On the patio, my father had likewise engaged Mr. Abdulaziz in conversation, about lord knows what—it was something he did with enthusiasm: talk to men, men of every stripe. He did it by feeling his way to the other man's interests and then expounding on some tangentially related topic. If Mr. Abdulaziz loved race cars or horticulture, then Dad would recall, in detail, an article he'd read three years ago about fuel shortages or agribusiness.

"You should think about joining a sports team," Courtney said. I hadn't realized she'd come outside, but there she was behind me.

She picked up a plastic fork and speared a bite of chicken salad out of the bowl and ate it.

Jamila raised one of her dense eyebrows, and then Courtney added, "It's what keeps me sane."

Their eyes met: it might have been a look of recognition or one of antagonism. And what was Courtney talking about? She was the sanest person in our family, or so I thought at the time.

I saw Dick Mitchell, on the other side of the pool, watching my sister. That summer she had a regimen. She'd studied women's magazines with the same tenacity she studied everything else, and from them had learned all about feminine maintenance. She shaved her legs every other day. She squirted Sun-In highlighting spray in her hair and stashed lip gloss in the downstairs bathroom. She wrote down everything she ate in a food diary (*1 NF yogurt 5 carrots 1 Eng muffin w FF cream cheese 1 med apple*) in which alcoholic drinks were given pseudonyms (*3 ginger ales*). Sporadically I would imitate my sister's rituals (*1 juice 3 pickles 3 slices pepperoni pizza OOPS 2 cookies OOPS!!!*) with poor results.

I stood up, then launched myself into the deep end of the pool. I was again wearing my *RELAX* shirt. When I came up with a gasp, my shirt billowing around my body, no one was looking at me. I swam the length of the pool underwater, surfaced, and glanced back to where I'd come from. Just Courtney was there, picking at the chicken salad, and then Dick Mitchell was there too, putting some food on a little plate and chatting with her. Jamila had gone back to her mother, who was still perched on the edge of a lounger. The two of them sat with their soft arms intertwined.

Our mother no longer touched us. The hugging and tickling and sitting on laps, the sprawling on the bed together, the kisses on the cheek and the nose, had gradually dried up. We'd all forgotten one another's smells.

The sky was hazy, crossed every once in a while by slow birds. With my eyes I was saying to Courtney, "Jump in!" and she was saying, "No way," until I dunked myself and rose from the water with a mouth full of T-shirt. The kids saw me, and I pretended that I'd meant to do it, for laughs.

Mom stood close to the house and took stock, squeezing her own finger, her hands all too idle now that she'd made the lemonade, wiped down the chairs, put out the forks. Her hands were biding their time. Shyly, dutifully, she approached the lounger where Mrs. Abdulaziz and Jamila were stationed and spoke to them from above, as though she were their nervous teacher, the sleeves of her cotton blouse fluttering along with her gestures.

She spoke loudly: "It must be very hot in Saudi Arabia this time of year!" They nodded.

"Mom," I said as I approached her from behind, dripping wet, and touched her arm, an experiment. The arm stiffened. "Hello there," she said.

"Can I go inside?"

"Why don't you stay out here and talk to our guests?"

"I want to change. I want to put clothes on."

"Maybe Jamila wants to go inside too."

Jamila didn't give a shit, I knew that much. I showed her where the television was and left her there. Then I slunk past Dick Mitchell and Mr. Abdulaziz, who were standing in the kitchen talking— about the weather in the desert? About the freedom fighters of Nicaragua? Dick might have questioned Mr. Abdulaziz about his view of the current policy.

Which current policy?

The president's.

It seems your president is incapable of choosing a policy. That's the trouble.

My father might have joined them. What's that? What trouble? And then Dad would've taken hold of an indisputable truth (that the president hated to disagree with anyone, that his hands weren't on the wheel but rather waving hello to whoever had come to visit) and blunted it, blaming Congress for one thing and another, and emphasizing the administration's strong commitment to its friendship with Saudi Arabia.

I clambered up to my room and exchanged my huge wet T-shirt for a dry one of normal size. Then I put on a tape and stared in the mirror, making faces, watching myself sing along for a few lines, *hello, hello again*, but I didn't like my face when it was singing. It was all mouth and nose.

Courtney, Maggie, and I shared the hall bathroom, which stank of Noxzema and acne cream. In that mirror I was yellower, and I could see the outline of my bathing suit under my shirt, and my little tummy, and, in the hopes of improving myself somehow, I took one of Courtney's razors out of the medicine cabinet and started to shave my damp legs at the sink. I'd done so a couple of times before, not very well—later I'd find remaining patches of hair on my ankles or knees. In trying to be more thorough this time, I nicked my shin. A red drip of blood traveled slowly toward my ankle. I watched it fall into the sink. Then I hopped over to the toilet paper and held some to my shin until the bleeding stopped. I trotted back down the stairs until I reached the third step from the bottom, and from there I jumped to the floor. The men weren't in the kitchen any longer, and in the family room Jamila was watching a black-and-white Western on Channel 5.

"These movies are so boring," I said. "It's like, men with hokey accents arguing, and then they get on their horses and go shoot people."

"I love Westerns. I've seen this one, like, five times." Her purse was lying on the table next to the sofa, on its side, so that I could see what was in it: a pack of gum, a tampon, a stubby pencil, and little balls of paper, like fortune-cookie fortunes or straw wrappers that had been crumpled into tiny wads.

I meandered back into the kitchen, where the watermelon my mom had bought for the party was sitting on the counter, unsliced. I would be helpful, I thought, as I was so often urged to be, and I took the largest of the knives out of the knife drawer and a cutting board from the dish rack. I made my first attempt through the middle, and the knife got stuck in the melon and I had to wrestle it back out and start again, but the cuts after that went cleanly through the fruit. It was a sharp knife, satisfyingly effective. Watermelon juice dribbled onto the cutting board as I made the pieces and stacked them up.

All of a sudden blood was pooling with the watermelon juice, crimson into pink, and it confused me—how could my shin have bled on the cutting board?—before I saw the source, the stinging middle finger of my left hand, its tip liquid red. I stuck my hand under the faucet to wash it off and realized the blood was still flowing. I hadn't seen blood come so steadily out of me before. My stomach turned. There was, I noticed, a little nugget of finger flesh clinging to the side of the knife.

I moaned, and from the family room Jamila asked what was going on.

"I cut myself. Pretty dumb."

"Is it bad?"

"Maybe."

She came into the kitchen and peeked over my shoulder as I pulled paper towels from the roll to wrap around my still-oozing finger. "Oooh. My father went to medical school. He can tell you if it's bad," she said.

"I probably just need to find a large Band-Aid."

"I'm going to get some ice."

"I don't think I need ice."

"I like to chew ice when I'm nauseous."

"You mean nauseated."

"What?" She pulled open the freezer and leaned over it, while I started to cry a little, because of the blood and because I didn't want to present myself to my parents and their guests this way. I sat down and watched TV for a couple of minutes, but the blood kept coming through the paper towels.

"Mom?"

Outside, everyone stared at me. Suddenly there were gnats everywhere, gnats in my eyes. My mother sat me down on the deck and crouched there, lifting up the paper towel bandage, which was already soaked. Mr. Abdulaziz stood next to her.

"I'm sorry," I said, inhaling through my nose and then trying to wipe my nose with a bit of the paper towel.

"What happened?"

"I was cutting the watermelon."

"Why were you doing that?"

Mr. Abdulaziz kneeled next to my mom. Lightly (and distaste-fully? Or did I imagine that?) he took my hand in his. My tears dried up and not only that, I felt my whole self shrivel, sensing some violation of his religion or mine. There was an unwelcome message in his cautious attention. Like it or not I was some sort of woman.

"You should go to the emergency room," he said. "They'll get you sewn up, don't worry. For now you should keep your hand elevated."

There was a brief negotiation over who would take me to the hospital. Every adult there volunteered him or herself, even Mr. Abdulaziz offered to go. I wished they would just send me to the hospital with Courtney. It fell to Dad instead: "I'll do it, I'll go," he kept saying, with a martyrish note in his voice, as if repenting for not having kept his house in order. Although Mom objected, saying it made more sense for her to go, he went inside for his car key. The Abdulazizes announced they were leaving. "Oh no, stay," my mother said, fooling no one. For some reason Dick came with us to the ER, maybe to keep my dad from panicking, since he was so wound up, while Dick sat shotgun, making jokes. I was in the backseat, holding up my hand, and he would say, "This girl keeps giving me the finger!" and so on until he leeched a smile out of me. He was there the whole time, there in the emergency room, and right outside the door as the doctor took a piece of skin from my arm and grafted it over my fingertip. It may not have taken any special valor for him to be there, but even now when I think of him it's with a fondness, because of his company that afternoon, his reassuring attention. Dad, on the other hand, was so anxious he hardly said a word to me—he only began to relax on the way home, rolling down the windows and playing the Beach Boys and stopping at a McDonald's for soft-serve cones and coffee.

Later, in retrospect, that abortive pool party would seem unreal, a hallucination. It was one occasion when my family's history may have intersected with that of Iran-Contra, but the stories seemed all but impossible to put together. To bring my dad—the dad who fixed things around the house, washed the cars, ate chips—into that tangle of secret machinations and planes full of weapons parts, meant recasting him as a different kind of person, a naive gringo in a geopolitical melodrama. Yet to work the other way, to try to reconcile the bigger picture with the kitchen on Albemarle Street, with our life circa 1985, seemed just as distorting, the product an erratic family comedy in which a cartoonish Oliver North had an odd cameo. I could inflate everything or I could minimize and poke fun. It was the same thriller vs. satire problem I'd had with the screenplay.

But this much I do know: eighteen months after the party, the joint select committees' investigators learned that my parents had entertained the special assistant to the Saudi ambassador, and they made a point of asking both my dad and Mitchell about it in the depositions each gave in advance of the hearings, as though perhaps a deal had been done poolside, i.e., my father and/or Dick

Mitchell might've solicited an illegal contribution to the Contras from Mr. Abdulaziz. The suggestion seems outlandish to me. No way did that happen: I'm convinced. Still, I wonder whether they could've possibly meant to do it, intended to make their own free-lance solicitation, until I'd interrupted them with my injury.

(From the deposition of Richard Mitchell, March 9, 1987)

MR. LEGRAND. What did you hope to gain from your contact with Mr. Abdulaziz? Or is it Prince Abdulaziz?

MR. MITCHELL. I was never clear on whether he is a prince or not. They have a lot of princes over there. He may have been one.

MR. LEGRAND. But in terms of your objective.

MR. MITCHELL. I would say that I was pursuing a relationship but not that I had a specific objective.

MR. LEGRAND. Did you notify your superiors at the State Department?

MR. MITCHELL. Yes. My boss was Elliott Abrams and I told him about it.

MR. LEGRAND. Did you notify anyone on the National Security Council staff, other than Mr. Atherton?

MR. MITCHELL. I personally did not. I believe Mr. Abrams may have mentioned it to Ollie North.

MR. LEGRAND. Were he and North friends, to your knowledge?

MR. MITCHELL. To the best of my knowledge they had substantial professional contact, which was friendly in nature. I would describe them as being close, on a professional basis.

MR. LEGRAND. And were you friendly with Mr. North?

MR. MITCHELL. Our interactions were always friendly.

MR. LEGRAND. Would it be fair to say that your friendly relationship with Oliver North ran counter to the prevailing attitude at the State Department?

MR. MITCHELL. He had his detractors, but it wasn't a universal attitude within the department. Certain people considered him an activist.

MR. LEGRAND. Activist in what sense?

MR. MITCHELL. Very operationally driven, and capable of manipulating people in order to get done what he wanted to get done.

MR. LEGRAND. Did you share that view?

MR. MITCHELL. I saw him as someone who was very passionate
and very effective.

MR. LEGRAND. Would it be fair to say that his detractors included
the secretary of state?

MR. MITCHELL. I was present at a meeting during which the secretary of state told Abrams to "watch Ollie North."

MR. BENNETT. Can we go off the record?

MR. LEGRAND. Sure.

(Discussion off the record.)

MR. LEGRAND. Back on the record.

The inquiry into the alleged solicitation was dropped, after it
was revealed that the Saudis had already been contributing to the
cause, secretly, for more than a year by the time of the pool party.
Only a handful of people had been briefed on the Saudi contribu-
tions, and my father and Dick Mitchell had not been among them.
Even the president may not have been fully briefed—at least that
would become his defense. Nobody had the big picture.

We never had anything close to a big picture on Albemarle
Street. I hardly had any picture at all. The scandal would bewilder
me, it would become entangled with the general confusions and fears
of adolescence, so that I still, all these years later, wanted to sort it
out, to arrive at some kind of big picture for myself. What had my
dad done—who had he been? I still wished we could collaborate,
which is to say I wanted Dad to tell me what had happened and then
I could write it, or both of us could, but if he chose to keep quiet I
would go on trying to piece it all together, assembling fragments
and figments.

I'm inclined to believe that Dick Mitchell was the type of person who would find older mentors he could flatter and profit from,
men who liked to see themselves in him. In the early eighties, he'd
met North, and though North wasn't much older than he was, not

a mentor exactly, Dick ingratiated himself with the lieutenant colonel. By that time my father was already on the NSC staff, and so it was easy enough for his friend to pull him in, to cut him a piece of the action. I'm not trying to blame it all on Dick, but had it not been for him I bet Dad might not even have known what North was up to. After all, there were plenty of NSC staff people who had no idea.

My quote-unquote manager called me while I was at the grocery store. I always felt a quick jab of hope at the sight of Phil Franklin's name on the phone display. Although I was not an optimist in general, I would enter contests (screenwriting competitions for one, but also raffles to win luxury cars or gourmet cookware, whatever was there to be won), and I answered phone calls from him in the same spirit, wanting to believe and so semibelieving that a studio executive had gone into raptures over an idea or a script of mine. That never came to pass, though. Now Phil announced he was quitting the entertainment business to help out a friend who'd started a custom yacht company in Marin County.

"You're going to build boats?"

"Of course not. I'm going to sell boats."

"Boats."

"It's a great opportunity."

Here I'd thought of him as one of Hollywood's enthusiasts, someone who would never leave the industry, but turned out he was just an enthusiast. His sentiment for TV and movies could be transferred to boats. And where did that leave me? Even though Phil had not actually helped me to become the working writer I'd hoped to become, his news was upsetting. *Now I have nothing to go back to,* I thought. It wasn't necessarily true, but I thought it anyway. There was nothing for me in Los Angeles anymore.

The house was empty when I returned from the store. I didn't know where Dad had gone. The answering machine blinked: *Tim, this is Roy Kotler, I wanted to let you know I won't be able to make it to*

the panel on Tuesday. I've got family coming into town, and . . . The event
was less than a week away, and acquaintances of my dad's kept calling to say they weren't coming.

It had been a while since I'd found myself alone in the house
where I'd grown up, and without my present-day dad to remind
me that the twenty-first century was well under way, I started to
feel as if I would wake up the next morning and have to get ready
for school. That my sisters and my parents would all be in the kitchen,
eating breakfast, reaching around each other for the milk—and
when I pictured that ordinary, harried, unfeeling moment I both
regretted what I saw there and longed to return to it, as though I
might better appreciate something about it or even inject a larger
dose of love into it than had been there the first time.

I drank a beer and watched TV, fell asleep to a report of another
roadside bomb somewhere in Iraq.

When I woke up, I went online to look for temp work. I was so
accustomed to making efforts that led to nothing, to writing pilots
and pitch documents that wound up in wastebaskets—and meanwhile to taking jobs in production that, unglamorous though they
were, I'd found by knowing the right people—that I'd almost forgotten there were other kinds of jobs that were more or less readily
available to college graduates, at least in D.C. in 2004 there were.
Although I was ten years too old for filing and Xeroxing, I sent in
a résumé. I touted my experience with the relevant software. I talked
to some woman on the phone for less than ten minutes, and the
next week I landed in an office in Crystal City, consisting of a handful of small rooms that had been modern circa the midseventies
and so were plain and dreary now, in a humble building linked
by tunnel to underground shops and the Metro, so that I came and
went without ever stepping out of doors, a working gopher. My desk
had nothing on it but a telephone and a file tray. Between tasks, I
watched the light change out the window.

went to that job on the day of Dad's panel, and after work I took the Metro straight to Farragut North and walked over to the S——Club, a private social club in an old mansion, where panel discussions were regularly presented for the benefit of its members. Standing before the club's elegant facade, I felt ungainly, a low-caste temp, but I went in, and up the stairs, and into the library, a high-ceilinged, plush, fusty room lined with mahogany bookcases. Collapsible furniture had been set up: a narrow table, with six vacant chairs behind it, stood underneath a line of track lights, and on the other side of the table were chairs for the audience, a handful of them occupied by white people in black coats. Others, still on their feet, mingling and murmuring, looked at me and looked away. Dad had probably invited sixty or seventy friends and acquaintances, but here, ten minutes before the discussion was due to start, there were maybe thirty people total, at least some of whom, surely, had come in support of the other panelists. I found myself making excuses on his behalf. It was early in the evening, when much of Washington was still at work, and it was two days before Thanksgiving besides.

I didn't see my sisters. They were both supposed to come—
Maggie was going to take the train down and stay until Saturday.
It took no more than this, their dual absence, for me to suspect that
they were out somewhere getting a drink and analyzing my deficiencies (such as: the very insecurity and self-involvement behind
that suspicion). A crackly "Helen!" interrupted my fretful reverie. It
was my dad's old friend Jodi Dentoff who, although she was quite a
bit older than the last time I'd seen her, appeared with her magic
intact.

Picture a stage, and now picture, in the wings, a well-seasoned
pixie of a woman who's seen the show a hundred times but still
seems absorbed by it, wryly fascinated: that would be her. She came
striding toward me wearing tall boots with tall heels, and even so
she was short, rasping, touching me on the arm and calling me
"sweetie," which was what she called everyone. She stood before
me as though there were nowhere she'd rather stand, and I sensed
that there wasn't a spot in the wide world where Jodi would not
have exuded the same sense of good fortune—*isn't this wonderful*,
you could imagine her cooing as she entered, for instance, a yurt—
and she fixed me with her big dark sponge eyes and instantly I was
ready to tell her everything I knew and some things I didn't know.
She was a reporter and had that talent for making people want to
talk to her, if you could even call it a talent, for it was as much a
part of her as her physical features, inherent in how she looked
and in how she looked at you, in her mix of sisterly warmth and
perfect chic, in her plucked, arched brows, which prodded you to
account for yourself, and in her very smallness, which put you
at ease.

"I'm so glad your father is doing this," she said.

"He's been looking forward to it," I said.

"How is he?" I had the sense that they were no longer very much
in contact. It wasn't a complete surprise, since I couldn't think of the
last time I'd heard him mention her, but there was a time when
she'd been a frequent guest of my parents', a good friend. Maybe

that was all before the crisis, I didn't remember. Or maybe the friend-ship hadn't survived my parents' divorce.

"He's good, you know, out and about, teaching his class. He's pretty much fully recovered." Was that even true? I wondered. I'd come home to see him, and yet I'd repeatedly felt myself refusing to really see him.

"Recovered?"

"He had a heart thing. A heart attack."

"What?"

"He's doing fine, though."

"Oh. Oh, I'm . . ." She stopped short. Her eyes went off some-place and came back. "Are you home for the holiday?"

"I'm here for a little while. I was kind of between things in L. A. and so I've been staying with my dad. I actually just started a tem-porary job, so. I'm not sure how long I'll be here. I'll probably go back sometime after the new year." Around my parents' friends I would find myself explaining my life in too much detail, trying to make it sound full and reasonable, though the effect, to my ears anyway, was to make it sound empty.

"How nice for your father." She reached into her small black purse and took out a card case, then handed me her business card. "Let me take you to lunch sometime, I'd love to hear about what you and your sisters are up to."

"That'd be great." I didn't think much of it, as I assumed that this was her way of ending a conversation, with the card and the indefinite promise of a lunch.

I claimed a chair in the row next to last, where there were three free seats for my sisters and me, and so placed myself directly be-neath (I noticed too late) a claustral lighting fixture that hung from chains and had put cracks in the ceiling plaster, a brass hazard I thought might well break free and plummet to the floor, or onto my head. The title of the panel—"Opportunities and Costs: Iraq Eighteen Months After the Invasion"—all but made me wish for such a catastrophe.

My father and the other panelists entered and were introduced: so-and-so from such-and-such, a fellow at the Center for X and Y, a former director of Z, the author of A, B, and C, a frequent contributor to D. Dad had been "an official in the Reagan administration," now "an adjunct professor at American University," which was far less of a biography than the rest of them claimed for themselves. As he was introduced he peeped at the audience, not seeing very many of the friends he'd hoped to see. I made my face as bright as I could, so that he would find me at least, but I was so far back, I didn't know whether I was visible to him.

The room seemed to vibrate subtly from ambient noise, from ancient radiators and pipes, and microphone static, and bodies in seats. The moderator (bespectacled, bald) joked that he was especially proud to have netted a panelist from the Department of Defense, "because these days, when you invite people to talk about Iraq, it can be hard to get anyone from the government to call you back." The man from Defense, who was maybe ten years younger than my father, smiled weakly, and once things were under way he made only brief sorties into the discussion. "The media needs to tell the positive stories about Iraq and not just the negative ones," he noted, mentioning the upcoming Iraqi elections and "positive outcomes" in Samarra and Ramadi before going silent again.

There were two other men on the panel besides Dad and the Pentagon official, while the fifth panelist, a visiting scholar in a wine-colored shawl, was an elegant woman who kept her delicate chin lifted during the others' remarks, in a show of listening. Her professional affiliations were with the University of Bristol and Johns Hopkins, her subject the failure to empower Iraqi women. She pronounced "nonnegotiable" with all six syllables, for example, "the inclusion of women in the political sphere is nonnegotiable," and cited statistics on the relationship between the level of women's education and employment in a country and that country's gross domestic product. She undermined herself, I think, by tossing out academic terms that wouldn't have resonated with that crowd—

subaltern, hegemony, subjectivity—yet even those sounded lovely coming out of her mouth. Once she referred to "carefully tailored operations," and I could only picture a company of soldiers dressed as she was, a flock of wine-colored shawls advancing across some desert.

She was the one talking when Maggie snuck in, as if by using those professorial words she'd summoned my professor sister, who with her loose blond hair, her motorcycle jacket, and her relative youth, not to mention the roller bag she had brought with her, stood out in that room full of the middle-aged in button-downs and blazers. She stationed her bag near the door, then slid in next to me, and we whispered back and forth—neither of us knew what had become of Courtney—and then turned our attention to the person now speaking, a straight-spined, white-haired man with a blockish head and a short beard, who said he'd been in the marines (years ago, it must have been) and who consulted his printed notes from time to time.

"There can be no doubt that security is the most important question in Iraq today," he was saying. "If we don't quell the insurgency, the United States will lose control of the country." He spoke of the mistakes of the Allawi government, the need for more U.S. military checkpoints and controls. My sister leaned into me. "Dad doesn't look too thrilled," she whispered. This was true. He frowned at what the ex-marine had to say, or possibly the frown had nothing to do with that. His eyes darted back and forth.

Even before the next man, this one wearing an argyle sweater, took a turn, it was clear that the panelists didn't care much about interacting. No doubt they'd all recently written essays or speeches related to Iraq and would now summarize their own work, the panel like a themed op-ed page come to life. Argyle Sweater's topic was Iraq's economic integration into the global marketplace—it was economic opportunity, he said, that would lead would-be insurgents to put away their bombs and open up shoe factories. Meanwhile we needed to train local police and military so that the Iraqis could take charge of their own security.

At this, the ex-marine sat up even straighter and interrupted. "Based on my conversations with a number of our military commanders, I'd have to say that any proposal to turn over security to the Iraqis would be premature. We have armored vehicles, they have pickup trucks. If we just stand by and let them get hit, then we're just going to cultivate even more resentment of American forces."

"Surely, though, we all recognize we can't occupy the country forever," said Argyle Sweater. "Maybe we provide them with some armored vehicles, but eventually . . ."

"First things first. More checkpoints. Secure the roads."

A pipe belched, and the moderator intervened: "Before we get into particulars, let's hear from the last panelist. Tim? Are there lessons from history that might shed light on the challenges of reconstruction?"

Dad took a deep breath. He had a strange grimace on his face. I knew that he'd prepared for the panel, that he had an answer to the question, but it was as though a fuse had blown. He stayed silent for some twenty or thirty seconds. Then he said, practically yelled, "I don't buy it. I don't buy any of this."

The moderator raised his brows and then followed with: "Maybe you could be a little more specific?"

"Specifically, I think it's all been a bunch of bunkum. We lied to ourselves and made a big mess over there. This idea that we can go into a country, take out the bad guys, and be welcomed by a bunch of would-be Jeffersons and Madisons who've just been waiting to remake their country in our image. The idea that we can create democracies out of whole cloth. When has this ever happened? It's a fantasy."

"Shit," I said under my breath, so that Maggie could hear. She squeezed my arm.

"Shit," she whispered.

"Arguably though, if you look at what's happened in El Salvador and Nicaragua—" began Argyle Sweater.

"We made terrible blunders in Central America," Dad said.

"But speaking about the policies of the 1990s as opposed to the 1980s, we helped foster greater transparency in those countries," the Sweater continued.

"You people are dreaming! When are we going to stop deluding ourselves?"

"We all have microphones," the moderator said. "So there's no need to yell."

"This administration has turned out one rotten idea after another, and our country has lost standing in the world as a result."

"Well, let's come back to that. First I think we should let Maryam have another chance to speak. Maryam?"

I do wonder why he'd been asked to be on the panel in the first place. Maybe an old colleague threw him a bone, someone felt sorry for him, wanted to include him in something: let him trade theses about geopolitics with a few wonks and a visiting scholar. As it turned out, a bad idea. It wasn't the first time I'd seen my father pissed off in public—hardly—but there was a tinny, plaintive quality to his harangue, the anger of a man whom no one hears, a man who believes he's been left alone on an island of reality continually circled by delusional people on party barges. When had my father started sounding like a cranky isolationist? The things he said could've been said by me or one of my friends, at a bar, but on this panel, and (I suspected) in Washington generally, he merely distanced himself from other people by saying them.

His vitriol did resonate with me. As an adult I'd followed politics with enthusiasm at times and at other times out of a sense of duty, but lately only out of duty. Never had I felt more removed from what was happening, more detached, than during the current presidency. The war, the torture, Guantánamo, it had stunned me, and while from time to time there was a petition to sign, or a form letter to send to my congressperson, I felt myself retreating from it all. Dad hadn't done that exactly, but I saw in his alienation a reflection of my own. He didn't utter another word until the moderator asked him to weigh in on a matter being discussed by two of the other men, something about bolstering stability.

"God knows how much money we're wasting, how many millions per week, that's what I think," he said. "Millions down the toilet, down some gold-plated latrine in the middle of the desert. We're not bolstering a thing, except for our egos."

"That's one way to look at it—"

"And these absurd discussions, these agency reorganizations—"

"All right Tim. Thank you. Let's move on."

"Yes, let's! Our government needs to move on, we all need to move on from the idea that we can better our interests through belligerence."

"I don't think anyone here has necessarily advocated for more wars, but we can't turn back the clock, can we? What we're here to talk about tonight is the question of postconflict strategy."

"Postconflict. Hah!"

It might've been an effect of light and shadow, but I thought I could see purple veins in his neck where normally I just saw his skin. His hands pressed down on the table. "Hah!" he said again.

"We have to do something," Maggie whispered to me. "Can we do something?"

"What can we do?"

"Pull the fire alarm?"

I thought it was worth considering. Then Dad noticed us and flinched, which led me to think that he hadn't seen us before then, that he'd believed even his own daughters hadn't shown up. He opened his mouth a bit, in such a way that you couldn't see his teeth, just a darkness between his skimpy lips: for a moment he looked like an old, toothless man in pain.

"Hah!" He pushed himself to standing and stepped back from the table, shoving the folding chair out of the way, and started toward the door. "Hah!" he declared again. He walked out, leaving behind a hushed room. Maggie and I stood up and went after him. People watched us go. I held the door for Maggie as she fetched her suitcase. We should hurry, I thought, we have to catch him before he makes it back to his car—but when we stepped into the hallway we found him sitting in a wing chair. He was gripping his knees and breathing in and out through his mouth, and as we walked toward him he continued to stare straight ahead.

"Are you okay?" I asked.

"I'm having some twinges," he said.

"What kind of twinges?"

He didn't answer but inhaled sharply.

"I'll call an ambulance," I said.

He said he didn't need one, it wasn't that bad. I said I would call the ambulance just in case. He objected again, and I could tell he had a horror of having an ambulance come there to the club, of being seen leaving in an ambulance. "A cab," he repeated. "It'll be faster than waiting for an ambulance to get here."

Maybe it was foolish of us to give in, but we did, we took a taxi to the emergency room.

Four hours later, after Dad had submitted to a series of tests, a doctor told us that there was no evidence of ischemia, as she called it, in other words she could find nothing wrong, but given his recent history, they would admit him overnight for observation. Dad protested, arguing that he didn't care to be observed, but by then Courtney had joined us at the hospital, and Courtney could tell him what to do in a way that Maggie and I couldn't. He listened to her—sometimes he even seemed intimidated by her—so that when she said, "Don't be ridiculous. You're staying," he gave in practically at once and started filling out the admissions paperwork.

If it had just been me, I might well have let him go home. I hated hospitals, they were full of their own risks, contagions, mishaps, and besides, as soon as Dad had left the club and settled into the front seat of the taxi he'd seemed better. He'd carped about what idiots the other panelists had been, not to mention the moderator (that thumbsucker, he called him, whatever that meant), while Maggie and I said nothing. And then once he'd talked past his anger, all the knowledge he'd failed to tap during the panel, the contents of his restless, pack-rat brain, came bubbling up, not in any organized way but because of something he happened to see out the window or just one thing reminding him of another thing.

He'd pointed to what had once been a hardware store, then to the former Chinese embassy (paid for in cash and occupied immediately, he noted, so that the CIA couldn't bug the building). He remembered a party he'd gone to thirty-five years ago at the Hay-Adams (though we were nowhere near the Hay-Adams), where he'd met Robert Bork, at that time the number three man, or some low-numbered man, at Justice. This prompted a digression about Bork, whom Dad said would have been a better pick for attorney general than John Ashcroft, never mind the man's baggage or the fact that by the year 2001 he'd been a little old to be nominated for anything. It was the kind of counterintuitive position that my father liked to stake out at parties. He would anticipate a skeptical response and then deliver up a polished gem of an argument in support of his peculiar thesis. As he talked in the cab, I could picture him saying the same words at a cocktail reception, a fund-raiser for this or that, leaning into another man, Senator Richard Lugar even, intent, tactless, impressively clever. I could see the other man parry once or twice and then make his escape, and that made me want to listen to Dad, to appreciate how smart he was, even as I was, of course, not quite listening to him, but rather half-listening to him while picturing him elsewhere.

Once he'd filled out the admissions papers, we waited with him until a nurse came to take him to his room. As he and the nurse walked down the hall and then disappeared around the corner, my own chest tightened—*wait!*—and I wanted to run and get him and take him home after all. I didn't, though. Courtney drove us back to get Dad's car. By then it was close to midnight, and I was too tired to ask her where she'd been, why she hadn't come to the panel. If she'd been there and we'd all sat in the front row then maybe everything would've gone fine—I hardly believed it, deep down, but even so I resented my sister for that reason, and when she asked me to fill her in on what had happened, I said, "I don't even want to get into it." Before Maggie could tell her, I turned on the radio and started fiddling with the knob. One of the low-bandwidth stations at the bottom of the dial was playing Al B. Sure!, of all things, and I said, "Al B. Sure!" too loudly, and really I couldn't have said why it was such a relief to hear that airy voice from one of the worst years of my life, singing *I can tell you how I feel about you night and day*, but it was, and I started singing along, and then Maggie did too. Courtney said, "Christ," and drove the car.

When we picked him up the following day, Dad complained that he hadn't slept at all, had lain awake for hours listening to the beeping of the hospital machines. This was on the eve of Thanksgiving, and nobody was much in the mood to cook or even to risk the madhouse grocery stores, so I'd made us a restaurant reservation. But on Thursday morning, Dad wandered groggily downstairs in his robe, long after he usually woke up, and asked whether we'd defrosted the turkey. I told him we hadn't bought one, we were going out. He hated the idea, and I felt sure that one reason he hated it was that he didn't want our mom to know that we hadn't pulled off a proper feast. So at the last minute Maggie and I made a run to Whole Foods to try to cobble together a holiday meal. Although we'd hoped to find a smoked turkey, they were sold out. The available substitutes were rotisserie chicken or a vegetarian "field roast," and so we bought a couple of the chickens, along with some prepared sides and a pie, and walked out with a meal in a bag like you might deliver to a needy family, plus a chocolate chip muffin that we split in the car.

Back home, we waited most of the afternoon for Courtney and Hugo to show up. It was part of what we did at that house, what we'd always done, waiting for Courtney. When we were young she would always take the longest to get ready, and any time we were going someplace as a family one of us would stand by the bottom of the stairs and yell up to her. She was meticulous about her clothes, and not only her clothes: before leaving the house, she wanted to arrange everything just so, to straighten her bedspread and line up her stuffed animals, and to go to the bathroom, sometimes more than once, because she hated the feeling of having to go when she was in the car. Although I made fun of her for it, I also coveted her room, it was so clean and orderly, and sometimes when she wasn't home I would go sit in there instead of in my own mess.

I felt the same covetousness as I talked with Maggie about Courtney and Hugo's new house.

"She sent me pictures," Maggie said. "It's something else."

It was unclear to me how much money my older sister and her husband had: more than I did, but the same could be said of anyone with a positive net worth. Hugo had spent ten years doing something in finance, then had left to pursue a doctorate in anthropology or maybe it was archaeology. His family was rich too, though I didn't know how rich.

"I hadn't even realized they were looking for a house until she told me about this one," I said.

"I don't think they were. They just saw it for sale, it's right by where some friends of theirs live. The ones with the twins. They went to an open house and one thing led to another."

"Where did Dad go?" I asked.

She didn't know. "Look at this giant mound on my face. Every month before I have my period I get these monster zits, I hate them," she said. I couldn't see any giant mound, only the beautiful face that I might've had myself, had the genetic cards been dealt differently— except then I wouldn't have been myself. I was often, too often, aware of other ways my life might have gone, but around my sisters that awareness was most acute, because I could clearly see some of the other ways my very face and breasts and legs might've gone.

"There's no giant mound."

"There is! Sometimes I look forward to menopause."

"Uh, not me. Is he in the kitchen?"

"For some reason I thought he was going to take a nap," she said.

Dad emerged from the kitchen with a mouth full of cracker, holding a bottle of wine and a corkscrew. How many times in his life had he done that, I wondered, walked out of the same kitchen with the same bottle of wine.

The doorbell rang and then the door, which hadn't been latched, swung open. "Hellooo!" Courtney cried out, as though calling to us from the opposite bank of a river. Hugo followed along after her, a half smile on his oddly wide face.

Here came my older sister in a hive of wool and silk and perfume and—was there such a garment as cashmere tights? Under her layers of fine clothing were more layers. She made a present of herself, one you couldn't unwrap. Maggie and I had once confessed to each other that we both feared her arrivals a little bit, though after ten minutes or so she softened. We had to steel ourselves for her entrances, her way of breezing in and saying things she'd thought of to say beforehand, mostly for Dad's benefit. Around her I always wished I'd worn something else. After college she'd gone to Italy for eighteen months, and it was there that she developed a taste for fashion, high heels, real jewelry, even as I kept dressing the way she used to dress, in sweaters and corduroys. We joked that she'd applied to business school to increase her clothing budget, and sometimes I wondered whether that notion was so far off.

It might have been the longest conference call in history, she was saying. "Do you know who we had on the phone?"

She named the former chief executive of an oil company, and Dad smiled in wonder. He loved that she consorted with such people, or at least sat in on calls with them.

"He was only on with us for ten minutes, but then we had to spend another two hours dissecting every little thing he said." I couldn't understand why she would've been on a conference call on Thanksgiving morning. Another minute or two passed before I

understood that the call had happened Tuesday evening, that she
was explaining why she'd missed the panel. She'd had to work. It
was her bulletproof excuse. For her (and honestly for most people I
knew), having to work was the universal defense—in almost all
cases, in any nonemergency situation, it was understood to be a
perfectly good reason for letting you down, not calling, not showing
up, though she would claim to feel badly about it and try to make
up for it in ways that were irrelevant at best, or that exacerbated the
slight.

I brushed cheeks with Hugo, who, as he drew back, had the
same moony look on his face he often had. I could never tell whether
that moony look was intended for me (and if so what did it mean?)
or whether he mooned at the world in general. I sometimes thought
of him as the Hugo-knot, and I had a fear that someday I would
address him that way out loud, by accident.

Hugo pronounced my father's name "Team." As in: Team, how
are you doing? What can I tell you, Team?

Dad asked Courtney and Hugo what they wanted to drink.
"Unfortunately we missed the boat on turkey," he said, "but we're
heating up some of those rotisserie chickens."

"Hmm. I'm not really eating meat or dairy these days," Courtney said. "But that's all right."

"Didn't you have short ribs the other night, at the restaurant?"
I asked.

"It's since then that I stopped. I had a bad reaction to the short
ribs. Then I started reading this new book on plant-based eating."

"We also got green beans and mashed sweet potatoes," Maggie
said.

"Is there butter in them?"

"Shoot," Dad said, and he meant it. "Why don't I run to the
store and get something."

"No, that's okay."

"Really. What do you want?"

"I think the stores are probably closed by now," I said.

"Sit down, Dad," Courtney said.

He stood there as if he'd forgotten how to sit.

"I'll make a salad," I announced, rising from my chair. "Sit here, Dad."

"Now you all are treating me like a damn geezer. Sit down, sit down, sit down. I prefer to stand, thank you."

"Okay, stand," Maggie said.

"Team, I stand with you!" Hugo announced. Then he marched over and stood right next to Dad, as though they both were presenting themselves to a superior officer. Our father, who was still getting used to Hugo, made a *hmm-hmm* noise and sat down.

I'd spoken too soon about a salad. We had none of the relevant vegetables. The best I could come up with were a few oranges, a red onion, an ancient can of hearts of palm—I found *Use by 09/97* printed on the bottom and threw it out—and a jar of peanuts. I started to peel and chop the oranges and the onion, while the conversation in the other room floated by. After a minute Courtney came in, opened the refrigerator, and seemed to ask the refrigerator how it was doing.

"All right," I said.

"Is there any more wine?" she called to the living room.

"What?"

Courtney yelled her question more loudly.

Dad said, "What?" again, and Maggie told him, and he said, "More wine?" and Maggie said, "Is there any," and Dad said, "I don't think so"—and then I could hear Hugo trying to convince him he didn't need to go out and buy more wine, which only convinced him that he should do it, until Maggie cut in and said that she and Hugo would go, if any place was open they would go.

"Maggie looks skinny, doesn't she?" Courtney said.

"She's always been skinny."

"Yeah, but did you see how loose her pants are? Do you think it's the Lexapro?"

"She's taking Lexapro?"

"But I always get fatter on SSRIs."

Courtney had lost weight before her wedding a year earlier, then put it all back on again, with interest. Her body had become bulky in the middle, but not at the extremities, which were delicate and carefully adorned; she had the designer shoes, the gold dewdrops in her earlobes. She seemed to me like someone who'd grown up wealthy—not that we had ever wanted for anything when we were kids, but there was a difference between that and really rich, as I'd learned at college, where I met that second type of person, whom Courtney now resembled. The rings on her fingers, the scarf around her neck. An airiness to her voice now, one that hadn't been there when we were teenagers. It was as if all throughout our childhood she'd been leading a secret moneyed life.

"You're not putting those nuts in there, are you?" she asked.

I had poured a little mound of peanuts onto the cutting board. I looked them over. "There wasn't a lot to work with. Dill pickles are also an option."

She picked up the peanut jar and held it away from her body. "They dump these chemicals on before they roast them."

"You mean like salt?"

"I'm serious."

"I'll put them on the side," I said. "In a separate dish."

"Thanks."

As a teenage jock Courtney had been mischievous, at least some of the time. She'd also been repeatedly disappointed, for though she had tried again and again to elbow her way to the top, she had always landed in the number two or three slot, third in her class, second in the voting for lacrosse team captain. Each near miss had prompted nonchalance in public, tears at home, and a redoubling of her efforts. I think it had always confused her that I didn't have the kinds of ambitions she had, though if she'd ever had the chance to observe herself from the outside, if she could've seen how miserable her perfectionist tendencies had made her, then maybe she would've understood. Besides, I did nurse some ambitions of my own, just ones that she didn't recognize as such. They were unwieldy ambitions, and I downplayed them, even as I conducted clandestine operations on their behalf.

"How's that new job going," she asked, and I told her about it. She stared at me, no doubt wondering at the fact that I was being paid to do such things, and impulsively I told her I had another project on my proverbial plate, something that had started out as a screenplay but that I was now attempting to turn into prose.

"Prose—"

"A prose narrative," I said.

"A *prose narrative*?"

I'd bought myself a notebook, and I'd started to write sketches, partial scenes, much of it crossed out the next day. So far I hadn't told anyone what I was up to, nor could I have told them exactly. I certainly didn't want to call it a novel. An Iran-Contra novel was worse than an Iran-Contra feature film, and only an Iran-Contra epic poem or maybe an Iran-Contra operetta would have been less promising.

"Like a book," I said.

"About?"

"Iran-Contra."

"Seriously."

"What happened to Dad, his whole story. And I also would want to include what we went through, that whole thing of growing up here."

Once I'd started thinking about Dad and Dick Mitchell, I'd found myself remembering other times I'd seen them together, mainly at the parties my parents used to have, and then I was remembering myself at those parties. I wanted to bring in those memories also, even though my notions of Dad's past and my own didn't seem entirely compatible. I didn't know whether I was aiming for one book or two.

"You wrote a screenplay about all that?"

"The screenplay was more limited to the political side, but now I'm expanding on it."

"I think we had a good childhood."

"I didn't say we didn't."

"You've implied it plenty of times, and now it sounds to me like you're writing this book about 'what we went through.' You say it in a certain tone of voice. When I think of growing up, I think about us playing in the snow, going to school, swimming. We had our own pool! We were lucky."

"Sure, but—"

"We had it pretty good, I think. No one's going to feel sorry for us."

"I'm not saying they should."

"We had it good, even if Dad effed things up," she said.

"I don't know—"

"He totally did. But whatever. The pity party ended a long time ago."

"It's not—"

"I mean, get a grip. We're adults now."

This sounded like something she was in the habit of saying to herself: *get a grip.*

"Speak for yourself." I meant that as a joke, but she didn't respond.

"Anyway, we should do something, you and me," she said.

"Sure, let's go out," I said, but she had another idea. She said she'd organized a blood drive at her office but had been sick that day, and so she was planning to go give blood the Saturday after this one. Why didn't I come with her? We could have lunch afterward.

This was another of Courtney's compulsions, one she'd inherited from our mom, who'd worked for many years as head of development for the American Red Cross. I glanced at my salad. "You okay with oranges and onions? They might have been sprayed with something, you know, more chemicals."

She grabbed a section of orange and put it in her mouth, then made a stricken, bulging face as if she'd been poisoned. I made a face back at her. Then she told me there was someone at her office she wanted to set me up with, a guy named Brandon or Brad or Brent, some name I didn't find so promising, but it was less the name than the fact that my sister, though she'd married a man from Mexico, would try to nudge me toward the Waspiest of guys. I'd thought I might tell her about Rob at some point, but I held back. Before, it hadn't seemed so significant to sleep with someone she'd dated years and years ago, but maybe I'd just been telling myself that, to give my wants the go-ahead.

Just as we were finishing dinner, Mom called from Philadelphia, and we passed the phone around and took turns having the same brief back-and-forth. She was calling from a friend's house, and I could hear festive noises in the background, a man's deep laughter, the clank and echo of somebody's good china, good silver. My mother was having a lively meal with friends while we were eating microwaved things from a deli case, which, in a way, we were doing for her benefit, so that Dad could tell her we were having Thanksgiving at home. I didn't say much before handing the phone to Maggie. Anyway the connection was poor. When Dad took the phone, he kept asking, "What?" and "Say again?" And then he told her, "Oh, we're having a fine time here." There was a gentle quality to his voice that I'd never heard him use with her when they were married, and now it bothered me to hear it. He didn't mention his overnight stay in the hospital.

We hung up, and then Courtney announced that she and Hugo had to get going.

"It's only quarter past nine," I said.

"I'm on an early schedule these days."

I wished she would stay a little longer, if only to please Dad, but she left all the same. Afterward he went into the kitchen for something, and Maggie and I nestled into the couch and finished off the wine.

"They should have a kid," I said. "We'll be maiden aunts."

Maggie winced at that, then rallied. "Speak for yourself. I want to be a dowager," she said.

"What is a dowager again?"

Dad had come up behind us, unnoticed until he protested, "You two ought to be a little less worried about your sister and a little more worried about yourselves."

"Dad!" I said.

"I'm serious," he said.

Only with a couple of glasses of wine in him would he say even that much, but I knew that what he wanted, maybe what he desired most of all in this world, hell-pitched handbasket though it might be, was that his daughters marry and procreate. Now, under the influence, he began to deploy some of his old diplomacy—or a more erratic and wheedling variation of it.

"Did you watch the news last night?" he started. "That accident in Herndon?" A kid had been stranded for hours in the back of a pickup truck, and as if that very kid were the grandchild we'd so far denied him, he began to talk about auto safety.

"What does that have to do with us dating?" Maggie asked.

"This is not about dating!" Dad said. "This is about people out there just driving around and hoping for the best! They are not prepared. Do either of you even know how to change a tire?"

"You get out of the car," Maggie said, "and wait for someone to stop and help you."

"What if there is nobody, what if you're out in the middle of nowhere?"

"I live in New York City. I don't even own a car."

"I left mine in L.A."

He looked to the ceiling in exasperation. What is to be done? That was his question. He had gone by the book, followed proper procedure, or mostly he had, and the rest of us had not held up our end of the bargain. The rest of the planet had not. Nobody was going to come help us change the tire.

And that was how we found ourselves standing in the driveway, watching Dad jack up the Camry. He marched us out into the mist-marbled night and went to work, while Maggie and I stood behind him, still holding our wineglasses. It was the same inscrutable demonstration he'd given each of us when we turned sixteen, in which he kept his back to us and didn't explain what he was doing, only this time it was late and it was cold and he was having trouble with the job. Periodically he would mutter "Hold on" or "Now watch" or "You see?" All I saw was Dad fumbling with the tools, the three of us washed up on the small island of artificial illumination created by the driveway security light, which on its own was insufficient for the task at hand, since its beam didn't quite reach the side of the car where Dad was squatting. Maggie offered to hold the flashlight, but before he passed it over he felt compelled to demonstrate how to turn it off and on, even though it was already on, and a young child could have figured out how to press its big orange button. Once he'd turned it off, though, it wouldn't come back on, much as he pressed the button and shook the flashlight and said "Give me a break."

So we retreated inside to refill our glasses and look for batteries, and I went upstairs to use the bathroom, or so I said. Really it was just to hide out for a minute or two.

In my room I fell on the bed, then lay across its width, my head hanging over the side. I wriggled backward, so that more and more of my upper body was hanging off the edge, and my entire trunk was stretched out, a position I used to put myself in, it now came back to me viscerally, when I was twelve and thirteen. I used to *read* like that, for the sheer pleasure of being upside down, a pleasure that was inaccessible to me nowadays—now what I felt was the blood rushing to my face and my nose starting to itch—but that had to do with feeling disoriented and dizzy but safe at the same time.

After half a minute I rolled over, in flailing-porpoise fashion, until I was hanging over the bed facedown and could see underneath it. I hung there with the side of the bed pressing into my stomach. I was a bit drunk, I noted. I took in the usual cobwebs and obligatory stray sock—how long had it been there?—which I pulled out and did not recognize.

And in retrieving that mossy old sock I realized I'd been reaching for my diary, one of the diaries that I'd kept irregularly in high school and stowed under my bed. I didn't know what had become of them, they were in a box someplace, but I could picture my old handwriting and the embarrassing lists, of foods I'd eaten and boys I liked and resolutions to self-improve, to work harder, to be kinder.

Back then I'd had an imaginary person whom I tried to emulate. Not an imaginary friend, exactly, because she was always ahead of me, rounding a bend, slipping out of sight, but an imaginary double. The person I should have been, if I'd been better. She was a more sparkling Helen, thinner, blonder, taller, free of Courtney's shadow. I'd thought of her as my idol, my goal, Platonic Helen, though as I recalled her for the first time in years, she seemed less like any version of myself and more like the generic blond popular girls I'd had little in common with, her elusive image just another tool I used to undercut myself.

I got off the bed, shoved open the window, and climbed out onto the section of roof that I could access from there, a shingled slope above the family room. In ninth grade, I used to sit and try to communicate telepathically with my future boyfriend. Later I would sneak cigarettes, less from actually wanting to smoke them than on principle. In the driveway, my father and my sister were out changing the tire again, and I thought about calling to them but didn't. I was freezing. A blurry crescent moon hung above the hulking forms of houses, above the streets I'd known as a girl, the brick sidewalks and holly bushes, and though I'd come back to the city it was as if I'd left this domain of well-off families and would not be allowed to reenter. People like my older sister were buying the kind of house our parents had bought, while I'd gone off track. And this teenage girl I'd been, the things she told herself, and the story I continued to tell myself about her—as I sat there in her spot on the roof it all started to seem too pat, the tale of the gawky, second-rate girl I was. I'd made up that story in high school, just as I'd invented the story of her better double, and told it to myself ever since. I sank my head back, stretched my chin toward the sky, and stared at a star that turned out to be a satellite. And I thought of all the nights I'd sat out here, resolving to eat nothing but apples, or nothing at all, to become weightless, to replace myself with a perfect, gossamer copy.

You should come up to New York with me," Maggie offered, at breakfast. Both of us felt more hungover on Friday morning than we'd felt drunk the night before. Dad had made us eggs and bacon, then left to run errands. Especially when we came to visit, he was a compulsive provisioner, always going out to buy lightbulbs or Dijon mustard, his random needs usually met by an eclectic grocery on Wisconsin Avenue that might as well have been built just to cater to him, with two floors of anything and everything. Maggie and I picked at our eggs, preferring the stale almond cookies I'd pulled from a cabinet. It was overcast outside, a blunted light entering the room by way of the window over the sink, but then a thin shaft of sun broke through and hit my sister's cheek, as though she'd been selected for some special assignment.

She was taking a midday train. There was a dinner party she'd been invited to, that was her excuse for leaving early. And papers to grade.

"I've got to get out of here," I said, knowing I wouldn't go to New York.

"Did you ever hear back from that guy?" she asked.

I'd been proud of myself for not bringing him up, and so no doubt sounded oddly proud when I told her that I had not. "Possibly he's just been busy, but . . ."

"These busy men."

"Yeah."

"We just need to move someplace where there are more men than women, and people are not that busy. I'm wondering about the Dakotas."

"You'll never move to the Dakotas. To either Dakota."

She tried to break a cookie in half, and it fell apart, into crumbs.

"I didn't tell you, though, who he actually was," I said.

"The guy? Some D.C. d-bag, it sounded like."

"He's not so bad."

"Not a douchebag."

"Maybe a little bit of one. A douchebaguette?"

Maggie waited, and I told her who it was.

"Courtney's Rob? Her ex?"

"They didn't go out for very long," I said. "I doubt she'd even call him an ex."

"Wasn't he like a drug dealer?"

"I wouldn't say that. He was not a full-on drug dealer."

"I know I was only in junior high at the time, but my understanding was that he gave people drugs and they gave him money."

"It was just among friends, though. He was not a real dealer."

The sunlight had left her face, and I could see that she wasn't going to accept my distinction between offhand drug sales and genuine dealing, but she wasn't going to pursue it either. In that way she was more sensible than Courtney and me, who would've spent another five minutes debating the point.

"Did you tell Courtney?" she asked.

"No. I shouldn't, right?"

"I wouldn't. She's been so prickly lately. I know she's still upset about losing the pregnancy—"

"Wait—"

"Oh."

"What?"

"You didn't know."

"No."

"I assumed you did, but then last night, when you said she should have a kid, I wasn't sure . . ."

"Fuck."

"Maybe I shouldn't—well, whatever, I already said it. She had a miscarriage. It was pretty early, but still."

"She told you about it?"

"It's probably just that I happened to call that day?" Maggie said. "I guess they'd been trying for a while."

"I thought she didn't even want kids."

"She was on the fence at first, but Hugo wanted to, and she came around."

I was having all the wrong feelings. I felt bad for Courtney, but a miscarriage was something I had no experience of and could barely fathom, and I was nearly as envious as I was sorry, mainly of my sisters' intimacies with each other, but also of the whole idea that marriage, even to an oddball like Hugo, could nudge a person past her ambivalences and propel life forward. Courtney in her lifetime had attracted more—I don't want to call it tragedy—let's say adversity, more than her share and certainly more than I'd had to deal with, and in my worst moments I envied that too. More adversity was still more life. More adversity made more life happen. For my part, I'd always thought that in some nebulous future I would have kids, picturing two boys, but now that I found myself in my thirties and single, I could sense, not a ticking clock, but those boys themselves fading away.

Something had curdled, and we fell quiet. Dad came home with his haul (batteries, a case of seltzer, razor blades, printer paper, and two chocolate bars) and then took Maggie to the train station.

"See you at Christmas," I said to her before she left, and she told me again to come up and visit her. "I will, I will"—I said that and meant it.

There were dishes from the night before in the sink, along with the pans that Dad had used to make breakfast. I left them for the time being, put a spare key in my pocket, and stepped out for air, still woozy as I rambled around, and pissed off and sad in the same muzzled way I always felt pissed off and sad after family occasions, holidays especially—and add fifty points for a hangover. It's not right! It's not fair! Those childish complaints rang in my head without referring to anything, the "it" was life as a whole, and so I was walking around and waiting for those emotions to clear, what else could I do?

I could run, I thought. Running was much better for metabolizing all that crud, and so even though I was wearing jeans and boots, I started to run down the street, my boot heels clopping against the sidewalk, my jacket drawstrings bouncing up and down, my hair flying everywhere, dogs barking as I loped by. I ran after those imaginary little boys, who were so much faster than me, around the block and down Reno Road and past my old elementary school.

Coming back to Washington had not quite had the effect I'd hoped it would have—I'd hoped it would help me clear more space in my head. Now, though, I just felt like a woman who'd come to the end of the line. I had ridden back home disguised as myself and could ride no farther, having arrived at the shore to find the horizon flat and empty, not a ship in sight. They'd all sailed. It was too late for me, I couldn't stop thinking that. What else was there for me to do in the meantime but keep busy? I'd gone on temping, I'd read about Iran-Contra, and I'd tried not to ruminate too much on what my long-term plan might be—which is to say I didn't think about it at all, because I didn't want to go back to California, back to what I'd been doing, but when I imagined changing my life what I thought to change was the past.

But, I told myself, life is no stationary bicycle. Rest assured, change is the only constant.

But: I was not resting, I was not assured.

But! Only later do the toings and froings add up to a direction. You change and you don't notice, other people see it first, and you're someone you never expected to be, and at the same time you're the person you always were. I told myself this, believed it too. More or less. Even so I was terrified.

I didn't think of myself as missing L.A. I did miss the Honda that I'd left with a friend. I missed my old duplex apartment. I missed my L.A. friends, I missed Griffith Park and taco trucks, I missed my fruit guy, and I missed that balmy weather that sometimes felt like a benediction and at other times felt unnatural and menacing.

And now, because I'd grown up in D.C. and then left, it was both the place I belonged and a place I didn't recognize. I'd been raised in a well-off white blister attached to a black city I hardly knew, but the blister had since burst. Starbucks and yoga studios everywhere, and all these new apartment buildings, cute new shops. Defense contracts weren't the only thing that had brought them here, not every young professional in D.C. was part of the national security workforce, but I still felt as if the wars on the other side of the world were indirectly underwriting the colorful awnings and the artisanal ice cream; and though ten years earlier that fact would have disgusted me—I would've felt outrage, refused to eat the ice cream, etc.—now I reacted with the same learned helplessness I felt toward the stupid movies they kept making in Hollywood. I had no say in the making of war or in the making of stupid movies but had lived most of my life in cities sponsored by one or the other, and though stupid movies were not as damaging as stupid wars, my options seemed to be the same in either case, I could watch them or I could not watch them, and if I felt so inclined I could make comments about them in an online forum.

I'll acknowledge that this line of thinking seems a little pat. I could see that it might be flawed, but I couldn't shake it loose. I was the sty in my own eye, I'll say that much. And there were days when it all piled up, it all seemed too much, returning a phone call like lifting a car by its bumper, retrieving a prescription a trek across the tundra. The difficulty came not in spite of the trivial nature of these activities but because of it.

I walked the last stretch. I was not in shape, and not until I'd almost made it home did my breathing return to normal. Looking up at the house, our impervious, oblivious house, I thought: I should not be living here. This place could swallow me up.

Dad had come home while I'd been out. Because he wasn't on the first floor, that I could see, I called "Hello-o" in the direction of the stairs, and waited for his reply. He didn't answer. "Dad?" Still nothing. I climbed up halfway to the second floor. "Dad?" I heard the toilet flush.

"Helen?"

"Hey, I'm back."

"Could you clean up those dishes please? The kitchen is a mess."

I was silent, until he said "Helen?" again.

"Okay!"

"Thank you."

PART TWO

Dick Mitchell was Dad's best friend—I heard Dad say that once. I don't know whether the best friendship was mutual. The Dick Mitchell of my memory is a bon vivant, a joker, not really the type to have a best friend, though no doubt he was more complicated than the affable operator he'd seemed to be. The main thing I know about him is that he killed himself; I don't remember how I learned it. After he died, our parents told us that he'd been sick. But we found out, somehow everybody at school seemed to know that Rob Golden's stepfather had committed suicide, a fact that kept circulating because none of us could absorb it. There were two girls at our school who'd tried to kill themselves but survived, and there was Ernest Hemingway, but before Dick Mitchell died I couldn't have conceived that a man like that, a friend of my parents, might take his own life.

The funeral took place at a narrow, slate-gray church in a transitional part of downtown, a sparse few blocks lodged in between more residential and more commercial neighborhoods. Outside the church, on a blackboard shaped like a pope's hat, white lettering spelled out Richard James Mitchell, 1938–1988, and I remember the strangeness of seeing the current year written that way, as the year of someone's death. Courtney was away at college by then. Maggie and I wore Jessica McClintock dresses, lace bibs falling over floral prints, as if we were much younger than we actually were. We wore stockings and black Mary Janes.

I saw my father press his shaky lips together, look down at his shoes. I had the impression that he was supposed to give a eulogy, but he never did. We sang hymns, and I could barely hear his voice, though my mother's was strong, maybe a little too strong. Rob Golden was there too, of course, home from whatever school he'd gone to—Bennington, I think, or was it Wesleyan? He'd dyed his hair platinum blond and had an earring in one ear, and was sitting in the front row, his hair all the whiter by contrast with his black-suited shoulders. I didn't speak to him, too shy and also embarrassed by what I was wearing. Mom had bought us those little-girl outfits, and after the service we became little girls. We ran giddily, giggling, around a park across the street from where the reception was, sweating and scuffing up our shoes. We waited there while our parents drank wine and talked to people. We came home with bloody ankles because of those stiff shoes and had to throw out our stockings.

An obituary from the Branberry, Connecticut, *Weekly Record*, dated September 27, 1988, for Richard J. Mitchell, fifty:

Richard J. Mitchell, a former deputy assistant secretary of state, died suddenly at his home in Bethesda, Maryland, on Sunday. Mr. Mitchell had been an aide to the assistant secretary for international security affairs at the Department of Defense, an executive assistant for policy planning at the Department of State, and a deputy assistant secretary of state. He also served as a trustee of the St. Albans School and as an officer of the Metropolitan Club.

Mr. Mitchell was born in Branberry. He graduated from Milton Academy in 1956 and from Harvard University in 1960, where he was Phi Beta Kappa. He entered the doctoral program in political science at Cornell University and received an M.A. degree before discontinuing his studies. He then went to Washington, where he was an aide to Senator Leverett Saltonstall and later worked for the U.S. Arms Control and Disarmament Agency.

Mr. Mitchell is survived by his second wife, the former Martha Golden, his stepson, Robert Golden, his mother, Mrs. Wilbur D. Mitchell, and two sisters, Lillian McCrory and Marjorie Reiss. A service will be held at the Christ Church of Washington on Friday, September 30, at 11:00 a.m.

I found this online. The *Record* from that era had been scanned whole, and so I read from an image of that week's actual page B7, set in one of those round 1980s typefaces, with halftone-dot shading around the names of the deceased. On the same page were three other death announcements and two advertisements for local businesses. *A world-class bank with a hometown feel.* I read and reread Mitchell's obituary, as if by starting again I might find the story changed, though he died every time, suddenly, at his home in Bethesda, Maryland.

My father had always looked up to him, that was my impression—albeit an impression based in my protean childhood ideas of who looked up to whom, and maybe an adult would've noticed that Dad had other feelings about his friend as well. I remember Dick's once tossing a dollar into the lit charcoal of our grill, making a joke about inflation. My dad never would've done that. And yet, as dutiful as he was, Dad still cared about what Washington cared about, whether you call it power or whether you call it a compulsion to get as close as possible to the action, and here was Dick, who found the action as if without effort.

I thought of him as the pied piper who led my father to Washington. Dick Mitchell with his long neck, his confidential smile. At

Cornell, they'd both been members of the College Republicans. Mitchell rarely went to the meetings but always seemed to know everything that happened at them, my father once told me. He was one of those guys who soaked up all the members' personal information, the dynamics of the group itself, the political nitty-gritty. There was a rumor, Dad said, that he'd managed to fix a campus election, though Dad hadn't believed it—vote stealing seemed beneath Dick. Then again, I discovered later that there were other things that would've seemed beneath Dick Mitchell but which, in fact, he did.

They were both in the thrall of Gerald Sayles, the nuclear strategist: for his famous course on technology and war, in which the assigned reading included his own writings as well as Wohlstetter's and Markov's, a hundred or more students would crowd the lecture hall, among them Dick Mitchell, in the back row and without a notebook, and Tim Atherton, who would show up early to claim a spot in the front row.

I could see it, my dad and Dick at Cornell.

. . . Sinewy old Sayles is a campus celebrity, technocracy's champion and prophet. His winged eyebrows and the deep crease between them contribute to his aura of genius. Trained as a physicist, he favors quantitative analysis, he likes to assign a probability P and write formulas on the blackboard in noisy, jabbing strokes, yet he emphasizes that these equations have "unknown terms," because so much information is not available to the public. *The body of secrets* is one name for that material, as in, "Any public assessment of military policy is of limited significance, given the body of secrets within the U.S. and Soviet governments." At other times he speaks of "the expanding frontier of secrecy," his tone approving. Some knowledge is and should be the special province of the elite, he implies, and part of his mystique is the implication that he has some larger access to the body of secrets—that he belongs to that elite, or at least knows it intimately. Mitchell can often be seen in Sayles's office, cross-legged in the chair opposite the great man's desk. He has the smoothness of wealth as well as the premature lines that appeared on his face during an extended stay at McLean, the psychiatric hospital, during which time he submitted to shock treatments that left him pretty well stripped of any memories of his years at Milton Academy. Mitchell takes note of a bright undergraduate named Tim Atherton, who asks questions he hasn't thought to ask, and what begins as discussions in the corridor after class would grow into walks across the quad and then beers at night . . .

That was what I started with, the two of them way back when. Even in death, Mitchell still had this magnetism about him, so that I could picture his life in a way that I found it difficult to picture my dad's—and then, once I had him, I could put the two of them together. It's true that these images, conjured out of bits and pieces, led me away from the small set of facts I had about my father's past. Although I considered my project to be biographical, I was inventing much of it as I went along. I decided—not at the outset, but as I scrawled and scratched out—that the best way to improve upon the kind of I-was-there! bullshit served up in *A Call to Honor* would be to create a more honest story, even if it was an honest invention. My aim was to flesh out the book that Dad had stalled on, to finish what he'd started. That I didn't know the full story, that he was reluctant to tell it to me, that we remembered those days so differently—these were not trivial obstacles, but I started to think I could write my way around them.

Which is not to say I was pulling it all out of my ass. I continued to consult outside sources. I'd lugged my dad's dusty old course reading up from the basement, textbooks and technical papers that he and Mitchell would've been assigned. Studying with the likes of Gerald Sayles and others had steeped them in a set of methods, an approach to geopolitical conundrums, the arms race in particular. The threats against us became terms in equations. Computers were programmed to evaluate the likelihood of nuclear war.

"The Delicate Balance of Terror" was the name of one of Albert Wohlstetter's widely circulated papers, from 1958. I found it online and printed it out in nine-point font, and of all things I climbed into bed with it. "I should like to examine the stability of the thermonuclear balance," he begins—and then he goes on to suggest that it's hardly stable at all. The postwar world, that happy land of big cars and big refrigerators, rests on a fulcrum made of uranium. I read the whole paper, every tiny word. The sentences washed over me and away, but the tone, the assumptions stuck, the crazy (to me) clash between the grand pessimism of overall outlook and the optimism about methods. The ongoing threat of global apocalypse could be countered with quasimathematical analysis. Numbers of missiles, payloads: what faith in their own calculating! It was a doomsday algebra they invented, to combat our math-savvy antagonists behind the Iron Curtain.

To one side of my bed was a window, an old ivory-colored shade covering the upper half while in the lower half I could see my reflection in the glass, my knees drawn up and the paper resting against them. When I saw that, I felt as if I were acting, putting on a show of studiousness for an audience of one, i.e., myself. And yet, haphazard as this whole course of research was, I did learn from it. Some remnant of that midcentury military-industrial mind had stayed with us, hadn't it? A machine inside a ghost. This was how some people who were still in power had been taught to understand the world, long ago, in different times. This was the rug that had been yanked out from under them. Secrecy, quantitative analysis, the best plans made by the best men.

I was drawn to the jargon my father would have learned then and also later, after he went to Washington, terms that cropped up in selected circles in the seventies and eighties, like *procurement* and *operationalize* and *off-the-shelf covert capability*. All those words that meant nothing but pointed to something, the confidence disguised as procuring and operating, the belief in our ability to analyze and control. To manipulate other nations like numbers.

And in his stiff old textbooks, I found Dad's underlining, the odd phrase penciled in the margin. Alongside the densely printed text of a book called *East-West Relations in the Atomic Weapons Era*, for instance, he'd written short notes, indicators of what was discussed on that page, like *nuclear aggression—consequences* and *reflexive choices*. Or was it *reflective choices*? These notes also got to me, though here it wasn't the words but the handwriting, recognizably my dad's, if neater and firmer. That script belonged to a twenty-year-old student with his mechanical pencil, the eager debater in his bilateral world of pro and con, west and east, good and evil, all or nothing.

With the help of the Internet I found a place of my own, and I told Dad I'd signed a lease on an apartment, a semi-furnished studio I could rent month to month. It was in one of the few remaining areas of D.C. that had not yet been thoroughly gentrified—that process was still in the early stages. When I explained where the apartment was, he scowled. No, he said, you shouldn't live over there by yourself. And then he said I needed to be mindful of "the security situation." Explaining that it was now home to a few artists' studios and a coffee shop had no effect. He insisted he would help me pay for a place in a better neighborhood, I said I didn't want him to do that, and in this way we circumscribed the subject of my departure without ever addressing it.

I wanted to live where I chose to live. During my childhood it was an area we'd driven through and never stopped in, which lent it a mystery that, for me, had always had as its wellspring the House of Wigs, a store on a corner that displayed tiers of faceless plastic heads wearing every sort of hair and, in some cases, fanciful hats. When I moved I was pleased to discover that the House of Wigs was still in business, though now the store, much dustier than in my

memory, seemed to cater to cancer and head-surgery patients. I
took up residence a few blocks from there, on Vane Street North-
east. Faded town houses that had been divided into apartments
lined most of the block, but mine was a corner building of brown
brick, with bars over the first-floor windows.

Dad helped me move in, and while he was there he checked out
the apartment, the suspect locks, the windows that according to him
should have been constructed differently. He was very much dissatisfied. He left me with a list of demands he thought I should make
to the landlady, demands I did not make, and from time to time
after that he would leave long messages in the middle of the day
about exploding water heaters and other hazards. Naively, I saw this
as a good thing, his preoccupation with the apartment, because it
focused all his worries about my life on what was, to me, the least
worrisome component, and so I was content to hear him out.

On the phone he was a different father. He would call to check
on me, and although we'd chatted plenty when I lived in other cities, these calls from across town had a new quality to them. I could
practically hear our nearness, the way you hear static or breath. He
might've been gabbing about any old thing, the Redskins' running
game or airline fares, and still there was this underlying sense of *I'm
right here, I'm right here.*

Loosely defined as the whole book project was, I began working in earnest, staying up late to crawl through the underbrush of
an imaginary bureaucracy, as memories of the eighties brewed, and
I brooded, at odds with myself. For no reason at all I pictured the
small white stickers that had appeared on bus stops and trash cans
when I was in high school, which had on them an ugly caricature
of the U.S. attorney general and below that the slogan: "Meese Is
a Pig." These came later, after Iran-Contra, in response to a lesser
scandal, but still. Rained-on, halfway scraped-off, melting Meeses
were with me as I wrote.

The afterimage of those stickers suited my twilight leanings,
the sense I had that the scandal marked the end of something. At

least, that was a sense I wanted to have. I wanted the scandal to pos-
sess historical weight, to mark the End of an Era, even if I couldn't
name the era. I wanted to tie it to the decline of the so-called Washington Consensus, to see the NSC mandarins' secret activities as the
reduction to absurdity of an older way of doing things, back when
policies had been fashioned by a small chummy group who dined
at the homes of Georgetown hostesses. I wanted to understand Iran-
Contra as a parody-triumph of all that, militarism as the new pa-
ternalism, the inner circle outdone by a junta. But even if there was
a case to be made (and I would be out of my depth trying to make
it), what did it matter? As best I could tell, one sort of ruling caste
had just been replaced by another, more corporate one. And much
as I wanted meaning on a grander scale, my terminal feeling had
not arisen sheerly or even primarily from my spotty understanding
of history. It came from sources and experiences closer to home.

The downside to my microapartment, for me, was not its loca-
tion or its window glass but the fact that I slept poorly there those
first nights. I don't know what the cause was—not street noise, not
the bed—but after I moved in, sleep was coy, a tease, and I would
spend half the night chasing it around those three hundred square
feet, only to sink deep into dreaming just before dawn, then wake
up again as soon as the sun infiltrated the room. I rose in fits and
starts; I dressed petulantly. To actually wake myself up, I relied on
a morning walk and a double espresso: before that beverage I was a
muddled brain weakly bleating out instructions to a distant and
uncooperative body.

I will go ahead and admit that I was reassured by the sight of
other white people in the neighborhood. I wasn't sure who lived
around there now, and I'd had a fear that I would feel extremely
conspicuous every time I went out. Instead I only felt somewhat
conspicuous. At a nearby playground, I saw a white girl shooting
baskets at a hoop without a net, in a taut ponytail and a headband
and shiny red shorts that fell almost to her knees. And there was a
man, I'd guess in his midforties, who lived in the town house next
to my building and who on some mornings would come out the

door just as I was coming out my door. I would follow in the same direction until he turned left toward the Metro station and I kept on walking straight ahead, toward the nearest coffee shop, a coffee shop that aspired to the status of cultural center, with shelves of left-wing reading material and movies for rent, and was populated by hipsters, kids in their early twenties wearing mismatched clothes from Value Village. It seemed these people were biding their time until they could move to some even more blighted neighborhood in Brooklyn or Queens. Hence Voltaic (this was the name of the place) had the feel of a train station or a dock, one where the awaiting passengers read Chomsky and discussed recent sexual endeavors and community organizing. On two or three hours of sleep I was never in the mood for any of that, and so I would down my espresso and be on my way.

Soon after I moved in I met the neighbor I'd noticed walking down my street, in fact more or less collided with him. I hadn't seen him when I left my building, and I was proceeding along my morning route when at an intersection I nearly stumbled into traffic. My eyes had been locked on the walk signal ahead of me, not the orange-smocked police with their whistles and their outstretched arms, not the approaching motorcade. Just as I was about to launch off the curb, someone took hold of my arm. And then a police motor-cycle zipped by, right in front of me, and for a moment I had one of the stranger sensations I've ever had: it was as though the sudden backward thrust had ejected some part of me right out the rear, so that I was watching myself from behind, for a second or two. If even that long. No sooner had the feeling arrived than it was gone.

I sucked in air. And I turned, with a keener interest than I might have had otherwise, to face that gangly guy I'd tailed on previous mornings. His eyes were hard to see behind his glasses. I had the impression of someone who, like me, didn't exercise much. His pants were baggy and woolen, and his chest bowed beneath a brown worm of a necktie—in fact everything he wore was brown, aside from his shirt, a faded blue, although none of it exactly matched. (But consider what he would have seen in me, a dazed girl—woman, I should say, but I have always had trouble saying it—hugging a tote bag.) He rubbed his forehead and apologized.

I asked him what he was sorry for, and he began, "For grabbing you in such a . . ." and then paused. As he searched for a word his hand moved in a circle. "Such an *adverse* way," he said.

Better than death by cop, which, I told him, would have been very adverse. It might have seemed to him that I was poking fun at his way of talking. But that was just my way of talking. We watched the vehicles go by, a series of motorcycles followed by three of those long black cars that reminded me of crocodiles. Attached to one of the limousines was a fluttering green and yellow flag.

"There go the generals!" he said. He put his thumb to his lips and mimicked a bugle fanfare, *doo do-do doooo.* There was something embarrassing about the way he sang out like that. I don't know why he thought there were generals in those cars.

Between the flaps of his brown blazer I could see a lanyard around his neck, a bureaucrat's work badge at navel-level. Silence swelled up between us. I considered then rejected the idea that we would fall improbably in love. No we wouldn't. He told me his name, Daniel, and I told him mine. I thanked him again, and we hastened away from each other.

That evening I called my mother, which I didn't do often. When I was in a good mood I didn't want to be brought down, and when I was in a sour mood I didn't have it in me. I called only when I was in a middling mood, and after a drink. Typically the conversation went better if I had news she would approve of, such as my having found a job and an apartment. Now, though, it only seemed to confuse her.

"So are you going to stay in Washington?" she asked me.

"Not forever, but—"

"I never really pictured you living there as an adult. It doesn't seem like the right place for you."

"I think I can adapt, at least for now."

"God knows it wasn't the right place for me."

But hadn't it been? My mom had molded herself into that exemplary Washington wife, blond and underweight, who favored crisp shirts and cardigans paired with the pearls she'd worn since college, who swam laps at the Chevy Chase Club and knew the number for Ridgewells, the catering company, by heart. Who met every unfortunate turn, whether it was a blighted azalea bush or a sick child, with the same semidetached poise.

She was a self-made WASP, not a born one. Her stock was Swedish, by way of Texas: an ancestor had hopped on the wrong boat, or so I pictured it, and instead of making his way to Minneapolis or Chicago or another of the communities where his countrymen were clustered, he'd landed in Galveston, met and married another Swede, and settled with her in Houston, where they begat a clan of functional alcoholics. Like a lot of her family, my mom had a hybrid manner, mixing Texan forthrightness and surface warmth with a more intrinsic Nordic cool. She got by on industriousness and denial, and having hoisted herself out of the Lone Star state with good grades and good manners and a law degree from Southern Methodist, she'd become a different kind of woman from the women she'd known as a child, namely a white-collar professional. And then she lived all those years in a city that was so starkly two cities, Washington and D.C., especially during the mid- and late 1980s, when D.C. won the grand title of murder capital while Washington remained the stodgy, blossom-ridden seat of government. In our dual metropolis it made perfect sense for a lady to be lost in Mario Puzo while waiting for her hair to set at Elizabeth Arden, the same way it made sense for white boys to blast rap from out of their parents' European station wagons. She gobbled up crime novels and sent us to dance classes, followed the news of every shooting and bought dresses at Garfinckel's.

"How's your new apartment?" she asked.

"Cozy," I said.

"Your dad said it was small."

"You talked to Dad?"

"Sure. We do talk."

"What about?"

"You girls, mostly."

As a kid I used to walk a few feet behind my mother, watching the backs of her narrow legs, tracking her down sidewalks and across parking lots. When she would stop so that I could catch up to her, I wouldn't understand why she was stopping. I would halt too, a few feet behind her, and we'd stand like that, separated, until she stuck her hand back for mine and pulled me forward.

"Hey, do you remember Rob Golden?" I asked.

"Courtney's friend?"

"I ran into him."

"You did? What's he doing now?"

"He was in Iraq."

"He's in the army?"

"No, he did something with the reconstruction authority."

She laughed outright: this was incredible to her. "That obnoxious kid!" To her he was still a teenager, and often it seemed as if she also thought of me that way, as a kid with my little friendships and crushes and hobbies.

"I was going to ask Dad about Dick Mitchell."

"Dick? Why?"

"He was Rob Golden's stepdad."

"Oh, that's right. God. I can't believe I forgot that," she said. "Dick Mitchell. Do you know I met him on the second date I went on with your dad? Your father took me to—I mean this was not a date by any normal standards. It was a meeting of the committee for—what was it? American, no, new American peace. The Committee for a New American Peace. All those guys, they were so full of themselves!" She brought her voice back down. "Dick Mitchell especially. He's the one that started it. How old could they have been, twenty-seven? Twenty-eight? They all went straight from taking the bar exam to deciding how to run the world."

"I think either you or Dad mentioned it before."

"They would get together and shoot the breeze, and they thought they were reinventing our foreign policy."

"You still went on a third date," I said.

"Yes, I liked him. He took me on better dates too. But we kept going to those meetings, we went to those damn meetings for how long, three, four years? Of course all the wives would be in the kitchen, wives and girlfriends. We used to roll our eyes at it all. Almost all the men had gotten deferments and were self-conscious about it. They needed to feel like they were part of a cause, fighting for something."

"Soldier envy."

"If you think about it, your dad's had a chip on his shoulder about guys like Jim Singletary for years and years. I don't know if he's mentioned Singletary to you."

"What chip on his shoulder?" I asked.

"If you didn't fight, you were always a guy who hadn't fought, and you had to prove yourself in a different way. Singletary was one of the army guys. There were a lot of men at that time, and now I'm talking about the late seventies and eighties, a lot of men around the White House who'd come from a military background."

"I bought his book. Singletary's. I started reading it."

"You did? Why?"

"I was just wondering what it said. Dad seemed kind of ticked off about it."

"That's an understatement. It's been driving him crazy. How is it?"

"Like all those books are."

I don't know what I'd been expecting when I read it—a sudden, direct attack on Dad? Of course there was nothing like that. In the few paragraphs devoted to Iran-Contra, my father's name came up once, in a matter-of-fact list of some of Singletary's NSC colleagues who'd been caught in the independent counsel's high beams. What I did detect in his short recap of the crisis was an acceptance of it, a note of satisfaction, even. He never said it out-right, but you could tell that Singletary thought some of his colleagues had had it coming.

"It's not as if I don't understand why this is driving him crazy," she said. "I get it. Why should Singletary have done so well for himself? The man is an idiot. Not I.Q.-wise, but he invents his own reality. Back then he was kind of paranoid: they used to call him Red Menace. And now instead of the Russians it's somebody else, the terrorists, whoever. It's all a big video game. Shoot the bad guy. Now let's invade Iran too. And then he gets to dine out on his extremism, they'll put him on TV precisely because he's in-flammatory. If you're a total wack job, they won't put you on those shows, but if you're seventy-five percent there, and you're good on camera, well then.

"Here's a man who was in the same pickle your dad was in, back then, but instead of being dragged down by the scandal, it all just rolled right off him," she went on. "I still don't know how he managed that."

"When you say the book is driving Dad crazy . . ."

"Did he tell you he bought a gun?"

"What?"

"A handgun. I have no idea where he could have gotten it, eBay? It isn't legal, he doesn't have a license for it. I don't know what he's thinking. He's out patrolling the neighborhood—"

"He leaves the house with it? I can't believe he leaves the house with it," I said, though that was the least part of what I couldn't believe.

"I don't know whether he does, he won't tell me. I asked him to promise me that he'd keep it in the closet at all times, and he said, 'What good is a gun if you can't take it out of the closet?'"

"But you've never seen the gun."

"For all I know he's driving around with it."

Judging by the hour and the sudden dramatic turn, I figured that Mom must've been into her second or third glass of wine. And after that she began to make arbitrary, disconnected disclosures. She told me that she'd bought a new pair of shoes and that learning Spanish was something she still hoped to do. Then she said that Dick Mitchell used to flirt with her.

"Even I can remember that," I said.

"You can?"

"He was not subtle."

"He was Dick. And really, you know, he was kind of a dick." She sighed at some specter I couldn't see. "And then he—well, he died."

"He killed himself, right?"

"I think your dad blamed himself a little."

"He did?"

"It wasn't rational. As far as I could tell it was just, they were friends, and maybe he could've been a better friend, that sort of thing. He never talked about it." She took another sip of whatever she was drinking and then asked, "So what makes you so curious about Dick Mitchell all of a sudden?"

"Like I said, I ran into Rob—"

"Oh, right. The stepson."

"But I've also been sort of thinking about writing something."

"About Dick?"

"Not only about him, but about Dad too, and you know, like, the whole Iran-Contra thing . . ."

"Huh," she said. I tried to say that I'd been provoked by reading Singletary's book, that there were so many hollow accounts like that one, and surely there was some value in telling a real story about someone who was more than just the sum of his jobs, but as I went on my mom was so quiet that I finally started to wonder whether she was still on the line.

"Hello?"

"Have you told your father you're doing this?"

"Kind of. Actually I was hoping we could work together on something, but he wasn't that into it."

"Huh."

"I guess you think it's a bad idea."

"I'm not trying to tell you not to, I just—it was just a very hard time, harder than you can imagine."

"I was there."

"I know you were."

After that we both reverted to chitchat, and soon hung up. How little access to her life she'd ever offered my sisters and me! She and my dad considered their past to be beyond my grasp, the past and for that matter most of what was interesting about the present. Sure, I'd sealed myself off from them too. Yet hadn't they invited that by sharing so little, by hiding it all from us? They started it.

I encountered another of my neighbors. I was walking from the Metro, back to my microapartment, when I saw the girl, the one I'd seen shooting hoops by herself in shiny shorts. She was coming from the opposite direction, ambling down Vane Street with all adulthood still in front of her. A girl dressed in black and blue, her lips puckered, whistling a tune I couldn't make out. (Not that I tried too hard: I can't whistle myself and have never much liked the sound of it coming from other people.) I don't think it's too much of an exaggeration to say I was immediately captivated by her, this girl in the lamplight, wearing a baggy sweater of faded black wool that might have been her father's, and tight jeans, and canvas sneakers written on with marker. There was a confidence in her stride and a lack of it in her rounded shoulders, and a kind of happy-go-lucky-screw-you in her whistling. Her straight hair, which fell down her back, looked brown to me from a distance, dark blond closer up, and she had that blank-slate teenage skin that I wanted to jump inside of, to remember what it was like to live in it.

She couldn't help but notice the way I inspected her. She looked right at me and called, "Hel-lo," in a singsong. My reply tripped in my throat, a froggish "Hi."

We passed each other, then she mounted the stoop of the town house next to my building. As I took out my key she took out hers. We lived next door to each other, apparently, and when I glanced at her one last time her expression contained a latent laugh, as though she found it funny to be the object of my attention.

My father and Dick Mitchell both moved to Washington in
1963, Dad to start law school at Georgetown and Dick to
work for a Republican senator. They were already familiar
with the city from summer internships and doubtless captivated by
the place, by the sense of being in the thick of it, even as under-
lings. The marble, the bustle, the diplomatic cars gliding in circles,
the stone creatures with their fittingly puffed chests guarding the
bridges over the Potomac, the crises large and small, a thousand men
in corrective lenses deciding the future of America.

For the most part, my father's 1987 testimony in the Iran-Contra
hearings addressed what he did or didn't know about Contra resupply operations in 1985 and 1986. But in one digression, he confirmed that he was present at the first meeting of the Committee
for a New American Peace, at Dick Mitchell's apartment.

From the hearings transcripts:

MR. COHEN. Are you familiar with the Committee for a New
American Peace, or CNAP?

MR. ATHERTON. I was at the first meeting.

MR. COHEN. That was when?

MR. ATHERTON. I believe it was in 1968.

MR. COHEN. And what were the qualifications for membership in this organization?

MR. ATHERTON. There were none, I mean it's not a formal membership process. A group of us who were at that time young staff members and students, who were interested in policy, started meeting informally.

MR. COHEN. Was Richard Mitchell a member of that group?

MR. ATHERTON. I guess you could say he was the leader of it. Again, we didn't have a formal structure, but he was the guy who got the ball rolling.

MR. COHEN. And what was the purpose of this organization?

MR. ATHERTON. As I mentioned, it was to discuss policy, discuss the direction our country was headed, propose solutions.

MR. COHEN. What do you mean by solutions?

MR. ATHERTON. We were young and believed every problem had an answer.

So here he is, Tim Atherton, venturing inside the grand but decayed Woodley Park building where Dick has rented a corner apartment. Chandeliers and fallout shelter signs decorate the halls, and Roosevelt-era tenants hide behind their doors. From the television comes a low voice, Cronkite's, reminding everybody where they aren't: Da Nang, Phu Bai, Can Tho.

Instead they are sitting on Dick's mismatched furniture, drinking jug wine from paper cups and eating Triscuits and canned olives, a half dozen young men. CNAP was Mitchell's idea, his baby, and notwithstanding the grand title it's essentially a discussion group for young men on the rise, one that allows them to take part in the central pastime of the political set, which has always been very much occupied with talking to itself.

Let's write to Melvin Laird, says a young professor wearing a brown smoking jacket.

The man doesn't know a damn thing about foreign policy.

What about Haldeman?

Vaht about Haldemaaann?

Dear Bob . . .

Tim sticks a finger into his wine: a piece of something has fallen into it, cheese or maybe plaster, and he drags whatever it is up to the edge of his glass, leaving it suspended there, for he doesn't see any napkins or plates to put it on.

Dick carries a typewriter out from his bedroom and sets it on top of the coffee table, then inserts a piece of stationery—he has actually had stationery printed, with *CNAP* in block letters at the top of the page.

What are you writing? somebody asks.

Our first press release.

Press release! Everyone laughs, but Dick is intent.

While men discuss national security in the living room, women smoke in the kitchen. Jan Mitchell, Dick's wife, has set out Chablis, cold cuts, and an ashtray. All the women roll their eyes at the men's pretensions, but Jan takes it the furthest, scoffs at Dick and his stationery. You'll notice the word *nap* is in the name, she says, feigning a yawn. A lawyer herself, who dresses smartly during the day, she doesn't bother to put on nice clothes or shoes for Dick's get-togethers, but carries out her assigned duties in a kind of peasant dress and house slippers.

The more Dick drinks, the more fluent he becomes, more urgent with his ideas, even as his consonants start to bumble into one another. Sprawled across half the sofa, in shirtsleeves and loosened tie, he gossips. He knocks William Rogers, Nixon's secretary of state, by saying that Nixon has tied Rogers's hands and won't let him do anything of significance. The president wants to run everything out of the White House, Dick says. He's got ol' Hank Kissinger in there to take care of it for him.

But Rogers and Nixon are old friends, Tim says. They were law partners.

Yes they were, but Rogers was always on top. The alpha-friend. You wait and see. Now that Nixon's got it flipped around, I bet you anything he'll rub Rogers's face in it.

Where'd you get this?

I've got a buddy that works for Kissinger.

Isn't that what they'd want to believe?

Trust me, Dick says, coming to his feet and walking to the window. Or don't. You'll see.

Now he actively scans the street as though waiting for somebody down there to give him a signal. Some assistant to Kissinger, maybe, come to relay more privileged horseshit. Tim is skeptical of Dick's gossip, but in the time he's known Mitchell he's learned that the things he deems impossible often turn out to be accurate, while unremarkable statements turn out to be lies told for no reason, or not any reason that Tim can figure out.

Mitchell moves nearer to the window and places one palm on the glass. Christ, he says softly. The street is deserted but for a young woman in a short fur coat and a short skirt who walks toward the building on skinny stork legs. Very young, maybe twenty or even younger, and beautiful, at least from a distance she is. Thin and fair-skinned like Dick himself, with dark brown or black hair piled on top of her head. As she walks her pocketbook swings on one axis, her hips on another.

Look at her, Dick whispers.

Pretty, Tim says.

Gorgeous. Let's go down and talk to her.

I don't think so.

We'll invite her to come up. We'll make her recording secretary.

Your wife is in the kitchen, Tim says.

Mitchell reflects on that fact but isn't ready to relent. I just want to see her close up, he says.

Tim puts a hand on his arm. I don't think that would be in the organization's best interests, he says.

Dick snaps out of his trance, smiles, says of course he was kidding. He returns to the room, to the making of pronouncements.

But a year or so later, after Jan leaves to join a commune in southern Virginia, Dick shows up at a party with a too-young girl who reminds Tim of the girl they saw that night, she might've been the very same girl. He couldn't say for sure. Dick Mitchell, he hears another friend say, has a weakness for the poreless. Tim doesn't understand at first. *For the young gals.*

By the midseventies Dick Mitchell has completed his transformation from a son of wealthy Democrats to a denouncer of the liberal elite. Not that he's given up his pretty clothes and refined demeanor, but he stays on a rightward course, and is rewarded with jobs at the Pentagon and later the State Department. He is staunch in his thinking and genteel as ever in his social life. Tonight, Dick announces one evening when Tim and Eileen are over for dinner, as he tends to a pot of boiling water, we're having *pasta al détente!*

MR. COHEN. Isn't it true that in 1976 your good friend Mr. Mitchell was appointed by Vice President Bush, who was then serving as CIA director, to a commission assigned to evaluate arms control policy?

MR. ATHERTON. I believe the CIA director named people to the committee and that they then hired their own researchers. Dick and several others from our group were researchers.

MR. COHEN. So did the CNAP group help produce this research?

MR. ATHERTON. There was no direct involvement, to my knowledge. Only an overlap in the people involved. I was not part of it.

MR. COHEN. This was the commission known as Team B.

MR. ATHERTON. Yes.

MR. DESHAZO. What is the relevance here? Mr. Atherton has already mentioned, he was not part of this.

MR. COHEN. What I'm getting at is that these kinds of views, the conservative position that our national security policy was too soft and that seeking a broad consensus was actually a grave threat to the country—this same type of thinking that apparently motivated some of the actions we're here to investigate—has a history.

MR. DESHAZO. My client is not here to testify about historical trends. He is here to discuss only the things, the limited things, of which he has firsthand knowledge.

MR. COHEN. In point of fact, even participating in this, whatever you would call it, this young men's debating club begun by Mr. Mitchell, turned out to have more serious ramifications.

MR. DESHAZO. Is that a question?

MR. COHEN. It's a statement. We'll move along.

had nocturnal bouts of sister-nostalgia. All those hours we'd spent lying around in front of the television in our nightgowns. All the mornings waiting for the bus. The afternoons at acting class or art class, held in an old house in Cleveland Park repurposed as a community center. We dreamed of stage lights, sang "Maybe" in the tub. We sent away for the K-tel Superhits on cassette. We fell asleep to the tick-tock of a shifty-eyed cat clock, its tail going to and fro, to and fro. We were sent to ballroom dancing school, in our white gloves and Mary Janes, and paired with one beet-cheeked boy after another.

But now that I think of it, each of us was sent to dancing school in seventh grade. We weren't there together. For that matter, only I sang in the bath. Still I include my sisters in all of it: we ate the same food, breathed the same air, went to the same places in the same cars, and I walked around with their sayings, their jokes, their accusations in my head.

Courtney would've scorned all that as false feeling. She saw herself as pragmatic and oriented toward the future, though the way she lived, the clothes she wore, the house she'd bought, these all seemed to express a wish for things to be as they had been thirty years ago or even before we were born.

I'd hoped that she'd forgotten about taking me to give blood. In fact I'd just misunderstood which day she meant to take me. She'd called me on Friday and said she would pick me up at ten the next morning.

"I'm squeamish," I said. "I'd be ill."

"That's silly. It'll be quick, and then after we can go shopping," she said, as if that were a good trade, your vital fluids for a sweater or a handbag.

"I'm broke," I said.

"They don't charge to draw your blood."

"What if I have a disease, like an STD?"

"You have an STD?"

"You never know. Do we need an appointment or something?"

"I already made one."

The day was cloudy and dull, the city sketched out in crayon strokes. Courtney pulled up outside my building in her clean white car. She wore unnecessary sunglasses and watched impatiently as I put on my seat belt. She lived according to that principle that a body in motion wants to remain in motion. Back in her sports-playing days she'd had this gift, and how she came to it I don't know, for perceiving the geometry of an instant, the sudden pocket of space between lacrosse defenders: she could see the opening, you might say, though really it was more instinctual. She knew it was there before it was visible. She slipped right through it, barreled toward the goal. Now as she drove I thought of her fierce and red-faced, with that chimpanzee look her mouth guard gave her, cradling her stick; I thought of this while she accelerated too much for the distance before us and braked too severely at the stop signs.

"I think if you turn right, up there, that'll get us onto Mass Ave," I said.

"How can you stand driving around here?"

I didn't say anything. She knew I didn't have a car.

"Right, right, go right."

She swerved and the car screeched, but she kept her cool, asking, "Is that it?"

"I think so."

"You think so?"

"I'm pretty sure."

I rummaged around for a question to ask her. "How's Hugo?"

"He's fine."

"Does he ever get, like, homesick? It must be exhausting having to speak a second language all the time."

"He's fluent, though. He speaks English. When he speaks."

"I didn't mean he doesn't speak English, just, it's not his first language."

"*Language* is not his first language, if you know what I mean."

I did not. "Oh."

We parked in the garage of a medical building on Foxhall Road. Courtney marched inside and I bobbled along behind her. I had never been to a blood bank before and so had pictured a clone of a regular bank, with tellers behind windows. Instead it was a small office where a nurse in a festive smock of a shirt tried to talk me out of not only my blood but also extra platelets and maybe, she hinted while glancing over at a poster of a frail, hairless child, maybe I could also spare a little bone marrow? I half-expected her to request in addition my hair and a couple of toes. As she waited out my hawing and humming she pecked at a form with her pen, leaving a trail of black dots around the spaces where my refusals would be marked with an *X*.

She told us to take a seat, it would be a few minutes, and Courtney asked, "Do you know how many minutes?" Her way of talking to people behind desks and counters made me cringe. Her voice took on this high pitch, and her eyes widened, she would be "sweet" in a way that seemed obviously fake to me. The nurse took it in stride, though.

"No more than five or ten," she said. "Fifteen at the most."

"Because our appointment was for eleven," Courtney said.

Courtney had a kind of authority, or two kinds, a false authority and a true: there were the high-pitched and bossy phrases that jumped out of her mouth, but then there was her physical authority, a latent, athletic power to which people responded. It was a simple enough mistake, for her to conclude that the respect had come about because of what she said and how she said it.

But her physical grace, why couldn't I have had that? Even reclining onto a gurney-type blood-draw table in a clinical box of a room, she might have been sunbathing; someone might have come to dangle grapes over her lips—but never over mine as I scooted my butt up toward the center of my table, crunching and tearing the paper bedding as I went.

When we were young, the saying "The one with the most toys wins" had been printed on notepads and coffee mugs—a joke, but one derived from real desires, real fears. The peculiar warp of those fears had made us the peculiar children we were, stalked by the greeds we'd grown up around. I would like to offer into evidence Courtney's crocodile boots, jutting off the end of her table.

The nurse tied a length of rubber so tightly around my arm I thought there would be no blood left in it, but before she stuck me she patted the vein inside my elbow almost tenderly, with as tender a touch as can come from a stranger in latex gloves. Then the needle went in.

The room was all corners and sharp things, my sister the sharpest. Like a long, elegant pair of scissors. She was saying, and I realized she'd been talking this out in her head ever since the car ride, that Hugo just didn't engage, didn't really even speak that much. If he would just ask her how her day had gone, that would be something at least. And it was like he constantly needed instructions, she said, she was always having to tell him what to do.

She started to full-on vent about her marriage, veering back and forth between generalizations—"lack of trust" was one—and minute particulars, e.g., she didn't like that Hugo sometimes put large items, such as padded mailing envelopes, into the bathroom trash can. Honestly none of it seemed so bad to me, but I understood her to be saying that she wasn't sure she loved him the way she once had, and I also understood, by the way she was saying it, that she really had loved him and maybe still did. I'd never given her full credit for it. Some part of me resisted believing in her feelings, preferred to think that she didn't actually have any.

I wasn't entirely sympathetic, though. She'd been giving instructions since she learned to speak—so far as I know she'd wailed them out before then—and it was inconceivable that she could have married anyone who was not inclined to take orders. Moreover, she was, based on my own experience, a difficult person to live with, given her particular food needs and missionary enthusiasms and fast-changing moods. Aware that I had to agree with her but not say anything negative about Hugo that might be held against me later, I said as little as I could.

"But. There are good things," she said. "And I mean we've got the house now."

I couldn't tell whether she meant that the house was one of the good things, or whether she'd said it to refute some other, unstated possibility. And then, from where I don't know, a ray of warmth passed over: it felt, for a moment, as though the venom might be cleansed out of us, whatever spoiled old things were in our veins might be sucked up into the sterile bags that hung beside us on poles. Who would protect me in this world if not my older sister? My sudden wish was to climb onto her table with her, get under the covers as we had in our parents' bed, back when they shared a bed—but there wasn't room for two on a gurney.

I am an optimistic sibling this way. I've always maintained an ideal of sisterly affection, like a photograph of a model in a bikini taped to the edge of a mirror.

"How's your place?"

"It's all right. Dad hates it."

"He probably wishes you'd stayed at home with him," she said.

"Yeah, I just couldn't stay there."

"I thought that's why you came back, though, to look after him."

My body tightened. "That's part of it, but . . . Anyway he's okay. He doesn't need someone looking after him twenty-four seven."

"He did end up back in the hospital."

"That was a false alarm," I said. "I was never planning to stay there, like, long term."

"Why did you come back here then? To write a book?" She made it sound like writing a book was an exotic hobby, along the lines of paragliding, and I chose not to answer the question.

"Honestly it seems like he's doing fine."

"Really?"

"Really."

She sighed the most irritating of sighs and then said, "You know, you haven't been around."

"What does that mean?"

"What does it mean to say that you haven't been here? That you can just run away from everything and do whatever the hell you want?"

"Is that what you're mad about?"

"I'm not mad," she said, and raised her knees, boots resting on the end of the gurney. I looked over at her and saw that her eyes were closed. I couldn't tell if she was thinking things over or falling asleep. After a long pause, she said, "I'm not mad at you."

"Okay."

"I do feel that you have distanced yourself from our family."

"I'm here now," I said.

"I'm just trying to tell you how I feel, so please don't argue with me. This is how I feel."

"Right."

We were silent for a while, and the next time she spoke there was no trace of the frost from before. Abrupt changes of heart—or at least, of tone—were normal for her, while my temper shifted much more gradually. "So what else is going on?"

"Not much," I said slowly. "What else is going on with you?"

"Actually there's this guy at my office—"

"Michael?"

"I've mentioned him before?"

"A couple of times."

"I don't know if I told you, I went to Chicago last week for a meeting? He went too, it was just the two of us from our office. We flew out and back together. And he's handsome, at least I think he is. He's married, it's not like anything happened or would ever happen, but on the plane, it was like, oh shit. I mean, we weren't even drinking, but—"

"Planes are romantic."

"It's weird, isn't it? It's so weird. They're so gross, airplanes are nasty. How can they be so gross and still sexy?"

"Gay dudes hook up in men's rooms."

"There are some things that sound cool to me about being a gay man, and having sex in a public restroom is definitely not one of them. Anyway. We talked the whole flight there, and the whole flight back, and it was clear that if we'd been single . . ."

"You're not, though."

"I'm not. I'm married."

"You are married."

"It was like I could tell him everything. I can't remember the last time I talked to somebody like that. And there was that thing, I was so painfully aware of every time he moved a muscle, I knew exactly where his arm was, his leg was. It was like being in eighth grade and having a crush on the guy next to you in class."

"Sounds flirty," I said. I was trying to sound more neutral than I felt.

"It's not cheating, to flirt."

"How would you feel if Hugo flirted like that with some woman on a plane?"

"I don't know. I think it can spice things up a little. I mean, when I got home we did have really good sex, better than we've had in, like, a while."

"So are you still flirting with this guy?"

"There is such a thing as context," she said.

"Context. Okay."

"I hate to tell you this, but—"

"I just don't get it because I'm not married."

"That wasn't what I was going to say."

"Yes it was."

She didn't respond, and I realized there was a radio playing, tuned to one of those soft-rock stations that play the blander tunes of the 1970s and call it "magic."

"You know, we're going to have plenty of room in the new house, if you need a place to stay for a while."

"I have an apartment."

"But if you wanted to look for someplace else."

"I don't think I need to do that," I said.

"It's not a great neighborhood you're in."

"Sorry I can't afford a house in Spring Valley."

Both of us lay back and were quiet again as the blood went gurgling out of us. I closed my eyes and then opened them. After the draw was done we were led to another room, where we were supposed to wait out any dizzy or fainting spells—or in our case a silent spell, with a silent spell's invisible heft. We were sentinels of the space closest to us, tacticians at a yard or so, and cared thickly for each other from ten feet away—but don't come any closer, please. We oscillated, each of us by turns crowding the other one, or shutting the other one out, or both at once.

An old lady volunteer offered us cookies and juice. Courtney declined and I accepted, munching loudly. After I took one, the woman rearranged the remaining cookies on the plate in such a way that they were evenly spaced, then offered the plate again. She asked whether we were sisters. Maybe only siblings and spouses sat in that kind of silence, not the silence after a fight but the silence that substitutes for fights you might as well just have in your head, shadow-boxing with your shadow sister.

"I feel kind of funny," I said. "Dizzy." The volunteer assured me it would pass. Her double chin and wide neck made her face into a kind of pliable rectangle, all the more rectangular because she had a boxy masculine haircut, pouffed at the top, Clintonesque. How did she know it would pass? What if they had taken too much out of me? I asked whether it was possible to get my blood put back in.

"You can't get it back," Courtney said.

"Why not? They're going to put it in somebody, right? I just think I want it back, in me," I said. "Right now."

"I'm not sure that we can do that here," the volunteer said.

"I really don't feel right. I think I needed that blood."

"Get a grip on yourself," Courtney said.

"It's my blood!"

"You donated it."

"You pressured me into it."

"No I didn't."

"I think I remember my acupuncturist in L.A. saying that I have a blood deficiency," I said.

"I don't think that means you have a low volume of blood."

"Why wouldn't it mean that?" In fact, I had no earthly idea what that, or anything else my acupuncturist had ever said to me, truly meant, but I did want my blood to be reinstated. Here was a part of myself I'd given away without enough forethought, and in that light-headed moment I felt that if I could just take those pints of blood back, it would mean something.

"I want it back. I just want it back." The volunteer regarded me with what appeared to be genuine concern in her milky eyes. I bowed my head. "Please."

"I really don't think it works like that," Courtney said.

"I'm not like you!" I said. She was wrong, wrong about everything.

The old woman plodded into the other room to ask the nurses about my request. She came back and explained that they'd offered to examine me, and while it was unlikely that I would need a transfusion, if I did receive one, for medical reasons or bureaucratic reasons or what have you, it would not be my own still-warm blood but somebody else's. I declined the exam and ate a couple more cookies, which were too sweet and too dry.

Courtney's sun came out again as we left that place and drove down to Georgetown, or maybe it was just that shopping made her perk up. I can't say the same for myself. She was an ace shopper, pawing her way through racks of clothes as though there were something very particular she knew to look for and seizing, say, a shirt, which she would examine closely and, if it passed the examination, carry over to the dressing room for further assessment. She could spot imperfections that I could barely see, then convince me they were there, tiny holes and loose stitches. Finding something defective seemed to give her almost as much pleasure as finding something she wanted to buy. Meanwhile I pulled shirts, skirts, pants out at random, each one representing a possible new style, a new look—I never did know what it made sense for me to wear. When it came to style I had a developmental delay: fashion trends would arise, cuffed jeans or off-the-shoulder tops or high boots, and while other women went prancing around in them I would dismiss them as silly, overpriced, wholly unnecessary, but one or two years later, after Courtney and her ilk had moved on to the next look, I would find myself plucking from the sale rack, admiring, and ultimately buying nothing other than an off-the-shoulder top. In the end I would regret buying it, though. I regretted buying just about anything that wasn't edible. It was never that far from my mind that one day we'd all be dead, while so many of these off-the-shoulder tops would remain.

As we were leaving a store, Courtney asked me about the temping.

"I know it's kind of lame, it's the kind of job you get when you're twenty-two, but . . ." I said.

She told me it wasn't too late to make a plan for myself. You could go back to school, she said, or get an internship.

"An internship."

"But soon it will kind of be too late, I mean I think you're pushing it if you want to have, like, a career, and not these random kinds of things."

"People reinvent themselves all the time," I said. "They go back to school in their forties. It's not so late. Just because I'm not on the same track you're on—"

"I know you've spent a lot of your life trying to do things differently than I did."

"It's not like I'm just doing things to be different from you."

"I didn't say that."

We were walking down M Street, which was crowded with women younger than us.

"Do you want to stick with TV?" she asked.

"No. I don't know. I mean I want to write, but I know—I'm realistic about the odds of selling anything."

"I guess it's pretty hard, isn't it. You know what my fantasy job would be? Opening my own café. I always thought that would be cool, you know, I'd want it to have healthy, organic food, but not too hippy-dippy. Not, like, with sprouts on everything. I'd want it to be elegant. Elegant and fresh."

My sister hardly ever cooked. It was hard to picture her a restaurant proprietor. But what the hell, why not. "Why not?" I said. "Why don't you do it then?"

"That's a daydream. It's not going to happen. Besides, I like my job, it's just—"

"What?"

"Sometimes I feel like my life has become kind of joyless, you know?"

I didn't know what to say. Joy? That was a word I read in self-help books or poems, describing an experience that other people were having. I didn't rule out the possibility that I had felt joy myself, but in feeling it I hadn't bothered to label the feeling and now found it hard to recollect whether those high moments had been truly joyful or just really good. There hadn't been too many of them lately. I didn't want to say something obvious, like *maybe you should work less.*

Courtney said it herself: "I guess I should work a little less hard. But then—I don't know. It's what people expect. And if I didn't work all the time, I feel like there'd be that void."

"I see," I said, though I didn't really. "Guess who I ran into?"

"Who?"

"Rob Golden."

"Oh god. Such bad news."

"I thought you guys had a thing in high school."

"He's an asshole."

"Well, that was high school. He seems all right now."

"It's nice how you always see the good in people."

"Thanks."

"Where did you run into him?"

"In a bookstore."

"And?"

"And what?"

"Is there something you want to tell me?"

And then it all came out like so much swill, I described our encounter in general terms, I attempted to cast myself as reasonable and at the same time tried to present the case in such a way that it might seem possible he really did like me and was just too busy to contact me? Like an idiot I went on, like I was draining a wound, and I suppose I was waiting for my sister to respond in some affirming way or at least reassure me that my behavior hadn't been completely stupid. But it had been, or at least that's what she thought, and all she would say was that it was good he was keeping his distance. "I'm sorry but he is toxic," she said.

I went on. Though I'd been reluctant to start talking, now I couldn't stop, I felt myself searching for another avenue of analysis, another set of significances, a possible interpretation in which this all had a happy conclusion, even though the more I prattled the more hopeless it seemed. It was as though I were scattering my own self: there was something that I'd made too available with Rob and was once again letting dangle and spew. As though the tryst and this conversation about it were both symptoms of the same ailment, a failure to maintain my integrity in a sense that was practically structural; it was not sex I'd given away but my muscles, my membranes. As though some part of me only existed so long as I didn't deflate it with so much blabbing.

"He is toxic," she repeated. "Stay away. I'm serious."

"I don't know. I feel like I'm just not attractive these days, I don't feel attractive, I mean," I said, suddenly about to fall apart. It was my own fault for trying to get her to reassure me, when I should have known better. Courtney was not the reassuring type. She looked at me and nodded—nodded!—and said, "Well, marriage also has its challenges."

"I know that," I said. Why was it that people who weren't alone always forgot what it was to be alone? I told her I would just take the Metro home, because I needed to stop at a store on the way back, though the real reason was that I couldn't stand her, my sister with her husband and her house and her money. In that instant I could not stand her.

All her jabs at me seemed semiconscious, meaning they weren't the product of forethought, and she would forget them afterward, but they were still jabs, even if the reasons for them remained obscure to me and probably to her too. There was one mishap from high school that I felt sure she'd never forgiven me for (though she would've denied it), and then no doubt there were a whole slew of other events, most of them unremembered, that continued to influence us. I did still think about that one accident from the beginning of tenth grade. It had not only made her furious but had cemented my family identity as a hopeless bungler.

Mid-August, 1986: the city a swamp, window units rattling, buses gasping for breath. Everyone with wet skin, chugging soda from wet cans. The disk drives whirring: Courtney worked on her college essays, composing them on the Apple IIe computer my father had bought and put in his study. There was an unspoken agreement not to speak loudly, or play music, or otherwise disturb her when we were nearby. I would creep past and hear the patter of the keys as she typed. Or I would hear her letting out a long sigh.

Or I would sneak into the room. She sat there in front of the black-and-white screen, intent, immobile, not even noticing that I'd come in—or so I thought.

"Get out," she said, without turning her head from the screen.

"I was just checking if you needed anything."

"What's another word for *achievement*?"

"Um, *feat*?"

"*I'm proud of my feats during high school.* I don't think so."

"How about *conquests*?"

"Shut up."

"If you need me I'll just be enjoying my summer vacation—"

"Get out."

Her applications became a family obsession. For us the process of applying to college had been vested with outsize significance, as if the overwhelmed junior administrators who made up the admissions committees at top schools were in fact deciding our ultimate worth, as if there in some dank New England basement they were weighing our souls on silver soul-scales. It's hard to even express how feverish, how snobbish, how riddled with collective self-importance, how idol-worshipping that whole business was, at our school and all the more so at home, where Dad looked forward to our matriculation at colleges as a kind of anointment—for these would be Ivy League colleges, book-lined palaces out of which we would one day stride triumphant in our mortarboards, with snappy a cappella numbers ringing in our ears and our tentative footholds in the overclass made solid and permanent.

When Courtney was just a freshman in high school, Dad led our whole family on an Eastern seaboard trip that just happened to include Cambridge, New Haven, and Princeton, where we were the youngest non-Asian kids on the campus tours. Dad had graduated from Cornell, but he never took us there, even Cornell wasn't good enough. He wanted something else for us, more ease, more access, a status-granting vitamin X that had not been part of his youthful diet, but he didn't really know what it was, or where we might acquire it. He decided it must be at Yale.

As a seventh-grader my interest was limited to the pizza we ate in each town, and I was young enough that I was not overly mortified, or at least not as mortified as Courtney was, by Dad's endless questions for those backward-treading tour guides. I do remember that after we passed a science building on one of the campuses he asked a question about "the new physics." The guide, ever cheerful, didn't have an answer for him.

During Courtney's junior year, the college bulletins started flocking to the house, in bright, chirruping clusters, and Dad's anticipation grew all the keener. At night he would nestle into a chair and open those bullish gazettes as if peeling the wrapper from a fine cigar, reading even the brochures for schools we never would've considered. "Juniata College!" he would announce bluffly as he turned the pages. "Let's see here." My own leafing through the brochures had revealed them to be nearly identical; at every college, winsome students tossed Frisbees across a grassy quad, performed plays, and conducted experiments in science labs. But Dad would actually read the text—sometimes aloud, when a sentence struck him as funny. "A dedication to harvesting the seeds of intellectual inquiry!" he'd snort. "Why wait for them to grow?" (He'd go on in that way until he had beat the thing to death.) "Educating the leaders of tomorrow," he'd say, and then, lowering his voice: *"with tomorrow's curriculum."* Or he might hold up something for us to see: "A nice picture here of their new parking garage."

Yale was his first choice and Courtney's. Her application for early admission was due in mid-September. By the time the school year started, she'd more or less finished the essays, but she kept tinkering with them when she was at home. She didn't let anybody else read what she'd written. Soon, though, I had assignments to do, and one afternoon shortly before her deadline, I went to the study to type up a history paper while Courtney was at tennis practice. The computer had been left on, and one of her essays-in-progress filled the screen.

"My intellectual interests are wide-ranging," it said. "One of my favorite courses in high school was 11th grade English," it said. "I also believe in the importance of community service," it said. "My participation in athletics has taught me invaluable lessons," it said.

How jarring it was to read those sentences, written by Courtney, about Courtney, and yet containing nothing of Courtney. I didn't recognize her in those polysyllabic assertions, the candidate-speak. It made me feel strange, to see all the games she'd played reduced to invaluable lessons.

Those were the early days of home computers, and I'm still not sure how it happened. I opened a new document, typed my paper, printed it out, closed the document. Maybe I'd closed the word processing program as well, I don't remember. But that evening, a wail sounded from the study. The essay wouldn't open. A message on the screen told her the file was password-protected.

I sat under the kitchen lights, staring at the vinyl tablecloth.

"What did you do?" Dad kept saying to me.

"I don't know," I said. Soon I was crying too.

Then Dad was on the phone to the software store, to the company that had made the software, but the file still wouldn't open. At some point my sister had printed out a draft, but we went through the garbage and couldn't find it. She had to rewrite the essay in two days. She'd stared at the lost essay for so long, she must have known much of it by heart, and the next day Mom called her in sick to school, so that she could stay home and finish—what I'm trying to say is that the rewriting she did, of a two-page personal statement, was not a superhuman feat. Yet we all treated it as though it were. She would've never done anything in such a slapdash way, writing entire paragraphs at the last minute, though that was the way I wrote everything. She finished, and my father drove the application to the post office, and all was calm.

A day later, however, she went back and reread her essay and discovered two typos, which she'd missed in the rush to finish it. An essay with two typographical errors had been sent off to Yale, and there was nothing she could do. I was to blame, I knew. I had ruined Courtney's application.

Later on (and I mean years later) the loss of the original essay would come to seem emblematic, in that so much Atherton family data was eventually lost. All our papers and letters and records from those years were stored on five-and-a-quarter-inch floppies, while technology moved on, until the files could no longer be accessed and the disks were thrown out. Whatever history of our family was contained in those documents, it wound up in the garbage.

No one else could rile me the way Courtney could. It wasn't anything she explicitly said or did, so much as the attitude, the superior stance. She was the older sister with her shit together and I was the incompetent, self-absorbed, lost one. She'd found this place for herself, a fancy pouf to park her butt on, and from it she watched me and criticized me and offered up stupid suggestions until I just wanted to kill her. I don't mean that only figuratively. I can remember fights we had as girls, the kicking and the biting that would begin tentatively and then turn vicious. The urge to annihilate each other had always been there, tamed over the years but never uprooted.

I e-mailed Rob. A half day with my sister had left me wanting a treat, better yet the one treat that would stick it to her. I sent the e-mail vengefully, not expecting a reply, much less one with exclamation points.

Hey! I broke my phone/lost your info! What's up?

Though I wasn't proud of my meager studio I invited him over, excited not only by the prospect of sex but by the realization (and it did feel like a Realization, a bell going off) that I'd come to the wrong conclusions about him, and that probably all my judgments over the past several weeks had been clouded by living with Dad and seeing so much of my family. I felt newly righteous about having found my own place. Maybe the apartment had changed everything after all.

In bed, after we'd slept together, Rob put his hands behind his head and started telling me something about his work, and I was content enough to have him there, to hear him talking, to look at his forearms or his chest the way I might look at a diagram, discovering the way one part was connected to another. He got up for a glass of water, and when he came back he was holding a few pages I'd printed and left on the table.

"Don't read that," I said.

"What is this?"

"Just something I've been working on. Don't read it."

"Sorry," he said, still reading.

I got up, took the pages from him, then asked him whether he remembered coming to our house for a pool party. "You and your mom and your stepdad came over, this one time."

He said he didn't remember the party. He did remember an argument that his parents had once had about going to our house. "My mom didn't want to go," he said. "And my stepdad said that your dad was the one decent friend he'd ever had and damned if we weren't going to go."

"Do you know why your mom didn't want to?"

"Probably because she hated leaving me alone."

"When you were sixteen."

"Fifteen, sixteen. Unless I already had other plans, she always wanted me to come along to everything. She worried about me staying home and getting into trouble, getting high."

"Your stepfather didn't have other friends?"

"I guess he didn't think they'd stick by him. Honestly, he was right. After the shit hit the fan, they all ditched him. Or that's what he thought. He was depressed too, and he wasn't leaving the house at all except to see his lawyer or his shrink. And he wasn't taking his meds, we found that out later, though why the fuck my mom wasn't on top of that a little sooner, I have no idea. It was the same thing with me, she was sort of in denial about the drugs I did and about my stepdad not taking his pills, but she knew enough that she was always hovering. She'd try to keep us around her so she could watch us. I guess she thought she could keep us from doing any-thing really stupid, but she was wrong about that."

"She was probably doing the best she knew how," I said.

"No she wasn't."

"Okay."

"God forbid she actually get out of her comfort zone." He'd been standing halfway between the kitchenette and the bed, and then he walked past me, to the window.

"I know the feeling. It's a drag."

"No, it's more than a drag," he said. "It's called enabling."

"I'm sorry."

"I should probably get going."

"You don't have to," I said in a voice that conveyed more than I wanted it to convey.

He turned back and gave me his head-tilt, and although I now recognized that as a mannerism, he snagged me with his fond—or fond-seeming—eyes. I wanted him to stay whether or not they were actually fond. He sat on the edge of the bed and lay back across it, so that his hair grazed my foot.

"It drove me nuts. Her and my stepdad, no matter how bad it got, they would pretend to me that nothing was wrong."

"Where was your dad in all this?"

"In Ohio. His company moved him out there. My mom would always threaten to send me to live with him, so that he could dis-cipline me. Actually I would've much rather lived with him, I just didn't want to change schools or live in Columbus."

I listened to him go on, assured by his voice that he was still there with me. I'd asked him to stay, if not in so many words, and he did stay.

It's true that my bar could've been higher. I did wish to find someone with whom I might reproduce and/or purchase real estate and/or adopt a medium-size dog, and yet all too often I chose to spend time with guys who were obviously not that person, because they were the guys who happened to be around, and I was very susceptible to a certain kind of confidence.

Exhibit number one would be the disaster of a man I'd been dating before I left L.A.

Lessons learned in sunny California: Never go a-trysting with a man who keeps looking at his watch. Never trust a man who hesitates before saying your name, as if he's not a hundred percent sure, and then says it three times in a row. Never trust a man who always walks one step ahead of you, in fancy loafers. Never trust a man you meet at a mall—that was where I'd met Gary Doyle, at the Grove, buying coffee.

But I was always analyzing my extinct relationships this way, shaking my failures out of them. Does being single force a person to adopt regrets at least as hypotheses, tried on for size? *Was that what I'd done wrong? Or that? Or that?* I wish I could be more toler- ant of myself, but in this instance I know that I am at least partly to blame. There were warning signs aplenty.

Helen, he would say to me, Helen, Helen. As though he had to keep reminding himself. I bet you raised hell in high school, didn't you. Was he kidding? Nothing could have been further from the truth. The first syllable of my name had led him off track. But he was funny, just his delivery was funny, so that even things he didn't intend as humor cracked me up, and he was brash and very success- ful, and there was something poignant to me about the way he was always starting a new diet. I wanted to help him make healthier choices.

Or did I really just want to pig out with him? I now wonder whether that one night, our worst night together, had been caused by a food coma—or maybe there had been something in the nachos. We'd had Tex-Mex delivered, just before everything went off the rails, and after we ate I felt extremely drowsy. Incapable of operating heavy machinery, and Gary Doyle himself was something of a heavy machine. This was our fourth or fifth date, we'd already slept together a couple of times, and it came after a terrible weekend in Santa Barbara, it was his friend's forty-fifth birthday and Gary had turned mean, badgering me because I'd never seen *Taxi Driver*, because I didn't actually know what happened at a seder (this even though Gary himself was not Jewish) or who Stu Sutcliffe was, whatever assorted things he knew. I was letting him down left and right. He'd imagined I was something else and so I'd found myself trying to be that something else even though I didn't know what he'd imagined. Somebody more conversant in the history of popular culture and the basics of other religions, I guess. My point is, there were signs aplenty, and yet I ran deeper into the maze, chasing after the bull-type animal.

Then came that one bad night. The man had strange proclivities, and yes, I would have cut it short had it not been for the silk ropes around my wrists and the fact that I was just so tired. But I wouldn't want anyone to think, or think that I think, that one evening of unduly prolonged nudity and some unwished-for splooge on my face counted more than it did. I'd agreed to the ropes. I wasn't protesting as it happened—at least I don't think I was, though now I'm not sure what I experienced and what I dreamed.

What I do wonder at now is less the weight of my mistake than the obviousness of it—the fact that I'd gone back for more after the weekend trip. I'd been more afraid of ending things than of what the badgering portended. I was willing to put on those black fake-leather chaps he'd ordered from some tawdry website and later to scrub off the streaks of black dye they'd left on my thighs. I was willing to indulge the whims of a vaporing man who'd jerked away too many Sunday afternoons watching porn. A man who kept the radio tuned to the classic rock station even as he undressed me, none other than Cheap Trick playing as he enacted his tacky little fantasy. What I regretted, much more than the experience itself, which was merely kind of gross, was the fact that I kept remembering it.

Even more regrettable was what happened two weeks later. He called me, and I picked up the phone so that I could yell at him, but after that he wound up coming over, one last time. We hadn't communicated since then.

What I'm trying to say is that in comparison to Gary, Rob seemed like a peach, a prince, and I was ready to cut him all kinds of slack.

One evening I came home from work to find a squad car parked in front of the building. A thin, dripping fog had spread, and I took in the scene as if through wax. On the stoop stood a woman who lived downstairs, and a lady cop in a cop hat who was interviewing the woman and making notes on a clipboard. I felt my throat pucker. Everything was blue and darker blue, save for the blinking lights on top of the police car, with their feathery halos.

A second policeman stood by the stair rail talking into a radio. A robbery, he told me. Because of the yellow police tape across the front door I awarded myself a kind of importance, that of a person who, unlike the handful of nonresident spectators who'd gathered to gawk, was entitled to cross the do-not-cross threshold. Except that I wasn't: the policeman explained that they had reason to believe the intruder might still be in the building, or at least no reason to believe he or she wasn't in the building, and I would have to wait "just like everybody else." This exile was, he implied, for my own safety, despite the fact that it would consign me to wandering the streets after dark.

Come back in an hour, two at the most, said the policeman. At the most! It didn't seem possible that this was proper procedure, barring someone from her own hearth and home (or: hotpot and television), but these were law enforcers, and I was law-abiding. I slunk like some yellow-eyed nocturnal creature toward the Hunan Palace, a restaurant I knew only for the electronic OPEN sign that seemed always to be lit above the door. From the sidewalk you couldn't see the dining room—the door was soaped over, and inside the single window was a display of cheap paper fans, with a

partition between that and the rest of the interior—and it occurred
to me that for all I knew the Hunan Palace was a front for something other than fried rice and green tea. But I entered to find an
ordinary Chinese restaurant. A boy jumped up from the table where
he'd been doing his homework to show me to a booth. I sank into
a bench, one buttock met by a feisty old spring. Only two other
tables were occupied by diners: an old woman drinking tea and the
man from next door.

He was eating with the basketball girl. His daughter! Even
though I knew they lived in the same building I hadn't put that
together, for I'd pegged him as a man alone in the world, a man
who ate his meals by himself, in front of the television. Yet he had
a child, and I was the one who, truth be told, dined most nights by
the changing light of the tube. My staring led to waving. Awkwardly,
we waved; more awkwardly, he invited me to sit with them; and—
how could I decline?—I bumbled over to join them. Nina was the
name of the girl, who acknowledged me with her eyes but didn't
say anything. Sitting with him, she seemed a different girl from the
one I'd seen striding down the street, younger. A kid.

One day she would be striking, I thought, but her face was
still indeterminate. She was at a stage when a few different potential
women are contained inside one suit of skin. She had studious
brown eyes and a looseness to her, for instance in the way she nodded, tracing a large arc with her chin, hair swaying. She said very
little at first, while Daniel and I tried to shovel things forward. I
explained I'd only recently moved to Vane Street.

"You used to live in Los Angeles? What was that like?" he asked.

"It was okay," I said. "It had its plusses and minuses."

"Nina wants to move to Paris, doesn't she," he said, and she
tucked her chin closer to her neck, self-conscious, and I wanted to
tell her not to be, not to worry about a thing.

"I used to want to live there," she said, surprising Daniel and
me both with a quick spill of syllables, "but now I want to move to
Brazil. Or Ireland. My friend went to Ireland."

"I've heard good things. About Ireland."

"I wouldn't like a place that had too many trees, though," she said. "I get creeped out by forests."

"Because you might get lost?"

"I like to see the sky."

Was it because we met in the company of her father that I felt like a suitor, a supplicant for her affections? That evening in corduroy pants and Chucks and an old Senators T-shirt under her black hoodie, she was hunching and bashful. She kept tucking her hair behind her ears (triple-pierced, pink at the tips) and talking with her mouth full.

"I wish I lived someplace where I could walk to school," she was saying. "Right now I take the Metro, and I get, like, *smushed* by secretaries every single morning."

"When do you get your driver's license?" I asked.

She looked down at her food and moved a slick piece of broccoli from one side of her plate to the other. "Probably never," she said.

I waited for an explanation but didn't get one. She was hard to read—they both were, she and her father. She excused herself to go to the bathroom, and he leaned toward me, then paused, reconsidering. He leaned back, stared at me with that stare of his, and attacked a pile of rice, his fork shuttling between plate and mouth.

"She likes you," he said. She does? As though I'd asked it aloud, he said, "She does."

He fell silent and then un-silent again, asking could he ask me something. "What did you want for your birthday when you were sixteen, turning sixteen?"

I would've liked to give an original answer, but I'd been an unoriginal girl, one who'd wanted cassette tapes and books with detailed, informative sex scenes. I gave a little shrug and told him clothes.

He looked at the table. "I wouldn't begin to know how to buy clothes," he said. "What about a watch, would you have wanted a watch?"

Boring. I mentioned a store that sold girly things, clothes and novelty books and candles and baubles—"Of course I don't know your daughter," I said. "But maybe something from there? Maybe a gift certificate?"

He took a notepad from his coat pocket and wrote down the name of the store.

After Nina returned from the bathroom she was quiet again. Those good feelings toward me had faded, if they'd ever existed to begin with. Then it struck me that I'd been one hundred percent wrong, that fathers shouldn't try to buy their daughters cool presents, that the attempt would only backfire. A watch was fine. A watch was perfect. Yet I could see no way of communicating my epiphany to Daniel.

Who this girl's mom might have been, they didn't let on. That Daniel was so eager to educate himself about girl-mysteries suggested to me that he didn't speak to her mother much, if at all. There was something uncomforted about him. He spent his days at the Department of Justice, I learned, and apparently spent his evenings guarding this rare bird of a daughter. Yet he didn't quite know how to talk to her, didn't know how to give her gifts—like my own dad, that way. I got the feeling he'd made a home for himself in whatever well he'd fallen into, but every so often, when his eyes met mine, I thought I saw something in them, directed not at me but past me. He was like someone who needed a ladder but didn't know what a ladder was.

"I think I've seen you out shooting baskets at the playground," I said.

"Nina just made the varsity team at her school," Daniel said.

"Oh yeah? I played basketball in high school," I said. Then I remembered that for her, my going to high school was a thing that had taken place in olden times, before she was born, even though I still considered it recent. I might as well have been talking about the kind of basketball my mother had played, with three girls on offense and three on defense. "I wasn't great or anything. You're probably better than I was."

She shrugged, that is to say she made a face that conveyed a shrug.

"But I felt like it was the one thing I was allowed to love wholeheartedly."

"Yeah, it's good to be into sports," she said, which was less than what I'd meant, but what had I really meant? At least she'd started talking again.

"What position do you play?"

"Post."

"When's your next game?"

"A few days from now."

"You should come watch," Daniel said.

Nina seemed embarrassed. I told them that I didn't know whether I could make it, but that I would love to, maybe, I'd try.

We left together and walked back to our buildings, the blocks made brassy by the street lights, so that it felt as though we were crossing a stage, the trash cans placed just so, and there was HOME-LESS MAN, who'd forgotten his line, and RED-HOT MAMA COMING OUT OF A STORE, peeling the cellophane off a pack of cigarettes, preparing for her monologue. And there I was, rudely, mechanically performing, recalling for Daniel and Nina my high school basketball days. Mundane stuff, which schools had been good and which bad, who had been rivals, and so on, but it was more than I'd realized I had access to—if you'd asked me beforehand I would've said I didn't remember much of that. But in my awkwardness, under those municipal spotlights, I felt a pressure to produce memories and grab hold of them. Which must have made me a bore, for those two, but maybe they were also relieved, since it wasn't like they'd had so much to say.

I'd all but forgotten about the break-in until I was back at my apart-ment, where I felt suddenly alone and unnerved. Out of pure in-stinct, I called my mother and told her about it. "They took a woman's computer," I said.

"Oh no, that's terrible. I would be lost without my laptop."

"Yeah, me too."

"I'm so bad about backing it up. I need to do that more often," she said.

We talked about backing up files and then about other things, and I never got around to telling her that the break-in had scared me.

"You remember we were talking about Dick Mitchell the other day?" she asked.

"Sure."

"You reminded me of something I hadn't thought of for years. You might remember it too. We had Dick over to the house a lot of course, and a lot of times he and your dad would wind up off in a corner, talking politics, lost to the party. You couldn't penetrate their little conference, or at least I could never break it up. But Courtney, when she was about ten or eleven, would just march up and say, 'Hey, what are you guys talking about?' It was the funniest thing. And they would try to explain it to her, and she would give her opinion on it. Like she was one of the adults. One of the men!"

"She did? I don't remember that at all."

"You were probably with the rest of the kids. But she always wanted to find out what was happening, what these grown-ups were all about."

"She doesn't now," I said.

"What?"

"Nothing."

"I just hadn't thought about that in so long. I miss that age."

She seemed to forget, briefly, that she was talking to me, but I understood what she meant. I missed that age myself, and I wished I had video of eleven-year-old Courtney, all legs and pigtails, talking about the 1980 election with my dad and Dick Mitchell.

I did wind up going to one of Nina's games. Another morning, I saw Daniel walking to the Metro, and he saw me too, and we walked together. He was exceedingly friendly, not hitting on me (at least

I don't think he was) but brimming with things to say and grins and gestures. He asked me again to come to a game, that very night. And when I walked into that gym and saw the girls in their uniforms warming up, my ambivalence vanished. It was like walking into a room from my own past. In a good way. Even after I was home again, I still felt stirred.

Rob called, and I told him all about it, that I'd been to a high school girls' basketball game with my neighbor. He found this almost unbelievable. "You know your neighbors? Didn't you just move in?"

"I met this father and daughter. The dad's kind of a dork, but I really like the girl, she's cool."

"Are you sure it wasn't a date?"

"You mean with her dad? No. I mean yes, I'm sure it wasn't. There's—no. It wasn't."

He asked whether I wanted to come over. "I think I'm going to stay in," I said. I told him I was tired, though that wasn't it exactly.

"I'm sorry about the other night," he said.

"What about it?"

"How I went off on my mom, for one thing."

"It's okay."

"Come over. We can talk about something else."

"Such as?"

"Recent Supreme Court decisions?"

"That's tempting." I did want to go—I did and I didn't—but it was late, and I had to work the next day, and then there was the queasiness I had about him, which was part my old infatuation and part something else. I said I was going to bed, and then I invited him to come with me to a Christmas party the next week.

"I'd rather go to a girls' basketball game," he said.

"Teenage girls in shorts?"

"I'm not opposed to that. Are you really going to bed?"

"Yes."

Less than a minute after we hung up, the phone rang again. I saw Rob's name and assumed he was going to try one more time to cajole me, and I felt myself starting to relent. But when I answered, the call ended, and there was no knowing whether it had been an accidental redial, or whether he'd called back just to hang up on me.

S o Dad," I would say to my father on the phone, the *so* announcing a new foray. Then I would lob questions at him and hope for a response. I was playing the odds, the likelihood that one out of every three or four tries he would tell me something.

"So Dad, when did you first meet Oliver North?"

By then I'd read a lot about the lieutenant colonel. He orchestrated all manner of stratagems from his outpost in the Old Executive Office Building, and he won over half the country by acting the part of the good soldier during the televised congressional hearings, although the other half didn't buy it: I can remember my high school friends making fun of him. To left-leaning teenagers in 1987, North had been a pitiful liar, just like the president himself. Years later, when I began to read more about him, I felt less decided. I wouldn't go so far as to say I had a lot of sympathy for North, but I saw him differently, as an ambitious, God-fearing egotist, his background provincial, his energy astounding—a passionate man, at times deluded, who'd thrown himself into a questionable venture, believing it was for the best.

"I suppose I met him around the office. People knew who he was. There was never any shortage of talk about him," Dad said.

The way he said it, I assumed that was all I'd get. He paused, and I prepared for him to change the subject, but he surprised me. "Then there was a trip to Miami. That must've been the first time I interacted with him in any substantial way."

Dad was pulled into it at the last minute, he said. Another person from the NSC staff was supposed to go and then couldn't. North knew he'd be arriving late, and he wanted to make sure to have someone else on hand when things got started.

Late for what? When was this?

Dad didn't remember the exact date, but it must've been around February 1985. The point of the trip was to meet with a group of Nicaraguans at the Howard Johnson near the airport. I'd read about the same hotel, which was said to have offered certain guests a special guerrilla rate.

There were concerns about the Contras' operations, my father told me. We were trying to straighten things out.

His instructions were to convey Washington's misgivings—about the lack of a clear command structure, for one, the rivalries among different Contra factions. In order to sell this thing they needed a unified force battling against the communists, against the odds, but not against one another. There had to be a public relations strategy. Slide presentations. David slinging rocks at the Soviet-sponsored Goliath. And the funds had to be accounted for, that was imperative.

My dad in Miami, with the Contra brass. As an old boss of mine used to say: infuckingcredible.

. . . Let's say there are eight or ten men assembled in one corner of a banquet room, joshing awkwardly about the girl wiping down tables, as they wait for the meeting to start. Outside, a strong wind tosses sand and grit and pieces of plastic against the slanted glass wall. People—who are these people?—show up at the hotel with gifts for the Nicaraguans: a box of glazed doughnuts, a stack of blue jeans wrapped in cellophane. Someone brings them Cuban coffees in take-out cups.

My father has shown up with a bundle of traveler's checks and a list of talking points, which now seem all but impossible to say. Two other Americans, based here in Miami, have arrived, but he's never met them before and doesn't understand exactly who sent them. There's a rattling that might be caused by the wind or by some loose connection inside his head. He didn't sleep the night before. His skull feels like a piece of china.

Like him, the Nicaraguans have come straight from the airport, but in a truck fitted with reinforced windows. There were more of them than could squeeze into the cab, and two rode unprotected in the bed, sitting solemnly upon the wheel wells in their suits.

He was assured beforehand that these men understood English, but the one who answers him, the most senior among them, speaks in florid generalities, which might as well be in Latin. His voice will start out low and cordial, and then it will spike as he puts forth some urgent declaration of principles. Liberty. Freedom. The more he says those words the more they shift shape. It's possible to agree on the meaning of grenades, sixty-five-horsepower outboard motors, magazines: the *comandante* gives him a written inventory of needed supplies, much of it misspelled. Liberty, however, can't be brokered or shipped or invoiced.

The commander, who appears now and again in press photos, is as tall as his Anglo counterparts, a large forehead and a strong chin framing his face. "A bit small-minded" one of his fellow officers would later call him: he is strapping, determined, and blinkered. Older than he looks. He makes frequent trips to Washington and Miami, and between trips he writes lengthy missives on Fuerza Democrática Nicaragüense letterhead. His rebel army is the protector of thousands of peasant families, he insists—it really is humanitarian aid he's seeking, even the grenades and mortars are for a humanitarian purpose.

There are pauses, there is small talk. Tim mentions his daughters to the commander. Maybe they can chat about their kids.

So you didn't have a son, the commander says.

And the response?

At no point does the conversation go smoothly. At no point does Tim feel he is on solid ground. He stares at his big, empty palms, not knowing how to read them, and listens while the man recommends his favorite vacation spots, as though they haven't just been discussing the war in that same country.

Look here, my father says. I want to make sure we understand each other.

The commander has been massaging his own shoulder. He drops his hand and says, Of course, of course.

It's nearly 10:00 p.m. when Lieutenant Colonel North arrives. He's flown down on an air force jet after a full day at the office, and though in Washington he rarely dresses the part of a marine, he is wearing his service uniform—did he change into it on the plane?—garrison cap and greatcoat and all. The glass wall has gone black and buggy, and in front of it stands North, his hands planted on a folding table. He is all haste and certitude, in his stars and bars and medals. His voice isn't loud. It is a low, urgent voice that draws people in and makes them complicit. He greets everyone and then lays into the Nicaraguans.

You folks need to clean up your operation, he says. You had better. I'm holding this whole thing together by a thread. Clean up your act, or you can kiss all of it *adiós*.

For the most part, people are either devoted to North or else they loathe him. There's a fellow back in Washington, an army veteran whom everyone calls Red Menace—in combined reference to his stark assessment of the communist threat, his auburn hair, and his irritating behavior. His political stance puts him only slightly to the right of North, and he's former military on top of that, and yet he can't stand North, can't mention the name without adding that the man is full of it, in his opinion. So ignorant, he says, with the air of a jilted admirer. But the boss, McFarlane, loves North—in 1985 he still does, loves him like a son. Tim understands that sentiment, and in that understanding is a piece of the love itself. He's heard enough about the tours in Vietnam to hold North in high regard for his military service alone. But it's all too easy for the lieutenant colonel to blow right by the facts, and everybody knows it. He's drawn to emergencies, invented or actual, always just coming from a meeting with the vice president, always about to catch a flight to someplace, he won't say where. Everything a covert operation: Operation Go to Work. Operation Eat Potato Chips. Operation Take a Dump, probably.

In the hallway a man and a woman are arguing in Spanish. Or maybe the woman is angry at someone else, maybe she's telling the man about it, for every so often the woman's voice surges, while the man's remains barely audible. At one point, her harangue coincides with a pause in the discussion, and some of the Nicaraguans smile, as though what she said was foul-mouthed or sensational.

I think we'd better clear the perimeter, North says. Tim steps out of the room to ask them to leave. The woman is much smaller than her voice led him to expect, and she wears the uniform of the hotel restaurant—khaki pants, a white blouse, and a colorful necktie. She carries herself erectly, while the man, slender and bald, with gold rings on his fingers, slumps against one wall.

When Tim comes out, they both turn to look, and as he doesn't know how to speak to them, he makes a tentative, sweeping gesture with his hand. The woman regards him with flared nostrils. Excuse me, she says, simultaneously an apology, a sneer, and a genuine request. Then they walk away, down the hall.

You can kiss all of it *adiós*, North says. Back in the room he is now admonishing the Nicaraguans about something else. My son's Boy Scout troop could do better, he says. Without logistics you don't have anything.

The white-haired *comandante* purses his lips and pouts. You see, he interrupts at last, that's all very nice, but without the funds, what can we do? He holds out his hands. He alludes to targets and quotas, while North wants to discuss moving more troops from rural to urban areas. They weave around and around each other, arguing about supply and resupply, about end-user certificates and the best way to take down a helicopter, until finally the Nicaraguans stalk out of the room.

But North stays, with Tim and the other Americans, talking on into the morning about how to tighten oversight of the rebels' operations. They are a few men in a hotel, trying to administer a foreign war. They move out of the conference room into the lounge and then, when the lounge closes, into a guest room, and there they sit on two beds and a desk chair and consume beers and snacks they've bought at a convenience store. Tim doesn't say much. He came to Miami, after all, as North's surrogate, and since North's arrival, he's had no other task than to listen. He's been thrown into this arena midgame and is still trying to glean the rules. And that's what he wants to do, he's not dwelling on the ramifications of all this, just figuring out his place.

The room is stuffy, and when North tries to turn the knobs on the AC unit, nothing works, not even the fan. Tim calls down to the front desk and is told the repairman won't return until the morning. Do you have a screwdriver? he asks. Pliers? He runs down to pick up the tools, and back in the room he dismantles the unit and manages to get it running again. It's the first useful thing he's done all day.

The talk grows looser, and every so often he joins in. At around three in the morning, he offers up a story he heard from his friend Jodi Dentoff, about a cabinet secretary, a deliberate, weary man, telling a joke after a press briefing. This was the same man who typically greets the president's zingers with an awkward nod or a "right," who is maybe trying to learn a new skill, straining as everyone is to ingratiate himself with the jokester in chief. The joke is one step removed from what you might find printed on the inside of a Bazooka wrapper.

Q: *What did the elephant say to the naked man?*
A: *How do you breathe through that thing?*

When Jodi told the story it was poignant, a miscalibrated attempt at camaraderie by the secretary, but upon leaving Tim's lips it contorts into ridicule. The other men guffaw and grab for the last of the salted nuts.

To my own surprise, I'd developed a kind of respect for North. Not for his patriotic posturing, certainly not for his later career as a right-wing radio host—I hadn't kept up with that—and not even for his military service, valorous as I gather it must have been. It was just that this man, this midlevel puffer fish in an inertial bureaucracy, someone whom I have trouble picturing as anything other than a comic character, managed to more or less run a war in another country! I couldn't help but think of its unfolding like an episode of *The A-Team*, like something that would've been on TV in the mid-1980s, in which a ragtag group of renegades pulls off some impossible rescue.

My quasi-admiration would've been treacherous to confess in 1987 and maybe still is—in my generally urban, generally liberal circles, at least. I can hear the objections: Any number of fascists have been *effective*. We don't give them points for that. But North wasn't a fascist, and much as I wouldn't want any more like him, I'll secretly tip my hat to him. To North, who loved secrets. The guy got shit done.

Of course this had everything to do with my dad, with how I thought about my dad, in contrast to how I conceived of a Dick Mitchell or an Oliver North. Different as Mitchell and North were, they both knew what they wanted to do and how to do it. I was exaggerating that quality in them, exaggerating their talents and minimizing my father's, so that even as I tried to write a book that would somehow rehabilitate Dad, I was subtly undermining him at every turn.

t's fifty percent pure bullshit," Jodi Dentoff said to me, speaking about James Singletary's memoir. I'd asked her whether she'd read it. "You might say that makes it a hundred percent impure bullshit."

When I'd run into her at Dad's panel, I hadn't expected that either of us would follow up on that wispy promise of a get-together, but then I'd found her card in my purse and sent her an e-mail, and she'd replied at once. We met for a drink at a downtown hotel, the same hotel I'd been taken to for birthday lunches when I was in middle school, and I was sorry to discover that the dining room had since been renovated, turned into something more generic, more mauve. My memories were of velvet drapes and long shrimp ringed around a pewter bowl, and when I was twelve it couldn't have seemed more fancy. Now it was nothing special. But Jodi made it seem classier, or clubbier at least, leaning forward so that her chin grazed the yellow blooms that had been placed there, and talking in barely more than a whisper.

"To be expected, with any of these guys and their books. They have selective memories, obviously, like anybody, and big egos, and then there are the unfortunate conventions of the form. If I know one thing from too many years of journalism, it's that any time you try to write the story of a life you distort it," she said.

I mentioned I'd been reading her recent articles. Jodi was still working at *The Washington Post*, as she had been for years, and recently she'd been assigned to cover the hearings and legal proceedings that had followed the revelations of abuse at the Abu Ghraib prison. She'd seen so many tempests blow through Washington, she said, and so she had low expectations, predicting that none of the evidence or testimony or reports would lead to any genuine accounting, that the end result of all the agitation would be to bury the facts in heaps of paper, that the public response would amount to a kind of distracted fatalism, if not sheer indifference.

"At what point is it all just more entertainment? I'm beginning to think of myself in those terms. As a pornographer," Jodi said.

She'd tried out this speech before, I sensed.

"Jodi Does D.C."

"Basically."

"But you're still doing it."

"The alternative would be what?"

Jodi was very much of the 1980s, even two decades later. She had made her name then, coaxing secrets out of retired two-star generals and discontented agency staff. Her sense of style, while of the type a magazine might have labeled "timeless"—black shifts, anorexic litheness—recalled another notepad slogan from my childhood: *You can never be too rich or too thin.* Her writing was as spare and chiseled as could be, avoiding the lyric and the folksy in equal measure. Again: timeless, according to the ideal of a particular time. Out of all the adults who had showed up at our house for parties when I was young, Jodi had been the one I'd been most curious about, maybe because she was so small, not much larger than I was at age nine or ten, but also so modish (I remember in particular a tasseled suede cape and snakeskin heels), with a husky voice that made everything she uttered sound like an extraordinary disclosure.

Now an older, huskier echo of that voice curled out of her throat, dipped in butter and ash. "The system always works the same way," she said, back on the subject of scandal. "A few lower-level people get hung out to dry, while the higher-ups . . . let me just say I'm not worried for Rumsfeld."

"He'll land on his feet, I guess."

"Those guys always manage to cover their asses. Almost always. They misrepresent things, and they end up believing their own misrepresentations. They publish them even, write memoirs and wind up in some law firm or a consulting firm, they do a little lobbying. In the end everybody's fine except for the poor bastards who drew the short straws.

"But," she added, "your dad knows a little something about that, doesn't he?"

I felt as though I were exaggerating my expressions, my nods, making faces and bobbing my head up and down in lieu of responding. I didn't want to seem as ignorant as I felt. Then I confessed to her I was trying to write something about what had happened to him, and she didn't say anything for a long time, so that I imagined she was testing out words in her head, working out the best way to let me know it was a dumb idea.

Instead she started to tell me, disjointedly, something of her own past. She'd come to Washington in 1966, as a cub reporter, that's how she put it, though the term sounded quaint to my ear, movie-musical romantic, like she'd arrived hanging by one arm from a Pullman car, wearing a fedora with a pencil in the brim. It was the first time I thought of Jodi as a transplant. She was much more tightly bound to the city than I was by the accident of having been born in it.

She paused and sipped her wine. "I met your dad when he was at State." She paused again. "And then he went to the NSC and then, as you know, some shit went down. What questions did you have?"

I felt foolish for not having come with any questions. Struggling to produce one, I asked her what part of the Iran-Contra story she'd covered. She stared back at me.

"I was not assigned to it," she said. "I filed a few related stories, nothing major."

And then how could she have said what she said next? Stating so matter-of-factly, "Of course your dad was wrecked by it."

"Wrecked?" Damaged, yes, but *wrecked*? As a father, he'd remained intact. Sometimes crazy, sometimes a pain in the ass—but intact. I didn't know what to do with her remark, and maybe I didn't even want to talk about Iran-Contra, maybe neither did she.

"His career I mean, it never recovered. I always wondered why he didn't just move, get out of this town. That's what I would've done. Then again he had his family to consider." She looked at me, part of the family in question. "And now he's so upset about that book, Singletary's book. I mean, who even takes Singletary seriously anymore? He's totally on the fringe. The fringe of the fringe. When he asked me to write some kind of takedown—"

"Singletary did?" I asked.

"Your father, he wanted me to write an article about the book, about the errors in the book. It's not the kind of thing I write. He was very insistent, but . . ." It seemed she was trying to apologize to my dad through me, or else she was trying to convey to him, through me, why she couldn't have done what he wanted her to do.

"Yeah, when my dad disapproves of something, he can get pretty agitated," I said. "Sometimes I think it's because he grew up in a small town, it was a lot of German immigrants, and there were all these unwritten rules for how to behave. So when he has these big reactions, it's because someone did something you just wouldn't do in his hometown."

She looked at me from under scrunched brows, as though what I'd said didn't parse, or maybe she found it distasteful, this daughter's offhand analysis of a father. I'd been trotting out that theory about Dad's small-town background for years, I realized, ever since high school or college when I'd developed it, believing I'd solved the puzzle of him.

"Or that could be part of it," I added.

"Mmm," she said into her glass, before taking another sip. "He would always talk a lot about you."

I smiled at the mistake. "Not me. My older sister, Courtney. She was always—the impressive one. He saw himself in her."

"No, not her. The middle one. You."

"He talked about me?"

"He worried about you."

I didn't know what to do with that. "Were you friends with Dick Mitchell?" I asked.

She inhaled slowly and exhaled his name. "Dick Mitchell," she said. "Why do you ask?"

"I remember him, but after he died it was like he'd never existed, my dad never talked about him."

"I haven't thought about him in a long time."

"But you knew him."

"We were friends. Back in—the early eighties, I guess it was. He wasn't a close friend, but we would meet for lunch or for a drink from time to time. We would talk about whatever was going on, what we knew. He was a big flirt too, not that I minded that, or ever took it seriously. I also used to have lunch with your father, though there was not so much flirting with him, of course. He was always more proper. And since they were friends, Dick and your dad, sometimes we would get together, the three of us, which was always a lot of fun. It was also very interesting to see those two together. Sometimes they would vie over me, like boys trying to get their mother's attention. They knew they were doing it, and they could be funny about it, but I saw the rivalry there long before . . ."

"Long before what?"

"Before their falling-out."

"They had a falling-out?"

"That was my understanding, that they stopped speaking around the time of the congressional hearings, the Iran-Contra hearings. After that I didn't see much of either of them."

"I guess my dad had been kind of in Dick's shadow, right?"

"No. I wouldn't say that."

"I was just a kid, but he had this larger-than-life thing . . ."

"Dick Mitchell lived under his own shadow," she said, and then she said that Iran-Contra had poisoned more relationships than just theirs, and she warned me away from what she called "the swamp" of the scandal.

My dad had been sucked into it, and so had a lot of people, she said. Now none of them could even remember the truth of what had happened—they were retired or semiretired and had too much time to revisit the big drama, their trauma, they were victims of this or that, they were misunderstood. They might tell you something they consider to be factual, but beware. Not to mention, there was a whole demimonde of researchers, she said, Iran-Contra obsessives who'd fallen into the bottomless pit of the scandal, who'd been poring over documents at the National Security Archive for years and years, developing their own theories. Time had stopped for them.

"If you want my advice, and I'll understand if you don't, forget about all that. The craziness, the secret deals: no one could ever digest it, other than to say that covert action and democracy make uneasy bedfellows. My advice would be to write what you remember. Stick to that."

I told Jodi I would try, i.e., try to anchor the story to my own memories—but what were those? *Say goodbye a little longer, make it last a little longer, give your breath long-lasting fresh-nessss . . . with Big Red!* Jingles and sayings from an era when people kissed each other with chewing gum in their mouths (or so I was convinced), in other words so much residue, hardly sorted or prioritized. In the midst of which, the scandal that tripped up our dad seemed to be, at a very minimum, some kind of organizing principle, even if it was only a connection to another mess, a jumble of activity for which no one could agree on a meaning.

Afterward I took a circuitous route back to the Metro station, past a number of grand old edifices of our federal bureaucracy. It was cold and late enough that the nearby streets were sparsely traveled, but for the odd black Infiniti wheeling softly in or out of a garage, the driver clutching a travel mug. Here were both the grand mystery of government and its little human movers, with their travel mugs, so small compared to the massive buildings.

The approach of the new year made me newly conscious that I was still in D.C., now working, renting. This unremarkable fact came to me in the guise of a remarkable one. I've never really gone in for epiphanies, nevertheless I was struck by the obvious: *I was living in Washington now.* I'd been thinking of myself as someone taking a break from real life, which would resume sometime in 2005, but now it was almost 2005. This was my real life. It was. And I had to start treating it as such.

The first thing I did was to retire my white jeans and my polka-dot shirts. One evening after work I ventured out to look for Washington clothes, at a Talbots store. In a curtained stall I tried on flare-leg trousers, I tried on silk blouses, then a double-breasted jacket, a sweater set, all of it black, red, cream, charcoal, and/or navy. One pair of pants combined all these colors in a plaid. In the corner of my stall there was a chair, and on it I heaped the clothes I'd already removed, a growing mound of boiled wool and micro-velvet that gave off a pleasant, almost woodsy perfume. Like a forest inside of a government building. I tried on something called "bi-stretch pants," which forgave me my back fat. I tried on pumps styled like loafers, called "loafer pumps." I could sense the sales-woman's excitement, or perhaps she sensed mine: a real transformation was taking place, an inside-the-Beltway makeover! I left there with two bags full of prissy-wonky lady apparel, and then at another store I bought a few black headbands.

That I conceived of "real life" in this way, as an exercise that required me to dress up as somebody else, in clothes I didn't like clearly it was this idea that needed the makeover, much more so than my wardrobe. But where was the store for that?

———

It was a long while before I managed to follow Jodi's advice. I was still drawn to what she'd called the swamp. I went to the American University library, where I found the transcripts of Dick Mitchell's deposition, from March 1987, and his testimony before the congressional committees, from July of that year. The thick black tomes of the official record spanned three shelves, so that for all the disclosures they might've contained, the total effect was of a black wall. Iran-Contra, this barricade of books announced, was too much for any one person to consume. The depositions alone took up twenty-seven volumes, organized alphabetically, Richard Mitchell following two men named Miller who followed former attorney general Meese.

I toted Mitchell's deposition to a carrel, next to a window overlooking Nebraska Avenue. There was a familiar low hum coming from someplace, a smell of—old carpet? Book bindings? Possibly I'd sat in that same chair in high school, looking up facts about African nations or the Missouri Compromise for some assignment, even as Mitchell had been giving the very deposition I was about to read. Whether or not that was precisely true, I was motivated, in my haphazard research, by the knowledge that important things had gone down back then, practically right under my nose, while I let myself be distracted. (It did not escape me that now I was here looking up testimony from seventeen years earlier, and so no doubt missing out on important things of the present.)

Jodi had mentioned a rivalry between Dick and my dad. That was the most recent addition to my mental list of facts about Dick Mitchell, which I kept returning to, because I had this nagging intuition that there was something I'd missed about him.

MR. EGGLESTON. Your job was to coordinate humanitarian assistance to the Nicaraguan resistance fighters, is that correct?
MR. MITCHELL. Through June of 1985 I worked under Assistant Secretary Abrams at the State Department. I started as director of the Nicaraguan Humanitarian Assistance Office on July 1.

MR. EGGLESTON. And that was also part of the State Department.

MR. MITCHELL. Correct. But we were in a separate building. We were relatively independent.

MR. EGGLESTON. Can you tell us what were your responsibilities in that office?

MR. MITCHELL. Congress had allocated approximately 27 million dollars for humanitarian assistance, and we were in charge of distributing that.

MR. EGGLESTON. How did you determine what would qualify as "humanitarian assistance"?

MR. MITCHELL. There was not a set rule. We used our best judgment. Food, clothing, mosquito nets, it was those sorts of items.

MR. EGGLESTON. Was everything purchased before it was delivered to the Nicaraguans, or were there cash transfers as well?

MR. MITCHELL. There were both.

MR. EGGLESTON. And how did you determine that the money you sent was used for humanitarian purposes only?

MR. MITCHELL. That was a challenge. The people we were working with down there, they weren't exactly trained accountants.

MR. EGGLESTON. Nonetheless, according to a Government Accounting Office report from July of last year, some of the recipients of this aid did manage some rather artful invoicing. In fact, fraudulent.

MR. MITCHELL. With this type of aid, regrettably, a certain level of fraud is not that unusual. Maybe in the future we ought to send some GAO people down to work with our recipients directly.

MR. EGGLESTON. That's not a bad idea. I don't know how they'd feel about it.

MR. MITCHELL. Oh, they'd love it in the jungle.

MR. EGGLESTON. Right, right. Getting back to my questions. Did you coordinate many of your disbursements with Oliver North at the NSC?

MR. MITCHELL. We were in contact with Colonel North. I wouldn't say we coordinated with him, necessarily.

To judge by the transcript, he was confident of his answers. He joked with the lawyers, and they responded in kind—Dick Mitchell, humanitarian, and his genteel interlocutors, peers from the same slice of Washington society.

How I imagine that world to have been in, say, the spring of '85: a giant tangle of crossed wires. The more I read about that period in government, the more it seemed that the right hand didn't know what the left hand was up to, though I assume most governments share that quality, to one degree or another. Even so, Dick Mitchell and my dad would have been, at that point, still (relatively) young, full of potential, full of good intentions—after all, who in Washington did not have good intentions during the first part of his career?

Nobody sleeps. The men tasked with running the country, they are in bed a few hours a night, if that, which they occasionally supplement by snoozing on an office couch or nodding off in a meeting. Night after night they deprive themselves, until more than a few hours of sleep are no longer even an option, for they've replaced their steady circadian rhythms with staccato, erratic beats. Their heads buzz and ache and echo. Other countries, distant wars, twirl in the dreamless kaleidoscopes of their minds, as they write memos and more memos.

Most days, Tim drives to work. At six, six-thirty you can usually still find a space not too far away. From behind, with its fountain not yet turned on and the East and West Wings half-hidden by trees, the famous building is just a house. Often the sunrise is the last thing he sees before he goes inside of it, joining a slew of nervy workers in coats and badges. And once he passes through the portal that is the west entrance, through security, he finds himself in the midst of an alternative civilization, a hive, with fluorescent lights buzzing and the presidential seal everywhere, on the walls and the coffee cups. Men in dark suits walk briskly to and fro as brisker couriers retrieve and deliver the great daily burden of paper documents, waves of memoranda and briefings parceled out in manila envelopes, bound dossiers, file folders, naked stacks still warm from the copy machine. Here are the graying viziers of the free world and their minions, their staffers, their secretaries—eager Southern girls changing out of their Reeboks into navy-blue pumps. Here a lingering odor of scrambled eggs from the breakfast trays.

Tim works for McFarlane, the national security advisor, a.k.a. the assistant to the president for national security affairs. It bothers McFarlane to no end that the president has not yet established a clear set of policy goals, leaving his own office without an agenda. The advisor tries to seal away his grievances, his fear that he isn't accomplishing anything, and yet he takes such pains to present a calm facade that the underlying turmoil is all too apparent, as if he were continually declaring that he was not upset, no, not in the slightest. Not at all! At times the force of his anguish and the force of his efforts to swallow the anguish combine to make him hover just above the ground, or so it seems to Tim. He returns from the president's morning security briefing with his jaw locked and his Florsheims floating over the carpet: out of sheer frustration, the assistant to the president for national security affairs is levitating.

He is mysterious to the people around him. He speaks in abstractions, makes general pronouncements in a flat voice that stops, backs up, starts again, and does everything it can to avoid any slithering, biting emotion. His jaw clenches. But every so often, a vent opens and he releases a quantum of steam. His voice grows more insistent, though no louder, and his ears redden. Tim doesn't necessarily know what (or who) caused it. His boss, as he's confided to Jodi Dentoff over lunch, is an honorable, thoughtful man, but his desire for the president's approval runs so deep it can never really be satisfied.

McFarlane would return from a meeting and lament, The president has been misinformed! It's bad policy!

All right, Tim says. Let's put together some information for him. But his boss bristles at that, ever loath to contradict his commander. Instead he contradicts himself: It's not a matter of information, he says. And then, just as quickly as this upset emerged, it is suppressed. Redacted. A thick black line is drawn over his covert turmoil. McFarlane places the studious mask back over his face and asks Tim to locate an unrelated document. Then he asks whether Poindexter is in, nodding at the closed door to his deputy's office.

I believe so, says Tim.

The deputy is a taciturn man, a vice admiral more inclined toward technical questions than politics, his mouth frequently plugged by a pipe, the door to his office usually shut. Tim doesn't know—almost never knows for sure—whether he's there behind that door or not. At the end of the day, Tim is distantly, quietly fond of McFarlane: he's rooting for the boss, hoping he'll drone and frown his way out of the administrative straitjacket he's been forced to wear, unlikely as that may be. But with the technocrat in the deputy's office, who mostly communicates, if at all, through short sentences scrawled on memos, Tim rarely finds common ground.

McFarlane heads toward his own office door, then reverses direction and asks Tim to lend him a quarter for the vending machine. He takes a series of deliberate breaths, as his eyes peer out from their cool caverns. Before he marches off he says—to Tim, to Poindexter's closed door, to nobody—I believe it is necessary for us to follow a coherent course of action, in accordance with the president's objectives.

His voice becomes lower and slower as he continues. That's of the utmost importance, he says. Clear, decisive action is needed.

In the courtyard at the Tabard Inn, Tim drapes his arms over the back of his small chair and clasps his hands behind him. He tilts the chair onto its hind legs. It's a balmy day, and the light lusters the two friends he's met for lunch. He listens to them trade tattle, between bites.

Because what I hear is, Schultz has been offering to resign on a daily basis, Jodi says, referring to the secretary of state.

I wouldn't call it daily, says Dick.

He's spinning his wheels.

It's not like Schultz is the only guy who's got problems.

The clusters of iron furniture are like big spiders that screech every time they move. He and Dick and Jodi meet up once a month, sometimes more, for breeze-shooting purposes. The Washington breeze: the braid of information and misinformation and you-didn't-hear-it-from-me, the airstream of open secrets. Flirting also plays a part in it, the weightless, daytime flirting that keeps things interesting.

Look at this woman eat, Dick says.

She is a tiny woman with an enormous appetite, now making short work of a cheeseburger. For Tim it's like watching his daughters when they were younger and had hands as small as Jodi's and ate real food—before all the diets. Do Jodi's feet even reach the floor? He is a giant by comparison.

She takes a sip of her iced tea. I'm still recovering from last week, she says. I was in Phoenix, which was like Satan's armpit. So hot I couldn't eat.

What were you doing out there? Dick asks.

Talking to loons, she says. These people had their own logic that I couldn't follow. I understood what they were saying on the face of it, and going from A to B it made sense, but once they got out to F or G it was just gobbledygook. This group called the United States Council for World Freedom, they're out there in the desert plotting how to eradicate communism globally.

I hear they've got Scottsdale pretty well cleared, Tim says.

When you're out in that kind of heat there's a different thinking process that happens, she says.

Tim dreamed, once, that he and Jodi were standing together at a cocktail party, a fund-raiser in a great empty plain of a room, with a huge marble floor and no one else there but the waiters. When he awoke he retained that image, and it has stayed with him as though it's a secret they share.

And how goes it in the inner sanctum? she asks him.

I wish I knew. You know how many people are on our staff, Tim says. It's one hundred eighty-something. And McFarlane talks to maybe half a dozen of those. The rest don't know what the hell they're doing. I mean, some do, but we've got guys who are literally wandering the halls.

She narrows her eyes, even as she eats and eats. It's an impossible situation, she says.

Exactly, he says. That's off the record.

Mitchell scoops up a bundle of Jodi's fries and eats them one by one out of his hand.

If you want any fries, just help yourself, she quips.

On paper Tim and Dick Mitchell have the same credentials, same track records in Washington. Tim would never swipe fries off someone's plate without asking, though. At work, he relies more on diligence, while Mitchell has his card shark's memory, his agility, and a talent for endearing himself to older men.

There's been talk about your hardworking marine, Jodi says to Tim. They're saying that the lieutenant colonel has gone operational, she says. That he's been jetting off to Ilopango and Tegucigalpa. They say his ass is way out on a limb.

How people relish the sheer insiderness of inside information, the specialized lingo of the agency and bureau, the acronyms within acronyms within acronyms—and inside the innermost one, a rumor about a petty feud or somebody's drinking problem. Or North's irregular (since nobody really knew what was illegal) activities. Every fact has its own, erratic momentum. It sticks to other facts, and they drag words along behind them. For instance: after the president was diagnosed with intestinal cancer he said that he did not suffer from cancer. He later clarified that while he did have cancer, he did not *suffer* from it. He didn't feel that he had suffered.

Jodi has stopped eating: Any chance you could confirm—

I can't, Tim says.

It must make you uneasy, she says.

I see the guy sometimes. I barely know him.

You know what the complaint is, she says. You've got all these military officers, ex-military working over there—they don't understand politics. They resent it. They see Congress as the enemy.

Tim nods. It's a familiar rap on his bosses, but to him it seems superficial, a description as opposed to a diagnosis. I don't think anybody really knows, he says. Knows the whole situation.

You're talking about North, Jodi says.

North isn't so bad, he says. Everything's happening interstitially now.

Jodi notices the time. She lays cash on the table, stands up, and backs away, smiling. Gentlemen, she says. It's been a pleasure.

After she leaves another spark lights up Mitchell's face. He taps the edge of the table twice, with both hands, and tells Tim: You managed that well enough.

He isn't aware that he tried to manage anything. He doesn't think of it that way. But he can see from Dick's expression that his friend knows all about North's game, maybe more than he himself does.

There is too much to know, too little to do. Every morning the agency staff descend from Annandale and Arlington by the thousands, with their lunches in brown bags, and succeed by dint of their long memories and regulatory vim in maintaining what the outsider might take to be stasis but what, to these balding Virginians, is a delicate equilibrium. A hippopotamus perched, just so, on top of a pole. Required to maintain the balance are strategic delays, lunch at one's desk, gallons of sour coffee, thousands of ballpoint pens, careful ignorance of what might be happening in other departments, and countless memoranda with titles like "Initial Proposals Re: Preliminary Steps to Prevent Negative Consequences."

Tim's position is superior to those of the pencil pushers, yet he has limited authority; it is not for him to direct policy or to be captured on camera as he marches from a doorway into a waiting black car. He is a platinum conduit, a fancy connector, through which top-secret matters ooze their way along, and as they go past, small adjustments can be made, suggestions offered, deposits of information amassed. He is close enough to the peripheral bureaucracy that he nurses a fear of becoming engulfed by it, of turning into a numb-assed, forgotten desk rat, to whom none but the most inscrutable and irrelevant documents are routed, and routed last—the fear that his would be the desk where disregarded memos go to die.

(From the testimony of Timothy Atherton, June 24, 1987)
MR. RUDMAN. What is the PROFS network?
MR. ATHERTON. PROFS stands for "Professional Office System." This was a system of IBM computers we installed in, I think it was 1984.
MR. RUDMAN. How were these machines used?
MR. ATHERTON. Instead of putting everything on paper, members of the staff could send messages by computer.
MR. RUDMAN. Just to be clear on this, one computer could send a message to another computer?
MR. ATHERTON. That's correct. Meaning one person could send a message to another person, directly through the computer.
MR. RUDMAN. And did that alter the way work got done?
MR. ATHERTON. Traditionally, we had a procedure in place so that memos would be seen in a certain order, first this person and then that person. Once the computers were there, some people stopped following the procedure.
MR. RUDMAN. Were you aware at any point of efforts on the part of your superiors to destroy sensitive computer messages?
MR. ATHERTON. I was not, no.
MR. RUDMAN. Were you aware that copies of the messages were stored on the system's mainframe?
MR. ATHERTON. I was not aware of that. I don't think anyone was.

A few years earlier, the White House had been no more technologically capable than a bank branch, but just recently a man who'd worked on the president's campaign promoted, then installed, an office computer network. Now every desk has a machine, its rounded screen traversed by letters and numbers, a glowing green armada of characters arranging themselves into directives and updates and schedules. Now messages can be sent directly from one person to another, rather than by the standard routing arrangement. Nobody has oversight over the flow of it all.

It was part of Tim's job to review the documents intended for the national security advisor, forwarding some of them along and rerouting others. He has tried to maintain an equivalent control over the computer messages, but often he'll ask for a document only to be told that it has been sent straight to the boss. There's no controlling the little green characters. North, he knows, sends everything directly to Poindexter and McFarlane.

The men who do still observe the old procedures come to Tim with their complaints. Exhibit A would be Red Menace, who works in one of the staff offices across the street. He has a way of darting into the White House, of standing at the threshold before he enters a room, making quick, dull eye contact before stepping softly inside, reaching behind him to shut the door. Then he presses his hands against his gray blazer and stares at the wall and insists that there are bad actors at State, undermining everything the president has set out to do.

Has McFarlane read my memos yet? he asks.

Tim has received paper copies of four memoranda from the Menace, directed to McFarlane. If memory serves, they all outline variations on a theme: the threat of a communist takeover of Mexico. It is one of the Menace's bugbears—today the villages of Nicaragua, tomorrow the beaches of Cancun.

I'll ask him when I see him, Tim says.

Will you?

Yes, I will.

And as for a meeting—

He's traveling with the president all week, Tim says. It's unlikely.

All I'm asking for is five, ten minutes every so often. Otherwise why have experts on the staff?

It's not just you.

It's my duty to keep him informed. I have twenty years of experience in the region. For all I know he hasn't even received any of my updates. He's spending all his time with the news media. At least he could learn enough to speak intelligently to these reporters whose company he so enjoys.

I will ask him, Tim says.

I know it's not just me. I've been talking to some of the others. We have no access. We are spinning our wheels.

Tim keeps most of the Menace's memos in a file drawer. He rarely passes them on to McFarlane, who dislikes their tone, the implicit suggestion that the national security advisor isn't doing his job properly. He knows that the Menace has been whining to people on the outside, people like the U.N. ambassador, about the way things are going. It's not as though Tim doesn't have sympathy for the analysts whose white papers and memoranda McFarlane barely skims, but this one does himself no favors by piping up in every single meeting or flooding the boss with written appeals.

He goes across the street, looking for North.

Inside the Old Executive Office Building, the grand rooms that once housed the Department of War are themselves embattled, in disrepair, spattered with bits of chipped-off paint, stalactites of dust in the corners. Distinguished area experts bring in box fans during the summer and space heaters during the winter. Exposed wiring dangles from the ceiling in one of the men's rooms.

Within this massive and sodden building the rhetoric of crisis is slung about. He waits outside a meeting of the Outreach Working Group on Central America, where North is holding court, and after the meeting breaks up he intercepts North. He wants to discuss the computer messaging system. Let's walk back to my office, North says. In his head he has rehearsed what he means to say. *I think we need to get something straight. These are the rules. An organization has to abide by its own rules, or else chaos will result.* But those are words in his head, spoken to an image of North, and here is the man himself, swaddled in his noble causes. Rules and procedure and caution

are impediments, obstructions to right action. Tim has to portray
himself as a fellow warrior.

All messages from you are considered high priority, Tim says.
I'll see to it that he gets everything right away—

You bet, I'll route everything through you, North says.

I only ask because that hasn't been the case recently.

What happens is, I'll be working late, I'm here at ten p.m., or
on a Sunday, and since you're not here I just send it directly.

But if you route it to me, it'll still go to the boss as soon as he's in.

You bet.

Room 392 is North's command center: There are multiple terminals and a printer with paper spilling out onto the ground, and
several different-colored phones, one of which is answered by the
prettiest woman in the building. As they walk in, she calls out messages like numbers in a bingo game, ending with, And you-know-
who came by to say that Motley still hasn't sent the draft directive
you asked for.

That's just what we were talking about upstairs, this BS from
State. If we didn't have one or two friends over there, I don't know
what we'd do.

Then he turns to Tim and grabs him by the forearm. Hey, listen to this.

He proceeds to tell Tim a variation of the story Tim told him
in Miami, but now it's the secretary of state making the joke about
the man and the elephant, the story exaggerated and turned into a
parable of ineptitude. He clearly has no idea that Tim told it to him
originally, and that it was about a different man, no memory of that
at all.

My neighbor Daniel didn't seem to observe the same rules and precautions, socially, that the rest of us did. He invited me to do things with him and his daughter, and had I been in L.A., or some other place where I had more friends, I would've been more leery of his overtures. I probably would've avoided him. But at Nina's basketball game, he'd asked whether I wanted to come along with the two of them to a museum that weekend—Nina had a school assignment that required her to go there—and I said that I would. I didn't have other plans. As it turned out, Daniel had to catch up on work that day, and so I went just with Nina.

The stone archway that spanned the museum entrance was decorated with bas-relief figures of every kind: bulls, cherubs, small-membered satyrs, miscellaneous pineapples. Nina studied a poster about upcoming events, as though she might go to one of them. She wore the same Converse sneakers drawn on with marker that she'd worn at the Hunan Palace, the same black hoodie. She was just a girl, I kept being reminded of that.

"You have so many buttons," I said as we presented our bags to the security guard.

"Yeah," she said, "I don't even know how I got all these." On
her backpack were at least a dozen pins, one with a rainbow, another with a peace sign, some with demands (End the War), others
with band names that I only knew to be band names after she'd
told me so. If I said she carried the weight of the world on her back
I wouldn't only be referring to all the buttons. What is that one? I
asked, pointing to a white squiggle on a black background, and she
said it had something to do with political prisoners.

We made our way to the basement. For all the pomp of the exte-
rior, the museum's lowest floor was as plain as a county administrative building, except that the gray, low-ceilinged halls had been
lined with oil portraits of deceased Americans. We prowled around
in search of the people f.k.a. Indians. There was a special exhibit,
demarcated by dark brown walls and dramatic lighting, with headdresses and spears and maize grinders and such things on display,
which Nina noted in a notebook, while I began to feel accosted by
fatigue and by a suspicion that Nina might want to get away from
me, since after all she was not the one who'd invited me to come. I
watched her stare hard at a specimen of pottery, then pat down her
hair, and I realized she hadn't been looking at the pottery with that
unmerciful face but at her own reflection in the glass.

Hanging on the walls were paintings by George Catlin. The
name had been only vaguely known to me beforehand. A sign explained that in the middle of the nineteenth century he had attached himself to Western expeditions so as to paint portraits of
tribesmen and tribeswomen, on the eve of what was then called
"the Removal." He had completed more than six hundred of these,
his gallery of a "vanishing race," and had taken the paintings from
city to city, lobbying the government to purchase them. The government declined, then bought them after he died. Sixteen of those
portraits now hung in a grid. *Mash-kee-wet. Man of Good Sense. He
Who Kills the Osages. Little Wolf. Black Coat. Old Bear.* In the other
rooms were paintings from the museum's permanent collection,
among them portraits of the nineteenth-century statesmen who'd
done the removing, all equally dead now, though the vanished na-

tives in their pelts and headdresses seemed much more remote than the Clays and the Calhouns.

Nina turned back to me. "That one, Black Hawk. He kind of reminds me of our principal."

"Why?"

"I don't know, he just does."

"Your principal doesn't dress like that, does he?"

"Only on Fridays," she said.

"I wonder what they thought of Catlin?"

"Maybe they didn't. Maybe they just sat there and got painted, and they were thinking about what to have for dinner, and then he left and they forgot about him or made fun of him or whatever."

Tossed off as this was, I found myself envying her. Nina bought into the reality of these paintings in a way I did not, she saw her principal in Black Hawk, while I saw the Oppressed as Depicted by the Oppressor, and for a moment I wished I'd never gone to college.

I decided to give her some space, so that she could take notes for her assignment. I roamed around the other rooms, strolling past slaves and soldiers, statesmen, stage actors. When I circled back she was still glancing at the same wall of Indians and writing in her notebook.

"Are you getting what you need?" I asked.

"I guess so," she said.

I told her I was going to look around a little more and would meet her back there. This time I wandered farther and found myself in the middle of Reconstruction. There were portraits of black congressmen and white Klansmen, carpetbagger cartoons, a display about rice growers. All that nation building, it made my head hurt, and I returned to the room where I'd left Nina. Only she wasn't there any longer.

I did laps of the downstairs and upstairs, at a speed too quick for museums, until a security guard asked whether I was looking for a tall girl with a backpack. She pointed to a nearby room, and inside, yes, was the girl in question, seated on a bench, baroque backpack by her side, gazing up at a painting not of a Sioux or a freedman but another girl. Actually a society woman on a sofa, but a young one, clean and fresh-eyed, though she was trussed in an elaborate gown, arms stiff by her sides.

When I reached the bench I saw Nina's face, and there was such a left-out look in it that I felt a throb in my chest. I sat down. I didn't say anything then. I hadn't completely forgotten what that age was like, before you learn to wrap your heart in something hard. I waited. For an instant I swear she glowed like something just pulled from the fire. Peripherally I could see this without looking, feel it on my skin, and I was overwhelmed by images of my own self-pitying tenth-grade existence, listening over and over again to a cassette of Chopin nocturnes, plastering myself with makeup and then scrubbing it all off again, etc. I hadn't wanted to be sixteen but also hadn't wanted to grow any older, hadn't viewed adulthood with much optimism. Even now I resisted it. So please don't blame me if I wanted the light to stay lit, if I didn't want her to cool to gray like the rest of us. But seconds later the sadness had disappeared from Nina's eyes, and I wondered whether I'd really seen what I'd seen, or whether I'd just been seeing what I wanted to see.

And then we were hungry. On the ground floor of the museum was a cafeteria that opened onto an atrium, formerly a courtyard but lately covered and climate-controlled, so that it was just the sort of place I imagined future humans would inhabit, a simulacrum of the outdoors closed off from the threat of genuine air. I bought Nina a sandwich and chips, and a cookie for myself, and we sat down at a table "outside."

"So it was your birthday? How was that?" I asked.

"It was all right."

"What'd you do? Did you go out?"

"My dad took me to dinner. It was sick."

"You got sick?"

"No, I mean the dinner, it was really good."

"Just you and your dad?" I asked.

"My mom died, of stomach cancer. When I was six."

She took a huge bite of her sandwich, as if to fend off the expressions of sympathy she'd heard too many times already. Ten years of pity from strangers. That didn't stop me from saying how sorry I was, but I kept it brief and then tentatively changed the subject.

"Did you get your driver's license?"

"My dad won't let me."

"Why won't he let you?"

"He keeps saying he's going to teach me but then he forgets or else something's wrong with the car. Something's always wrong with our car. We really need a new one. I want him to get an El Camino."

"Can't you get lessons from one of those driving schools?"

"He says it's a waste of money when he can teach me himself."

"That sounds frustrating."

"My dad's not very organized."

A few tables away from us, a tray full of plates and cutlery and drink bottles tipped over and fell to the floor, and without giving it a thought I jumped up and scurried over to that place where everything had spilled and scattered as though I had been the cause of it, not the employee in a dark green uniform who was now crouched next to the mess. I dropped to my knees. One might suspect that my effort was for show, and maybe no good intention is free of vanity, but it's also the case that in life as in lunch venues, I've tried to make the accidents disappear. The woman in uniform recoiled from me. "Is okay, is okay," she was saying, and more than once she craned her head around, perhaps to check whether her supervisor was watching, yet I stayed there on the floor with her, holding a bunch of forks and knives in one hand and trying to keep my unbelted pants up with the other. Under my knees it was wet. Her expression was three parts dismay to one part disbelief, and I could tell that if roles had been reversed she would never in a million years have stooped to assist a cafeteria employee, and because she felt that way, or because I felt she felt that way, the roles *were* somehow reversed, I the flunky and she the superior, and no she wouldn't have been dressed the way I was or confused the way I was, she would have worn nice jewelry and stylish things and avoided cafeterias altogether. (Oh, but I loved sliding a tray along metal rails, I did, and even more than that I loved to see all my options lined up there in a row.)

Nevertheless: the fact was that I had in typical American fashion intervened where I didn't belong, the solicitous fool in my sliding-down pants and too-small shirt, and I was only making things worse by handing that woman pieces of silverware, by sticking my knee in a puddle of Coke as not only Nina but also a puzzled German or maybe Dutch family looked on, and really, what was my excuse? I felt again how improper it was for me to pose as any sort of role model, and I wished I could reassign Nina for instructional purposes to the small scornful woman in uniform, who had at least remembered to wear a belt.

When I got back to the table Nina was eating her chips, and I formulated apologies without speaking them, without knowing what exactly to apologize for. "So can you teach me to drive?" she asked.

I probably should've given it more thought before I said that I would.

Unfortunately, Dad found out about the break-in at my building. I blamed my mother for that. He called on Sunday and insisted he was coming over to check my locks, and though I tried to discourage him, suggesting we do it the following weekend, by which time I hoped his too-urgent state of mind would've passed, he refused to be postponed.

He appeared at the door wearing a windbreaker loaded with pockets and snaps and zippers, and carrying a black messenger bag. I let him in. He walked around without saying anything. He'd seen the apartment when I moved in, but it looked even worse now. Some flowers that I'd bought the week before in an effort to brighten things up had wilted, and it smelled of dying flowers and microwave dinners.

He pressed his forehead with thumb and finger. "Remind me, how much are you paying for this dump?" Then he inspected the door bolt and both window latches and told me one of them was busted. "There are three empty bedrooms at home."

"I'm fine here. And the landlady's cool."

"The landlady is not cool. The landlady needs to keep up the place."

"So I'll call her. It's not a *dump*."

"It's a damn rathole," he said. "Pardon my language." He set the bag on the table. Something inside it went thud. He opened the bag, and I flinched.

"I think you should have this," he said.

"Oh god."

"If you're going to live all by yourself down here—"

"Oh my god. No."

"You should be able to protect yourself."

"No way. Absolutely not. I don't think that's legal for me to have."

"All anyone needs to do is turn on the news to get an idea of how they're enforcing those laws."

He took out a package of bullets. "Let me show you how to load it," he said.

"How about I get a baseball bat. I wouldn't be able to sleep with that thing here."

"You could move home any time."

"Dad."

I'd seen hundreds of them on-screen or in policemen's holsters, but I'd never been in the position to touch one. It was a small pistol, something I could picture a Barbara Stanwyck pulling from her purse. I'll acknowledge that I was not completely uninterested. In the Barbara Stanwyck idea, that is, the pulp glamour.

I looked at my father. He was sweating. Something he'd always had in him had been amplified. He'd always been anxious, as though whatever had kept all of us healthy and more than adequately fed and clothed might disappear at any moment, and it was his singular

burden to hold up the roof over our heads. And now he was still
straining to hold up that roof, only there were four different roofs,
five if you counted my mother's Philadelphia condo, all held up by
one hand while with the other he kept opening door after door,
looking for the one that led back to the life we'd lived together,
under just one roof. Yet each one he opened led to an empty room
or a crummy apartment or a brick wall. I had this sense of my dad
wandering around Washington with that tiny gun, wishing to rec-
tify the present, to bring it in line with what he'd pictured for his
so-called golden years.

But there. I heard him breathe. Saw him seeing. Saw him trying to tie my shoelaces again and for once didn't resent it. Saw how
confusing it was for him, to find me like this. The daughter who
should have been someone's wife by now, someone's mother too,
living in a house with three or four bedrooms and a pool in back.
Saw for the first time how in not doing those things I hadn't just
chosen a different path for myself but had in some way left him all
at sea.

"I just—" he began.

He sat down.

And then—what else could we do?—we sat there at the little
table that was my dining table and desk, that had (dis)arrayed over
its surface salt and pepper shakers, a gas bill, a newspaper, a dirty
paper napkin, and now a handgun. I offered to make tea. He opened
the newspaper. It was almost okay, but then every so often I spotted the gun again and felt frantic to get rid of it.

He stood up and went to examine the busted window latch a
second time. "Where's the nearest hardware store?" he asked. "I
bet I could fix this."

"I promise I'll call my landlady and get her to take care of it,"
I said.

"I'll even pay for it." He took out his wallet. "Here, here's a
couple hundred."

"Dad!"

Near the window was a stack of books, my research materials, and too late I saw that *A Call to Honor* by James Singletary was right on top. Dad hadn't noticed it there—until he did, turned and looked at it.

He picked up the book. I waited for him to say something. He set it back down.

"It looks like this latch has been broken for a while," he said.

"It's not very good."

"No."

"I mean the book," I said. "The book's not great."

"I can't say I'm surprised."

"I wouldn't recommend it."

"No." He avoided my eyes, preemptively deflecting all the questions I wished I could ask about Singletary, about the lying that Dad said he'd done.

I tossed one at him anyway. "What was he like to work with?"

"A pest."

"What about your book? Have you been working on it?"

His look was remote. "I could give you what I've done," he said, sounding as if he were recalling something. He was repeating a suggestion I'd made.

"That would be great. I've been thinking about it a lot, actually."

"About what?"

What indeed? "I guess, the choices you would've had to make, or—I'm sure you didn't agree with everything, but you were there and, well, you know . . ."

"I was there," he echoed, musingly. "I don't make any excuses for that."

"But I'm sure there's a lot to say that isn't even about blame or responsibility. So much time has passed."

"It has," he said. "It has. I wanted to write something, but now—"

It occurred to me that we were both stalled writers; that was something we had in common. "What about you?" he said abruptly.

"What am I writing?"

"How are things?"

"They're good."

"You need money?"

"Dad. Really. I'm working."

"But it doesn't sound like—listen, maybe you need to quit that and figure out what it is you actually want to do."

"Doing nothing has never really given me much insight—I just get depressed."

"Everybody's depressed, everybody. When did that happen?" He came back to the table and sat down.

I told him I didn't know.

"Are you depressed? Like right now?" he asked.

"No. Not really, I don't think. But I'm not even sure I understand what counts, technically, as depression."

My father squinted—or winced? "Have you eaten? Is there someplace to eat around here?"

"Actually I'm—I have plans this afternoon," I said. It was a lie.

I asked him to take the gun with him, but it was still there on the table after he left, and he had managed to stash the two hundred dollars underneath it while I wasn't looking. Whatever neutralizing effect had been achieved by talking was now unachieved; there was a little pistol on the table. I didn't even know whether it was loaded, whether there was a bullet in it already, whether it was cocked, was there a manual for it online? I didn't know how to determine such things. I wanted to just throw it away. I found a pillowcase and deposited the thing inside, gingerly twisting the fabric around. I put that on a shelf in the closet. I took it down and jammed it under the bed. I retrieved it and set it back in the closet. I plucked it out again. I stuck it under the bed.

I turned on the television. A gray compound with smoke flushing from behind the walls: armed men had attacked the U.S. consulate in Jeddah. They'd rear-ended a truck as it was about to pass through a gate and then sped into the compound, throwing grenades, killing five "non-U.S. employees." I pictured some Filipino groundskeeper on a work visa, with a wife and three kids who were now fucked, they were there in my head for an instant and then they were gone, poof, replaced by the statement that our president had made: "The terrorists are still on the move."

On the move, I repeated to myself. And here was Deputy Secretary of State Armitage at a press conference, Armitage whose name cropped up everywhere lately, the name itself so perfect, like the name of some upscale arsenal, a swank hotel for surface-to-air missiles. *The Armitage.* He'd been at the Pentagon back in the eighties, I'd read that somewhere, the same time my dad was at the White House. A friend to all the old freedom-fighters. A survivor. Now there were those who considered him too cautious—not enough froth at the corners of his mouth. But he'd hung in there. He stayed on the team. Perhaps I'd underestimated the burden of that, of loyalty I mean, since I'd never had to be loyal to much of anything. I let him finish talking, this other dad, before I turned the TV back off.

Was it loyalty that had compelled my father to stay in his job at the White House? Or inertia? Or did he just fail to realize how far things had gone, until after they'd gone too far?

lthough Tim is the one who works on the NSC staff with Lieutenant Colonel North, it's Dick who befriends North and who later ropes Tim more fully into the operation. It's Dick who one afternoon sits in the dusk of an unlit government auditorium and watches, from a metal chair, one of North's slide shows: scenes of war on a pull-down screen. There are the slides of the boys in the jungle, preparing for battle, and then there's the one of a lone wooden cross planted on a new grave. He listens to North urge in his throaty near-whisper: *We've got to give them more . . . than just the chance to die.*

Mitchell's boss, the assistant secretary, lets him help out with some of North's activities. As an employee of the State Department, Dick is bound by certain rules, but those rules don't prevent him from learning of the more than $27 million recently deposited in a Credit Suisse account in Geneva for the benefit of the Contras. Nor do they keep him from strategizing about how to take down the Sandinistas' Soviet helicopters, nor from weighing in on North's idea to detain or maybe even sink a Nicaraguan merchant vessel suspected to be carrying arms shipments. It's as though time itself runs faster in room 392, as the rest of the capital plods on, mired in debates about welfare, warnings about drugs, and endless analyses and forecasts in re gas prices or farm subsidies or the interstate highway system.

You ought to come see what we're up to, Dick brags to Tim, making it sound like they are designing some secret weapon. All but smacking his lips. He tells Tim about the weekly meetings of the Restricted Interagency Group, in which a dozen people assemble on an upper floor at Foggy Bottom to discuss training programs, the southern front, the availability of Maule light aircraft, getting Costa Rica to cooperate. A peculiar, febrile logic prevails in those meetings, and so for example nobody sees any contradiction in enlisting a couple of businessmen to set up a vaguely defined covert operation involving a mesh of shell corporations and that account at Credit Suisse, and calling it "Project Democracy."

At State, the RIG men are known as the cowboys.

In the middle of the summer, Dick is promoted to a new position. During that same pool party that might or might not have been thrown as part of an ill-conceived and redundant effort to raise money from the Saudis, he tells Tim the news. It's a special office for aid to Nicaragua, he says, his voice low and burbling. It's just been funded by Congress to do humanitarian assistance.

Humanitarian assistance? Tim asks.

As far as I'm concerned, everything we've been doing is humanitarian, Dick says, as he stares through the patio doors at the girl by the pool, Tim's oldest.

You're not kidding, are you.

Not at all.

Tim himself is not so sure, in the summer of 1985, about everything they've been doing. Inside North's office, people joke that they're all going to wind up in jail. Is that funny? For Tim a hole of worry opens up, and the wider the hole becomes, the more he wishes to tell Jodi. He believes he would never improperly give up sensitive information, just as he would never cheat on his wife, but whenever he meets with Jodi, the possibility of both transgressions buzzes through him, and he returns to his desk more energized than he was before lunch.

He never has to explain much to her. Trying to tell Eileen about work, it's like trying to describe a sport she's never seen played, while Jodi knows the game intimately. Not that work is the only subject. When I can't sleep, he finds himself telling her at one lunch in July, I imagine I'm back home, in the town where I grew up. I go through the downtown and remember what each store was, and I'll go in and out of them, and then walk over to the park or the school or our house.

Sometimes I try to picture the ocean, Jodi says, but I can never hold on to it. I go back to thinking about what I have to do the next day.

After she has emptied her plate of everything but the parsley sprig, she wipes her mouth and takes a reporter's notebook and a pen out of her purse.

All I want to say is that we've got a whole lot of talent over there that's going to waste, Tim says. Not to mention people being paid to do essentially nothing, and this is the process by which the president is being advised on national security issues. It's . . . it's a mess.

It certainly sounds that way.

He continues: But it's not all McFarlane's fault. He's not getting what he needs from on high—he's stuck.

Right.

But that's not to say, I mean—he could at least talk to them. You don't just stick your head in the sand either. I want to make sure this is on background.

Of course.

Tim is tempted to say more. Everyone suspects everyone else of leaking anyway, so what's the difference? And then Jodi all but says it for him.

So instead you've got North making up the Central America policy as he goes along—

I don't know if I would put it quite that way, Tim interrupts. I'd just say he's been kind of the point person on it. The thing is—

You could do a better job, couldn't you? she says. Better than McFarlane.

That's not what—

But it's true. You'd be great at it.

Maybe someday.

Tim heads back to the office entertaining a vision of himself in eight or ten years, serving as national security advisor. It is possible, isn't it? Ascent. A good seat in the Sit Room. To deliberate at the highest level. All that infighting and backbiting he sees around him: Does he think he could rise above it? Not exactly, but he thinks that he could, in time—and in another administration—manage it. When he was younger, what he'd said to Eileen was, *I want to make a difference.* Well, who didn't? But now that he knows the process intimately, knows that so much of it is convening meetings, requesting studies, updating intelligence estimates, conferring over the phone, negotiating, wheedling, manipulating . . . Still it is remarkable, that he works in the White House; it still makes his heart rattle. He has a tiny surge of feeling every time he walks in the building.

Have you seen tomorrow's paper?

Dick Mitchell is asking Tim. The two men are drinking at a small, dim, nominally Irish tavern, which does most of its business during the day—but where the painted green door remains unlocked into the evening for the benefit of a few people, mostly men in their forties and fifties, who stop in after work. A pale woman with deep-set eyes and a halo of dark brown frizz is tending bar. She looks as though she's spent her whole life reading in bed, and is appealing in her lazy, yolky way, especially to men so estranged from their own bedrooms that half of their desire for a woman is a longing for sheets and pillows and the untroubled sleep that might follow sexual release.

Why would I have seen tomorrow's paper? Tim replies.

Remember how that reporter in Miami wrote about North's trips to Honduras? Guess who wrote a follow-up for *The Post*?

Something about the building is off-kilter. Maybe the floor is uneven, or the ceiling is, or the liquor shelves were installed at a barely perceptible, but then again perceptible, angle. From the doorway the wooden bar itself looks higher at one end and lower at the other, though when you are up against it, the effect disappears—liquids are level with the glasses that contain them.

Sitting targets: those words came to Tim shortly after he arrived, as he pulled out the bar stool and lifted a wet coaster off its seat. He then sat without moving, a well-mannered pupil, while Mitchell waved his hands around and said it was about time they had a drink. It's been weeks since we've seen each other outside the office, hasn't it. About time. There was an element of performing for somebody, even after the bartender returned to her science fiction novel. A television flashed footage of airplanes and Arabs.

Our little friend Jodi. She never mentions him by name, but it's clear enough, Mitchell says.

Earlier that summer Mitchell brought his new wife and her son over to the house. The boy—was his name Ron?—quickly started after Courtney, and Tim spent the afternoon gripping things (his beer, the frame of his chair, Eileen's arm) too tightly. The two kids went into the house together, and Tim wanted to go after them, but Eileen held him back. It's all right, she said. But how did she know? People were always saying it was all right, as if you could make things well just by speaking the words. The boy had been too confident.

And then Mitchell concocted that scheme to hit up the Saudis for Contra money, appealing to a diplomat he'd met at a party. Tim couldn't remember at what point Mitchell had become a Contra booster, much less why he let Mitchell persuade him to go along with it, but the party was a bust, and now Tim thinks of it with embarrassment.

Mitchell himself never blushes or breaks a sweat. On his broad face the features have been carefully molded from fine, northeastern clay. His eyes are clear blue. He's always all right, always makes Tim feel that really there's nothing to get worked up about, no knot they can't cut their way through, given their degrees, their network of contacts, their important positions—it was like this even when they were summer interns at what was then the Department of Health, Education, and Welfare.

Dick starts talking about his vacation, for some reason. What's remarkable is that he went on a vacation, and not even at Christmas or late August when everyone leaves town. This was in the spring. So we were out in Carmel for a couple of days, Mitchell says, and Tim's attention wanders, until he goes back to talking about tomorrow's big news.

Just wait until you see tomorrow's paper, Mitchell says. Tomorrow's going to be a big day at the office.

Another Nicaragua story.

There's some strong stuff in it. No names, but you'll see. It'll get some reactions from your pals at the Capitol. Barnes. Definitely Barnes.

The hell with Barnes. What's in the article?

I don't want to misquote, Mitchell says. Wait and see.

As they are leaving the place, they see in the distance Red Menace, headed away from them. His walk is a military scuttle, erect and quick. There's a restaurant in town called the Dancing Crab, a name that would also suit Singletary with his air of trotting on two claws.

Look at him, Mitchell says. When are they going to get rid of that guy?

You think he should be fired?

It's the government. Transferred.

He knows his stuff, even if he is a nuisance.

Mitchell swipes one hand out in front of him and says, He's a bloviating idiot. I said as much to him the other day.

You told him that?

He came to me looking for a fight. He hates North. I guess he hates me. His purpose in life is to be against things. Have you seen the memos he writes? Twelve, fifteen pages single-spaced. I bet no one has ever read one.

I have. They're overblown, but he's well informed about the region.

God. You're probably the only person who's ever read one.

Tim stifles his urge to stick up for the Menace. He agrees with Dick for the most part, and (as he reminds himself) it's probably a waste of time to dwell on the ten percent he finds too harsh. And by now the Menace has turned a corner, he's out of sight.

What does Tim tell his wife that evening? To say that he is no longer sure that his colleagues are on the right side of the law, that would scare her. And how to explain that what he fears, more than lawbreaking, is that in a moment of carelessness he might have said something he shouldn't have to Jodi Dentoff and that it will appear in tomorrow's paper? That even without his name attached, his colleagues will know that it was he who spoke too freely?

In the summer he'll come home at eight or nine or later, and some nights he'll change straight from suit to swim trunks and do a few laps in the pool. It's a small pool, and so he hardly gets going before he has to turn around and swim the other way. His strokes and kicks make heavy splashes. Everyone inside can hear him. Sometimes Eileen is already in bed by the time he towels off and goes back in the house, but other evenings he finds her in the kitchen, sucking on a piece of chocolate. He might take some potato chips out of the cabinet, and she might wipe up the crumbs that have fallen onto the countertop. He almost never has a chance to eat dinner when it's actually dinnertime, but he does love the taste of potato chips after a swim.

While in the pool he snorted some water into his nose, and his throat still stings.

He is sitting at the kitchen table and she is standing at the counter. He's always admired her profile. Although she is self-conscious about the skin starting to loosen over her jawline, what she's lost in beauty she's gained in softness, resolve—the two combined. She has picked up on his mood, but she doesn't ask about it. She doesn't want to find out just yet. She doesn't feel like having a serious talk, you can tell by the set of her head, the way she is inspecting the linoleum.

She works so hard. He works longer hours, but she is like an athlete training for something, an endurance event that keeps being postponed. He wants to spare her any more. She would agree to bear his fears along with everything else she is carrying, but he doesn't want her to. He says nothing.

The next morning the newspaper has not been delivered before Tim leaves for work. He usually reads an office copy anyhow, but on that day he drives downtown and then walks straight to a newsstand. There it is, not just on the front page of *The Post* but also in *The New York Times*: "NICARAGUA REBELS GETTING ADVICE FROM WHITE HOUSE ON OPERATIONS."

Both articles teem with anonymous officials. "A senior Administration official said . . . Another senior official . . . A former senior White House official said today." Tim wasn't the only one who'd talked to Jodi—naturally—and he didn't tell her anything as significant as what these others had said, these unnamed officials, probably the chief of staff's people. The chief of staff himself maybe, Regan, who started in January and went for McFarlane's throat almost immediately.

"Various officials confirmed that a marine officer on the NSC staff has played a key role in formation and implementation of U.S. policy in Central America . . ." Tim stands there on the street, reading one story and then the other. Things have gone further than he realized. He glances at his watch: the morning meeting is about to begin. He rushes back and enters the room just in time to hear McFarlane declare that there is no truth to this morning's big headlines. Then McFarlane recites one of his standard lines, about how it is the cabinet that makes administration policy, and the NSC staff implements the policy. It's what he'll later say to Congress. Yet there is a new threat here, palpable in the room.

He should get out, Tim thinks. He could give Jodi a little more of the story, a parting gift, a token of his admiration, and then resign. Or resign and then talk. After all, what has his life been over the past two years? He holds it in, holds it together. At night he grinds his teeth. He shouts too loudly at the girls' basketball games.

Tim calls Jodi at midday. I can't tell you anything right now, he says, the "right now" a promise of later indiscretions. They agree to get a drink at 6:30, the first time they've ever met in the evening. He hangs up but holds on to the handset, then starts speaking into it, to the dial tone, when McFarlane comes out of his office. Regular work has come to a halt. The sound of phones ringing is practically the only sound. He takes a slow sip of his lukewarm coffee and watches the green letters file across the screen.

There were times in his life when he felt warmly toward his colleagues, as though they were friends of his, but in fact they are not. He is on his own.

He goes to the restroom and then wanders outside, into the summer swamp, the air not so much hot as it is wet. As he walks, his shirt moistens, and his feet turn warm and clammy. After a few minutes he sits down on a park bench and unties his shoes, which is as much as he intends, but then comes the impulse to slide his feet out and peel off his socks. He puts the damp socks under the tongues of the shoes and probes the mangy grass with his feet. Tourist families shuffle past with their bags and cameras and arguments—it is the kids who notice the barefoot man. He sees one girl pause and survey him from necktie to naked toes and back, with a quick, shy glance at his face, before resuming the family march to the Tourmobile stop.

Could his life have gone a different direction? How much leeway is there for anyone?

He doesn't immediately recognize the man in the blue serge suit. It's rare for him to run into anyone on the street: the work sucks them inside, and it takes effort to leave.

"Getting some fresh air?"

Red Menace has inserted the tips of two fingers into his shirt, between button holes. In the humidity his hair has formed thin, damp cords. Though his demeanor is languid, there is a suggestion of things roiling underneath, a hint of rocking back and forth, of lifting up onto toes and back down.

He could have been one of the story's sources, an unnamed official. Then again Tim doubts that he knows enough.

It's been quite a morning already, hasn't it.

Washington in August, Tim says. Everyone gets cranky.

Like little children. They're like kids, all of them.

Tim has never asked before whether the Menace has kids. What a thought. Pigeons have descended and are closing in on them, indirectly, waddling around and coming nearer and nearer.

You've got nothing to worry about, says the Menace. Your friend Mitchell, on the other hand—

What are you talking about?

He's up to his ass in it, isn't he?

Whatever you've got against him, I'm not really—

It's nothing personal. Mitchell's just running with the wrong crowd.

Then, ever the name-dropper, the Menace tells Tim that he's meeting the head of a think tank for lunch and prances off on his claw-feet.

August isn't the worst time for a story like this to appear. The president is recuperating from surgery at his Santa Barbara ranch. Most of the political class has flown north on vacation. Still, Congress begins to clamor and squawk, demanding that the national security advisor explain what his staff has been doing. A House member makes it known that he wishes to review every memo that North has written on Central America. And so during that August of 1985, everything that will happen fifteen months later, the big crisis to come, is foreshadowed. It's practically a rehearsal: the clamoring investigators, the tight-lipped officials, the remote commander in chief. A drama played out for the benefit of the news media.

As soon as the stories about North and the Contras appear, the climate in and around the Old Executive Office Building shifts. Whirligigs of smoke generated by a slow, secret fire are seeping out through the building's jambs and vents. And what clouds there are in that heavy August sky take on the shapes of axes waiting to fall.

People speak out of smaller mouths. They glance back behind them before they say anything of consequence.

The next day, Poindexter springs the assignment on Tim. Maybe if he'd anticipated that he would be asked to do such a thing, or if he had more time to think it over, he would have hesitated. Instead he says yes right away.

Though computers have come to the building, most official business is still committed to paper. There are files upon files upon files, in steel case drawers, with typed labels; hundreds if not thousands of files at the office and more in temperature-controlled storage facilities. Tim spends the rest of the week reviewing lord knows how many files, one after the other, until he is overcome by typographical nausea, until his neck and shoulders ache. He pulls out anything about the Contras, anything that might be seen as incriminating, and then he goes back over those flagged documents, examining them in light of the ban on military aid. In the end there are six memos from North to McFarlane, reporting on Contra-related operations, that Tim hands over before returning the files to their drawers. He doesn't ask what will become of the memos. He doesn't need to ask.

A few days before, Tim went to meet Jodi as planned, to tell her he would be quitting. He arrived ahead of schedule at the low-lit hotel bar: wood-paneled, smoky, and not as well air-conditioned as

Tim would've liked. Because he was early he assumed that he'd beaten Jodi there, and he was halfway across the room before he saw her sitting with Dick Mitchell. They were at a table in the corner, and their glasses were nearing empty. Jodi was smiling. Maybe Mitchell had just said something he shouldn't have said, something that Jodi very much enjoyed hearing. Her hair fell forward into her face.

The speed and force of Tim's jealousy surprised him—he wouldn't even have been able to say what he was jealous of, exactly, or why the sight of them made him change his mind. Not that he changed it on the spot: he just turned around, left the bar, left the hotel, and went home to his family. What had he been thinking? What integrity would be gained by jumping ship? He didn't want to leave and he didn't want to be like the Menace, lamely bitching about one thing after another. The next day he went to work, with newfound loyalty he'd willed into being and that buzzing, biting worry shoved into the shredder.

Dad had received all the usual holiday invitations, to the same parties he'd been dragged to by our mother for years and years. Now he actually wanted to go to them, or so he said. He'd asked Courtney and me, weeks ahead of time, whether we would tag along to the Morgans' Christmas party, "because the Morgans would enjoy seeing you girls," though we knew it was that he wanted us to come, so that he wouldn't be there alone. It was the party I'd invited Rob to, without thinking. I was relieved he hadn't said yes.

That party, any party: a bulwark against the rest of it, against dreariness, against solitude, against dogs barking and drizzle-slush and the wet wheezing breath of the capital city in the last month of the year. The house was stately stucco, with a broad porch and two dozen steps bisected by a dripping black handrail, holly in planters, bare bushes. And the glow at the top of the door! Inside there was goat cheese, there were flatbreads and the gentle timbres of glassware, and men rumbling and rustling in their sport coats, and women cooing over one another's jewelry. Where did you find that? In Santa Fe, in a little store on the Vineyard, oh, David bought it for me in Oaxaca, on that trip, could it really have been five years already? I know, I know, I know. How the time goes. There was music, Count Basie, and whiskey streaming like hot honey into tumblers. Everyone's heartaches salved by the warm little egg of evening.

I'd come with Courtney and Hugo, and the three of us waded into a pride of people I still thought of as other people's parents, and for all my preparing I wanted to turn tail, for they could be counted on to speak of their children's careers and marriages and babies in such a way as to put in relief my not having a comparable curriculum vitae, and I felt sorry not for myself but for my mother and father, who'd been suffering the comparisons for some years now. Maybe it was just as bad, maybe even worse to have to keep reporting on your child's single, freelance state to achievement-minded peers than it was simply to be the child giving evasive answers. It had been all right when I was younger and *in school*, less so when I was *working in Hollywood* and *dating someone*, and now what was there to say? (I was best glossed over in favor of my sister, the married one with a good job at a big-name nonprofit.)

But I'd gussied up, worn earrings. I was prepared to feign an interest in official acronyms, to palaver about current events, to do whatever it took.

"Where's your father?" Hugo asked, over the din.

"Maybe he's not here yet," Courtney said.

"He gave me a gun," I said.

"What did you say?"

I saw that she had taken in my words but rejected them, and I thought the better of making myself clear. "Let's get a drink," I said.

I saw a head, a younger one with stubbly sideburns and impish eyes, floating above the crowd, attached to a tall man (though not too tall, his head perhaps not actually so lofty as it seemed in that moment). Our eyes met; instantly I blushed; and into my own head came the thought that this might be a different sort of evening than the one I'd anticipated. My heart accelerated for maybe five beats until I saw next to him a pregnant and pretty companion.

But of course. Courtney ran over and gave him a hug. It was apparently someone she knew. I followed behind her, loopily, my voice rushed and cracking as I introduced myself, and I knew my sister was watching, wondering what the hell. I couldn't help it.

How's the food? was what I'd meant to ask, I swear, but what I in fact uttered was, "How's the fetus?"

Well, fine, they said, smiling, as Courtney stepped deliberately on my toe. In fine fetal fettle. Just yesterday it had caught the hiccups. And then I made a joke so poor I can't bear even to repeat it here, all I'll say is that they excused themselves then, and rightly so, leaving me with my sister, who asked, "Am I going to have to take you home?"

"Just five more minutes. Who was that?"

"You don't remember Ted Wexler?"

"*That's* Teddy Wexler? He was a lot less hot in high school."

"What's the matter with you? He's about to have a baby."

"That doesn't disqualify him from hotness. It doesn't de-hotify him. What is he, like some do-gooder lawyer now?"

"Actually I think that is what he does."

"Where do these men hang out when they're single?"

"Not in the neighborhood you're living in."

"That's helpful, thank you."

I stepped away from her, then glanced at my phone and saw that Rob had texted, asking for the address of the party. I sent it to him and then instantly regretted it.

In no time at all came the phase of the party when all the rented glassware had been distributed and was in use or abandoned on tables, smutched with fingerprints and lip balm, while standing by the bar pouring red wine into a coffee mug was a rosy Nordic giant in a bright red sweater and wide-wales, his face flushed with his own good fortune. I had a feeling that this was the sort of man I ought to be talking to, if I wanted to improve my prospects in Washington. But before I could work up the resolve to introduce myself I was distracted by a balding fellow in a down vest who'd found a birdcage under a worn yellow towel and was proffering, to what I think was a cockatiel (or was it a cockatoo?) a blanched haricot vert. And then rather than speak to either man I got caught up in a swell of women ascending the stairs to admire some just-completed renovations of the upper floors.

A small, sparkly woman led the way—our hostess, Rennie or Ramie I think her name was. Her youngest son was still in high school and lived on the third floor, which was its own apartment practically. A tricked-out living area at the top of the stairs had a leather sofa and television, also a sink and a refrigerator and a stretch of marble-topped counters. There, a thin scapular boy with a pierced lip stood pouring a vodka and coke.

"Say hello, Jonathan."

"Hello, Jonathan," the boy said. The mother paused, her face crinkling coolly. Then she clapped her hands together and led us down again. "We let him drink at parties," she confided, though as soon as we were back on the first floor she whispered something to a man who'd been handing out cocktails; he went bounding tightly up the stairs. When he returned, holding the bottle of Grey Goose, his eyes had gone glassy, yet he went into the kitchen and after a minute came out dimpled and hale once again.

I saw my father bending another man's ear, spinning some theory no doubt. The other man was noticeably well-groomed, not a stray hair on his head, and as he listened he polished off a slider, neatly, and touched his lips with his napkin afterward. I pulled out my phone and texted Rob again:

party no bueno, let's meet up after?

The bird fancier was still standing by the cage, still wearing a down vest over his shirt, but now the bird had perched on his hand. And all at once the sight of that obliging tropical specimen with its curled pink talons and clipped wings filled me with a childlike sadness. At the same time I wanted to take the bird on my own finger.

I couldn't place the man, but I'd seen him before, either he was someone's parent or else someone who had at one time or another been in the margins of the spotlight: a campaign advisor, a special counsel. And now I felt I might as well be the bird, looking to perch on somebody else's status-callused hand. Did I actually begin to trifle with the man in the down vest? If so it wasn't intentional. Or else he started it, passing the bird off to me, so that we were attending to it together, and the lies began pouring out, that I was applying to law schools, that I had loved college, that I had missed Washington, that I was interested in what his sons were doing: Who the hell were his sons? Who was he? It was one of those party exchanges that go on and on before you get around to names. Finally, I told him mine.

"Tim Atherton's daughter?" he asked, and when I nodded he said, "Your dad's a smart guy."

I knew that, but the man's tone gave it weight. I wished I could get him to say more. Just then Hugo approached.

"What a beautiful animal," Hugo said, and in no time at all he started in on some question of trade with China. I hoped he would shut up, but the man in the down vest seemed as eager to discuss trade with China as Hugo was. I myself had a mental block on trade with China—any time those two words, trade and China, showed up in the same sentence, I started to fade.

My sister's husband had thick coppery hair and a highly audible voice, and early on I'd wondered whether Courtney had ended up with him for no better reason than that she'd noticed him, whether it had taken this emergency signal of a man to divert her from her agenda. His eyes were wide-set, roaming, forever trying to anchor themselves in some impassioned conversation that I didn't want to have. They shared that interest, he and Courtney; they made a point of speaking about the war, about third world disasters, about the environment. Few people I knew in L.A. talked much about these things, not once they were past thirty.

I excused myself.

But how did I end up on the second floor—and inside our hostess's closet? Having gone upstairs in search of a bathroom, I opened the wrong door and was welcomed by dry-cleaning bags, smells of cedar and perfume, a chorus line of shoes, each toe even with the next one. A mother's closet. Even this strange one, though it was missing the particular belts and boots, purses and jackets and hose I knew best, was a very comforting place to stand. I stayed in there a spell, the noise of the party below barely reaching me. It seemed as good a place as any to finish my eggnog, to make a few notes, to try on—why not?—my hostess's shoes. They pinched a bit.

Of course in any tale worth its salt, the person hidden in a closet or behind a curtain becomes privy to some business she shouldn't have seen, and so when I heard footsteps approaching I pulled the door almost closed, and I spied with my little eye.

It was my dad. He sat on the bed and balanced his drink between his knees. I could hear his exhales. He took out his phone, its blue display a beacon in the darkness. His hands were slow: I always forgot that he was no longer in his forties, that I was closer to my forties than he was to his. He stopped, stared at the phone again, and at last made a call.

"It's me. Tim. It's, ah, Saturday at around nine p.m. I'm at the Morgans, which made me think of you. I just had a very interesting talk with Al Barnett, I was telling him about my book, the one that I've been working on, and he thought it sounded very promising. I think . . . well. I know you're busy. But please give me a call at, ah, your earliest convenience."

Earliest convenience? After ending the call he waited a moment, as if he expected an answer. Although I couldn't be sure, I believed that I had just seen my dad drunk-dial my mom. And was he still working on his book, in spite of what he'd told me?

Who was this person?

Everything I'd written about him so far, I'd written by looking away from him, and now my Tim Atherton seemed all wrong. The outline of a body on the floor, from which position my living dad had stood up and wandered off. Surely this was why it was more typical to write about your parents after they were dead and could be pinned down, I thought—even if that was an illusion, that they could be specified, you could still manage it without confronting them, without having to compare your meager version to the living one.

I waited until he left the room to emerge. I spotted a landline phone on top of a dresser, picked it up, and listened to the dial tone for a while. It occurred to me that I remembered Gary's number.

I didn't expect him to answer, but he did. "Hello? . . . Hello?"

The sound of his voice paralyzed me. Then someone else got on the line, waited, and then said, "Hello?"

"Hello?" Gary repeated.

"Who is this?" It was the boy upstairs, I realized. Jonathan.

"This is Gary Doyle, who is this?"

"You sound lame."

"You sound a little old to be making prank calls, asshole," Gary said, and hung up. A mysterious cheer resounded from below.

As I walked back downstairs, Hugo appeared at the landing, carrying a little plate with little veggies on it. His tie was covered in circles: dark, filled-in circles surrounded by the outlines of larger circles, like dozens of eyes. Instead of meeting his real eyes, I looked at the tie. I thought, as I'd thought in the past, my sister sleeps in a bed with this man. *Every night.* But I passed judgment so readily, even when—especially when—the person I was judging could be said to be better off than yours truly. About Courtney that certainly could have been said. It had always been sayable, implied if not said outright, and though I would've preferred to be free of any negative feelings about our lifelong inequality, Courtney > Helen, I was not.

What a human I was turning out to be. So what if her husband was taking baby carrots with him to the bathroom, what did that matter? He turned himself sideways and backed up against the wall so that I could pass—out of politeness, but it was as though I weighed three hundred pounds. I felt enormous.

Downstairs Courtney was at the bar, mixing the feeblest of cocktails in a plastic cup: seltzer with a tiny splash of vermouth and a lemon wedge. I picked up the vodka and started pouring it into the glass. "You forgot this."

"Stop. I'm not drinking that."

"Yo, check out the boots. Those are tight."

"I got them in New York," she said. She'd gone up to New York for work and had seen Maggie and I guess had gone shopping with her. I knew it wasn't that they'd left me out on purpose, and still it pinched at that thing in me.

"What are you wearing?" she asked.

I tried to explain about the bi-stretch pants. I'd worn those.

"Are they comfortable?"

"I think if I gain weight over the holidays, they'll just keep stretching. In two directions," I said.

"I'm so ready for the holidays to be over. Hugo and I were thinking we might just go away somewhere."

"You? A vacation?" I'd gone upstairs in a strange mood and come back down in a stranger one.

"I'd still have to work some, but I could bring my computer."

"No, come on, don't. You should totally go on a vacation. A real one. You wouldn't even have to go anywhere, you could just take a little time off, lock your computer in a drawer, and do the whole holiday jam for once. Do it up."

I knew what she thought, that I was always on vacation. It wasn't true, I worked all the time, but my work wasn't like hers.

"It's nothing but eating and drinking and buying shit and thinking of all the things you meant to get done but didn't in the past year."

"Honey, if you're against Christmas, you're against America. And eating and drinking and buying shit are what you do *instead of* brooding over the past year. You gots to chill, my sister. Chill out and have some alcohol. Have a treat." I held up a gingerbread snowman.

"I'll pass."

I waved the snowman in her face and then bit off its head. From across the room Hugo was watching, I noticed, with a fond bug-eyed expression that might have been for either one of us, or for us both.

It had been easier when we were girls and I was simply trying to emulate Courtney. I borrowed her clothes, I copied her speech, I listened to her tapes, I followed her and her friends around the house until they sent me away. Or else we fought. At the corner where the school bus picked us up, she once gave me a black eye with a broom handle we'd found. Another time I almost managed to pull down her pants just as the bus was coming. Always parked at that same corner was a secret service trailer assigned to an ex–vice president who lived nearby, and just in front of the trailer we would fight each other, possibly observed by the agents inside, we never knew.

Our father found us, and came to shore. "You know who that is, the fellow you and Hugo were talking to earlier?" he asked me.

"He said he runs some kind of data management business."

"He was at Treasury for years. Pretty high up, by the end. He was Frank Lake's boss."

Who Frank Lake was, I had not a clue, but I pretended to remember.

"Are you having a good time?" I asked Dad.

He seemed confused by the question. "I'm having a fine time."

"Is the semester over?" Courtney asked.

"Just final papers to grade."

"That's good," she said.

"So girls," he began—it was usual for him to address us that way—"what should our plan be for Christmas?"

"We need a Plan B?" I asked.

"Maybe we could do a little more this year, you know, make it nice. I'm planning to go to the cathedral the night before if anyone wants to join me."

"Isn't Mom coming down?" The past few years, she'd taken the train to D.C., and we'd had an early dinner with her on Christmas Eve. Then she would take the train back.

"If you wanted to join me afterward, I meant. It's a late service."

"I think Hugo and I might go to St. Bart's," Courtney said abruptly.

"St. Bart's?" Dad asked.

"It's an island."

"I'm familiar with it. For Christmas?"

"It's been so hectic with work, and the move, and everything, we could use a few days on the beach."

"Sounds nice. Maybe we could all go!" Courtney stiffened, and he added, "For the weekend at least, and then you two could stay longer . . ." She closed her eyes and whispered no, her face less sorry than irritated.

"Okay. Scratch that."

"Why do you have to do this?" she asked.

"What? Do what?"

"Is it so wrong for me to spend a holiday with my husband? That's something that people do. Hugo is my family now."

We all looked over at Hugo, who had made his way back to the birdcage and coaxed the cockatiel, or whatever it was, onto his long tan finger. He was leaning his head forward and talking to the bird, probably about trade policy with China.

"Of course, he's your husband," Dad said. "Of course. If you haven't bought your tickets yet, why don't you let me get them, as a Christmas present."

"Stop it! Just stop it!"

"What is up your butt?" I asked.

She ignored that and kept after Dad. "I don't need you to buy the tickets. I don't need you to do anything for me." She turned away and walked over to Hugo, to tell him it was time to leave. The bird seemed reluctant to let go of Hugo's finger, until my sister nudged it with the side of her hand.

I understood that an old ugly argument had crawled out of the depths and taken hold of Courtney, and I wanted to say something reassuring to Dad, something about how this probably had nothing to do with him, but before I came up with anything he went off to get another drink.

I felt a draft but was slow to recognize that it had come through the open front door. I had failed in my watch, such as it had been, for here came Rob, already in the house, already shrugging off his coat. He'd had a haircut. It made me think of school, of the entire breed of private school boys and in particular that clan of handsome, lacrosse-playing, beer-pounding, boisterous ones, who floored their parents' cars at 1:00 a.m. on Western Avenue, and flirted with the Spanish teachers, and set off on summer service trips to Central America that they would later describe on their college applications. The kind of kids who bug the shit out of people—*born on third base and thinks he hit a triple* was a criticism lobbed at our prepschool president, but I don't remember those boys taking credit for their own exceptional luck. Yes, some of them had been arrogant dipsticks, but most had been merely obnoxious, often winningly so, and while I'm sure that they'd felt more confusion and angst than they'd let on, life had been good to them and they hadn't denied it. They'd had fun, something I hadn't had much of a knack for in high school, which is to say that while I had little spurts of fun, I never was able to relish, say, getting wasted or getting high or driving very fast. I didn't feel superior: I'd always believed there was some worth in these activities, not for me but for the guys who experienced them with delight, guys who'd been living it up while I wrote in my journal.

As best I could tell, Courtney hadn't caught sight of Rob yet, and instead of going straight to him I cut toward her first, wanting to block her view. He saw me and watched quizzically as I made my zigzag, and then once I'd come close he leaned over to kiss me hello. I gave him my cheek and then glanced back.

"Are we being discreet?" he asked.

"Let's go over there," I said, pulling him into a throng of backs and shoulders near the drinks.

"What the hell are you wearing?"

"D.C. drag."

"Nice. Is there someplace I can put my coat?"

"We won't be here long. Did you get my message?"

He pulled his phone out of his pocket and read it, as if for the first time, though I had a suspicion that he'd come precisely because I'd told him not to come. We were being continually jostled, and next to us, a man and a woman were yelling back and forth about the lamentable state of the Occupational Safety and Health Administration. The woman was much taller than the man, and they had to project to make themselves heard.

Insofar as my sister had been about to leave the party, I think my plan to hide Rob from her, silly as it was, might have in fact succeeded, had the crowd been slightly less oppressive, the OSHA critics not quite so noisy. But Rob took my hand, insisting we move to another spot, and when we came out from the pack, she was standing right there. He still had my hand in his. Her face, the narrower, cooler variant of my own face, managed to flay me while barely shifting its expression, until finally she turned to Rob.

"I would introduce you to my husband, but we're on our way out."

"Next time, I hope," he said.

"Next time."

She gave me another eye-smack before she strode past us. "Now that's some real holiday cheer," Rob said.

"She's had some stressful things to deal with lately. She's not always like that," I said, which was true, much as I sometimes made her out to be a full-time ice queen. "Let me go find my dad and tell him I'm leaving. We're leaving, okay?"

My father found us first, and I introduced him to Rob. "Remember I mentioned him to you?"

"This is—you're Dick's . . ." He stared at Rob, as though he might find a resemblance.

"Stepson, right."

"I think we're taking off, Dad."

"I see. Do you have a car? Can I give you guys a ride someplace?"

"That's okay," I said. "Stay here and enjoy the party."

"It's no problem—"

"I do have a car, actually," Rob said. Dad seemed sorry to hear it.

———

At my apartment Rob grinned and grabbed me, then started to unbutton my blouse. He had this invisible ribbon he was winding around me. A chrysalis was forming, and meanwhile I was so full of questions, itches, feelings without words; they overwhelmed me, and I had trouble saying anything.

As prey I wasn't challenging enough, I hardly struggled. I found myself performing to keep him there, even though I didn't necessarily want him there. In my head I'd started explaining myself to Courtney, making excuses: it wasn't my fault, I had tried to un-invite him.

What followed wasn't especially nice or especially anything. Afterward he took a shower. By then it must've been midnight or later. I lay on the bed as I listened to the sound of the water, nestling into the gap in time this shower offered. It seemed to me that these gaps in time, the blank spaces inserted into the middle of the night, were the best part of hooking up. He came out of the bathroom rubbing his hair with a towel, naked the long dripping rest of him, and then found his BlackBerry. He was easily bored.

I knew better than to ask him about Courtney, and still I asked him. When had they started going out?

"Mmmm," he said.

"You guys totally went out."

"Uh-uh."

"Yes you did."

"We fooled around a few times."

"But I remember you picking her up from our house, I remember you calling."

"I might've done those things, but we weren't . . . You know how your sister was in high school."

"What are you talking about?"

"She got around."

"Wait. That is not—it's not like she was some slut." He'd turned toward me by then, and I detested the look on his face, which managed to be innocent and superior at the same time, his brows lifting in surprise, or mock surprise, while the word *slut* hung there unrefuted. "Are you kidding me? She was not."

"I didn't use that word."

"You're wrong if you think that. She was into sports. She was a big jock."

"That's not the only thing she was into. She got kind of out of control."

I felt suddenly furious. "That is so—"

"I'm not making this up."

"You'd better leave," I said.

"You're kicking me out?"

"I am."

"You're kicking me out of your apartment for saying that Courtney Atherton got around in high school."

"No, I'm kicking you out because you're being a dick."

"Okay-bye," he said quickly.

As soon as he said that, I changed my mind, but he already had his pants on and was reaching for his shirt. By the time he left I was wide awake, still hearing him say *out of control* and trying to call up the nights I'd seen my sister with her boyfriends. But there was too much interference. I kept replaying in my head the proceedings of the prior ninety minutes, and everything I thought about it, i.e., about Rob, was just a bunch of cliché junk from pop songs. He was the worst person I'd ever liked, I thought, but then I remembered that he wasn't even close to being the worst. He was merely typical of the men I liked, men who were always going away from me, often at my own insistence. And he was someone I'd liked all the more, presumably, because of my unshakable desire to compete with my sister, although now I didn't exactly feel like I'd won anything.

Then I remembered how I'd left my dad behind at the Morgans' so that I could bring Rob home with me. I wondered how long he'd stayed after that. I wondered whether he'd been sober enough to drive home. I had an urge to call him, but it was the middle of the night.

When we were kids, our father had spent what time with us he could: Saturdays on our bicycles, Sundays at Roy Rogers. And then later, he'd spent on us, opening the billfold time and time again, the cash inside always brand-new as though the bank were minting it just for him. Money having come to him later in life, during his postgovernment years at Intelcom, he seemed eager to get rid of it. No end to the meals, clothes, anything we happened to express a wish for in his presence.

Even before then, we could always lean on him to get us the stuff our mom wouldn't. She was the in-house IMF and he was the backwater potentate who couldn't quite give up his old spendthrift habits. Sometime in the eighties he'd gone from economizer to granter of wishes, like he was trying to buy back what had already been lost, during all those hours at the office or in the car, in elevators: he'd stepped inside, the doors shut, he went up and down and stepped out again to find we were little girls no longer. We were mysterious creatures holed up in our bedrooms, the phone cord snaking under the door; we climbed out our windows, we burst into tears, we tramped through the kitchen with packs of friends, we giggled and protested and whispered and thundered down the stairs and then we were gone.

For better or worse (in the end, probably worse) he stays at the NSC. He doesn't quit in August 1985, and after he makes that choice he is confronted by a second one: he can stay at his desk shuffling memos, or he can ally more closely with the people who are doing things. It isn't enough to be smart, not if you aren't willing to engage. He chooses to side with the activists—I don't blame him for it. Well: I do and I don't.

It's the national security advisor who quits. At the end of November, McFarlane, who has become ever more strung out and unhappy, who's started smoking again, who is unable to mask the swells and crashes of his disappointment, resigns. Quite a few people saw it coming, including Tim, who was along on what should've been a rest day, a visit to a boys' school in Virginia where McFarlane spoke to the assembled student body about the meaning of public service. On the drive back into Washington he started to raise his voice, he yelled about the recent arms talks in Geneva but also seemed to be yelling at life itself, *The hell with this, the hell with this,* and they had to pull over so that he could calm down.

Not long after that he throws in the towel, and Vice Admiral Poindexter replaces him. My dad starts reporting to North, not officially but as a practical matter. He buries his reservations about the man.

Meanwhile Dick Mitchell is running his little office, administering what is termed humanitarian aid. He has learned to bend the rules without really thinking of it that way. He does certain things on the clock and certain things off the clock. Food, medicine, apparel are on the clock, magazines and grenades are off. The same L-100 or C-123 transport can carry the approved supplies and, on a second leg, the freight provided by outside donors. The M-2 and its magazine weigh ten pounds total. You can fit a hundred of those on the plane, a thousand pounds. On paper it's a no-brainer. In reality, though, there are frequent malfunctions, and so Mitchell is grateful to have a friend on the NSC staff who can help fix them, who can, for instance, travel to New Orleans to check up on things.

(From the testimony of Richard Mitchell, May 21, 1987)

MR. BOREN. Were there concerns about how the money was being spent?

MR. MITCHELL. There had been a lot of rumors and speculation that some money was going where it shouldn't go. There was no proof, but Colonel North always wanted the Nicaraguan resistance to be as clean as possible, and he was concerned about their image.

I think in hindsight much of this program, ever since the beginning, its inception, has probably been done—well, obviously not as well as it could have been. So I think we all had regrets.

MR. BOREN. I believe you talked about a plane being used that had been used previously to run drugs?

MR. MITCHELL. Yes, sir.

MR. BOREN. I have before me exhibit number 11, a memorandum to Colonel North in which you stated that you feared that for some of the top Nicaraguan commanders, the war had become a for-profit business?

MR. MITCHELL. Those were not my exact words. I did come to the conclusion that compared to the *campesinos* putting their lives on the line, some of the leaders were acting out of self-interest and some of the money was not accounted for.

MR. BOREN. And nonetheless you decided to keep pursuing these activities, in secret?

MR. MITCHELL. Senator, I think that there are times when there is the necessity for secrecy.

Of all the scenes from my father's government career, his trip to New Orleans is the strangest, I think, the hardest to conceive of, it's like I'm trying to insert my dad into one of the García Márquez novels that all the Washington wives were dreamily reading in those days, fictions they hoarded and savored like South American caramels even as the husbands fought proxy wars in the territory between here and there, here being the United States and there a magic land of jungle loves and yellow butterflies.

They send him to New Orleans to talk to the *comandante*'s cousin, who is running—just barely—the procurement side of things. Some of the supplies for the Contra rebels have been warehoused out of New Orleans, in a dingy corrugated-aluminum hangar off Interstate 10.

The middle of May and already the air is like warm, dirty jelly. Driving his rental car to the address he's been given, Tim sees two boys fishing in what might have been a ditch full of sewage, under a bright red industrial sunset. He arrives at the warehouse to find the gravel lot empty and the dock door shut. No sign of the man who told Tim to meet him there. It takes Tim two hours to find him and another two before he sobers up enough to make any sense. By then it's close to midnight. The man is blaming corrupt Teamsters for what he calls, with a buzz of rolled *r*'s enclosing a barely pronounced *o*, "errors," and claiming that the reason he's acquired frozen as opposed to canned food, when they have no means of transporting frozen goods, is that the vendor delivered something other than what had been ordered and then refused to take back the shipment.

The man's glistening white Mercedes smells brand-new. A holster lies on the backseat, as well as a small black shopping bag. A month earlier, unbeknownst to anyone, this man invited an NBC news crew to come along on the initial supply flight to Tegucigalpa. The plane door opened and out popped a cameraman, in a Yankees cap no less.

I'm going back to my hotel, and tomorrow I'm going back to Washington, Tim tells him. Is there any reason you can give me for not recommending this whole operation be shut down?

The man, uncomprehending, shouts, To help the people!

Which people do you mean, the frozen food people? The Teamsters? The employees at the Mercedes dealership? Much as all those people I'm sure appreciate the help, that was not the intent here.

You give me time, the man says. I fix it, I fix it. Then he starts to bellow about how they are being fleeced by the suppliers, and from there he launches into complaining about what a shithole the city is and you couldn't expect magic and why aren't they warehousing out of Miami, you think I like to live here? He switches to Spanish, slurs the locals. Do I look like a black to you? he asks.

Tim writes to North that there are some serious concerns about New Orleans, and afterward he never hears a word about it. The same thing happened some weeks earlier, after Mitchell reported similar misgivings in a memo, writing that he'd found many of the Contra leaders to be untrustworthy, that some of them were greedy and deceptive. False receipts have been sent to State, and hundreds of thousands of dollars are unaccounted for, he wrote. But North would not—and maybe could not—digest that.

The bad news disappears. Tim keeps his head down. The song they keep playing on the radio goes *throwing it all away, throwing it all away*, the melody slow and wistful—Tim hears it at a deli downtown and again at Peoples Drug and again echoing in his head just before he goes to sleep.

Christmas was a challenge, as ever. It deflated us. We would participate in the standard traditions just enough to more or less fail at them, to remind ourselves that we were not exactly one of those loving families gathered around a tree in matching sweaters, whose cards and photos arrived every December at Albemarle Street and were piled in a basket on top of a radiator. Much as I felt sure that those other families had troubles of their own, we still had to contend with their cards. And there were no kids at our Christmas, which I think made everyone feel aimless and cranky, and made children of my sisters and me.

Yet I knew Dad hoped for something better this year, he'd said as much at the Morgans' party, and so I wanted that for him. It was as though he were the kid, only not one to be satisfied with a new toy truck or a dollhouse. Worse, he told me over the phone that he had a special gift he was excited to give me, which I feared would be something wrong and expensive that I would ultimately return. I had a break from work, and I sank into the holiday spirit as into a sugary trance. I looked at websites with adorable tips and pointers and DIY crafts, I consulted cookie recipes, I made plans and lists. Although I am not a crafts person and hardly ever use an oven, I made a supply run and then got down to business.

The bourbon balls bombed. Greasy little cow pies. I left them to cool and attacked the next project, which meant spray-painting white a couple dozen pinecones—having sampled a good bit of the bourbon by then, I also managed to paint parts of the table and, somehow, my pants. I set the cones out to dry on the previous day's Style section of the paper and then proceeded to eat half the non-pareil candies I'd bought to decorate the gingerbread house, which I had not started making yet. And so it went. Fast forward to that afternoon, and what you would've seen in my apartment was: a giant mess of bags and dough bits and tinfoil, a kicked fifth of bourbon dappled with floury fingerprints, a bowl of white pinecones with bits of Style section stuck to them, a gingerbread Depression-era shack, and me passed out on my bed.

On Thursday Maggie took a train to Union Station and I met her there, toting a supply of clothes and the pinecones in my overnight bag so that I could stay for a few nights at Albemarle Street instead of schlepping back and forth to my apartment. The city mouse in her motorcycle jacket: I found her smoking a cigarette out front, while men coming and going assessed her furtively, or not so furtively. As did I, admiring her jeans and her new haircut—and more than the particulars, the way it all cohered. She *looked* like an academic from New York City, and although hers was no more secure a life than mine, it made more sense to me.

That wave of thought came and went, and then I was so glad to see her. As we took the Metro to Van Ness, she told me about some old duffer on the train who'd talked at her without ceasing. Then she showed me his card, from some foundation.

"Was he hitting on you?" I asked. She made a face and told me he was our father's age. "Well dressed," she said, "and very . . . genteel."

"A genteel man on the train. Don't those usually turn out to be murderers?"

"I was bored. Listening to him was better than this." She showed me the book she'd brought along—*Jacques the Fatalist.*

"Why are you reading that?"

"This dickhead left it at my place. I can't get into it, though."

"Was it that kid from your class?"

"No. I wish," she said. "But not really. I don't really wish that."

She had on fingerless gloves, very *Breakfast Club*, a kind of joke about looking tough that still conveyed something of the referenced toughness. Once when I was visiting her in New York, she'd taken me to a packed yoga class in an overheated room above an electronics store, and everyone in the class, my sister included, had seemed to be straining and striving and agonizing. They were there to master yoga, to conquer it, and they threw themselves into difficult asanas I would never do, as I crouched in child's pose.

At the house we clomped around in our coats for a while. Maggie was a great praiser: she praised, in her admiring-younger-sister way, things that I saw as shortcomings, or evidence of shortcomings. "I love those pinecones!" she said when she saw me pour them into a salad bowl, bits of newspaper and all.

Another thing about her was that she was solicitous toward our father, attentive in a way I didn't know how to be. That afternoon he'd gone to his office and come home just as the sun was setting, and as soon as he walked in and saw her, his face softened. They hugged, and she went to get him a beer.

"Here you go, sir," she said as she delivered it.

"Thank you very much," he answered. He asked her about the train ride and she told him she'd met someone who worked for the C—— Foundation.

"Aha," he said, as if she'd named an old classmate he were struggling to remember. Finally he summoned up some related information. "They used to have their office right over on 16th Street," he said, and then continued on from there.

After he'd finished his beer, we went out together to look for a tree. With two days left before Christmas, the pickings were slim. We stood in a parking lot behind a Catholic church, surveying the sparse, lopsided product.

"That one," Dad said, pointing to the most robust—but also the tallest—tree on the lot.

"It's got to be ten feet," I said. "It won't fit in our house."

"We can trim it to size."

"Then it won't have a top."

"Not if we trim it properly, from the bottom."

"I don't know, Dad."

Maggie had wandered over to a scraggly specimen and was circling it. "How about this one?" she said. "I love this one."

"That runt?" Dad asked.

I remembered her at six, seven—she'd always had the most natural enthusiasm of anybody in the family, which meant that we made fun of her attachments but also deferred to them. She was the reason we'd brought home our first dog, and in junior high when she joined the softball team and became an Orioles fan, we started going up to Baltimore for games in the summertime. She pointed to that sad little spruce, and I went along. "Let's get it," I said.

"You girls need corrective lenses," Dad said as he opened his billfold.

That evening she tied strings around my pinecones and hung them on the tree, along with some old yarn ornaments from our childhood, and though Dad kept on grumbling about the eyesore in the living room, I think he secretly agreed with me that it was perfect. He went about his Christmas improvement efforts in the meantime: he strung white lights around the porch and put a wreath on the door, and he came back from a shopping trip with a three-foot plastic Santa that lit up when you plugged it in.

"Oh god. What is that?" Maggie asked him.

"They had these on sale. Fifty percent off."

"Where are we going to put him?"

Discount Santa went on the front porch.

Maggie helped me bake a more successful batch of cookies, and then we went for a walk, and it was so nice having her around that I started indulging a vision of moving to New York and rooming with her. I did sometimes wish I lived there. We would console each other in our struggles, bake treats in her tiny kitchen, go out to bars together and bring home dickheads with French classics in their messenger bags.

In the kitchen, we talked about Courtney. She and Hugo had decided not to go to St. Bart's after all. But when were they coming over?

"She's probably avoiding Dad," Maggie said, and when I asked why, she answered, "Because that's what she does." I remembered how short she'd been with him at the party.

"She might be avoiding me."

"Why?"

"I think she's pissed."

"Did you tell her about Rob?"

"That's part of it."

"And the rest?"

"I don't even know."

What Maggie did, what Maggie would do: shift very dramatically from light to dark. She could be the best, most helpful, most genuinely cheerful person to have around, and then, for no reason that you could discern, some unseen change in barometric pressure maybe, that person would disappear, nine-tenths of her normal personality would submerge and what was left was a sulking, walled-off clone of my sister.

It happened at Whole Foods. The store was packed, treacherously so. The Northwest matrons might have been admirals in a shopping-cart navy, the way they maneuvered for their Swiss chard and flageolets and steaks. Maggie and I made our way through the sections. The matrons turned to watch her as we went by. Beauty fades, I imagined them saying to themselves. I could tell Maggie was getting frustrated, with the crowded aisles and the looking-askance, with the very purgatory that was the Tenleytown Whole

Foods, and I was irritated too, and even so I felt that Maggie's
mood was my fault, that I and not the store had somehow caused it.

Then a woman with a corona of thick white hair and a granite
face and a tight grip on her shopping cart hit our cart with hers, or
else we hit her. There was a collision. Wine bottles rolling against
each other, ringing out. She must've assumed that Maggie, who was
pushing our cart, would stop sooner, and Maggie must've assumed
the same of her. These had been faulty assumptions. Maggie, rather
than apologize or move out of the way, just kept going (or tried to)
and nudged the other cart again, not so much aggressively as out of
distraction, as though she were simply trying to continue moving
forward and hadn't noticed that the obstacle was attached to a person. The woman gasped at Maggie's boldness and took a couple of
unsteady steps backward and collided with a tower of Parmigiano
Reggiano. She landed on the ground, theatrically, I thought, more
or less choosing to sit down on the floor—what would be called, in
certain sports, a flop. This lady was trying to get the foul call from
an invisible referee. She sat with her legs sprawled and a half-dozen
plastic-wrapped Parmesans spread over her skirt. It was a long, black
skirt she was wearing, which gave her the look of a violin teacher
who'd been caught trying to boost all that cheese.

"I'm getting the manager," she kept saying. I went over to her
and tried to help her up, but she refused my hand. An employee had
come out from behind the cheese counter—a cheese partner, I guess
he was—and was heading toward us. "Could you get your manager,
please?" she called to him. He said something into a walkie-talkie.

"I'm really so sorry," I said in a low voice. "My sister's a little
out of it right now. Her dog just died."

"That's bullshit," she said, insightfully. She pushed herself up,
gave us each a cutting look, and huffed away, no longer interested
in the manager.

I looked at Maggie, thinking we would share a moment, but
she was staring upward, toward the trelliswork of crossbeams and
lights and occulted security cameras, and I couldn't tell what her
face contained, whether she was shaking her head slightly or try-

ing to discern something up there. Even my younger sister had faint
lines on her neck now, that much I could see. Other shoppers pushed
past us, saying "excuse me" in harried voices.

As we left the store and eked our way out of the parking garage,
she remained absently somber, staring out the window at all the
SUVs or else staring past them. "Next time we'll go to Safeway,"
I said.

"Mmm."

"You okay?"

"Mmm-hmm."

"Good," I said. We didn't talk for a bit, not until we were halfway home, when Maggie noticed she'd missed a call from our dad.
"Should I call him back?" she asked.

"We'll see him in a couple minutes. It's probably okay to wait."

"Poor Dad."

"What do you mean?"

"Like—that plastic Santa!"

"I know."

"It just makes me think of the way he wants to be appreciated,
how he's always wanted that more than anything," she said.

"Yeah," I said, "of course." I don't know how to explain why I
was so struck by those words—*the way he wants to be appreciated.*
Naturally he wanted that, who doesn't? But from time to time one
of my sisters could say something about our parents and it would
seem revelatory to me, even if the statement would've sounded
mundane to anyone else. There was something deep and true
under the words, something I'd seen before but only partially, and
now here was another facet all lit up. I wanted to talk about it more,
to analyze our dad's need for appreciation, but Maggie had moved
on, now she was trashing Whole Foods. Whole Foods and its
fucked-up people buying their fucking *ciabatta* and their fucking
fair trade coffee, people who thought they were so superior when all
they had was money, not culture, they'd confused ciabatta with
culture. With art! *Ciabatta is not art,* she was saying. I didn't argue,
though obviously we were those people she was denouncing, insofar

as we'd been buying the same food at the same store. And she'd probably paid at least a hundred dollars for that new haircut she had. But she hadn't published all that she needed to publish to advance in her career, and she was worried about money, and angry that she had to worry about it, and though she kept her anger under wraps, every so often it lurched out of her.

Was everyone angry in every family? I didn't used to think so. However: it did sometimes seem that way, in this country at least. People might've still been happy in Corfu or Uruguay, but here we all felt we should've gotten something we didn't get, and though I hadn't voted for him I sometimes thought our current president was just the leader we deserved: the feisty son, the shorter one who'd struggled in school and drunk too much and once challenged his dad to a fistfight. Our peevish commander! There was a little W. in all of us, during the holidays especially.

On Christmas Eve we met Mom at an Italian restaurant, one that had opened when we were in high school and that we'd been going to ever since. In the mideighties it had quickly earned a spot on the best-of-city lists, though it had since drifted into the honorable-mention category and was entering its senescence. Loyalists continued to eat there, generally older people who I suppose were as comforted as I was by the familiar, by the rosemary breadsticks at the center of the table, the fried calamari on the menu, the frescoes that decorated the walls, and the somber, long-suffering maître d', who in his pigeon-toed stance behind the podium had the air of an inbred aristocrat reduced to servitude at a restaurant in Washington. Between the frescoes were nooks with lit candelabra in them, a touch of Tuscan gothic, their long shadows fingering the walls behind.

When Maggie and I arrived, our mother was already seated with a glass of white wine before her. She looked up, then stood. I had her modest height and her habit of holding her hands up by her chest, and I too had a way of resisting when I was tempted to smile.

I could sense her bracing herself. Not that she was unhappy to see us, but greetings and farewells made her tense up, even with her own daughters. It was as though she were following dance steps that had been inscribed on the floor, positioning her feet over the foot-silhouettes and then looking past us. Her skin had a sheen to it, produced by her regular, rigorous facials, and her hair was smartly cropped and colored a blond that approximated what she'd once been naturally. She still looked the part of the Washington wife: the soft red sweater and black pants with velvet seams, the fancy flats, the fresh manicure. I guessed that she probably had male admirers in Philadelphia, and that she wouldn't have made half the effort for them that she'd made for us.

"Are we expecting your sister?" she asked, even though she knew that we were.

"She might be running late," Maggie said.

"Just this once," I added.

I was only partway through my first breadstick when Courtney and Hugo arrived, which is to say they weren't so late, by Courtney standards. She came in coldly. Her lips were pursed, her eyes hard, at least they were when she glanced my way. But Hugo, bless him, had brought a bottle of tequila, and though at first the waiter seemed uneasy about letting us drink it there, the holiday mood got the better of him. He brought us little glasses. I took a few sips, and it was like the smoke of some magic spell wafting down my throat. Hugo kept saying funny things and pouring more for everybody. This was before we'd eaten anything, and after a few sips, Mom's Texas accent came back to her.

We talked, though Courtney and I never addressed each other. We talked about people we used to know, and about a movie that Mom and Courtney had loved and I had not loved, and then during a lull in the conversation Mom said, "So how is your father?"

This only prolonged the lull. We all gazed at nothing. Then she followed up with, "Has he been exercising?"

Everyone looked at me. I was now the expert on Dad and his fitness habits. "I think he's been exercising, yes," I said. Before I'd moved to my own place, I'd sometimes heard the braying of his old rowing machine down in the basement.

"Good, that's really good for him. And seeing people. Has he been socializing?"

"Mom, stop," Maggie said.

"Stop what?"

"You're talking about him like he's debilitated."

"I am not."

"Like you're his social worker."

"I'm concerned, that's all."

"Did he call you the other night?" I asked. "From the Morgans' party?"

She plucked a bit of fuzz from her sweater before she answered. "I did get a message from him, a little strange. Why?"

"I just thought I heard him call you."

"He was talking about that book."

"What book?" Courtney asked.

"He said he's been trying to write something, a memoir I guess it is. He's been at it for a while." She didn't say *bless his heart*, but it was there in her voice.

"I thought he gave that up," I said.

Mom said she really didn't know much about it.

"I wonder if he's dating anybody," Maggie said.

"He did make some mysterious late-night calls when I was there," I said.

"He has a lady friend?" asked Maggie, not hiding her delight.

"Maybe."

Then Hugo piped up. "What about you, Eileen?" he asked. "I bet that you have been beating off men with sticks."

In spite of the accidental image—one that he and Mom were oblivious to and Courtney ignored, while Maggie and I stared at the table and bit our lips—there was a charm in the way he talked to our mother. I wondered whether he weren't in fact some secret genius, saying these things to amuse us and placate her at the same time. At any rate he was the hero of the evening, the source of the smooth liquor and smoothing-over remarks that kept our wheels turning.

"Oh no," Mom said. "I'm enjoying the life I have now. Why would I let some man mess it up? You should see these women I know, they go onto websites, date-oldsters-dot-com or something. Not me!" She laughed unpersuasively. "Who wants dessert?"

After dinner we opened the gifts we'd brought with us. As usual Mom had given my sisters and me the same thing in different colors. This year it was pashminas. Beige for Courtney, black for Maggie, green for me. I gave my mother a teapot. We all put the scarves around our shoulders. Then Mom said she had to leave, to catch her train back to Philly, and Courtney and I spoke the first word we'd said to each other all night—goodbye. Maggie and I returned to the house to find that Dad had left for the midnight church service already, and though it was not so late, we retired to our rooms.

There's not too much to say about Christmas itself. We traded presents quickly and apologetically. Dad gave me a handmade vase, which, he explained, he'd bought at a church holiday bazaar. It was cylindrical and had swirls of blue in the glaze, and odd though it seemed that this was the "special gift" he'd told me about on the phone, I could never tell what would strike his fancy—in this case he knew the woman who'd made the vase, and that made it special to him, I guess. Courtney was still cool, quietly bustling around and picking up other people's discarded wrapping paper until we forced her to open her own gifts. In the afternoon we made enough food for twenty people. My father was dissatisfied with the roast; he said that it was unevenly cooked and that the oven needed to be serviced or replaced. Although there was more than enough decent meat to feed us, he wouldn't let it go and at one point dug up a toll-free number for Whirlpool, which we had to convince him not to call. Then he went on a long thing about an army general who'd been in the news, how he thought the general was an honest guy who had gotten a raw deal. From there he skipped to another news item and then back to Whirlpool. Even so, I don't think he was disappointed with Christmas. He seemed grumpy and sanguine at the same time. In the middle of dinner he got the idea he should call Judge O'Neill and invite him for dessert, but the judge was busy with his own family.

We stuffed ourselves, then opened a bottle of port, which we drained while watching *Die Hard* on television. Whatever happened to Bonnie Bedelia? we asked ourselves; nobody knew, and that would've been that—except that this black wave crashed over me as the movie was ending, one minute I was merely drowsy and the next thing I knew I felt close to tears, though not close enough to get any relief from crying. It was that Courtney had disappeared too, just like Bonnie Bedelia, and had been replaced by this self-righteous, overdressed person who made me feel crazy every time I was in the same room with her. I glanced at her—she was half-asleep.

"So what are you guys doing tomorrow?" I asked her.

She blinked and yawned. "We need new tile in our downstairs bathroom, so we thought we might go look for that."

"Tomorrow? The stores will be a nightmare."

"Probably. We have jobs, though. We have to go to stores when everyone else goes," she said.

"I mean, I guess it just seems like the day after Christmas—"

"We're not going to a mall. We're going to tile stores."

"Okay then," I said, meanwhile pressing my fingernails into my palms. "Good luck finding some tile."

We just fell into these exchanges, it seemed. I wouldn't see them coming. The blandest of topics would still lead us back to *You're wrong. No, you're wrong.*

The next day, I was reading the paper on the living room couch when Dad came in to tinker with the thermostat, a new digital model he distrusted. Offhandedly I told him about a bit from the gossip column. "That's Washington for you," he said, and then he stared at the tree and said that he wondered from time to time how his life might have played out in a different city than this one. It was the kind of thing I wondered about all the time, with respect to my own life, but it startled me when my father said it, because I considered the course of his life, of both my parents' lives, to have been fixed. All but fated. I didn't like to think of their choices as choices. I sat there, staring at him, Dad in his sweater and jeans and slippers, hair uncombed, thumbs hooked in his pockets, and thought, *Even for you it wasn't all mapped out.* I'd been raised in a world of tests and competitive admissions and college career offices, maybe that's why I had to remind myself of the obvious—that our lives are shaped as much by other people and external forces and luck as they are by aptitudes and plans.

"I was offered a pretty good position down in Florida in, what was it, spring of eighty-five? An old friend of mine had a company that was doing very well, it was a distributor for medical supplies, and he invited me to interview for vice president of something or other. Operations? I had the sense that the interview was a formality, though. It paid very well."

"Did you think about taking it?"

"Oh sure. We had college tuitions to think about, and it was just so different, the private sector, Fort Lauderdale, all of it. I went down there and did the interview, talked to a bunch of guys. But your mother was happy in her job here, and you girls were in high school, and you know—selling things to hospitals. I just hadn't seen myself in that sort of business. But then again . . ."

He drifted off, and I thought I understood: had he taken the Florida job, he would have avoided the scandal, which itself had steered him into the corporate life, but only after many months of investigations and unemployment—and painful memories that lasted much longer. But he went on.

"Then again I was certainly tempted to get out. The White House was exciting, but it wasn't the best atmosphere. There were big egos, a lot of infighting. It could be hard to get anything done, or even keep in mind what we were trying to accomplish."

"Did you write about that, in your book?"

He stayed quiet for a bit, and then he said, "I didn't get that far."

"Maybe you should keep going."

"It's not about Iran-Contra, hardly any of it is. I wanted to write about the rest of what I did, the parts that got lost after the whole, whatever you want to call it. The whole shebang. I was going to give you some of it to read. That was going to be my Christmas present, but then I thought the better of it."

"Why?"

"These old-man memoirs. They're so funereal."

"It's not funereal."

" 'Let's go ahead and get it on the record while he's still got his wits about him. Then we'll self-publish the thing and never look at it again,' " he said. He'd started pacing a little. "Believe me, I've seen these things at other people's houses, and they're like long, first-person obituaries."

"Come on, Dad." He didn't say anything. "I'd just like to know more about it. When it happened, Iran-Contra was like this big thing that nobody had straight and people made fun of, at least the kids I knew would make fun of it."

He stood still and tall. "I'll say one thing about all that. My colleagues at the time, they skirted the law. They broke it, I suppose, and they covered it up, and they—we, I should say, since I did help them, we were caught. But those men did what they did for reasons they believed to be the right reasons. Moral reasons. I won't say I myself had all the conviction of an Oliver North, but I did believe in their good faith, if that makes any sense. I still believed I was working for and with people who had our country's best interests at heart. This may seem simplistic to you. We live in, I guess you could say, a more complicated world now, and we're more sensitive to how dangerous our convictions can turn out to be. At least some of us are. But then I look at your generation and I wonder what it's like—what do you even put faith in?"

I couldn't tell whether he expected a reply. I didn't have one. Faith? A pretty country singer. The shape of a fish on the back of a car. A musty old rocking chair that had not been handed down to me. I wanted to defend my generation, but all I could think to say was that there were other members of my generation who were better and more faithful people than I was.

Dad went upstairs, and I heard the printer going. He came back down with a small stack of paper and handed it over.

"It's not much," he said. "Fits and starts."

The pages were still warm when I took them in my hands. He was already heading back toward the stairs. "But you should be writing something of your own, not helping me with a book I might never finish."

I thanked him; I said I was really excited to read it, which truly I was. And then again I was reluctant. I took those pages home and didn't touch them for a long time. I also put my own book on hold. The more I'd written, the more the whole construct had threatened to collapse, maybe because I'd never actually been part of the professional world I was trying to re-create, though that wasn't the only reason. Iran-Contra was too convoluted. My father was too close and also too distant. And did it matter so much what he had done in his career, or had I just fallen into an all-too-Washingtonian trap, believing his career had defined him?

This wasn't just about his career. This was my family's encounter with History. The scandal seemed to me, in its mysterious, byzantine way, to be more than a political mess that had sullied my dad. I sometimes thought of it as a puddle in which a whole swath of sky was reflected, as well as, from certain angles, my own face.

Yet it was a relatively recent obsession. I'd only become compelled by Iran-Contra once I'd had the idea to write a script—in other words, my curiosity about the story and my urge to tell the story had presented at the same time, like two symptoms of the same illness, back when I'd hoped to convert our family crisis into Hollywood drama. The longer I stayed away from L.A., though, the less I believed that such a conversion was even possible, never mind desirable. I lost track of my three-act structure. I no longer knew who the antagonists were.

I set my book aside, but I didn't stop thinking about that time. Everything—the streets, the season, the smells in the air—reminded me of the past, and I was remembering things I hadn't thought about in years.

PART THREE

1986

I t was the year Len Bias died. Len Bias, All-American, star of the University of Maryland basketball team, was picked second in the NBA draft by the Celtics on June 17 and pronounced dead, at Leland Memorial Hospital, less than forty-eight hours later. The day after the draft he had flown with his father to Boston and back, and that night, while celebrating in a Maryland dorm room, he'd ingested enough cocaine to stop even a young athlete's unscarred heart. He collapsed on the floor. The friend who called 911 told the dispatcher, "This is Len Bias. He can't die," and though the dispatcher didn't recognize the name, countless other people would've understood: not only was it unacceptable for Len Bias to die of an overdose before he'd played his first game in the pros, it was inconceivable. Not Bias with his defiant hang-time, Bias who would bring off his perfect jump shot on one possession and on the next soar straight to the hoop. Bias, one of the two greats to come out of the Atlantic Coast Conference in those years, along with Jordan.

If you were a kid who cared about basketball back then, the death of Len Bias was another *Challenger* explosion—and a much bigger deal than the reports about weapons sales to Iran and covert aid to the Contras that began surfacing later that same year. *He can't die.* No one could believe that the demigod had been so crudely exposed as a mortal, that such talent could vanish so quickly from the earth, and that nothing would be left but the game tapes and a photograph of Bias at the draft, in an ivory suit and a green Celtics cap, not beaming like you might expect but smiling shyly, more Lenny the quiet boy who used to go home from college on the weekends and wash his mother's car than Bias the big-time baller. On the news they showed that photo over and over, the picture of a glorious beginning that would be snuffed two days hence. Poor dead Len Bias, his happy face was everywhere.

D.C. was nuts for basketball, at least lots of us were, and the same ardor that had produced a Len Bias infected many, many lesser athletes, even a contingent of private-school girls who were, practically speaking, playing a different game that just happened to have the same rules.

Our team tryouts were in mid-November: three days and thirty-odd ponytailed teenage females, in faded T-shirts and new high-tops, crouching and sliding sideways, zigzagging across the shiny wood floors. This at an "elite" secondary school. Most of us were daughters of privilege and most were white, a small herd of spindly-legged *jeunes filles* running around in a cloud of estradiol and the bright, fruity scents of our bath products. We ran and jumped desperately, desperate to be better than we were.

Each afternoon a skimmed light fell from the high windows and faded as we went on. Coach E—the varsity coach, Deanna Estes— pushed us until we were raw and heaving and more or less mute. We might make eye contact and stick out our tongues, but then it was back to the pain and the striving, each of us trapped inside our hopeless bodies, lashing at them, go on, go on, until the sky was dark and the air in the gym had thickened into a fug of sweat and nerves. There were two secondary authorities, the varsity assistant and the junior varsity coach, but Coach E, fortyish and wide-hipped and hoarse and intimidating to me, was in charge, and all business.

The year before, as a junior, Courtney had been the varsity's leading scorer. I'd been a freshman on JV and had come in off the bench, and so my hope was to start for the JV that season. But on the first day of tryouts I flubbed everything. I missed shots, I dropped passes, I stumbled around the gym like some sedated heavyweight, wondering whether I would so much as stay on the JV team, even as Courtney was nearly perfect. She moved through the drills matter-of-factly, like someone doing housework, like a charmed person doing housework. When it came time to shoot she hit shot after beautiful shot, lowered her head and ran on. It wouldn't be quite right to say that she was a superior athlete, or that she was ego-less, but she had worked very hard to become pretty good, and she was something like her best self when she played on a team, and you couldn't help but feel grateful for it. Her body was loose, easy, but if you looked at her face you saw her eyes always scanning, alert to the steal, the cutter, the shot, the hole.

In my room that night, I sat on my bed and rubbed at the red indentations my socks had left in my ankles, then wiped my nose against my sleeve. *Oh fuck it. Fuck me. Well as if anyone would.* I stood up and stalked around the room. I ripped a taped-up picture of the Georgetown Hoyas off the wall and crumpled it up, which was hardly satisfying.

I could hear him climbing the stairs. My dad, in his slippers.

"Knock knock."

"Go away."

"I'd rather not."

"Go away!"

"Aren't you going to eat?"

I shook my head, though he couldn't see me do it, a piece of my dark wet hair attaching itself to my jaw. He cracked the door.

"Your mother says you missed dinner."

"I'm not hungry."

He stepped into the room and, seeing my face, spoke more softly. "You should eat."

"I messed up. I did terribly."

"I'm sure you did better than you think you did. Courtney said things went well." He nodded to himself and started to look around the room. I'll eat later, I told him.

Because we were sisters who played basketball, people assumed that Courtney and I had grown up playing together. I can picture it myself, an alternate girlhood in which we unwound game after game of one-on-one from a fat spool of afternoons, sweating and squealing and laughing all the while. But when we actually tried to play, it sucked. We would come this close to punching each other, and between punching each other and killing each other was barely any distance at all. She was the older sister, and so she absolutely had to win. She did in fact beat me consistently, but she wasn't expert enough to win every single game: she wasn't quicker than I was or any kind of ball-handling whiz. I was more reckless, more physical, which sometimes worked in my favor and sometimes backfired. Every now and then I took the lead, but I didn't want to make her mad, and so I would start to giggle and do silly things. I would, when I had the ball, turn my body away from the basket and then back myself toward it, dribbling and backing into my sister until I got close enough to attempt an unlikely hook shot. Those hook shots infuriated Courtney. "Come on!" she would say. It didn't take long before she grabbed my hair, and I would exclaim, jovially, "Folks, now she's got her sister by the hair!" which only made her yank harder.

I wanted her approval badly, but instead of doing things she'd approve of, I did the opposite.

In other words we didn't play together much. Mostly, I ran. Ran the trails down to Georgetown and back up through the streets, ran along the parkway by the river, ran on Reno Road and Nebraska Avenue, ran around the grounds of the cathedral, ran up and down the hills in Battery Kemble Park. Ran in excess of what was necessary or even desirable for basketball, for I was overworking the wrong muscles. I had much more lung capacity than I had power. But in high school everyone has to find her own way to keep her head on straight, and my way was to lope around for an hour at a

stretch with a mix tape in my yellow Sports Walkman, taking refuge in those patches of woods that are scattered among the Washington neighborhoods, jumping over roots and skirting the muddy
sections and shortening my stride to skitter along exposed pipes.

And in the side yard Courtney worked and worked at her shot,
her moves, her dribble, even things like cuts without the ball. I'd
look out and see her jumping rope, or machine-gunning her feet, a
regular Rocky of Northwest D.C. Though her best sport was lacrosse,
and she'd already been contacted by lacrosse coaches from a few
different colleges, she was obsessed with basketball. Or: the city was
obsessed with basketball, and she'd caught the civic fever.

The second day of tryouts, I did better than I had the first day.
One thing I could do was follow instructions, and on that day I did
everything Coach E said. *Hustle up!* she yelled, and I dutifully hustled. *Hands up on D!* I put my arms in the air. *Boards!* I jumped up
and caught the ball. *Box out!* My butt was on another girl. I did as
I was told. On the third day, about halfway through the practice,
Coach E split us up into teams of five so that we could scrimmage.
I saw that the other four girls on my team were seniors, from last
year's varsity, which unnerved me. I started fucking up again. On
defense I ran under the basket toward the ball when I should've
stayed over on the weak side to rebound. Then on offense I set a
screen, squaring myself against one of the girls on the other team,
but she shucked me off and I fell down, fell on the floor with a thud,
and at that point I was ready to give up and head for the locker
room.

A hand appeared, someone offering to help me up. It was Courtney, who was on the other team. She pulled me to my feet and
then pulled me close to her and slapped my lower back, something
I'd seen her do with her teammates but had never experienced myself, and I experienced it now not as a simple gesture of solidarity
or support but as something greater, I want to say cosmic, though I
know that sounds overblown. It was as if my sister, and therefore
the universe, had for the first time in my life found a place for me.
Then I heard Coach's gargly chiding, *Step on the gas, people!* and I

did. I ran back on defense and blocked a girl's shot. I sprinted the length of the court, caught the ball, and fed it to the post player, who scored. And there was Courtney jogging by me, saying something, *N'est-ce pas*, I thought she said, but that didn't make any sense, and I refitted the sounds into our own language: *Nice pass*. Two syllables, and I bounded ahead like a dog running out of the water.

I didn't do anything spectacular, but I kept my girl from scoring and made a few shots and by the end of the game I felt good about it. After practice, the coaches posted the team rosters on the locker room bulletin board. My name was on the varsity list: I stared at it until it became unreadable, a pair of squiggles. I stood there in that humid cavern, in the swim of other girls' sweat, smelling everything. Courtney squeezed my shoulder and said, "Way to go!" It seemed like she was still deciding how she felt about it. She was in just her sports bra and shorts, looking around, thinking things over. "We're on the same team," she said, accepting the fact if not quite celebrating it. Our parents sounded the same way when we told them I'd made varsity. That's nice, they said.

It had been maybe a week earlier that we'd all sat in the family room, the radiator hissing and the ice cream on the coffee table going soft, as the president addressed us, via TV, from two miles away. Our buoyant leader had turned old and false and sarcastic.

I know you've been reading, seeing, and hearing a lot of stories the past several days attributed to Danish sailors, unnamed observers at Italian ports and Spanish harbors, and especially unnamed government officials of my administration. Well, now you're going to hear the facts from a White House source, and you know my name.

The family room: Where my sisters and I would sit on a small hound's-tooth couch and argue over whose turn it was to get up and

change the channel. Where plastic horses had been paraded, cray-
ons melted over the radiator, mittens clipped to parkas, damp pool
towels left on the floor, a shoe, thimble, and hat advanced around a
board, sleepovers staged . . .

*The charge has been made that the United States has shipped weapons to
Iran as ransom payment for the release of American hostages in Lebanon,
that the United States undercut its allies and secretly violated American
policy against trafficking with terrorists.*

In my scrambled memory, there is just a single, comprehensive
Reagan speech, raveling in the wake of a breathy *Well,* regarding
threats in the Caribbean and in Central America, the evil empire,
welfare queens, SALT II, crack cocaine, hijackers and hostages. And
somewhere along the way came the president's own failures to remember, the gaps—memento mori—in the sunny script.

*All appropriate cabinet officers were fully consulted. The actions I autho-
rized were, and continue to be, in full compliance with Federal law. And
the relevant committees of Congress are being, and will be, fully informed.*

Not true: my father must have known that was false. Or did he?
How much did he know, that evening, and how much did he anticipate? If Dad, that night—in his armchair, necktie loosened,
shoes off—foresaw what was ahead, he kept it from the rest of us.
He sat and watched and ate his ice cream.

Even as the weeks went on and the clouds gathered, then let loose
their storm, Dad remained a stalwart of the stands, just as he had
been ever since Courtney's freshman year. As far as I know, he

never left work before eight or nine at night for any other reason—
didn't ever go to the doctor, I'd be willing to bet, during the four
years that he served on the National Security Council staff—but
he'd come to just about every home game and some of the others
too. He would arrive while we were warming up, take off his hat
and his long wool coat, smooth his damp hair and loosen his tie.
He would shake hands with the other parents. And then, once the
whistle sounded and the ball went up, this otherwise slightly formal, Republican, whiter-than-rice bureaucrat would turn into a
zealot. He would stalk back and forth in front of the bleachers and
cheer his heart out.

The days were short. Darkness had blackened the windows by
game time. Beyond them lay our frosty, self-deceiving city, its marble walls sliced up by passing headlights, its statues watched over by
park police as angry poor people fired guns in the distance. But the
gym was lit up and warm. It had a faintly rancid odor, of furnace
heat and floor cleaner and damp anoraks balled up and strewn
about, of sweat and dried sweat. Our opponents would walk in
preening and joking and slapping hands. Then came the tumble of
feet, the sneaker-squeaks, the crying for the ball, the whiny bounce
of rubber against wood, the second of silence as a shot went up: the
game had started. On the sidelines, attorneys and economists in suits
would clap the chill out of their hands, calling out, "Good shot!"
"Get the ball!" "Go!" as their daughters ran this way and that.

Our dad didn't actually know much about the game of basketball. He was handy with a drill or a saw, but to watch him pick up
any sort of ball and try to loft it into the air gave me pangs. It was
only later that I recognized his clumsiness as partly a product of his
childhood, which had been full of work and church—no one had
ever taught him to throw. Yet at games he had picked up on various
cheers, a bunch of things he'd heard other people say and adopted
indiscriminately as his own. It was like he was speaking a foreign
language, badly but with gusto. He might start with a few cries of
"Let's go, ladies! Hustle!" He would round his large hands and clap
them slowly. He would roll up his sleeves. When he really got going,

there was no telling what might come out of his mouth. Sometimes he adopted a sort of announcer's yodel: "DEeeeeeeFENSE!" Other times he shouted, inappropriately, at members of the other team. "Hey you, pack a suitcase!" he hollered, and pointed a long finger at a girl who'd been called for traveling.

"PACK YOUR SUITCASE!"

Boys in the stands snorted and pointed. I tried to ignore it, but Courtney complained to our mom, who missed a lot of our games because she had to pick up Maggie from ballet school.

"He's blowing off steam," she told Courtney. There was plenty for him to blow off. Before long he would become a target of the investigation and lose his job, but in the meantime our gym was a refuge. Afterward he would ask whether we wanted to stop at Swensen's for ice cream, as though we were still eight years old.

Actually I wouldn't have minded a trip to Swensen's, but Courtney set him straight. "Dad, we just played basketball. We're sweaty and tired and want to go home," she said.

"Oh, okay," he said, humbled. He had a way of deferring to her, which he didn't with Maggie or me or even our mom. "Home we go."

That season we competed in empty, neglected gyms and small, crowded ones. The president's Special Review Board, tasked to make sure that "all the facts come out," started to gather masses of information. We competed in damp, echo-ridden buildings with faded pennants hanging from the rafters. An independent counsel was appointed, and John Poindexter and Oliver North and Robert McFarlane and Robert Owen and Albert Hakim and Richard Secord sought legal help, as did my dad. We competed on brand-new courts with shiny floors and cinder-block walls painted the school colors. Depositions were taken, huge quantities of documents were exchanged, and the House and Senate Select Committees were created. We competed at ivied old girls' schools, against thoroughbred girls coached by thin, steely WASPs, and we competed at glossy suburban academies, against fleet-footed soccer players with hairsprayed bangs, and we competed at the public school down the street, where black girls laughed at us, and at religious schools where the girls wore knickers and three-quarter sleeves.

And everywhere we played, people launched into the same cheer. *B-E! A-G-G! R-E-S-S-I-V-E! Be! Aggressive! B-E! Aggressive!* Whatever that meant. I chanted it too, lord knows how many times.

2005

After New Year's I returned to the office in Crystal City, and I was there when Nina called. I guessed that she wanted to schedule her driving lesson, but instead she invited me to go hear a band with her, an indie act popular enough that even I knew a few of their hits, minimalist ballads about breakups and the seaside and minor historical figures. Again her dad had planned to go with her, but he'd found out he would be in court the following day, which meant he had to spend that night preparing. "He said I could ask you," she said.

I had to keep my voice low, and we were on cell phones. The undercurrent was lost in a tower someplace. I agreed to take her.

God, it was cold that night of the show, not a typical mid-Atlantic cold but some ice-fanged front from farther north blowing right onto my eyeballs. I hurried out of my building and hurried up the stoop next door, and after I was buzzed in I hurried up to the second floor as though the wind were still gnashing its jaws at me.

Here was Daniel welcoming me with a kindness that made me feel very young, a friend of his daughter's. I couldn't conceive of growing up like this, in a two-person apartment, so quiet! But inside of it, I could feel the quiet warmth intertwined with the quiet sadness, the sloppy odd-couple care that father and daughter had for each other. The place itself had the indifference to looks that you might expect in the home of a man and a teenager: there were pillows on the floor and days' worth of schoolwork and legal documents on the dining room table, and on the wall next to the door they'd taped Nina's basketball schedule and a calendar from a Salvadoran restaurant. Daniel showed me to the kitchen, where Nina was eating a sandwich over the sink. "We usually eat together," he said, apologetically. "It's been a crazy week."

I'd been wishing I could get out of the whole thing, because of the weather and because I didn't care about the band and didn't want to stand for two hours in a crowd of its giddy young fans, but Nina had put on eyeliner and she'd pinned her hair back with a mishmash of barrettes, and by the way she was wolfing down her sandwich I could tell she was more excited about this than I myself had been about anything in ages. Seeing her that way, I tamped down my reluctance and let Daniel call the taxi company.

In the cab she clasped her hands between her knees and looked out the front windshield. The sidewalks were nearly empty, blown clean, while the streets were full of cars. Angry trees wagged at us. An unlatched chain-link gate blew open and shut. Nina listened to music in her head that I couldn't hear. The cold had pinched her cheeks, and in the half light of the backseat, in profile, she had the ghostly look of a fashion model.

"Have you seen them before?" I asked.

"I've seen videos from their shows."

"That singer is cute," I said, though I actually thought he was scary-looking. In the photographs I'd seen here and there, he was shaggy and skinny and so white he was almost a pale blue, and when he smiled it was like his face had been winched open, so that you could tell what a sneering, miserable person lived inside his too-small clothes. But it was the sneer and the misery in his voice that made the songs into what they were.

"I *know*," Nina said. "Adam is so adorable."

We were trying to find each other, but there were no doors. As the cab rattled over a series of potholes I gripped the seat, and she let herself be jostled.

"You have the tickets, right?" I asked.

She frowned, and at first I thought she'd left them at home. Slowly she reached into her small khaki purse and pulled them out, then studied what was printed there. "I invited someone, a friend of mine," she said.

I didn't get it. "Does your friend have a ticket?" I asked. Nina turned to me with so much pleading in her expression that I could barely stand it, and that's when I understood what she meant.

"My dad doesn't let me go on dates," she said. "All we ever do is e-mail, since he doesn't go to my school. We can never see each other."

"It would have been better if you'd told me about this before now."

She didn't say anything, rereading the tickets instead, until more words burst out of her. "It'll just be like, two hours, and we'll be inside the club the whole time. You can do whatever you want and I'll just call you when the show's over."

Just do this one thing for me, her eyes said, for young love and pop music.

People were clustered in front of the club, stomping and shivering as they waited to get in, smoking cigarettes with frozen fingers. Nina got out of the cab, and the mob ejected this boy come to meet her. Was he really in high school? I wondered. I couldn't tell anyone's age anymore. He was on the small side, his dark hair more neatly trimmed than any of the other guys' hair, his skin neither dark nor light, his ethnicity unclear to me, his jacket too thin for the weather—he looked like an engineering student from someplace warm. They beamed at each other without touching, he and Nina.

Oh shit, was all I could think. I bumbled after her and told her I'd pick her up at that exact spot at 10:30, no later. She started to say that she could just call me when—but this was me feebly putting my foot down. "Ten-thirty," I insisted. Then I stuck out my hand and introduced myself to the boy, who politely said his name, Sam. His tone was soft. Then he smiled so broadly that I wondered whether he might be high, but I couldn't tell, and before I had a chance to think it over they said so long.

Suddenly I was the nurse in *Romeo and Juliet*, only the nurse never had to spend two hours in a fricking Burger King on 19th Street, which is what I did, eating onion rings out of a cardboard pouch and reading an article from somebody's discarded newspaper, about a planned overhaul of government intelligence services, and asking myself why I'd let myself be manipulated by a sixteen-year-old kid. But then I remembered the question my dad had posed— are you depressed?—and I decided that no, I didn't think I was anymore, and that this improvement seemed to have come about less because I'd figured anything out about my life than because I was no longer sitting in my L.A. apartment watching election coverage. Even sitting in this Burger King seemed better. Even here I was busier, and while I did still want something more for myself, I had a new appreciation for the merits of keeping busy. I wondered whether this was one reason why everyone around me worked such long hours, whether they were all warding off secret funks.

My phone shuddered at me.

What are you doing?

The text was from Rob, and I was all too glad to get it.

Eating onion rings.
R they hot?
Yes. Want to come over later?

He didn't reply. Though I had bought a texting-enabled phone, I wasn't in the habit of texting and certainly didn't have the hang of text banter. For the next ten minutes I kept checking the phone, thinking maybe I'd missed a response from him. I walked back to the club. Nina came out at exactly 10:30, alone, her coat over her arm as if she could no longer be touched by the cold. "Thank you," she said.

"Okay," I said, not knowing what to say. For the first part of the cab ride home we barely talked. Then I asked her how she and Sam had met.

"He was my math tutor, last semester."

"Where does he go to school?"

"AU," she said. "He's a junior there, but he started college early. He's only three years older." She took a deep breath. "He's actually from Turkey. Samed is his real name but he calls himself Sam. He's like, the smartest person I have ever met."

I thought about Anthony Jaffe, my high school not-quite-a-boyfriend, and the things he used to say. "Did you know," he said to me once, "did you know that time is not a property of the universe? It is a property of clocks. A convention," he said.

But then how come I can't be rid of it, I'd wondered.

"Does your dad know?" I asked Nina.

"The first time we kissed, he walked in on us. Oops. That was the end of math tutoring. He thinks Sam's too old, even though hello, my mom was three years older than him. He says that's different, but I don't see why it's different."

"So you're not allowed to see him."

Her phone buzzed, and she took it out and read something that lit up her face. She thumbed a reply, then looked back to me. "Please don't tell," she said.

"I kind of should."

"I'm really sorry."

No, I thought, no you're not. She begged me not to say anything, and I refused to make a promise one way or another. I said I would have to sleep on it. She angled her head back against the seat and returned to the club and the boy with two names and the adorable-miserable singer, and the sight made me sentimental in spite of myself, late-night sentiment trumping the sense I might've had at another time of day or another time of life: though I was pretty sure I'd messed up, I also thought that now she would have this for the rest of her life, this night when she was sixteen and went to hear music with the boy she was nuts for, and who was I to take that away from her?

At home I checked my phone again.

I can't. Let's check in fri.

I felt out of sorts. I could still smell the onion rings. I put the phone away.

1986

Coach E used to lecture us on the topic of desire. What do I mean when I say the word *desire*? she would ask, with her arms folded and her chin out, her gaze aimed at the rim. I am not talking about lust. I am not talking about your *teenage urges*. Where does this word *desire* come from? From the stars. From the stars. Desire comes from the stars.

This is about something bigger than you, ladies. This game. This game! This game is greater than you. You reach for the sky, and that's desire. You ask the stars for help. That's desire. You strain with all your might toward something greater! That's what desire is. The *desire* to play the game with everything you have, and more.

For me one desire swirled into another. I would watch the boys' varsity team play basketball in a kind of terrific swoon. All those legs, the hairy, knobby legs and the smooth pillars, pale legs and dark ones, jumping up, up, up. I wanted to jump. I wanted a body that could hang in the air. It was amazing to me that the same boys who scuttled stupidly around the school in their stupid jackets could soar the way they did. I wanted to jump like them, and it's true, I also wanted to be jumped by them. At their games I used to swish my tongue around my mouth, imagining what another tongue would feel like in there, and press my hands into the bleachers, and feel all my skin, the entire surface of me getting warmer. But when they put their stupid jackets back on, I didn't want them anymore.

My friend Anthony used to come find me during free periods, and we would loaf in the student lounge or sometimes we would shoot around in the gym together. He had unruly blond hair and grasshopper legs and I guess a thing for me, ever since we were in math class together in ninth grade. I was quicker than him in math, which got his attention, and one day I'd found a screw on the floor and picked it up and said, Wanna screw?—then realized my mistake. The answer in his eyes was yes, yes, yes. But I'd just said it to be funny. He was really skinny, not that I was fat, but he had the kind of metabolism that made him susceptible to head-rushes and even fainting first thing in the morning. I was bigger than he was, that was one reason we never went out.

He was eleven months older and so had his driver's license well before I did, and he also had his own car, which he drove to school and to his job as a projectionist at an arty movie theater. His parents were doctors, a neurologist and a psychiatrist, and loyal BMW owners. He drove one that had been his mother's, a car that embarrassed him (though I cherished it, for it was like the car Cybill Shepherd drove in *Moonlighting*), with deep seats of cream-colored leather and a removable stereo and a car phone that didn't work. Anthony used to slap the seat, or the steering wheel, or his own leg, to emphasize something ridiculous or to punctuate the silence when he wasn't saying anything. "Mrs. Gonnerman!" he would say— this was our chemistry teacher—and then give the car a slap and then repeat, "Mrs. Gonnerman! Well, I never." He would just say these nonsense kinds of things and I would laugh. We drove around doing that, parroting phrases we thought were funny and listening to Whodini and the Fat Boys. "So should I go buy some Timberlands?" I remember him asking, making fun of the other white boys who borrowed whatever bits of black style they could get away with, but also I think genuinely wanting to know whether he too could pull it off.

Otherwise I was at loose ends socially. My best friend from ninth grade had transferred to public school in Virginia, and besides Anthony I had people I sat with at lunch, but none of them called me at night, or wrote me notes during the day.

In November Dick Mitchell went before the Senate Select Committee on Intelligence, and so did Assistant Secretary Elliott Abrams, who explained to the senators that the "State Department's function in this has not been to raise money" for the Contras. Less than two weeks later, Abrams went back to the committee and owned that he himself had asked the foreign minister of Brunei to contribute $10 million to aid the freedom fighters of Nicaragua. During that second appearance, the senators raked him over the coals. ("You've heard my testimony," said Abrams to Senator Thomas F. Eagleton of Missouri. "I've heard it," said the senator, "and I want to puke.")

Like most kids I couldn't have told you much about any of that, but Courtney was paying attention, she was piecing things together, and after she read about Abrams's second round, she had some questions for Dad. Why did he lie? she asked one night at dinner. Dad told her that Abrams may not have known what he was allowed to talk about and what he wasn't allowed to talk about.

"He didn't say that. He didn't say, 'I'm not allowed to talk about this.' He lied."

"If you look at the exact wording of what he said, I don't know that it was a lie. It was an omission."

Courtney looked toward Mom, who had a way of being studiously distant in those moments, who was serving herself some more salad.

"The thing is, at this stage, there's a lot we don't know," Dad said.

"I know it's lying," she said, and on her face was betrayal. Dad mashed his lips together and then said, "We are not going to talk about this at dinner."

Courtney didn't say anything more, in that case she wasn't going to talk at all.

After that, absurdly, our parents tried to shield us from what was going on. Not only did they pretend everything was normal, they pretended we were ten years younger than we were, or they treated us like that anyway. They imposed a news blackout—such a thing was still possible in 1986, insane but possible, though the gist of the affair did reach us eventually. They instructed us to cover our ears, and for a little while we went along with it, even as we learned also to read lips, to puzzle out what people were saying. Mom was the family censor: she no longer watched the evening news as she was making dinner, and every morning she cut out all the relevant articles, making lacework of *The Post*.

Of course she and Dad still read those snipped-out stories themselves, and after 11:00 p.m., the anthems of the late news seeped out of their bedroom. I used to sneak out to the hallway, trying to hear what was being said. I could sometimes hear Dad yelling, "That's a bunch of bull!" at the television, though I had no way of knowing who was being accused, the men in the story—*bull!*—or the news program itself—*bull!* Or both: everybody was lying. On Sundays, when he was at home, he would be looking out the window or into the refrigerator, and his brow would lower. His lips would move ever so slightly. You could see him getting angry again, silently having it out with someone, everyone, the president himself.

It was as though the background chatter of TV and print news had been a string knitting together the household. Once it had been pulled out, we lost our footing. Rules and rituals were forgotten. When was dinnertime? Were the Redskins playing? Together my sisters and I did chores that we'd argued over in the past, wanting to keep some kind of order. And as we washed and dried the dishes I would perform for Courtney, to make her laugh, peddling dumb jokes about how grody our refrigerator was, or about the way our dog wiggled her butt when she walked. We would cackle as Maggie shimmied around the kitchen, with an eleven-year-old dancer's grace, pretending to be the dog.

A year earlier, just before I started ninth grade, Courtney had handed me a piece of filler paper spritzed with Anaïs Anaïs. It contained a list of *HIGH SCHOOL DOS AND DON'TS ACCORDING TO MOI (COURTNEY ATHERTON)*:

1. Do shower daily, or twice daily in the case of severe B.O.
2. Neither a borrower (of my clothing) nor a lender be.
3. Don't stare at junior or senior boys even if you think they're cute (trust me they're all retarded).
4. Don't put any personal info about yourself in writing, even if it's a note to a friend.
5. Do take time for General Foods International Coffees. Ahhhh.
6. If life hands you lemons, stuff your bra with them! The Atherton females need ALL the help they can get.

I saved the note in my desk drawer. The boundary between us was always shifting, some days it was all tra-la-la and trips to Peoples Drug for no reason but to buy candy and Wet n Wild lipstick, but then the next day or week it was like she didn't even see me, or like she thought I was the dumbest creature she'd ever come across. And there were times when I was the one who snapped at her, sick of all her achievements, her useless superiority, her advice.

When I say Courtney was pretty, I don't mean that she was one of those skinny sylphs who came to school in teeny-tiny skirts on the coldest of days. She was muscular. She rarely wore makeup. Her smooth brown hair fell into place on its own, and her clothes all fit her just so. There was always some soft-spoken boy trailing after her—the shyer members of the lacrosse and soccer teams all loved her—but she only wanted to be friends with them. She liked a different type of guy.

She invited me to come along to a party—an unprecedented offer—and I yipped out a "yes!," then tried to gin up some nonchalance after the fact. This was early December. We'd played our first game that week, an easy win (to which I had contributed two rebounds in two minutes of playing time), and I was giddy as we sallied out in our mom's car, a Ford Taurus a.k.a. the Fortrus. First we drove to Courtney's friend Tanya's house, and I moved to the backseat, and there in Tanya's driveway we puzzled over the Montgomery County map book resting open on top of the hand brake. *Animals strike curious poses,* Prince sang as we started for Bethesda. My sister and Tanya talked about boys I didn't know.

It was Rob Golden's house, that is to say Dick Mitchell's, a big plush colonial, ivy on the outside and fields of chenille and carpet within—fibered surfaces where kids on the brink of a kiss could nestle their wads of gum, and these would lie undiscovered for weeks. Courtney and Tanya and I filed through the house, out the back door and into the yard. It was cold, but half the party had gone out there anyway. A keg sat on the flagstone, among patio furniture, guarded by one of those shy boys who preferred to spend the whole party priming the pump and squirting beer into cups, while around that outpost and its lonely viceroy radiated fleeting colonies of young bodies, moving erratically, huddling for a while and then breaking apart.

Tanya peeled off to go talk to some friends of hers, and Courtney kept several paces ahead of me. I could tell she wasn't sure whether it'd been a good idea to bring me along. I looked around the yard and saw only one other sophomore, a promiscuous Deadhead who liked to get high and then let some lucky boy deprive her of her tie-dyed togs. She was sitting up on a stone wall at the edge of the yard, in a row of girls who were swinging their legs and holding their red plastic cups with two hands, like bouquets, while swains in baseball caps lined up below them. In the moonlight the girls reared their heads and ran their fingers through their hair.

Aside from that one girl they were all juniors and seniors, people I had never seen at night. Their faces were painted over with shadows. They looked like bears and squirrels and dogs. I drifted across the yard, craning my neck as though I were looking for someone.

"There you are," a guy said, and I turned to face a person I didn't know, though I knew his name, Greg, as I knew the names of all the upperclassmen. "Oh, sorry," he said. "I thought you were someone else."

"It's true, though," I said desperately.

"You are someone else?"

"I am here."

He nodded solemnly.

On the other side of a bush something rustled, and a security light went on. Greg was taller than I was, but not by much, with straight brown bangs and a blunt nose, and the pale skin and slight doughiness of someone who spent his daylight hours away from the daylight. His face was taunting and dappled.

"Did you crash this fiesta?" he asked.

"Not that I know of. Were there, like, invitations?"

"Engraved. Delivered by footmen."

"I came with my sister. Courtney," I said.

"Courtney Atherton? You're her sister?"

"'Tis true."

He peered at my face, and I mugged for him, tucking my chin.

"Okay, I can see it," he said. "Wow. Amazing."

"How is that amazing?"

"She's just, like, an intense person."

"She's my sister."

"She's so—*literal*."

"What does that mean?"

He told me his first and last name, Greg Jacobs. On a whim I lied about my own name. I said it was Becca.

Inside, someone had put a record on, and through the patio doors I could see boys thrusting their shoulders forward and back, chanting the words to "It's Tricky."

On the patio itself, five or six weight-room regulars were in heated discussion. One of the guys clapped his hands slowly and repeated, "Let's do this, let's do this." A more prudent one said, "That's foolish, y'all." Then the one who'd been clapping abruptly pulled off his T-shirt. His muscles and his gut bulged. Jay Wood was his name, a.k.a. Woody, or Woody Woodpecker, or Good Wood, or just Wood, said pointedly—*Good morning, Wood.* All those boner jokes had done nothing to sweeten his personality.

Greg cocked his head toward the boys. "Some guy keyed Ben Sachs's Volvo, that's what they're upset about."

"Who?"

"I think they said he goes to Landon."

"Is it Ben's car or his parents' car?"

Greg didn't know. "Hey, isn't your dad the one at basketball games who—"

"I should probably go look for Courtney," I said.

"Nice meeting you, little sister."

In the kitchen I saw Rasheeda, our point guard, who waved and called out my name but had nothing much to say to me, nor I to her. We cast our eyes around the room and back at each other and exchanged speechless smiles.

I went looking for the bathroom, just to give myself a purpose, then returned to the kitchen. My sister's legs appeared on the back stairs, negotiating one step at a time. She was gripping the banister with one hand and holding her shoes in the other. Above her stood Rob Golden, studying her progress. He wore a letter jacket and a Duke baseball cap, and he had white tape over one ear. In the weak light I couldn't make out the flavor of his grin, whether it was affectionate or just amused, but my first impression was that he was curious to see whether she would fall.

"Hells bells!" she squealed when she saw me. "What are you doing? Are you drinking? Are you having fun?" A cup of beer had found its way into my hands. I didn't much like the taste, but I was doing my best. I took a gulp. "Yeah!" Courtney cheered. Then she said, "This is Rob." She gestured behind her, unaware of how far away he was, but just then he hopped down after her and handled her from behind. I wanted to pry his fingers off her arms. Then she herself shook loose of him.

We've met before, I wanted to say, but Rob wasn't looking at me. Close-up, I could see the deep dimple in his chin and the red vessels of his bummed-out eyes. What his disappointment had been about, Courtney explained to me later, on the drive home. Tanya had gone with her friends to another party. I was behind the wheel, even though I had only a learner's permit and wasn't supposed to drive after dark, and I went slowly through a maze of curving roads, hounded by headlights bearing down from behind. We had to pull over to consult the Montgomery County map book several times. It was so much darker than when we'd come, and the radio was off, and the meaningless names of suburban courts and circles glowered at us from small signs.

What Rob wanted, what they all wanted: "Not in a bathroom," Courtney said. "Uh-uh."

Certain boys may have hoped that by removing our hooded sweatshirts they would summon the lacy ladies of Cinemax, but that wasn't Courtney. Under her sweatshirt were a cotton bra and a complicated heart.

"Did you see they had those padded toilet seats?" she asked.

"Yes! Oh my god."

"Hey. Do you have any cigarettes?"

"Um," I said. "Do we smoke?"

"Maybe we should stop and get some. Let's, okay?"

"I think we're lost."

"Well there's got to be a 7-Eleven around here somewhere."

"Do you think you would . . . with him?" I asked her.

The sex talks we'd been given by teachers (not our parents, oh no) leaned heavily on the word *special*. When a man and a woman have special feelings about each other, they do this special thing with their special parts.

"He's very—how should I put this?" She twisted her face up and I knew exactly what she was getting at, or thought I did.

"Large," I said. "Humongous."

"That's not a word," she said.

"It *is*!" I said. "I bet he has a *humongous* cock. A big kielbasa!"

She lowered her head and shook it back and forth a few times, then brought it back up with a jerk and stared at the road.

"So what's up with the tape on his ear?" I asked.

"It's something from wrestling. Cauliflower ear."

"Is it, like, cauliflower in your ear?"

"Not actual cauliflower—"

"One time I had cheeseburger ear, and I had to tape this bun over it—"

"Seriously, you have got to stop talking about meat. I'm so going to hurl," she moaned.

"You are?"

"Just keep driving. Did you have fun?"

"I talked to Rasheeda. And this guy Greg."

"Greg Jacobs?"

"Yeah."

"What did you talk to him about?"

"He called you literal."

"What's that supposed to mean?"

"I told him my name was Becca!" I'd forgotten until then.

"That's cute. You're cute," she said, as though she'd just come to this conclusion. "Did Greg tell you you were cute?" She leaned her head against the window and then quickly straightened up and opened her eyes very wide. "I'm a dizzy lizzy."

"Do you know where we are?"

"As soon as we find a 7-Eleven, we can just ask them where it is."

"Where what is?"

"The 7-Eleven!"

"It's almost midnight. Mom and Dad said—"

"They're so asleep right now. They pretend like they're waiting up, but they fall asleep."

"Dad's probably up watching TV."

"Nope. Asleep."

It was so dark. I was afraid I might never find the way home, and that was hardly my only fear. "Do you think something's going to happen to him?" I asked.

"Don't *worrrrrry* about it."

"Don't talk to me like that."

"I'm just saying. The other people that he used to work with, they're the ones who did whatever they did."

"But we don't even really know what happened, or what Dad—"

"There's nothing else I need to know. It's like—"

She moaned again and told me to pull over. "Like, *now*." She lunged for the wheel and I had to push her hands away. Before the car had even come to a full stop, she opened the door and threw up neatly into the gutter.

"Are you all right?" I asked, when we were back on the road.

"Good thing Mom keeps the Fortrus stocked with Kleenex," she said, dabbing at her mouth with a tissue she'd taken from the glove compartment. "Where the fuck are we?"

2005

The girl was bold. I hardly thought Nina would pursue the driving lesson after the night at the club, that is to say her night at the club and my night at Burger King, but the following week Daniel called, to thank me for offering to teach her. I was wary, but I still liked her, and I thought I could be—I want to say *of service*, though that sounds too grand. She needed someone, not me exactly, but someone older and female and maybe I was as close as she was going to get. I agreed to it. And when I saw her the next Sunday I didn't feel uneasy any longer. I was all aflutter, in fact. Here she was in crepe-soled creepers, sauntering but bashful, bashful but sauntering, eyeing me with half a smile. A couple of broken leaves were caught in her hair, as though she'd been lying on the ground, and she wore a black peacoat with a torn plaid lining and bright pink pants she'd no doubt found at some vintage place. You could see a small bulge of skin above the waistband, her shirt was so short. Out of breath, coat sleeves pulled down over her fists, carrying an overstuffed backpack, she told me that one of her friends had come out as gay and that one of her teachers had not been at school in two weeks and was rumored to have had a nervous breakdown. Every so often, as if this were an inside joke we already shared, she spoke in the voice of a robot.

Her fingernails were painted blue and the sidewalks were damp, and we strolled in the direction of Independence Avenue, where I'd parked my father's car.

"Last year, I was such a loser," she told me.

"No you weren't."

"I was! And this year I'm still a loser, but now I like it."

"You're not a loser."

"Why shouldn't I be?"

I learned that the rectangular object in the outer pocket of her backpack was not an MP3 player but a deck of tarot cards. "I'm learning to tell fortunes," she said. Then she stopped to pick something up off the ground. a gray moth, with long antennae and a large, furry body.

"I'm naming him Vince," she said.

"Hey Vince, what're you doing out here in January?"

"Do you know that moths are messengers? They travel back and forth between this world and the afterlife," she said. She touched the creature and it rose a few inches, its wings sputtering. I stepped away as it fell back into her hand. She touched it again and this time it dropped to the pavement.

"Poor Vince," she said.

"He's neither here nor there," I said.

But then without another glance downward she skipped ahead.

"How's basketball?" I asked.

"I've been riding the bench," she said cheerfully.

The sun was on its way out by the time we began the lesson. An irony here was that I was known in my family as a poor driver: lead-footed, heedless of posted limits, a reaper of citations. Nor am I a natural teacher. *Okay, turn the car on. Pull out. Stay in the lane.* All my instructions took as their premise that she already knew how to operate the vehicle. Which she basically did, at least she was easier on the pedals than I was. Slowly she drove the car toward the stop sign at the end of the block, halting twice before we reached it, once because of a branch in the road she'd mistaken for a squirrel, and then some ten feet before the intersection, braking prematurely. I kept the radio off the same way my father had kept the radio off when I first learned to drive—though after one lesson in which I proved a less careful student than my older sister, he'd outsourced the job to an unflinching and deadpan instructor from Washington Driving School, who taught via sarcastic suggestion: you might want to try stopping *before* the stop sign next time.

Nina checked the mirrors every few seconds. And then we passed through an intersection, pleasure overcame her, and she said, "I'm driving!"

Because it was Dad's car, and I hadn't told him why I was borrowing it, I was especially cautious. First I directed Nina to a supermarket parking lot to practice, but there were so many shoppers and little children barely over bumper-height, and Nina was looking every which way, not at the shoppers and their kids but at entrances and exits and occupied cars. She was at an age when the world is small and run-ins are common, and you are always hunting for your classmates, your crushes.

But there we were, and we drove on, the river to our left with its drowned garbage and fallen tree limbs, the parkway below, a cloud-blanket drifting slowly to the east. People were pitched forward in the chill. A man in a long coat spit onto the sidewalk. When I'd learned to drive, I couldn't get out of my head how easy it would have been to kill myself and/or another person with a mere spasm of the wrist. Nina, however, seemed immediately confident.

I could've sworn that no time at all had passed since I had learned to drive, and yet red lights took forever to turn green.

We drove up into Northwest, and as we neared a playground she said she wanted to take a break. We let ourselves in through a chain-link gate, passed a stone water fountain—the sight of which recalled me to the smell of playground water fountains I'd drunk from twenty years earlier—and sat on the too-small swings, knees level with our bellies, chomping on Orbit but earthbound, our legs too long.

I picture us now not beached on a playground swing set but sitting high above the city on hanging platforms, the entire government small beneath us, grit raining from our shoes. She was smart, smarter than I was, she asked me what I thought of artificial intelligence and whether I liked Thoreau, who in her opinion was boring, and whether I believed in an afterlife and what was my take on some band I'd never heard of. Notions rolled out of her in one long stream. To be honest there's nothing that looks that good to me right now, she said. I used to want to be a professor like my dad used to be but then he became a lawyer. I don't know, maybe I could be a lawyer. Too many lawyers as it is, I said. But then I saw her face and backtracked and said some of them do cool things.

"It must be nice to have a sister," she said.

"Sisters are hard sometimes."

"What's hard about it?"

"I don't know. I have two, and sometimes we get along and sometimes we really don't."

"You mean you fight?"

"It's not even fighting. It's that you're bound to this person who you would probably never otherwise be friends with. And you bring out the worst in each other a lot more than you bring out the best in each other. My older sister still thinks that she knows better than me about everything."

"So do you wish she wasn't your sister?"

"I might as well wish that I'm not me."

Nina and I slid slowly from the swings and walked out of the park. My phone tickled my thigh, and it was a text from Rob.

Whassup?

I'm with Nina. My high school girl

What're you doing

Swinging

I heard Nina giggle. She had gone on ahead and appeared to be bumming a cigarette from some random guy, who must have been thirty at least. He seemed all too happy to oblige. What got me was the way she had positioned her hand on her hip, or maybe it was the way he was leaning over her. I froze: oh crap. Then I said her name, too loudly. Nina turned, and I saw she had the face of someone who knew exactly what she was doing, although she didn't really know, she couldn't have.

It happened so quickly, the transition from plastic horses and jumbo drawing pads to lingerie and lip gloss, from playing Marco Polo and holding tea parties underwater to lying beside the pool, soaking in the light. The magazines disclosed ten awesome beauty secrets and ten ways to tell if he really does like you and ten top accessories for fall. No more "tummy," "poop," or "mommy," but instead "bogus," "spaz," and "dick," or whatever they said these days.

Another text from him.

Let's meet up

Nina had only just passed through it, the time of girls' disappearing. They fell from the sky, from greater and lesser heights, and slid out of their girl-selves on the way to becoming someone's girlfriend or the vice president of the French Club. At high schools the expired shells were molted off every which place, in bathrooms and classrooms, stuffed into lockers, useless. One moment you were adrift in the airspace above the field hockey field, and then down you came, tumbling, nauseated, Icarus in kilt and cleats.

The man walked away from us. I told her to lose the cigarette.

"Why?"

"I just can't condone that."

"I could hold it farther from you."

"Put it out," I said, and then I asked whether she wanted to get dinner. A friend of mine might join us, I said.

I was driving now, because it was getting dark.

"So is this guy your boyfriend?" she asked.

"Unclear. Not exactly."

"What's it like to have a real boyfriend?"

Did I even know the answer?

"My dad is never going to get me a car," she said. "It's the Metro for-evah."

Eventually, I told her, you will have a car. And a nonsecret boyfriend.

The "pan-Asian" restaurant occupied a long narrow room with booths on either side, low-hanging lamps sheltering each booth from the darkness of the unfinished ceiling. Beautiful young women brought pots of steaming tea and bowls of food on wooden slabs to husbands and wives, to bright-faced students, to old friends. There was a sweet, hot smell. Rob had said to meet him there, and we found him at a table engrossed in his handheld device.

As we said our airy hellos and then read our menus, it was as though I knew every one of his motions already, each rustle, each breath, and I knew, therefore, that I was hardly out of the woods when it came to him. In fact I had barely entered them. In winter: storms coming and going, wires down, lines crossed.

I told him we'd been learning to drive.

Oh, where did you go? To Turtle Park and back again, up Reno and down Nebraska, over hill and dale and Rock Creek. Which we all agreed was a poor name for a waterway. I ordered stir-fry and they ordered soup, or was it the other way around, but theirs looked right and mine looked wrong.

"Can you do this?" Rob asked, and he took a few twined rice noodles from his bowl and stuck them above his lips, so that they dangled down like the tusks of a noodle walrus.

Nina copied him. I couldn't have joined in if I'd wanted to, not with what I'd ordered, but then again I didn't want to. I wanted them to stop. My companions suddenly seemed tipsy, though they weren't drinking. Nina was pink. Rob was tilting his head right and left, so that the noodles swayed. I was quiet, waiting for a beat I could catch, but I had no rhythm at all. Once again she ought to have been teaching me, as I was going about it all wrong and steering her toward the dragons besides.

Rob asked her what school she went to, whether she liked it there, what bands were her favorites. This had the feel of teasing more than questioning, which is to say I don't think he cared what the answers were. His directness made her shyer than she'd been a moment ago, and she answered shyly—coyly?—consulting her soup bowl before she spoke. Rob was an opportunistic listener, waiting for her to say something that grabbed him and then jumping in with his response, no matter whether she had more to say. He did the same with me, I realized, but when I was talking to him I got too tripped up to notice things like that.

When she was in the bathroom, I told him that Nina had a secret boyfriend. "Or not a boyfriend exactly. It's her former math teacher. Or tutor."

"What's his name?"

"Sam, or Samed."

"Am I supposed to choose?"

"He has two names. And he's older, which I don't know, is that bad?"

"Yes."

"I just mean, like, two or three years older."

"If I had a daughter, I wouldn't let her go out with some older guy with two names. No way."

Because I thought he was joking, I waited for him to ease up. He didn't.

"This guy is like a nerdy student from Turkey. I don't think he's too dangerous," I said. Rob didn't seem at all swayed by that. I saw Nina come out of the bathroom and lowered my voice. "Don't tell her I told you."

He drew his finger across his lips.

Although I offered to split the check with Rob, I found myself, in the bathroom afterward, resentful that he hadn't insisted on paying for all of us. By the time I walked back out to the dining room, he and Nina had already left the table. I could see them standing outside with their backs to the door of the restaurant. She was nearly his height, and they stood close enough that their silhouettes had merged into one. Granted, it was dark out, and they were wearing bulky coats, and as soon as I stepped out the door it seemed to me I'd been too sensitive, imagining things.

While Nina was distracted by something on her phone, I asked Rob did he want to get together later, after I dropped Nina off. He told me he had a breakfast meeting the next day. In other words, no.

I didn't realize how late it was until Nina and I started back. On Vane Street, Daniel opened the door to the building just as she hit the steps. "Long lesson!" he said, with false cheer.

"We had dinner too," Nina said.

"No accidents?"

"She did great," I said.

"Bye!" she said, walking past him, through the door.

I stood beneath him, at the bottom of the stairs, and though I might've come up or he might've come down, we both stayed where we were. "She did all right?" he asked, wanting more reassurance than I could possibly give him, not just about her driving but about her entire state of being. His worries were vast.

"She's a natural."

"I've been meaning to teach her, but it was just one thing after another, really. Thanks so much for offering."

"No problem."

"Maybe next time, if you do it again," he began, tentatively. "If you do go to dinner or something, if you could let me know . . ."

"I should've called you about that. I'm sorry."

"You have my number, right?"

"It's in my phone, yes."

"It's just that she sometimes forgets to let me know—"

"She's sixteen, I guess."

"Right! But she did okay?"

"She did."

I entered my own building, and as I went up the stairs something started to squeeze my insides, I was tetchy on the landing and passed through the door to my apartment with a full-blown sense of grievance I couldn't assign to anything specific. Since I'd come back to Washington I'd become more quick to anger, I noticed, and maybe that had a positive side—I wasn't depressed anymore! I was fucking pissed off!—but it wasn't so positive overall.

I got down on my belly next to the bed and looked for my gun. It wasn't there. I started to worry, until I remembered that one night I'd become unnerved by its presence and had stuck it under the kitchen sink, behind the spare paper towel rolls. I'd put it inside of a large freezer bag, like evidence in storage. I fetched it and eased it out of the bag and held it in my palm, then held it with two hands, posing.

I walked around like that, wanting to shoot, feeling like Elvis as I aimed at my pillow, my small TV, my refrigerator, my dirty dishes. *I have to stop digging in the muck*, I thought. A little less conversation, a little more action!

My head hurt. I put the gun down. I sat down. I looked out my window at the windows of Nina's apartment, where the lights were already off.

The next day I wished I were a wanderer, a rambler, a hobo out of an old song or a folk tale, nobody's daughter. I wished I were not in our nation's capital but out on the plains, or in some bleached-out motel on the Mexican side of the border. Instead I parked my dad's car on Albemarle Street. I was returning the car and meant to return something else too.

The neighbors' houses, stripped of their holiday lights, squatted grimly on hills of ivy. The steps to our own house needed hosing down. I didn't want to go inside. Much as I understood that my failings and failures couldn't be blamed on this house, I still felt as though it had sapped too much out of me and that I'd been hobbled by it. I bided my time in the car, the little gun in my purse.

Or was I just avoiding my father? His sudden outbursts, his unacknowledged, indescribable needs, his heavy heart—I didn't know what to do with him.

No one answered the door, and I let myself in. "Hello? Dad?" I heard footsteps on the basement stairs and then there he was, stumbling up from underground in his rowing singlet, his face reddish and sweaty and suddenly too large, with too much of that damp skin on it.

"Hello!" he said.

"Hi. I brought the car back."

"You didn't have to—I could've come out on the Metro to get it."

"That's okay," I said. I knew he would've done it, had I asked. "Thanks for lending it to me."

There was a basket of clean laundry by the stairs, not yet folded. I still wasn't used to it, his doing his own laundry. And out of nowhere I had the thought, *He needs someone over here taking care of him*, though it wasn't the laundry that was the issue, he was perfectly capable of laundry, and there was nothing about that basket of clothes or about the house generally or the way he himself looked that suggested he needed any special help. Even so, I understood in that moment why it had bugged Courtney when I'd moved out.

"Are you sure you don't need it for longer? You could keep it for the weekend."

I shook my head.

"Let me clean up a little, and I'll drive you back over."

"You don't need to—"

"I'm not busy."

"Weren't you exercising?"

"I was just finishing. Happy to drive you."

The heaviness I'd been dreading beforehand was not present now: sometimes he was suffused with it and sometimes not at all. You never knew.

He went upstairs to rinse off and change, and I sat in the living room. I reached into my purse for a magazine and then remembered what else was in there. I had to give it to him. And what could I tell him? When he came down I pulled the pistol out of my bag and said, "I brought this back. I can't have this." And then: "It freaks me out to have it."

"Oh," he said. He looked at it, then shook his head very slightly, almost talking to himself. "If you can't have it—"

"I can't have it."

"I'll put it in the safe." And up he went again, to his study, where he had a safe bolted to the wall behind his desk.

It was as though I were trying to unload not only the thing itself but some excess of maleness I'd been saddled with—because of my dad? Was it in trying to please him that I'd become more of a boy than was good for me? Or in trying to compensate for him? It was a subtle thing, for it's not like anybody who met me would've found me especially masculine, but there was a way in which I tended to tamp down those parts of myself I found girly, preferring to stand around making wisecracks. Although I couldn't really get rid of that by returning the gun, I felt better after I did.

I heard the phone ringing, then the toilet flushing, and so I went to answer the phone myself.

"Hello?"

"Hello?" echoed a woman's voice, surprised. "Is—Tim there?"

"He's not available just now. Who's this?"

"It's Valerie. Who's this?"

"Helen," I said, shortly.

"Ah. His daughter Helen?"

"Yes."

"This is Valerie," she said again. "If you wouldn't mind telling him I called."

"Sure."

"Valerie called," I told Dad when he came back. "Thanks," was all he said in response. Then he clapped his hands and asked me was I ready to leave.

"Who is Valerie?"

"She's the, uh, a woman who calls sometimes."

"A woman who calls sometimes?"

"We've had dinner together."

I couldn't get any more out of him. I was glad to know there was a woman who called him, though as it sank in—the fact of these occasional calls and at least one dinner—I grew tense. Oh please! I

scolded myself. For I knew what I was feeling and it was: abandoned. I let him drive me back. Mass Ave was deserted, nothing
but dark buildings. More Washington arcana spilled out of Dad as
he drove, and I let it wash over me, the sound of my dad when he
was feeling good, or good enough.

1986–87

A fatefully slim envelope, return address Yale, arrived at our house in mid-December. Courtney had been rejected—not rolled over into the regular applicant pool, or wait-listed, but denied outright. I think we were all shocked that such a thing could happen to my straight-A, near-perfect-SAT-score, lacrosse-prospect, exemplary sister. Nobody said a word about it. Courtney herself didn't let anything show: she bit down on her disappointment and finished her other applications. But Dad, oh Dad was so upset. They'd made a mistake, he believed, they'd mixed up her file with someone else's. Our mother, who was sorry about it for Courtney's sake but didn't take it so personally, had to entreat him not to call up Yale to insist that they correct the error. Probably he tried to, regardless. Did he blame me for her rejection? Did Courtney? Not in any overt way, but I can't say for sure. They blamed me, and the universe, and probably themselves too. The small blue pennant on the kitchen corkboard was tossed in the garbage.

By then we'd already played a few games of the type that always led off the season, against teams from outside our conference, which were often blowouts one way or the other. We'd lost a game by twenty points and won the next by more than thirty. Then came our first league game, at a girls' school in Virginia, and though we were ahead for most of it, we threw it away in the end. We were sloppy. There was nothing Coach hated more, and during the desolate van ride back home she delivered a droning sermon from behind the wheel, which was not on one subject but shifted here and there; it was about attitude, it was about respect, it was about commitment, it was about showing up ready to play. It was about hustle. And it was about respect again. Can't have a team without it. Can't win games without it. It's respect for the game that helps you comprehend your role on this team, she said. It's respect that keeps you from throwing up stupid shots, or throwing an elbow at your opponent. Those girls you just played, they weren't more skilled than you but they did use what they had. They weren't faster than you but they did hustle.

We were tired and brooding, half-listening. The city lights were colored smudges, and it was as if Coach's words were outside the windows too, filtered through cold glass. I started to dream the rest of her speech, it was about power and it was about fear, then about the color blue, it was about a trial taking place in the gym and about some papers I was required to alphabetize, and at last it was about loving one another as if we were all sisters—this just before the engine shut off and we were dispensed into the parking lot.

My actual sister was drifting away. Only a month earlier I'd thought we might become friends, something like friends anyway, but after the rejection from Yale she grew more distant. She started to play differently too. She'd always been a precise athlete, her form exact, deserving of an A grade in the subject of basketball, but now she had something she hadn't had before. She stole the ball, sometimes snatched it right out of an opponent's hands, she came home from games with bruises on her knees and on her arms. She never cracked a smile. She played angry, and we won the next five games in a row, three at a Christmas tournament and then the first two games of the new year.

Like everyone on the team I was drawn into Courtney's field. I started to play better, if only out of fear. But then came the absence of fear. The apologetic, chattering voice in my head had quieted, and I heard only *yes!* and *yes!* and *yes!* I was drawn to the ball, and it to me, and I hung each shot like an ornament on a branch. One day Coach said to me, "When you go against Courtney in practice, you're full of fight, but against anybody else you get nice. You're too nice. Pretend every single one of your opponents is your sister." And so I did, I saw Courtneys everywhere.

The relationship between my brain and my body shifted. In the next game, and in the next one after that, I *was* my body, which was strangely like being someone else and being no one at all. In movies these moments are given to us in slow motion, the sounds of the crowd muted, the ball crashing on the floor and swishing through the net, but for me it wasn't like that. It was fast, grunting, awesome.

Coach started pulling me off the bench sooner, usually halfway into the first quarter. I would crouch by the scorers' table, waiting for the whistle to blow so that I could go in the game, so nervous! Convinced, always, that my streak was about to end. As I jogged out, I would forget everything, all our plays, which girl I was supposed to guard, my own name, and then remember again. I didn't always do well, but I was a part of things. And because people saw Courtney, they saw me, and they talked about us as a unit, the Atherton sisters, though we were in fact not the unit I wished we were. For all that time we spent together at practice and games and driving to and fro, for all the shots sunk and high fives, Courtney had gone away from me.

Dad still came to watch us, but he was not so fanatical anymore— and at home he was likewise subdued. He slipped in and out of the house. He slept in his clothes sometimes. There were pouches under his eyes, and his hair turned from mostly brown to slush-colored.

He and I were the early risers of our family. Dad typically left for work before 6:00, and one morning I crept downstairs at around quarter past and went out to our porch to pick up the newspaper. It was a half hour or so before sunrise. I read by the porch light while my mother slept. But what was I reading? Five or six paragraphs about a downed plane, the role of the Israelis, the assertions of this or that official.

My father must have been sitting in his car. All of a sudden he came surging up the steps with rigid arms and a rebuke at the ready, but then I think he recognized he couldn't actually scold me for reading the paper.

"Let's go inside," he said.

He turned on the kettle, and we sat at the kitchen table, silently. He must have been trying to formulate an explanation. "I've been advised," he began, then stopped. "Okay. What questions do you have?"

It was early. It was dark. Things I'd read bobbed around my head, just out of reach. I wanted him to read me a story, or teach me to ride a bike again.

"What's going to happen?" I asked.

"We're going to be fine," he said. "Just fine."

That's a bunch of bull, I wanted to say.

Maybe he saw it in my face. He lowered his eyes. The kettle shrieked, and he stood to take it off the burner. He turned back toward me and asked, "How is school going?" His voice was as gentle as I'd ever heard it, but he didn't have any words to go with the gentleness. It was all he knew how to ask. The time we'd once spent together, such as it was, had always been centered on activities, on biking or skiing, or trips to Roy Rogers for burgers, but then he took a job that consumed all his hours, and then I was too old to want to ride bikes with him.

"It's fine." I wanted to say so much more than that. "It's okay."

"Good."

He started to spoon instant coffee into a cup, and then he asked me whether I wanted some. I said I did, so that I could drink it with him, and in the silence that followed, we discovered a new activity: that wordless coffee-drinking itself. I started waking up even earlier, listening for Dad's footsteps. I would pull on a long-sleeved shirt over my pajamas and go downstairs and into the kitchen, where I would mix a little of his instant coffee into hot milk. While Dad heated water in the kettle, I would put milk in the microwave and watch to make sure it didn't boil over, though often my attention would wander, last night's dream would for a moment or two retake my porous 6:00 a.m. brain, and the milk would spume over the sides of the cup. I would sponge the milk scum off the microwave carousel, and then we would drink our coffees, in loud, slurpy sips.

Because of the scandal my father would have to resign, but his new boss allowed him to give three months' notice, so that he was able to remain until early March, and his lawyer persuaded the joint committees to postpone the date of his testimony. We were living inside the temporary shelter of those deferrals, a lean-to of scavenged time. It was a chilly, exposed place. In spite of the restricted access to information on Albemarle Street, we all knew that it wouldn't be easy for our father to find another job. The thing that scared me was to see him pick up the comics and read them straight through, *Prince Valiant* and *Momma* and *Family Circus*, all of them. Or: once I passed by the study and saw him playing one of our computer games. He'd never had any interest in those things before.

In the short time that Courtney went out with Rob, she never seemed in love with him so much as preoccupied by him, waiting for his calls and then answering them briskly, as though he were a nuisance. My suspicion was that she undertook Rob in order to undertake sex, sex as another entry in her list of achievements. Deflowering: check. But after the deed was done, and done a few times, she found herself attached to him and irritated by him and confused about what to do with him. Which was not all that different from how she felt about me.

She stared into space. She fouled out of two games.

One night Tanya, who was our team's equipment manager, drove us home from an away game. I sat in a cramped backseat seemingly designed for the legless, making origami of my limbs and looking at Tanya's long neck in the space between her seat and the headrest.

"Your dad couldn't make it," Tanya said to Courtney, who was in the passenger seat.

"He had to meet with his lawyer. I'm sure he's hating it," Courtney said.

"He told you that?" I asked, but the two of them went on talking to each other.

"Why does he have a lawyer again?" Tanya asked.

"Somebody decided that he and some other people he used to work with aren't eligible to have White House counsel," Courtney said. "They hung them out to dry."

"I meant, what's he accused of?"

Courtney exhaled deliberately. "They are accused," she said, "of violating a law that said you can't give military aid to the Contra rebels in Nicaragua. But you know what? It's not even the law anymore! Congress overturned it."

It was as if she had learned Mandarin Chinese on the sly.

"How do you know all that?" I asked, louder this time. "Mom and Dad told you?"

"Yeah, right," she said. "I read the newspaper at school, in the library."

"You found out Dad was meeting with his lawyer from the newspaper?"

"No, Dad told me that."

"Okay," Tanya said. "There was a law, and now it's not a law anymore."

"But they broke it when it was a law, right? Doesn't that still count as breaking it?" I asked.

Courtney sighed again.

Only much later did I think anything of the fact that Courtney would've seen Dick Mitchell during that period, a period when my father wasn't supposed to contact him. She and Rob spent time at his house on the weekends. I thought about the plush suburban manor I'd seen when we'd gone to the party there. I pictured the two of them sunk into an overstuffed sofa, watching cable, this vision not sharp and realistic but fogged with envy: romantic, transcendent Saturday-afternoon cable.

My sister did mention Mitchell at least once. This was one evening when she'd come home late from dinner at their house. He'd let Rob and her each have a glass of wine, she told me, and had said the funniest things. He's so cool, she said.

Our own house had become gloomy. It sounded so much better over there, for even though Rob's stepdad was in the same bag as our dad, he was cool and our dad was not.

The goals were worthy . . . , said the president in his State of the Union address, *but we did not achieve what we wished, and serious mistakes were made in trying to do so.*

The first snow of the year came in late January. On the radio they warned of baffled traffic, dangerous conditions, abandoned cars. White out: the city was redacted. Tufts of snow topped the bus signs, and lost scarves lay wet and mangled in the road. People covered their little red ears.

School closed, and Anthony and I found each other outside, in a muddle of kids still deciding what to do with themselves. He said I had to come to Georgetown with him. Why would I do that? I asked. He thought the movie theater where he worked would still be open. His boss there would never close, not for a tornado, not for a tidal wave. He was going. There was no reason to go with him but for a snow-giddiness that drew me slipping and sliding, and we skidded all the way down Wisconsin, pushing each other, running in circles, burying snow in each other's necks.

Then kissing. In the projection booth, it was. He had his hand up my shirt, he murmured "Oh god" as he sank his face into my hair, and that seemed like something he'd seen in a movie, but he was trembling too, while in the theater below a lone man watched the film. I did let Anthony unbutton my shirt, I'd sipped the vodka he'd taken from a cabinet, and I snuck my hand under his shirt too, reaching for his thin waist, soft in spite of how skinny. Patchwork of temperature, warm, cold, warm, cold, his lips, my hands, his breath, the air that came from someplace. The room didn't seem clean enough for taking off clothes, everything black and metal, stacks of reels gathering dust, and there was dust on top of a file cabinet, thick and dense as a rug. Way too suddenly, his hand was inside my underwear and then his finger was in me. It hurt. Anthony! He pulled his hand out of my pants and leaped back. Shaken. We both were. I buttoned myself up. Here was this person who'd been sort of my best friend. And now what.

We stayed there, holding hands, for a few minutes after the movie ended, and when at last we zombie-walked down to the lobby, that man, the audience, was still shuffling around in his coat and hat, reading the blown-up reviews on the walls. He had on tinted glasses and hid his baldness under a maroon snow hat with a gold pompom.

"Did you like it?" Anthony asked him in that way of teenagers talking to adults, half ironic, half surprised that it is even possible to talk like this. It was his fourth time seeing it, the man said. There was something he wanted, he looked at us too eagerly, making me nervous, though all he did was pour some M&Ms out of a pack he was holding and push them into his mouth.

Although we tried to make fun of the man after he left, the joking fell flat. By then it was six or seven. We walked along the lit-up sidewalk, the darkness yellowed by the streetlamps and the headlights of the occasional taxi or SUV, the tires slurping through a stillness that made it seem much later than it was. The snow had stopped, it had been trampled, driven over, and we couldn't tell whether the buses were running.

"That was sad," I said.

"What?"

"That man all by himself."

"Lots of people go to the movies by themselves. I go to the movies by myself."

"Yeah but still. There was something about him."

"Maybe that's just your imagination."

"Really, everything is my imagination, though. I'm imagining you," I told him.

"And how do I look to your imagination?"

"Cold."

"I'm serious."

I didn't know the answer. I liked him more than just about anybody, but I wanted to get away. I wished that I could think of a joke to tell or that a bus would come.

"You're a fortress," he said.

"That's what we call our car."

"I'm not talking about your car."

His lips twitched. I nodded. Then we trudged very slowly up the hill. It was dark, and I assumed that by the time I got home my parents would be angry at me for coming in so late, and I also wondered whether they would see that there was something different about me, that I'd been drinking and messing around, but it wasn't actually that late, and they didn't notice anything.

2005

The trouble with sisters is this: any time you have more than one of them, the configuration is highly unstable. Were I a scientist of family dynamics, I might dedicate myself to studying systems of n sisters for $n>2$, which are continually perturbed by half-licked wounds and false fronts, secret competitions, unstated agendas. I felt this whenever I was in the presence of both Courtney and Maggie. Though I often looked forward to seeing either of them one-on-one, I shied away from the three of us. Still, there was this idea that it was good for us all to get together—not my idea, probably not anybody's, but it remained part of our collective thinking. And so when Maggie came down for a literature conference at Georgetown in mid-January, Courtney invited us both to dinner at her new house, on a night when Hugo had other plans. Maggie agreed to skip the gender studies cash bar, and I said of course I'd come along.

I met Maggie, who had borrowed Dad's car, at the conference, in a building lobby full of academics wearing paper name badges. There was a peculiar vibe in that lobby, which I chalked up to equal parts enthusiasm, ego, and insecurity, this inference drawn from my eavesdropping, while waiting for Maggie, on a few young men in V-neck sweaters who were absorbed in a conversation about sub-limated lexicons, etc., making noisy assertions and subtly craning their necks. On the way to Courtney's, I detected some of the same frenetic spirit in Maggie: she was flushed and spoke quickly. She told me Dad had come to her session, where she'd been one of three people presenting papers, and that he'd seemed to appreciate it, that is to say he had not fallen asleep, even during the other papers, like the one that had addressed the performance of ecstasis in colonial Latin American verse.

"Who among us does not enjoy a good performance of ecsta-sis?" I asked.

"I don't think he was all that into the presentation per se."

"Of course he was proud of you. I'm sure he was thrilled." Weeks earlier she'd told me the subject of her own paper, I'd for-gotten what it was exactly. She specialized in early Tudor drama.

She was at the wheel, sitting straight up like yoga had taught her to do and driving as though she'd gone to Courtney's new place a dozen times already. The farther we went, the taller the trees looked, scattered around ever-larger houses. "He said he hadn't seen much of you lately," she said.

"I saw him, like, a week ago. A week and a half," I said, feeling accused, no matter that Maggie was only reporting what he'd said. And then I remembered that I hadn't heard from Nina for roughly the same amount of time. I'd assumed she would call to ask about another driving lesson, or to tell me when her next basketball game would be, and after she didn't, I'd left a message for her. She hadn't returned the call. It made no sense to interpret her silence as any-thing but a reminder that she was young and busy, a sixteen-year-old not hugely invested in a friendship with me (which, to be sure, was an unusual friendship, with uncertain protocols). Even so I felt the lack of her.

"I'm going with him to the doctor on Tuesday," I said.

"The cardiologist?"

"Yeah. Just a checkup I think."

"So what's going on with all that?"

"I'm not sure. I'd like to ask him more about it. I don't know what to ask."

"Me either. I got a book about heart disease," she said.

"I should get a book."

"But really we need to get him to tell us more about what's happening with him."

She was right. Instead of asking about his heart I'd spent all that time trying to learn what had transpired during the Reagan administration, and now I began to confess as much to Maggie, in the hopes that she would absolve me.

"You want to write about Iran-Contra?" she asked.

"I was trying to write about Dad, you know. About what he did, and how it affected us."

"So did you interview him?"

"I tried to get in a question here and there."

She said the same thing our mother had said—"Huh"—but without Mom's note of disapproval. For Maggie it was straight-up confusion, which made me want to explain myself. I tried to.

"The past isn't even past?" she asked.

"Actually I think the past is past, but we don't have a handle on it. They never told us about it. I wanted to know—"

Just then we pulled up to the house, a doozy of a residence, three stories, red brick, two huge oaks presiding over a tidy yard. We parked but sat there in our seats for a moment, looking up at the place. And before we could reach the door and take hold of its brass knocker, it opened, and Courtney stood there gloating, or I took it for gloating. Inside she showed us around, while we were still in our coats. We praised the arched doorways and picture molding, the large windows, the kitchen the size of my apartment. She made sure to point out all the things that were not quite right and/or needed fixing—because of the trees the house didn't get good light in the mornings, there were issues with the bathroom tile, and so on. Maggie managed to sympathize, to be engaged by questions of paint color and furnishings, but I didn't have much to say about Courtney's decor. I couldn't tell whether she was still mad at me.

No doubt she was, but she didn't shoot me any loaded looks or hollow smiles, and I took this to mean we were going to aim higher than that, for the evening at least.

In the kitchen, I picked up a book from the counter, a thirty-day program for optimal wellness. My sister was into that kind of thing: on the advice of a book, she would throw away the cheese and crackers and fill the cabinets with brewer's yeast and kelp and herbal supplements. She would elaborate on the consequences of various vitamin deficiencies and exhort me to stop using a microwave. She would put arugula in the blender and drink the result. And then she would have a cigarette.

"Do you want to borrow that book?" she asked.

"I think I'm probably well enough."

"It's really good. I learned so much about how our hormones are affected by corn."

"Maybe not *optimally* well."

"Corn is in practically everything," Courtney said. "And it gets cross-contaminated by other toxins, from other crops."

"So corn is bad?"

"It's not quite that simple. You should just read it."

When we were kids, our parents had worked long hours, and Courtney had looked after us, in her way. She'd been the choreographer of our three-person dance routines. She'd chosen our games, booby-trapped our rooms. One time she'd found a plastic slide someone had left out on the street and dragged it home for Maggie to use. She'd picked a summer camp for us all to go to, after seeing an ad for it in *The Post*'s Sunday magazine. She put Band-Aids on us, liked to feed us snacks of marshmallows or salami rolled into flutes.

But by the time she started at Brown, she seemed to have forgotten us. During her first visit home, at Thanksgiving, she announced with a flourish that she had nothing to be thankful for. Dad said she might at least be thankful that she wasn't homeless, and a long argument about homelessness—and AIDS, and Reagan's legacy, and Marion Barry—ensued, during which Dad made reference to the *National Review* and Courtney to Jean Genet. After that, she rarely came back to D.C.

As far as I could tell she spent her undergraduate years doing just what people did at high-status private colleges in those days, reading the deconstructionists, dabbling in drugs. Then she went off to Rome and spent a year and a half there learning the language and shacking up with this scrawny Italian who had a receding hairline and glasses but also a sexual presence you don't often find in young American guys. When she returned she lived briefly with friends in New York, waited tables, applied to business schools, and chose Stanford. She kept smoking, though, and even sunny Palo Alto couldn't uproot her chronic discontent. Then she moved home to Washington, for what looked like the long haul. That had been the most surprising of her sudden shifts.

We sat down to eat and did some drinking along with the eating and then (alas) waded into the subject of the recent election. Maggie had become a little obsessed. Republicans had stolen Ohio! As she denounced the voting machine manufacturers and a certain county's Board of Elections, her voice became strident, though for all I knew everything she was saying might have been true. "They cut the number of machines, they purged the voter rolls," she went on.

"Bush won by three million votes," Courtney said. "Even if Ohio had gone the other way, would you really be satisfied with that? Another Bush–Gore?"

"If it got Bush out of office, then yes. Have you actually read about any of this?" Maggie asked her, then turned and looked at me. "Have you?"

"I guess it just seemed to me like Kerry conceded, so . . ." I said.

"You don't care if it's an illegitimate result?"

"I'm not as fully up to speed on this."

"It's over," Courtney said. She reached for the wine and refilled her glass.

"Even if there's nothing we can do about it now, the public deserves to know," Maggie said.

"Honestly I don't think the public really gives a crap," Courtney said.

"But this goes back to what you were saying in the car," she began, looking at me, then turning to address Courtney, "We need to know the real story, even if nobody gives a crap—especially if nobody gives a crap! Like, nobody gives a crap about Iran-Contra, which is why Helen's writing a book about it."

That wasn't quite right. I wanted to say as much, and I wanted to say that more people cared about Iran-Contra than about early Tudor drama, though I didn't know it for a fact.

Courtney pounced. "Good grief. You're not still working on that?"

My fork and knife were noisy on my plate—actually Courtney's fork, her knife, her plate, all of it sleek and Finnish, given to her as a reward for getting married. We were eating peppers stuffed with, I think, kamut.

"Maybe I am. Can we not talk about this?"

"I just can't believe you're so bent on doing that," Courtney said. She twisted to one side and then the other, stretching her shoulders.

"Can we talk about something else?"

"All right," she said. "Let's talk about what you've been doing when you're not working on your project."

"That's not what I had in mind."

"I mean, I worry about you, and I know Maggie does too . . ."

I shot a look at Maggie, who seemed to be trying to hide behind her wineglass.

"What is this, an intervention?" My throat stiffened, as did the rest of me. I stared at Courtney, and she stared back with her big, blank eyes. I broke away, looked down at my lap and tugged at my napkin, her fancy linen napkin, from both ends, as if to tear it apart. My thoughts, all the things I thought to say, to yell—*you bitch you bitch you bitch*—would've only gratified her sense of her own superior composure, and besides, we just didn't yell, we never had. That was our electric fence, and we stayed behind it, instead spewing little digs and behind-the-back insults, insults in the guise of analyzing one another's behavior. I checked my voice before I said what I said next. "You don't actually approve of anything I do, so."

"That's not true."

"Hey guys—" Maggie began.

"Why did you have to bring up the book?" I shot back. "Did she tell you to?"

Maggie flinched.

"Now that's just paranoid," Courtney said.

"That's what you think of me? That I'm paranoid? A paranoid fuckup?"

Courtney shut her eyes. "I think it's fine if you write a book about something. That's great. But Iran-Contra? Really? People did some dumb shit they shouldn't have done. Our dad was one of them. It messed up his career. The end."

I bit my lip and waited until she spoke again. "I mean, you have to put your own life first, right? This all feels to me like some kind of distraction," she said. "You're not in a real job, you're single, and instead of facing the music—"

"What is 'facing the music'? Facing the speakers?"

"You get so wrapped up in what things *mean*, and dwelling on things from a long time ago." She pressed her lips together as though she'd just polished off one of her arugula frappés. "And now you say *maybe* you're still working on it? Like you don't even know if you are?"

I was committed to my book, I really did want to make something of it, I just didn't know what. However: by that point in the evening, I had drunk two large glasses of pinot noir, and when I responded I was full of excess conviction, conviction with nothing but wine behind it. "Yes, I am working on it. It's the story of our family!"

"Our family? That doesn't even exist anymore."

"Um, it does."

"No it doesn't. I mean, you two will always be my sisters, Dad will always be our dad, and Mom is . . . what she is, but they're divorced. We're grown-up. The thing you're talking about, that family ended years ago. We can have our little nostalgic holidays, but . . ."

"Jesus, you guys," Maggie said.

"You don't even believe that," I said, and all at once I was on the verge of tears. "That's just something you're saying."

"And there's no mystery about what happened to Dad back then, by the way," Courtney continued. "He fucked up. He was too trusting, he went along with something he shouldn't have, that was not legal. So he lost that job, and then he went to work for Intelcom and made a whole lot of money. I mean, boo hoo. He and everyone he worked with are lucky they didn't go to jail! Honestly, I don't see why that would be something you'd want to dig up."

Because the last time I'd heard her talk about the scandal was in high school, and back then she'd been more generous to our father, I was actually more startled by this sudden lashing than by her other declaration, i.e., that our family no longer existed.

"Isn't that kind of harsh? I always thought he just, you know, got caught in a storm without an umbrella," Maggie said.

"He made mistakes, but we still don't really have all the facts. And it's not like he didn't suffer. He was publicly shamed," I said, still straining to hold myself together. "And then he spent all that time under investigation."

That Courtney thought of our father as a wrongdoer, and Maggie wanted to protect him, and I was somewhere in the middle, forever seeking more information as if there were some data out there that would clear it all up—for a passing instant everything was so plain to me that I wanted to laugh as well as cry. Fuck! Of course!

"Of fucking course!" I said.

"Excuse me?" Courtney asked.

Her cold eyes. Her chilly little nose. The tiny gold earrings in her ears.

"I'm just . . . I'm just sick of you," I said, finally starting to lose it.
"Okay—"

"I'm sick of being dismissed, and talked down to, and then you tell me you're *worried* about me? You love that, don't you? You love having something to *worry* about. You have no idea—"

"Here you go, crying so that I'll feel like the mean one."

"It's not on purpose!"

"I'm sorry, but I've been to therapy. I finished doing that. I'm no longer interested. I'm not even sure what your problem is . . ."

I buried my face in that linen napkin and then—ha! fuck this napkin!—I blew my nose into it. A small thrill went through me. "You're the problem!"

I scooched my chair back and thrust myself out of it, almost knocking it over. We were silent as it teetered. Its legs settled back on the floor, and I rushed out of the room. What I'd said wasn't strictly correct—Courtney wasn't *the* problem—but I felt as though it had been true up until then. I was still furious, and still kind of crying. My ribs had locked around that old, hot thing, even as my body tried to snake its own drain, to push the thing out through my eyes and nose. I lumbered into my sister's big, shiny kitchen and leaned against the island. In one hand I was still clutching the snotty napkin, and I dropped it there, on the countertop, then continued to the bathroom and slammed the door. I put my hands over my mouth and screamed into them, this with a twinge of self-consciousness, I mean, I could see myself in the mirror doing it, my loony red face, my red eyes, and even so I did feel (and was surprised to feel) some relief. She wasn't my problem.

When I came back out, I found Maggie in the kitchen washing plates. I started drying them. The light over the sink glared too brightly. Behind it was a window, and the light's glaring reflection.

"For what it's worth, she wants things to be better for you guys," Maggie said.

"For me and her?"

"Yes. She's said that to me."

It was plausible that she'd said as much to Maggie, but I didn't quite believe Courtney wanted that wholeheartedly. "Yeah, like if everything would just go her way, then it would all be better, right?"

"I know it's not easy."

"Where is she?"

"Out back."

I looked again through the window and saw her, in profile, lit from behind by the house. Her face was dark. "What's she doing out there?"

"Smoking?"

"It feels like now I'm supposed to go out there and be all con-ciliatory."

"You don't have to."

"Right."

Maggie watched her out the window.

"Maybe I should go out there," I said.

I left the dishes to Maggie and stepped outside. Courtney didn't acknowledge me. She stood with her shoulders hunched forward, and for all the luxury that enveloped her, the house behind us, the sloping yard with its canopy of oak trees, the bulky turtleneck sweater whose sleeves fell halfway over her hands, she struck me as unprotected. She squinted out at the yard, as if she were seeing something other than lawn.

"This is a nice yard," I said.

"Thanks."

"Are you . . ." I didn't know how to finish the question.

"I'm sorry if I made you cry," she said.

A bullshit apology, and still I said, "That's okay."

"Has Rob said anything to you about me?"

"What? No."

"Whatever he says about me is a lie."

"We haven't been talking about you."

"Not at all?"

"Not at all."

"Because it feels like this is a little bit about me, you guys . . . doing whatever it is you're doing. And I just want you to know, he thinks things about me that are not true."

"Like what?"

"I'm not going to say. I just wish you could get to know some guys who aren't, like, sociopathic."

"I don't really think he's a sociopath."

"Well, whatever the opposite of a sociopath is, he's not that. He's more sociopath than, like, socio*pal*."

But wait, I was the play-on-words sister! For a moment I felt infringed upon, and then I remembered that we were related, siblings, congenital infringers.

"So I guess he was kind of a dick to you in high school? I never really knew."

"That's in the past."

A perfectly ordinary thing to say, it nonetheless sounded strange to my ears—what else is there to be sorry about but the past? It was as though my sister were wearing a big signboard with an arrow pointing to our childhood and the words DON'T LOOK OVER HERE printed above it. Or maybe it said I'M NOT MAD ABOUT THIS. I thought of Courtney in our basketball team photo, with thick bangs over her forehead and that wide, guileless smile. A happy kid, that's what you'd think if you saw that photo. An athlete, cute, with a good solid life just up ahead. And now she did have that life, or she appeared to have it—she had a good husband, a good job, a good house—but she couldn't enjoy it.

"I started to fall for somebody else, while I was going out with Rob. Which made him mad. And then he did some fucked-up shit . . ."

"That sounds bad," I said, while silently wondering just how bad it was, whether it could be forgiven, whether all this was even true.

"When I think about it now I feel like he knew, of course he already knew how messed up things were for us. He knew I was an easy mark."

"You think he was that much of a predator?" I asked.

"I do."

"Things must've been bad for him too, since . . ." I started, even though I knew it was the wrong thing to say. She shut her eyes. When she opened them, they'd turned into stones.

"Why would you do that? Why do you have to take up for the other side, always?"

More and more Courtney and I were like puppets being operated by a malevolent puppeteer—I don't mean to say that I had no agency in this, but when we were around each other we slid into the same ditch, every time.

"I just—"

"Forget it."

"I'm sorry, I—"

"It's all shades of gray for you, all the time, isn't it? Which seems very convenient," she said. She wasn't actually crying, but she touched the back of her hand to her face and drew out her breaths.

"I'd like to think that—"

She cut me off. "Forget it. I'm just really tired."

"I'm sorry."

"I'm going to take a shower."

"Now?"

She nodded and went inside, and I followed as far as the kitchen, where Maggie was still washing dishes. Hugo had come home and was helping her, wearing an apron over his nice clothes. He seemed not at all fazed when his wife blew right by him and ran upstairs. I gulped some wine from what might or might not have been my glass. I heard the water turn on in a bathroom.

"She said she was taking a shower," I said to Hugo.

"Sometimes to calm down, she takes a shower."

"Maybe we should get going?" I said to Maggie.

"Do we say goodbye or not?" she asked.

Hugo led us upstairs and through their great big bedroom, then cracked the bathroom door and said we were leaving. "They are

going," he repeated into the steam. We stood in the doorway. Courtney's clothes were in a heap on the floor. She stuck her head out
from behind the white curtain and smiled, better now that she was
clean and I was leaving. You are such a fucking weirdo, I thought,
as I tried to stave off all these little emotional monsters that were
coming right at me. "Bye," she chimed.

Later on, back at my apartment, I called Nina again. No answer.
I hung up, then called a second time and left a message.

1987

All winter long I would tread over dirty snow in my loose-laced high-tops, across expanses of salted pavement, across empty parking spaces, in and out of gymnasiums and locker rooms, pulling sweatpants on or off, always short of breath, hurrying, lost. Blowing into the bowl of my hands. I was usually too cold or too hot or, somehow, both. In freezing buses and suffocating vans, wired from adrenaline, I would chant to myself: *don't fuck up today, don't fuck up, don't fuck up.* I had a way of holding on to the missed shots, the rebounds I didn't get, the times I let the other team score by giving some girl the baseline. I cared too much about all that. I wouldn't say that the team was a family, since I barely knew some of my teammates, but it shared some of the qualities of *my* family, of people yoked together with limited intimacy but with a kind of job to do. An occupation. The team consumed my time, it consumed me.

And it linked me to Courtney, who had stopped bringing me to parties or telling me anything, who'd reverted to just tolerating me. We still spent two or more hours together each day, at practice, at games, or in transit, and I would wish for her to sit next to me on the bus, or even just to walk into the locker room by my side. Instead she stuck with the other seniors, and I kept my eye on her. She'd started to look skinny—she was losing weight, I thought. She wasn't playing as well as she'd played earlier in the season. She'd jammed one of the fingers on her right hand, and her shots were often flat.

Every team in the conference played every other team twice, and in early February came our home game against the team that had handed us our ugliest loss back in December. This rematch was the high school game I would remember best of all as an adult (and then again I've presumably remembered it worst, by remembering it most often: no doubt all my later revisiting has altered, bit by bit, the picture in my head). The game started off just as badly as the December one had ended. Everybody was jittery and winded. The shots weren't falling for either team.

From a seat on the bench I watched Courtney air-ball a jump shot and then stay too long where she'd landed, frowning at the basket when she should've been running back to play defense. Because of it she lagged behind the girl she was supposed to be guarding, and as that girl caught the ball, Courtney tried to reach for it and got called for a foul. Her face mottled with—frustration? Remorse? Not a minute had elapsed before one of the officials slapped her with another foul, for leaning into another girl's back on a rebound. That call was questionable. There was booing from the stands. Courtney started stalking toward the ref to protest before she checked herself and went back to playing.

Coach beckoned and told me to go in for Courtney. I did want to play, but I also wished I could stay on the bench, to sit next to my sister when she came out, even if I couldn't really comfort her. I waited by the scorer's table for the next whistle, which, when it sounded, was simultaneous with the hinge and crack of the heavy double doors.

Another sort of official entered: into the gym stepped a broadly built, white-haired man in a plenipotent overcoat and black leather gloves. The man's dry, planar face would have been known to those who scrutinized the newspaper's political pages, and here he was in the flesh, now pausing to check the score as he pulled off his gloves, now striding along the baseline, as such men strode toward helicopters or up marble stairs, to the opposing team's section of the bleachers, where the spectators parted to make room for him, and where he took a seat, naturally, at the very top.

A U.S. senator. The people who'd been watching the game developed split vision, and would glance from the court to the senator, court, senator, court. And our dad, *oh god*, our dad who'd been sitting on our team's side, crossed the gym, climbed up to the top of the bleachers, and wedged himself in beside that other, more eminent father. Dad sat with his hands on his knees, pitched forward as if there weren't quite enough room to sit straight, twisting his head back awkwardly to speak. Even from a distance it was obvious the senator wanted to be left alone.

As is maybe clear enough from the fact that I was clocking all this business on the sidelines, my mind was not quite where it should've been, i.e., in the body that was running and jumping, catching and passing. I did, however, notice a shift in the game, for when I came onto the court the pace still seemed frenetic and out of sync—there were wild passes, forced plays, balls not saved before they rolled out of bounds—but slowly it settled, and at the same time it soured. The two teams had it out for each other, we banged around under the basket and steamed and cussed. The game was shaping up to be a low-scoring bruiser, the kind that isn't so much won by either side as it is terminated, and although one team can then point to the scoreboard and claim victory, there's not much pride in it.

We needed a run, a boost. Coach took a chance and put Courtney back in, though my sister risked picking up a third foul before halftime. I had assumed I would come out, but Courtney signaled to another girl, and I stayed on the court with her.

It was a minute or two before I realized she hadn't taken a single shot. Not a one. She caught the ball and then passed it. Her defender started to hang off her, and Coach was calling, "*Shoot* the ball." She didn't. Had she lost her nerve? It felt more like some strange protest.

From the stands came the rataplan of pounding feet: "Let's go Ea-gles" *stomp-stomp stomp-stomp-stomp.* "Shoot the damn ball!" Coach yelled, and I did. I made two baskets, and after that my defender started to tackle me whenever the opportunity presented itself. She was the senator's daughter—I think so anyway—and it was as though the refs knew it and granted her immunity. They didn't call anything. Meanwhile she sneered and elbowed me, and even then my dad was still cozying up to the senator, and it was all just too much. The next time that girl had the ball, I ran right at her, shouting, "You! You! You! You!" I tried to block her shot but wound up hitting her head with my forearm. The whistle blew, and she was about to charge at me, but Courtney nudged me out of the way. The girl went at Courtney instead, and I don't think either of them had any idea what to do when they made contact; they more or less grabbed each other's arms, and my sister tried to break free, then fell to the ground.

More whistles: they called fouls on both Courtney and the other girl. I held a hand out to my sister and saw her wince. I pulled her up to standing, and she walked back to the sidelines, stepping normally with her right foot and tiptoeing with the left.

At halftime, in the locker room, she kept walking, circling the rest of us until she was sure of her ankle. "I'm good, I'm good," she said to Coach.

"Okay," Coach said, "now listen. Don't let them throw you off your game. This is your game. You've got to go out there and *want it.* You've got to go out there and *assert.* That means shoot when you have the shot. That means hands up on D. You gotta want it, ladies."

The second half was even grislier, the players shrieking, the crowd wailing. The windows had fogged over. The floor shook. For a while the score didn't budge, and with every scoreless possession the pressure in the gym rose, the air became hotter, more fans stripped off their sweaters. The boys' team returned from their own game and pushed their way into the bleachers, whooping. I saw that Dad had made it back to our side, thank god, and still more and more people kept filing into the gym, as though word had been spreading about the game, as though all of Northwest Washington were on alert.

Courtney with her three fouls stayed on the bench for most of the third quarter. We held steady without her, but slowly the other team eked out a small advantage—three points, five points, eight— and I felt the first tremors of panic. Coach called another time-out. "Focus, people," she said. "Get in control of yourselves."

She looked at Courtney: "You okay?"

"It's fine. I'm ready."

"Here's what we're going to do."

I have no idea what she said after that, what offense she might have diagrammed, because it was irrelevant. Courtney went in—it was the other team's possession—and stole the ball on the inbounds pass and made an easy layup. Soon after, she scored again. And then she just took over. She owned the rest of the game. I'd never seen her play like that. I'd never seen anyone on our team play like that. She was everywhere—she would block a shot on their end and sink one on ours. It was as though she could jump higher, run faster than she ever had. Take after take: she missed nothing. Someone would feed the ball to her and she would get it to the basket, one way or another, spinning and contorting herself and hooking it over her head. And one. The other team called a time-out, in hopes of killing her momentum, but when the game resumed she was just as intent.

And our father could not contain his joy. He started cheering the way he once had, the way he no longer did, a pentecostal of the sidelines, sweating and shouting praise. He kept yelling, "Thank you! Thank you! Thank you!" Which wouldn't have been so bad had he not kept repeating it, and so loudly, in a voice that clambered up and over all the other voices.

My sister was something else, something unexampled, and when the buzzer sounded and we'd won, everyone on the bench and a multitude from the bleachers swarmed onto the court and surrounded her, reaching over to touch her, just to finger a piece of her sweaty jersey. Dad fought his way through all the people, beaming, and when he reached her he said something, I couldn't hear what, and then just stood next to her with a big smile on his face. He was so happy. That night, Courtney seemed like the savior who'd lifted Dad out of his distress, like the one person in the world who'd ever done right by him.

I don't know exactly when Courtney and Rob stopped going out. She never told me. I just stopped seeing them together. He no longer called or came by the house or showed up at our games. For a few weeks she was mopey. That was the one time she ever seemed to want our pity. But at the same time she rejected us, she snapped at us. I studied her all the more closely. I peeked into her backpack. I went up to the third floor when she was out. Her bedroom was tucked under the eaves. Unlike my own room, hers had shed its ruffled bedspread and dolls, and at her request our mother had redecorated it with white laminate furniture and gray bedding— teenage modern, livened with sports trophies and a bulletin board that she'd papered with snapshots of her friends and box scores torn out from the newspaper. I opened her drawers and looked in her closet, searching for something I could seize. I wanted a secret, any secret. A diary, a love letter, a condom. What I did find only bewildered me: a black floor-length nightgown, with spaghetti straps, folded up and wedged into the back of her desk drawer. In that same drawer was a big bottle of Tylenol and a change purse with some other pills inside.

Since the game I hadn't given much thought to her fall—the athletic trainer had given her an ankle brace, and she'd gone on playing. If she'd scowled more and smiled less at practice, there could've been other reasons for that. By then everyone in the family was high-strung, stepping carefully over trip wires that may or may not have been present, we were all nervous, we were all angry, so that at the very time we should've rallied around one another and mustered some Atherton solidarity, we were instead straining at our tethers. We didn't stick together and we didn't split apart, we just wandered around our big house, went off, and came back.

Then one afternoon in the locker room I happened to see Courtney unlace her ankle brace and peel off her sweatsock, and at first glance I thought she'd been wearing some sort of dark purple hose underneath, because there were big wine stains running up the side of her foot, which was also puffy and criss-crossed with grooves left by the laces. She very quickly put on another sock, and when she saw that I was watching her, I looked away. In the next moment she went on getting dressed as though nothing had happened.

That night Courtney came to my room and asked me to do her a "huge, huuuuuge favor." She took three twenties out of her bright-blue leather wallet and asked me to find Rob the next day and give them to him. He'll know what I need, she said. The same thing as before, she said.

"What is it?"

"He'll know. It's just to get me through the season."

"Can't you just—"

"It's like impossible for me to deal with him right now," she said. "He won't be an asshole to you."

"But shouldn't you—"

"Please?"

Around that time Dick Mitchell, or some lesser hologram of that man, appeared on the show *Evans & Novak*. He leaned back in his chair, like an old friend of Evans's or Novak's, as Evans explained to the camera that tonight's guest would offer an insider's perspective on the Nicaragua conflict. My father watched in the family room, staring at the screen as if it were an optical trick and he couldn't make out the trick. He saw only the bearded guy and not the fancy lady. He drained his beer.

So charming in person, Mitchell on TV came off as glib—every other word he uttered was "certainly" or "absolutely." Even though the interview was not the least bit confrontational, even with Novak tossing softballs at him, even when he said just what he presumably thought, he seemed slippery.

> Q: *Oliver North has been a star in this administration, has he not?*
> A: *I would certainly have to agree with that. He's absolutely been a key player vis-à-vis our efforts in Central America. No question.*
> Q: *And what was the involvement of the State Department in those efforts?*
> A: *The way I see it, if we're speaking about the State Department qua the State Department, I would say that its role has been to support, diplomatically, the policies of the Reagan administration.*

Our household media embargo had lapsed by then. My mother walked into the family room and took a seat. She had untucked her shirt from her skirt, and her face was flushed from standing over the sink. She didn't say anything at first, but during a break in the show she suggested to Dad that he turn off the TV.

He may or may not have shaken his head. The television stayed on. When the three men on-screen resumed, she cleared her throat.

"I really think—"

"It's Dick."

"I know who it is."

Maggie had an oral report due the next day, and she was practicing in the living room: "In 1831 Her Majesty's ship the *Beagle* set sail for South America." I'd been in the kitchen helping Mom with the dishes, then watching the TV through the doorway.

I saw my father's pursed face in profile. He disapproved, but I didn't know whether he faulted Mitchell, the show, the situation, or my mother for that matter. At the same time there was something childlike in his expression, he was so fixated on the screen, and maybe it was that youthful rapt attention or the angle, but I believe there was something hungry in it too. It could be that I misread his face, yet I would learn soon enough, if I didn't quite know it yet, that even when our friends are genuinely sorry for our misfortune, often they are not merely, plainly sorry.

Courtney entered through the back door. She'd been out with Tanya, and she walked in just like she always did, still bound up in the outside air and her outside people, and when she encountered us in the family room it irritated her, I could tell. She would've rather gone straight upstairs. Then she saw who it was we were watching on television. She paused. She sucked that irritation inside of her and, oddly, smiled.

"Why is Mr. Mitchell on TV?"

"He just is," our mom said.

Dad countered: "He's explaining our Nicaragua policy."

"Oh, we have a Nicaragua policy?"

But Dad didn't take the bait, nor did she wait for an answer. They were both too riveted by the show. Finally Maggie came in, planted herself right in front of the television, and said that she needed help practicing her report. "We're watching this," my dad said. My mom stood up and left the room with her.

Not long after that, Mitchell was linked to one of Iran-Contra's odd footnotes. It had to do with that part of the affair my dad was not involved in, the Iran side of things, the doomed negotiations and half-baked arms deals that McFarlane and North had arranged. During the secret talks, North had given the Iranians, as a gift, a Bible inscribed by the president (or, in the ass-covering language that was used at the time, inscribed "in the handwriting of President Reagan"). Of course when this detail came to light, the press had a field day with it, and at the same time word got out that Mitchell had known about this Bible and had maybe even bought it for North at a B. Dalton in Bethesda. When he testified, later that spring, the congressmen started asking about that, whether it was consistent with U.S. policy to hand out Bibles in the course of secret negotiations, and so on and so forth. They seemed more preoccupied with it than with any of the larger questions, presumably because they knew it would make better copy, get them quoted in somebody's column. A day or two later came the Herblock cartoon of Mitchell as a gap-toothed Bible salesman.

The inscription had come from Galatians: *All the nations shall be blessed in you.*

Mitchell became the star of his own sideshow. Though many things would bother our dad about the way the scandal played out, this was one that really got to him, the way his friend Dick Mitchell was mocked, lampooned, not for taking part in the supply operations but because he'd maybe purchased a Bible that had then been given to somebody in Iran.

The night that we saw him on television, he hadn't yet been brought low, at that point nobody knew what was coming. Mitchell was just commenting on another story of the week, and I'd watched him with the excitement that came from seeing someone I'd met talk on TV—but also with a premonitory shiver. I may not have been especially attuned to the subterranean shifts around me, but I could tell that Dick Mitchell was on the brink.

It never occurred to me to say no to my sister's request. It made me uneasy, but I longed to please her, and more than that: I thought that I was helping her. There were some false starts. I would spot Rob and head toward him and then chicken out, because he was with other people, or because I'd forgotten what I'd practiced saying.

Finally I found him by his locker. He looked so amused by me that I guessed he had seen all my prior failed approaches.

"Okay, finally. What is it?" he asked.

"Could we talk privately please?"

He steered me around the corner, to a short, empty hallway that led to the lunchroom, and I found myself backed up against the wall, Rob standing over me with one hand planted near my shoulder. I held my breath until I realized I was holding my breath.

"Courtney needs some of that stuff you gave her."

"I'm sure she does . . ."

I took the money out of my pocket. "She gave me this to give to you."

"You have your sister's lying eyes," he said quietly.

"I have my very own eyes."

"You have her mouth too."

It was as though he were going to kiss me, and in that moment I wouldn't have resisted. But we were standing right under a school bell, which rang, loudly, and he straightened up and took the bills out of my hand. "Come find me again tomorrow and I'll have it for you," he said. I had a notion that this was the wrong way to go about things, that I shouldn't have given him anything until he had the goods, so to speak. Yet it seemed too late to get the money back.

I countered: "Or why don't you come find me?"

He said no, I should find him, actually. Which I did, the next day as school was ending. He unzipped my backpack and put something inside of it, and later on, at home, I mounted the stairs with the sandwich bag full of pills concealed in my bathrobe, and I passed that on to Courtney. She took the bag and shut her bedroom door.

On the weekends she would go out with her friends and come home electrified or angry, in one high-voltage mood or another. She would return at midnight or later, after our parents had gone to bed. I'd be in the family room, not waiting but waiting.

"Where were you?"

"Adams Morgan."

"How'd you get home?" I hadn't heard a car come or go.

"I walked."

"You did?"

"It's a beautiful night."

I looked at her. "Dad would be so pissed."

"So don't tell him."

My thinner sister became a bat in our midst, flying away every evening at sundown to feed, ignoring our parents' (weak, unenforced) instructions to be home by nine on school nights. I never knew what to say to her. I worried about her sprain, but it was righteous worry, i.e., she was wrong to hide her injury just as she was wrong to hide everything else she was hiding from me. I judged her and feared for her and resented her, and finally, one Saturday, I told our mom.

She was down in the basement, shoving clothes into the dryer. I felt shaky and kept one hand on the table where we folded our laundry. My parents had let the housekeeper go, that's why Mom was transferring gobs of damp bath towels from one machine to the other—in dozens of small ways she was holding our household together, but she was unhappy to be doing it. And there I was, serving up another nuisance.

"It's sprained, maybe broken."

"But she's been playing on it, hasn't she? Could it be just a bruise?" my mother asked, hopelessly.

"Anything's possible."

"Christ."

Mom had confronted Courtney as soon as she got home that night and, after inspecting her big purple sausage link of an ankle, had dragged her to the emergency room. The worst part of it wasn't that my sister was put on crutches for the rest of the season, that for our last game and the league tournament I would start in her stead and she would sit on the end of the bench in her street clothes and ace bandages; it wasn't that we were eliminated in the first round of the tournament by a team we'd beat twice during the regular season, or that my sister was now treating me with a thousand cutting looks and under-the-breath comments, silences, snubs, slow rolling of the eyes, daily reminders of my zero worth. More than all that, it was that I'd set off a chain reaction: Courtney was furious with me, Mom was furious with Courtney and also (she couldn't help it) with me, Dad stayed in his study most of the time, and Maggie, we thought little Maggie had no clue, but of course she knew as much as anybody. A couple of times I saw her sucking her thumb, a twelve-year-old. Courtney refused to sleep on the first-floor sofa bed and instead hopped her way up

and down the stairs, which became the erratic drumbeat of our
distress.

In March Dad gave his first congressional deposition, which would
be followed by grand jury testimony in May and an appearance before the joint committees in June. Then would come a series of in-
terviews with the Office of the Independent Counsel. We never
knew what happened at any of them, we were never told. During
those months he spent hours and hours—billable hours—at his
lawyer's office.

Further cutbacks were imposed: Did Courtney really need a
salon haircut? What was the matter with last year's bathing suit? It
had as much to do with my parents' panic than with the actual cost
of anything. Mom still had her fund-raising job, and she started
working on weekends, which wasn't going to bring us any more
money but which served as a distraction, I suppose, an escape. And
she traveled more, visiting donors and going to conferences, two
purposes that were combined in my imagination. I saw her floating
through a ballroom full of wealthy donors wearing name tags, my
mother in a chiffon blouse with a sash at the neck, kissing people
on the cheek as she lifted the change out of their silk-lined pockets.

One day during that spring of our family's unraveling, I'd come
home from school before my sisters, and I walked into the first-
floor bathroom, only to find Dad sitting on the toilet. I shrank and
backed out before I understood what I'd seen. The toilet lid was
closed. He was just sitting there, in an unlit bathroom. I stood outside the door. "I didn't know you were here," I said.

"I came home early," he said.

My head was full of Shakespeare's Henrys and Richards, the rul-
ers of my assigned reading. It was as though Dad had come home
from a battlefield upon which glory had been exposed as a sham,
kings were only body doubles of kings, friends betrayed friends,
and cowards outlived the brave.

"Do you have homework?" he asked.

"I have some," I said.

"Is there anything you'd like some help with?"

He hadn't helped me with my homework in years. It had been years since we'd discussed my homework, or played card games, or done anything like that.

"Not really," I said.

"Okay."

"Do you want to watch TV?"

He said that he did. He got a beer and I got a Coke; we turned on the set and watched *Wheel of Fortune*, and before one puzzle had been solved (CHERRIES JUBILEE was the answer) he'd fallen asleep in his chair.

Dad was now under a kind of low-intensity, erratic siege by reporters, a zillion of them all rushing to develop their own angles. They called the house, they sometimes stopped by. There was a tendency toward conspiratorial thinking, an urge to make the big story even bigger, so that suddenly men my father had worked with on the NSC staff were being talked about as possible Mossad agents—I heard him rant about this to my mother. He himself was never accused of anything so exotic, though he was named in some of the articles: there was one piece in *Time* that referred to a phone call Dad had supposedly made to an official in Costa Rica. "Like many of the young bucks on the NSC staff," it said, "Atherton was tireless, committed to the cause, and sometimes arrogant." After that, Mom actually called an editor at the magazine, someone whose kids we'd gone to grade school with, and gave him hell for it. "Arrogant?" I heard her saying. *"Arrogant?"* As for Dad, he was less angry about that one article than about the sheer amount of classified information that had come flooding out of the White House, every last administration official suddenly unburdening himself.

He continued playing video games on our Apple IIe, late at night. *Apple Panic* was the name of one: you had to climb ladders and lure pulsating bad guys into holes and then hit them with mallets until they vaporized. One day I turned the game on and saw that he had all the high scores.

On plenty of nights that spring, just Maggie and I were home, while Mom worked late or attended a conference, Dad racked up more hours at his lawyer's office, and Courtney went out with her friends. We'd order a pizza and pay for it with money that Mom or Dad had left on the counter, and we'd watch fantasy households on TV, *Full House*, *The Cosby Show*, *227*, *The Golden Girls*. All those hijinks and misunderstandings and reconciliations. Sometimes I'd look over at Maggie, who'd be sucking on a Jolly Rancher, one skinny leg launched over the chair arm, and I'd wonder who she was, who she would be. She was the changeling of the family, fair-skinned and fine-boned, and when we were younger she'd been content to spend hours on her own, drawing elaborate maps of other worlds or talking to her dolls in an invented language.

Or, we made the mistake of treating her as that, as an imaginative child instead of as a full-fledged person. On one of those nights the two of us were sitting in the family room with the TV on, and she got up and went to the kitchen, and when she came back she had a bottle of beer for each of us. I'd never seen my twelve-year-old sister drink before, but I shrugged off whatever concern might've pinged at me. A single beer wouldn't kill her. And there was something about how we'd been left there alone, to guard the house that the rest of our family had abandoned, that made me think the hell with them. Cheers. I drank about half of my beer, rested my head on the sofa arm, and fell asleep.

When I woke up a different show had come on, and there were two more bottles on the coffee table—Maggie was on to her third. I found her in the kitchen, standing on the stool she needed to reach the wall phone, and dialing a number. As soon as she was done dialing she planted her free hand on the counter to steady herself.

"Is Brian there?" she asked, her voice all in flux.

I walked over to her and hung up the phone, then dragged her stumbling and protesting over to the sink and made her drink some water. Half of it went down her shirt. I grabbed a banana from the fruit basket and told her to eat it.

"No way," she said. "You eat it."

The stairs went slowly, and she was still talking about Brian, whoever that was, and suddenly I got angry. I told her Dad would notice how many beers were missing. Maggie turned her head back and forth.

"No. He won't."

At last we reached her room, and I told her to get ready for bed. I ran downstairs, gathered up the bottles, and took them outside to the neighbor's garbage can. Back upstairs, my sister had passed out. I took off her socks, then tried to take off her sweatshirt but it was too hard to do that. I put the blanket over her and then went to bed myself, though I didn't sleep for a while, thinking Maggie would wake up and be sick. I kept listening for puking noises. None came. Courtney returned, my parents returned, everybody went to their rooms and slept.

2005

Dad had been instructed to report to the cardiac imaging center at 7:15 a.m., earlier than I'd ever gone to any doctor. The
night before, I slept over at Albemarle Street, and in the morning we both came downstairs at around the same time Dad used to
leave for work during his White House years, the hinge of the day
just creaking.

There was a question of who should drive. I said I would, and
he hesitated but then took his seat on the passenger side, put his
hands under the flaps of his winter coat, and leaned his head against
the headrest. Both of us were quiet, and the streets were still, lined
with cold cars, everything crusted with frost. I wanted to ask him
about his health, specifically about this appointment, but it was so
early. He turned on the radio, which purred its bulletins from
elsewhere.

The sky over the hospital parking lot was dark, but by the time
we'd taken two different elevators and turned through hallways
and arrived at the waiting room, a watery early-morning light rilled
down from above, through skylights, landing upon a few synthetic
plants and groups of chairs upholstered in dull orange fabric.

Immediately, Dad was chuted into a Process: first he had to note his arrival on a slip of paper and place that in a plastic tray, then he had to fill out two forms, and then, heeding a sign that had been printed on pink paper, in an unusual font, he had to *Please Wait Until Your Name Is Called*. The sign put me on guard. I figured it had been placed there by some snippy person, dug in behind the reception desk, who had come to think of heart patients as needy morons and who felt under siege each time one of them had the gall to approach the desk *before* his or her name was called. It was true that these tyrants of the reception areas, in their jersey separates and scuffed pumps, had their antagonists (the ever-ringing phones, the hostile software) to cope with, and yet I did wonder at the fact that jobs of this kind, jobs that revolve around interacting with other people, were often filled by men and women who apparently despised other people. Had they always been so, or did the jobs make them that way?

Around the corner from the counter where Dad had filled out his slip of paper were two window bays with chairs pushed up to them, like the setup in prisons allowing visitors to talk to inmates. Only one employee was visible when we arrived, her small, froggy head attached to a large body. She was seated on her side of one of these windows; a middle-aged, sun-baked patient sat across from her, earnestly answering her questions as she recorded his responses on a computer.

My father and I were the only people in the waiting room besides that man's entourage—four other people, his family, sprawled across the chairs.

I said, "Seems like an okay place."

"I'd like it better if I could have a cup of coffee," he said. He'd been fasting since the night before. He picked up a magazine.

Another patient arrived, a woman carrying two big tote bags, and then came a wiry man with a beard, wearing a Hoyas sweatshirt and black sneakers. More people followed, old people mostly, each scanning the room as they entered, filling out their slips, taking seats, peeking over their periodicals, waiting for their names to be called, and I thought about all the vexed hearts beating beneath all the sweatshirts and sweaters.

The woman in the reception area dismissed the man she'd been talking to, and then she called the name of the man in the Hoyas sweatshirt, who'd arrived a full five minutes after us. I wasn't the only one to notice. Dad kept looking at her. Finally I went up to the counter. "Excuse me," I started.

"Ma'am, take a seat, please," the woman said.

"But my dad's been—"

"Take a seat and I'll be with you shortly."

Shortly indeed. Behind her was a poster of the human heart colored red and blue, a hunk of meat with a tangle of plumbing on top.

"Don't mess with her, is what I've learned," Dad grumbled when I sat back down.

"Got it."

"She's what your mother would call a . . . a . . ." At first he seemed to have forgotten this label of Mom's, but in fact it was just a word he was not used to saying, one that he uttered softly: "a bitch."

Then she did call Dad's name, his full name—the name of that person he was officially. His shirt had come untucked, and the wrinkled tail swung behind him as he made his way over to her. He took his time pulling out the chair and lowering himself into it, and once they got started, although I couldn't hear the rote questions and answers, I could hear their mutual impatience, Dad's and the receptionist's. They were well matched, Churlish v. Churlish, the two of them making no secret of their disdain.

When she was finished with him, Dad walked back toward me, rolling his eyes. It was a shared moment, and perhaps an opportunity—I could've asked him then to further explain the condition of his heart—but we were in public, and I was too shy to do it.

A man in sage-green scrubs appeared and led my father away. I read a pamphlet that explained what would happen back there: he would be injected with an isotope, a radioactive tracer that would diffuse through his vessels, and then he would be slid into a machine that would take pictures of the flow of his blood. Dad's veins and arteries, the cavities of his heart would be illuminated on a screen. A little while later they would have him walk, then run, on a treadmill, and the machine would take pictures again, after the exercise. Four or five people in addition to my father were being led through the same sequence of steps, which meant that the interior door kept opening and closing, these patients venturing in and coming back out again with needles in their wrists or dried sweat in their hair. And less frequently, the door from the hallway would open and a new patient would appear, to be entered into the cycle.

While Dad was still back there, a new man came in from the outside, satisfaction in the set of his mouth, in the calm mass of his forehead. The hearing aids he wore didn't take anything from his air of contentment. A woman in a velour sweatsuit accompanied him, and both had the faraway faces of a couple that had exchanged maybe three words since breakfast. They seemed well-off, and not merely in the financial sense. Comfortable in the world. Then I recognized the man, remembered who he was. In the flesh he looked very different from his author photograph.

It was the woman who had the appointment—she went to the window to be interviewed and returned to her seat, calmly. Then the interior door opened, and in it stood a handsome older man with hair that was still thick and eyes that looked just like mine. He grunted, and he was Dad again. For just a moment I'd seen him without knowing him, a stranger to me and at the same time more familiar than ever. I'd seen the cast of his eyes and been reminded of this thing we shared—a kind of yearning without an object. What in other people might grow into a spiritual tendency in us had been thwarted, misdirected. It coursed around those branching tubes I'd seen in the heart poster, lost in the arterial maze, and manifested as a general, constant ache in our chests—in my chest, at least, and I assume in his—and a damp, expectant look that came over his face from time to time, I gather it came over mine too. I don't mean to say that we were especially sensitive people. I mean that we were dumb about our sensitivities, we pretended not to have them, like people pretending not to have their own noses even though everyone else can see them plainly.

I was hoping against hope that Dad wouldn't notice James Singletary sitting there. He took two rigid steps into the room, then stopped by a pile of magazines and started to sort through them.

"Tim," the woman in the velour sweatsuit said. "Tim Atherton? Is that you?"

My father looked up, not bothering to pretend he hadn't seen them already. "Gail," he said. "Jim." Then he took a seat right where he was, well away from them and also, as it happened, across the room from me.

"Come over and say hello!" the woman said. Dad reluctantly got up again and scrutinized his own feet as he crossed the waiting area.

"It's been a long time, hasn't it?" said Singletary as he offered his crackled hand, which Dad took limply in his own and then dropped. In his other hand Dad was holding a *TV Guide*. "It's been a long time," Singletary said, answering his own question. He was shifting in his seat, narrowing his eyes, taking my father's measure. "You been keeping busy?"

The man in the green scrubs called, "Gail Singletary?"

My father blinked at them. Anyone would've assumed it was the husband who was the patient, not the wife.

"She's a nutritionist, a tennis player, healthiest woman I know, and they've got her coming in here for this deal," Singletary said. "I smoked for thirty years, ate steak like it was going out of style, sat at a desk, and they tell me I'm doing great. How's that for fair."

Gail, who had probably heard this little homily before, barely acknowledged it before she disappeared. Singletary took off his sweater, exposing a golf shirt and veiny biceps. "So what are you up to these days?" he asked Dad.

Dad's shoulders popped up and down. "I'm here, today," he said finally.

"Sure, sure."

My father glanced back behind him, at his original seat next to mine. I didn't know whether to go join him or stay put.

"And you?" Dad asked.

"One thing and another. I've got a book that just came out."

"Oh really?"

"The title is *A Call to Honor*. My editor came up with that."

"Well. Congratulations." Dad gestured toward me. "I'm here with my daughter."

"Your daughter? Holy cow. Last time we saw each other, your girls were in high school, I think." He started waving at me. It seemed he meant for me to come over there, and so I went.

"You live here?" he asked, and before I could formulate an answer he turned to Dad and said, "Must be nice. I've got two in the service and one in the Bay Area. I hardly ever see them. Any grandkids?"

"Not yet," Dad said.

"We're at two so far. I tell you, I am loving it. Kind of makes up for all the stuff we missed out on the first time around, you know? Always working around the clock, weren't we?" He looked at me. "Are you married at least?"

"No," I said.

"You've still got a little time."

More than you, I muttered to myself.

"Beg pardon?" he asked, touching one of his hearing aids.

"Thank you," I said.

He turned to Dad. "How's Eileen doing?"

"We're divorced."

"Ah. Sorry."

"Don't be."

"I should let you get back to your seat. It's nice to see you, Tim."

Dad tilted his head, as though puzzled by the idea that there was anything nice about it. He might've been working up to a reply, but just then they called his name again, and he seemed glad enough to be summoned.

I was left there with Singletary, who was staring at the door that his wife and my father had passed through. "I guess your dad's had some heart trouble—"

"He did," I said reluctantly. "He does."

He nodded. "Gail too. She's on this reversal diet now, where you reverse the disease. No butter, no oil, we've got none of that in the house anymore. No meat. No sugar. I've lost fifteen pounds."

"Does it work?"

"Who knows? They say it does. They've got her on Coumadin, Lipitor. She rides her bike all the time, does yoga. Oatmeal. Oatmeal every morning."

I stared helplessly at his shirt. "Are you a golfer?" I asked.

"Love to golf. You?"

"No—no."

"What do you do?"

I said I was a writer, said it plainly without my usual qualifiers (*trying to be . . . but my day job is . . .*). It felt good at first, less so when I realized that I would have to explain what sort of things I wrote. But before he could ask, Gail came out, and Singletary introduced us. We smiled politely.

Singletary said to her, "What did you do with the parking ticket?"

"You never gave it to me," she said.

"I absolutely gave it to you."

"I don't remember that," she said, opening her purse and pawing through the insides. "I don't see it in here."

"Maybe you put it in your wallet," he said.

"I don't think they validate here anyway."

"We still don't want to be charged for a lost ticket!"

"It's probably in the car. We'll find it when we leave."

"Check your wallet, please."

She did so, carefully, with no resignation or resentment that I could see, and then said, "It's not here."

They were still discussing the ticket when I excused myself. Maybe five minutes after that, my father returned. He was breathing heavily in and out. Only later did I learn what had happened back in the examining room: after he had been on the treadmill for a short time, walking at an easy pace, the technician sped the machine up, and though it wasn't going all that fast he began to feel light-headed, short of breath. The electrodes on his chest, it was like they'd been delivering little shocks, that's what he told me. He had to tell the technician to stop the test.

I could imagine that person, trained in what to do next, saying, "It's okay," and adding robotically, "You did great"—the way they so often did, these doctors and nurses, telling you that you did great, just for submitting, and even for failing to submit. Then it was explained to him that they were going to give him a drug to raise his heart rate, in place of exercise.

Dad sat down next to me without saying anything. A woman was exclaiming, "They want me to drink barium. I'm not going to drink barium!" and a little radio in the receptionist's area was emitting a tinny "Pink Houses." They called Gail's name again.

I started to feel drugged myself. My own clothes were too heavy on me. I looked over at Dad: he was studying the *TV Guide* so closely, he might have been cramming for an exam on its contents. His lips were parted, and I thought I could see in his face both the endless curiosity (the ability to be curious about anything, even this week's TV schedule) and the way in which, in seeking out information, he kept disappointment at arm's length. He kept the disappointed old man within him confined to a small area, fought valiantly against becoming only that.

Dad was still waiting to be called again when Gail emerged from the interior for the last time. She put her hand on her husband's shoulder. "Ready?"

"All set?"

"They're finished with me."

"Did you find that parking stub?"

"It's not in my wallet."

"Can you check one more time?"

"I know it's not in there."

"What about your purse?"

She glanced in Dad's direction. "I'll check one more time if it means so much to you."

Dad had been watching them, and now he stood up and retrieved our own stub from his pants pocket. "Here," he said, "take mine."

"How are you going to get out then?" Singletary asked.

"I can afford it."

"Don't be ridiculous," Singletary said.

"You sure you don't want it?" he asked.

"Don't be ridiculous, Tim," Singletary repeated. "For chrissake. You always did want to be the good guy, didn't you?"

"And that's wrong?"

"You sit on your high horse—"

"I'll withdraw my offer then." Dad put the stub back in his pocket.

Gail tried to usher her husband toward the door. "Let's go, Jim."

He and Dad were staring each other down. Now other people sitting nearby were watching the two of them, and what they saw, surely, was a pair of old guys arguing, a geriatric comedy. None of us could've told what Dad and Singletary were reliving just then.

Finally his wife managed to steer Singletary out of the room. Dad sat back down and looked straight ahead. He didn't move for a while. Then he took a pack of chewing gum from his coat pocket and offered me a piece before unwrapping one for himself. More patients came and went as a cloud of cinnamon smell formed around our heads. I looked at our matching knees, my knees smaller than his but shaped the same.

"I don't know how she could stand to be married to him for so long," he said. "Jim Singletary. Always looking out for number one. Which is not exactly unheard-of in this town, but he took it to another level."

I wished he would elaborate, but having swallowed much of the *TV Guide*, he was now an expert on the television industry and wanted only to engage me on that subject, i.e., which were the top shows and why were they successful and why didn't I go work on

Lost, and while this was annoying, it was less annoying than it had been when he'd hinted that I ought to do something entirely different with my life.

In the car, though, Dad told me more about Singletary, whom he painted as a scourge of the workplace, circa 1985. An alarmist, a busybody, a Red-baiting pest in the Old Executive Office Building, Dad said. Now that I'd met him myself, I couldn't quite reconcile the figure my father was rendering with the man in the golf shirt. To me he was just a gamecock of an old man. Dad picked up on my general attitude. "I might as well tell you. When push came to shove he really tried to screw everybody over."

"How so?"

"As the whole Iran-Contra brouhaha was starting, we had these meetings at the White House. I guess you'd call it spin control, though that makes it sound more organized than it was. Most of us didn't know all of what had been going on, and those of us who knew part of it found that some of our colleagues had a different idea of the facts. So we were all trying to get on the same page. The idea was, we all agree on one story that we can give to the media. It was supposed to be the truth, as much as we could agree on what would've been the truth.

"Singletary, he was always a schemer, always running off to meet with people from other departments, from the military, from intelligence, people who considered themselves the real conservatives. Then all of a sudden he wasn't with those people anymore.

"Suddenly he was with the chief of staff, with Don Regan. Singletary was strutting over to his office and feeding him lord knows what, all sorts of nonsense. Regan had never gotten along with our folks, and being the chief of staff, he saw it as his responsibility to cover the president's rear in whatever way he could.

"So Singletary teams up with Regan and they start telling this story that the whole Contra operation and the weapons sales to Iran were all the handiwork of my former boss Bud McFarlane, who'd stepped down by then, and North, with the help of Elliott Abrams and Dick Mitchell and myself. That nobody above them, the president, the vice president, nobody else knew. There was a big article that ran in *The New York Times* to this effect. Singletary was obviously the source of it. He wasn't named, but still. And you know, it was just one story, one theory out of a dozen or more that were floating around, but . . . the man had no loyalty whatsoever.

"There's no question that Dick and I would have been part of the investigation no matter what, but we got roped into it all the more because of that. Especially Dick. Jim Singletary wanted to bring Dick down, I know he did, and he helped do it. The investigators and the lawyers were asking Dick about these stupid rumors that Singletary had started. They made so much of things that I would consider to have been relatively insignificant.

"This is not—I don't want you to think that I'm saying that this is why Dick, you know, didn't make it. He'd always struggled. He had his demons, and from what I understand he stopped taking the medication he was supposed to be taking. But the nonsense with Singletary, and the silly rumors, it was all such, such . . . such *horseshit*! And then they indicted Dick, which was outrageous.

"People like Singletary, they don't even have any awareness of the damage they do, they just go around like, like insects, spreading disease. That man, to me, is an insect. A bloodsucking tick."

I said something unmemorable in response—yes, I see, how awful—and at the same time I was privately thanking Jim Singletary, bloodsucking tick, for having latched onto my dad and drawn this out of him. He was telling me this, at last, and as he did I felt something in myself unlock, because it seemed to me that once he was willing to tell me the story, I would be released, finally, from needing to know it.

(*From the deposition of James Singletary, March 17, 1987*)

MR. LEGRAND. At what point did you become aware of the negotiations with the Iranians?

MR. SINGLETARY. I was not aware of them until last fall.

MR. LEGRAND. After details about those negotiations were revealed in the media in November of last year, and also details about the plane that went down in Nicaragua, did you then become involved in preparing a chronology for Congress that would explain the NSC staff activities with respect to Iran and to the Contras?

MR. SINGLETARY. At first that wasn't seen as necessary. There were reports coming out of the Middle East, but because they contained a number of inaccuracies, we didn't expect them to hold up. At the same time there were some other things happening, a hostage was released. We also had the midterm elections. However, by the following week, it became clear that the president would have to say something about these news reports. We therefore had to assemble all the relevant facts and present them in a coherent way. And so internally within the White House we were putting together the chronology.

MR. LEGRAND. Who was assigned to be principally responsible for the chronology?

MR. SINGLETARY. It was North.

MR. LEGRAND. He was the author of it?

MR. SINGLETARY. He would do a draft, and then we would meet on it and Poindexter or somebody else would remember something else, and North would try to verify it and if he could verify it, he would modify the draft. There were several iterations.

MR. LEGRAND. And were there any disputes—disputes may be too strong of a word—any differences of opinion as to what should go in the chronology?

MR. SINGLETARY. No more than what you would expect.

MR. LEGRAND. Did you agree with the consensus on that chronology?

MR. SINGLETARY. In some places yes, in some places no. I would say there were some things left out of the official story.

1987

Another night when just Maggie and I were home, I stayed awake after she went to bed. I roamed through the house, picking up books and trinkets at random, peering into cabinets, closets, the freezer. At last I went up to my room and crawled out the window and perched on the roof, pretending to be at ease though the air was biting and there were shingles pressing into my butt, and I didn't want to move around too much because I was afraid of falling. I liked sitting on the roof, but I was also posing there, posing for nobody. Sometimes I would bring a notebook out with me and write wretched poems—once I'd torn one out and then lost my grip on the paper, so that it flew away and landed in the neighbor's pool. But that night I just sat with my hands around my knees and shivered and wondered what it would be like to fall, to go sliding over the gutter and land on the back deck.

I heard the phone ring and hoisted myself back inside. On the other end of the line, Courtney's voice was low and flat, steady like she was trying to keep it steady. "Can you get Dad?"

I told her he was still at the lawyer's office.

"It's almost midnight."

"He's not here."

"Seriously," she said, and then hung up. I lay down on my parents' bed, the bed upon which I'd been, or at least might've been, conceived. I listened to the clang of the heating pipes. I put my cold hands over my face, and when I did I saw Courtney's face disembodied and surrounded by sunbursts of yellow and pink, as if her head were inside some psychedelic television set. She wasn't in trouble and she wasn't smiling either. She was floating there coolly. I slid to the floor and went to the door of Maggie's room and peeked in: she was curled up in a lump in the middle of her bed. Her faint snuffle had a hint of melody to it, against the ticking of the clock. The phone rang again.

"He's not answering at the law firm," Courtney said.

"Where are you?"

Her voice took a cracked, woozy turn. "I don't know. I don't feel good."

"Okay. What do you see around you?"

"Wisconsin Avenue."

"Who are you with?"

"Nobody. I just need Dad to come pick me up."

"I can come in Mom's car."

"You don't have your license."

"Duh. I can still drive."

"I have the spare key with me."

"Then get a cab? Or do you want to wait for Dad? I'm sure he'll be home soon."

"Why are you sure?"

"Just tell me where you are."

She said, "I'm—" Then her voice cracked. "Shit. Shit."

"Should I call—"

"No! Don't call anybody. I just need to fucking get picked up."

"Just tell me where you are right now! I'm calling a cab!"

"I'm near the grocery store." It was another battle to get her to tell me which one she meant, and she kept saying she didn't want a cab, no, no, and so I told her I was coming to get her. I didn't know how I would do it. "Just stay where you are. I'm on my way."

"I need a sweater," she said.

"Okay."

"Or a coat or a blanket. I'm freezing."

I called Anthony. We'd been avoiding each other. Once in a while I'd catch him watching me, in the lunchroom or in class, with a look on his face that I would describe as forensic. Still, he had his own phone line, one I could call without waking his parents, and I knew he would help. He'd spent his summers as a camp counselor, and at school the teachers would entrust him with tasks like taking copies over to one of the classrooms or showing a new kid around. The sound of his sleepy voice comforted me, though when I told him why I was calling I got scared again.

While he was on his way, I filled a school duffel, the kind we used for our gym gear, with things I thought might be needed. I had become entirely practical but had lost common sense in the bargain, packing not just a sweater but also sweatpants, a plastic baggie full of crackers, a package of wet wipes, a handful of Band-Aids, and a bottle of room-temperature cranberry juice. Courtney was fine, she was fine, I said to myself. I'd just talked to her and she was waiting for us and I was bringing supplies and she would be fine.

I must've looked all too happy to see Anthony. He turned quickly away from me and, facing the windshield, asked me where to go.

The night was a forest of traffic signals diffusing in the haze. Anthony drove fast but not fast enough for me. At one point he slowed for a yellow light that he easily could have sped through.

"No rush or anything," I said.

"Where are your parents?"

"My mom's out of town and my dad's still with his lawyers, I guess."

"It's, like, midnight."

"They have a lot of work to do."

"Yeah, I'm sure."

"What does that mean?"

"I bet all those guys are going to get away with it. They'll get off scot-free," he said. He stared at the road the whole time.

"I don't know about the ones who did it, but my dad didn't do anything."

"Okay."

"He didn't. He wasn't in charge."

In his silence he was a bastard, and I couldn't believe him, despised him, what did he know? I might have said something, but we'd come to the part of Wisconsin Avenue where the Giant Food was, where Courtney had said she would be.

I didn't see her. I saw the supermarket's tall windows with that week's specials taped to them, and I saw a homeless person cocooned against the store's red brick wall. Oh god, I kept saying.

Anthony tried to reassure me. She probably got a taxi, he said.

We can't leave, I said, and we circled, driving past the store and halfway around the block, taking the back way into the store parking lot and then going around again. After three or four circuits I made Anthony stop the car. He tried to tell me that there was nothing I'd see on foot that we hadn't already seen, he said that maybe she'd been talking about a different store, but I got out anyway. It was windier than it had been when we left the house, and I didn't have any plan about what to do. I paced and waited for her to, I don't know, burst out of the ground like a crocus or a missile. And at the same time I had this view of myself, I saw myself from a distance, the middle sister in a fairy tale—a fucked-up fairy tale in which our girl in her jeans and rugby shirt wanders piteously back and forth in front of Giant Food, now the castle in which her beautiful sister has been imprisoned.

And then there she was, treading slowly from the shadowy end of the block, where the police substation was. She looked awful, and she had on this weird shimmery dress that had bunched up on one side, so that the skirt hung aslant. Her face was a smear of laments I'd never seen on her face before. Her hands were clenched into fists, and as soon as she saw that I'd seen her, she put her head down. I wanted to run toward her but didn't. I walked, and when I was close enough to touch her, I put my hand on the back of her thin arm and guided her to the car. And that meant something, to me at least: in spite of the fear and the unreal feeling I had the whole night, like we were in some strange play about the lives of other kids who had our same bodies, I would hold on to that sensation of my hand on her arm and walking right by her side, just like I made a keepsake of that little slap she gave me during basketball tryouts. Both times the contact was so brief, but in those moments I knew what we were, I knew we had a piece of each other.

Just as we reached Anthony's car, a black Isuzu Trooper pulled up behind, familiar to me because I'd seen Rob drive it. But it wasn't Rob who jumped out, it was Mr. Mitchell, looking dazed. He scrambled toward us and took Courtney's other arm, and as soon as he did she left my side and collapsed toward him as if he were her own father. And he was stiff but also kind, he told her she was safe, she was on her way home. He asked, "Are you hurt?" She shook her head, and shook her head again.

He insisted on taking her to the house himself. I asked if she wanted her sweater or some juice, she said no, and they climbed into the Trooper. I got back into Anthony's car. He turned off the tape player and drove so slowly, the car was like a boat on a still lake, skimming toward a rotten dock. Better to stay out on the water. I wished we would.

When we made it to Albemarle Street, the Trooper was idling at the curb. The doors opened, and as Courtney and Mr. Mitchell started toward the porch I stayed where I was. Anthony's eyes were tired and steady.

"See you Monday," he said. I could tell that he didn't want me anymore, and that his wanting me had been the furnace of our friendship. It was something I'd let burn too high. I'd wasted it. Still, the wanting, a remnant of it at least, had to be in there somewhere: I was looking for it in his eyes and didn't see anything at all. I leaned forward and kissed him. I felt it, but he wouldn't let it out. He pushed me back and said good night.

From the bottom of the stairs I saw the door swing open, and there was our dad. He saw Courtney and then he saw Mr. Mitchell. I don't even know how to describe the look on his face: it was all out of whack, anger and relief and confusion mottling him, hitting him in waves. What was his friend doing there? He must've wondered that. With all that beating on him from the inside he had to grab on to the doorjamb to support himself.

I hesitated to go up the stairs. I saw Courtney glide past him, and he and Mr. Mitchell stood there talking, though not for long. By the time I'd started upward, Mr. Mitchell was coming down. He gave me a tight nod as he went past.

Courtney had fled to her room, and so I was all Dad had left. "Where the hell were you?" he asked. He smelled like alcohol. I had no idea what to say, and so I just told him I'd gone to pick up Courtney but Mr. Mitchell had beat me to it. My father, uncomprehending, told me I should go to bed.

The next morning Courtney came into my room, very composed, with a sad, noble burnish about her.

"What did you say to Dad?" she asked, and then, after I told her I hadn't said anything, she fed me a story. "Here's what happened. Tanya's car wouldn't start, and so I was stuck at the party and you had to come pick me up."

"Where were you really?" I asked her.

"That's what happened."

"No, for real."

I didn't think she would tell me a thing, but then she said, "I just got together with the wrong guy. He was being a jerk, so I left the party by myself."

This hardly filled it all in for me, but I knew better than to press her. "So how come Mr. Mitchell showed up?"

"I wasn't sure if you would make it, so I called Rob. His stepdad was the one to answer the phone."

We were both grounded for two weeks, Courtney for staying out too late and me for leaving Maggie alone at the house. Not that it made Courtney any friendlier toward me—she mostly stayed in her room and listened to music. At school there was something in the air, I caught the scent of it now and again and tried to track it down. I would walk up to people and they would go quiet, and I'd know they'd been saying something about my sister. I just knew. What? I'd ask. And they'd make up something. There was a story about Courtney making the rounds, I could feel it.

Whatever happened that night, it didn't visibly traumatize Courtney, it didn't stop her from going out or from going out with boys in particular (there was Jesse, who had a band, and then Paul, who was Canadian), and eventually I came to remember that night as one of the last times I'd talked to Anthony, all but forgetting the reason I'd been with him. But my sister did continue down the path she'd already started down, one that led away from the rest of us. She let slide much of what she'd once cared about, everything from grades to shaving her legs. Her eighteenth birthday came and went; she barely acknowledged our presents and went out to celebrate with her friends. Her room started to look like mine: what had once been a showcase for trophies arranged just so, for books set with their spines all the same distance from the edge of the shelf, a desk with an absolutely clean surface, and the bulletin board on which photos of her friends and of Matt Dillon and a couple of mix-tape track lists had been perfectly aligned, this same room now had sweaters heaped over the unmade bed, candy wrappers on the radiator cover. A couple of times, when she wasn't home, I went up to her room and started straightening up, even though my own room was still a mess.

One day I saw that she'd thrown all her trophies and ribbons and certificates in the trash can. I couldn't help myself: I exhumed them and placed them back on top of the bookshelf where they'd stood before.

Of course, as soon as she came home and saw them, she guessed that I had put them there, and she barged into my room and told me I was not to go "trespassing" again. She said it like I'd gone deer hunting. Her speech lasted another couple of minutes. The carping was as familiar as could be, but the skinny almost-woman who stood before me was not my familiar sister. It was like somebody else had stolen my sister's voice. In my disorientation I hardly listened to what she said. I wanted the other Courtney back, the one who may not have liked me that much but who was my sister all the same. I wanted my old sister back, I wanted my old family back, and in that moment the wanting was so immediate and so total that I had a glimpse of mortality, i.e., that I would never get them back.

Then Courtney went out and banged the door shut behind her. Even from the floor beneath hers I could hear the clatter of the trophies as they went again into the trash.

2005

In the days following my father's cardiology appointment I found myself still contemplating his too-old body, where by *contemplating* I really mean *flinching from*: I would picture him failing on the treadmill, attached to an octopus of wires, or I would see him lying on a kind of man-size tray and being slid inside a big white machine that in my ignorance I pictured as a giant copier. I would see these things and then try to block them out.

I kept returning to what he'd said about Jim Singletary. When I'd read the memoir, wondering what Singletary had done to offend my dad, it hadn't occurred to me that the insult might have been personal, that it was Dad's loyalty to his old colleagues and friend Dick, rather than to larger principles or truth itself, that had made him so hostile. Singletary had helped bring Dick Mitchell down, that was why Dad hated him, even though (or maybe because?) there'd been a part of Dad that had wanted to see Dick Mitchell brought down.

This was moving to me but also dizzying: there were so many personalities and episodes involved even in my father's small portion of history, so many battles that had been fought over how to define the story even as it was unfolding, that I felt a new, or maybe renewed, hopelessness. I am no relativist—I do believe there is such a thing as the truth of the matter, not just a jumble of different versions—but that truth was seeming less and less available to me or to anyone.

I told the temp agency that I was leaving, moving back to L.A. I did think that I would probably go back sooner rather than later, although I had yet to buy a plane ticket. And then I arranged with Dad to borrow the car for a couple of days, because I had this idea I would take a long drive that weekend, out to Shenandoah, and do some thinking, some strategizing.

I drove the car to work on my last Friday of employment, then came home early, just after lunchtime, and parked down the street from my building. When I turned to shut the door, I caught sight of Nina headed my way, her backpack over her shoulder. As she came closer I saw that she was wearing eye makeup, which I hadn't seen on her during the daytime. It made her eyes look bigger but also aloof, masked. And with no real prompting, it hit me that I'd been wrong about her, I'd thought I had maybe half an understanding of what it was to be without a mother, but no, I only knew what it was like to be half-mothered, and that was different. She was fiercer than I'd given her credit for. Inside her an iridescent girl and a cackling, clawing bird shared too-close quarters.

I wanted to gush, I wanted to say *hi, hi, how have you been?* But something straitened me, and I asked, "Don't you have school?"

"Not today. It's parent-teacher conferences."

"Where are you headed?"

"A friend's house." I had the feeling she might keep walking, but she stopped and then asked, "You're not working?"

"No, I— No."

As I was fishing quarters from my wallet to feed the meter, I lost hold of the car key and it fell in the gutter. Nina went over and picked it up. She examined it, as if it were transforming before our eyes into something more than a Toyota fob, and even as I told myself it wasn't true I had the sense—by the way she glanced at the car, the way I could practically hear her gears turning—that she was tempted to take it, hop into the car and drive away. Instead she handed the key back and said, "See ya!" and headed on down the street.

The encounter troubled me, although I couldn't put my finger on the reason. I tried to distract myself. The pages that Dad had given me, his attempts at a memoir, had sat on the table ever since I'd brought them back to the apartment. That afternoon I finally read them. They were fragmentary, the first page a single paragraph:

> From 1966 to 1987 I worked in the United States government, first in the State Department and later in the White House. My tenure as a public servant coincided with a tumultuous period in American history, spanning the Vietnam War, Watergate, the Iran hostage crisis, the Iran-Contra Affair, and the end of the Cold War. Because I was privileged to observe from close up and at times participate in those significant events, I have endeavored to set down some of my recollections and reflections. It is my hope that these may provide a useful, and at times corrective, footnote to the existing record. Although there is no shortage of primary and secondary material regarding this period, it is my belief that the proliferation of accounts has sometimes had the unfortunate consequence of reinforcing, through sheer repetition, certain misinterpretations of what took place.

That I could recall, Dad had never showed much interest in writing. The books that he read were not memoirs, not even Washington memoirs, but histories or biographies of historical figures, books he didn't necessarily finish but absorbed a lot of facts from, adding to his mental stockpile. I couldn't reasonably expect him to turn out something top-notch, but I was hoping for something a smidgen livelier. What followed was a slightly longer effort, a page and a half in which Dad summarized his early life:

> I was born in 1941 in Trinity, Pennsylvania. My father, William (Bill) Atherton, worked at a dry goods store, which he later bought from the original owner. My mother, Dolores Kelley Atherton, grew up on a dairy farm, became a teacher, and met my father at a dance in Trinity. They married, bought a two-story house outside of town, and had three children, my older brother, Bill Jr., my younger sister, Edith, and me. Despite her country upbringing, Mother had a love of politics that she'd inherited from her father. She and my father were active in the local Republican Party, and I can recall passing out leaflets and attending candidate events from a young age.

This went on for several more paragraphs, in the same mode. He named the schools he'd gone to, the piano lessons he'd taken, his boyhood friends. His was "an all-American childhood," he wrote. "Bill and I went fishing and ice-skating at Mill Pond, dreamed up pranks to play on our sister, and worked afternoons in Dad's store." He'd done well at school. He'd been part of a championship debate team. He was accepted at Cornell, where he'd struggled his first year but eventually found his footing. Then Georgetown for law school.

I turned to the next page, glanced at its first lines:

> Churchill once said, "The whole history of the world is summed up in the fact that when nations are strong, they are not always just, and when they wish to be just, they are no longer strong." These words came to mind on November 13, 1986, as I watched President Ronald Reagan give his first press conference regarding the Iran-Contra Affair.

That was about as personal as it got. I skimmed the rest: no revelations, minimal detail. Nothing I didn't already know. I stacked the pages and set them back on the table.

The buzzer rang. I'd been making cheese toast when its obnoxious peal sounded. Over the intercom I heard Nina's scratched voice, asking could she come up. Of course, I said. I felt newly ashamed of my place. The moment she walked in, I thought, she would see how unsuited I was to be a big-sister figure, or whatever kind of figure I'd been pretending to be. When I opened the door, though, her face was like a sack full of stones. She made straight for my bed and sat on it and grabbed the edge with her hands.

"I really need to go to Wheaton. Can you take me in your car?"

To me Wheaton was a name on the Metro map, a suburb I'd been to maybe once or twice or maybe never.

"It's my dad's car."

"Please. It's important. We don't even have to take the car, we could go on the Metro."

"What's out there?"

"That's where Sam lives," she said.

"I don't think—"

"It's an emergency."

"Don't you have a friend with a car?"

"If I'm out late with my friends, my dad gets all frantic. He trusts you."

"It's not a good idea."

The stones in her face were shifting now, grinding against each other. "Sam hasn't answered any of my texts for the past week. I think he could be in some kind of trouble. I went to AU to try to find him today, but I couldn't."

I brought her a glass of water, even though she hadn't asked for one, and set it on the floor. Then I sat down next to her.

"You know, guys, sometimes . . . sometimes they just—"

"That's not what happened."

"One day they're all into you, and then the next day—"

"He wouldn't do that."

"It's not even about you, it's that men basically suck, most of them do."

"I did get a text from your friend Rob," she said, biting back, and that instinct to bite upset me as much as anything.

"Texted you. How did he have your number?"

"He got it when we were at dinner. You were in the bathroom."

I didn't know what to say to that. She crossed her arms over her chest and said, "So you won't take me."

"I'm sorry."

She sat there glaring at the wall and then launched herself to standing. "I guess I'll see you later."

My cheese toast was burning. "Why don't we do something else, like on Sunday?" I asked as I opened the toaster and waved my hand through the smoke.

By the time I turned back around she was halfway out the door. She called back to me from the hall, "Yeah sure," but it was as though she'd said *yeah right*. The door shut, and I was convinced I'd said the right thing in the wrong way, which was not much different from saying the wrong thing. Or was it that she'd said one thing and I'd heard another, I couldn't be absolutely sure. And wasn't it too late to take a neutral stance with Nina and her dad and Sam, now that she'd already dragged me into it? I should've either gone to her father and told him everything or stuck by her and driven her to Wheaton, but I couldn't bring myself to do either, and even without saying anything to Daniel I'd probably lost her, lost them both, because really there's no remaining neutral unless you're okay with remaining by yourself.

And then there was the fact (alleged at least) that she'd received a text from Rob, which confirmed some fears I'd had but tried to not have when we were all at the restaurant.

It took me a while, at least thirty minutes, to notice that the car key was missing. I'd put it with my own keys, in the middle of the

table, and now only my keys were there. Maybe I was misremem-
bering? Maybe, I said to myself, I'd set the car key someplace else,
on the counter, in my purse, left it in the bathroom. But it wasn't
any of those places.

I called Nina's phone and she didn't pick up. Then I called
Daniel. "Is Nina there?"

"Isn't she with you?"

"No. Are you at home?" He was. "I'm coming over, okay?"

1987

And then came another nighttime phone call from Courtney, this one later in the night and more desperate. I had a telephone in my room, a low-profile desk phone that I usually left in the middle of the floor. It didn't reach all the way to the bed, and so most of my calls were spent lying on the carpet and staring at the ceiling. I liked how all the sound was right there in my ear and up above me was just light and shadow. But I was in bed, not on the floor, that night. The phone rang at around two or three in the morning. Shoved out of sleep, I kicked the phone by accident before I answered—a little brawl between me and nobody. A recording said it was a collect call. Then my sister's first and last name: Courtney Atherton, calling from jail.

For once my parents were home. I went to wake them up. I think that was the only time I ever saw them both asleep at the same time—they were on their backs, under a comforter. The phone had half-roused them, and as soon as I said "Mom, Dad" they sat up, my mother leaning against the headboard, my father planting his legs on the floor, and once he got on the line he told me to hang up my phone and go back to sleep. Here was another problem they wanted to pretend didn't exist, but I couldn't possibly pretend that. After Dad left to pick up Courtney, I went down to the kitchen, poured a glass of juice, and sat at the table and waited.

Thirty minutes passed, then an hour, and I went back up to my room. I lay down on my bed with all the lights on. Just to rest, I vowed, but the next time I opened my eyes it was morning.

I crept up to the third floor. Courtney's door was shut. I went back down, back up, back down—she slept until noon, and when at last she appeared in the kitchen, still wearing her pajamas, she acted as though it were just a normal Sunday. I couldn't get more than a single word at a time out of her. She brought the milk and a box of cereal to the table and ate two bowls in a row.

Finally she said, "Surely you have better things to do than to stand there and watch me eat," and I could have countered with the truth, which was that I did not have anything better to do, but instead I took a basketball outside and started shooting.

What I didn't learn that day but found out over the next couple of weeks: Courtney had gone to hear a band play, and then on the way home she was pulled over for driving with no headlights. The policeman smelled alcohol, according to his report, and he brought her in. By the time they tested her she was well under the limit, but she was underage, and they'd found prescription pills in her purse that had not been prescribed to her by a doctor. They charged her with possession of a controlled substance. My parents hired a lawyer (another lawyer!), who got the case transferred to juvenile court, the charge reduced to minor in possession.

She told our parents that she'd just wanted to see what it was like to drive on Rock Creek Parkway without lights. They didn't understand that, and neither did I. There were still streetlights on that road, other cars with lights on. It seemed to me that by switching off your own headlights you would not experience the dark but merely raise your odds of hitting something or being hit. The judge suspended her license and made her attend teen Narcotics Anonymous meetings and do community service. She wound up going two afternoons a week to a big downtown homeless shelter and got involved with some homeless activists for a while, who tried to make a radical out of her, unsuccessfully, though they did convince her not to go to prom.

My parents were at a loss. In any other year, this would've been our crisis, but in '87 it was another blip on the screen. Courtney had been accepted by Brown, and briefly they panicked about whether that offer would be revoked, but once they had been assured that she could still enroll there, and once she had made it through the court system, they just let it go.

2005

Daniel met me at the door to his apartment, shoeless and stricken, intoning "come in, come in." That was it for hospitality. Next came interrogation. Yes, I admitted, yes, Nina had mentioned somebody named Sam, and yes, I believed she might have seen him recently. In fact I believed she might have gone to look for him.

He tore into me. The fact that his daughter had stolen a car, that I'd hardly condoned the mission—these things didn't matter. He brought his hands up by his head and then slashed them through the air, drawing out the word *irresponsible*, the word *negligent*, and while I sensed that every accusation he leveled against me was in some measure a charge against himself, insights like that are not much comfort when you're getting your ass chewed. He yelled until he was winded and his voice was breaking. He said he planned to call the police, as well as some of his daughter's friends, and he said he wanted me to leave and to have no further contact with him or Nina ever again.

———

Back in my own building, I called my father and told him the entire story, not very coherently. His car was missing and a girl was missing along with it, I said, and we needed to locate an American University student from Turkey who went by Sam or Samed and lived in Wheaton. When I was done talking I expected him to tell me that it would be impossible to dig up that kind of information, at night especially, but instead he spoke in a voice that I hadn't heard in years: his official voice. He said he'd see what he could do. His voice was responding to my voice, the undercurrent in it, the plea for help, more than the strange specifics.

Less than an hour later he called back, already on the way to my apartment. He'd contacted his colleague Dr. Mohammad, who had in turn called the head of an international students association, who had happened to know the roommate of Sam/Samed and had offered up a phone number as well as the address where they lived. Nobody had answered at the number, and so, Dad thought, we should just head out there ourselves. He'd borrowed a car from Judge O'Neill. It was a far-fetched thing to do, going to Wheaton, but we had worked ourselves into a far-fetched state, without knowing whether this was a real emergency or an imaginary one—it didn't matter, we'd found ourselves a crisis and were determined to act more effectively than we had in past crises.

I suppose I ought to have contacted Daniel to tell him where we were going. I did not. I went off with my dad into the night.

Those were the last days of paper maps, and as Dad drove the judge's black sedan I opened the glovebox and used the light from there to read the same Montgomery County map book my sisters and I had used to look for parties twenty years earlier, its pages faded and creased, a large rip jagging the middle of Bethesda. That book was another thing my Dad had kept in the house, in a drawer with old phone directories.

I was unexpectedly happy to be driven by him, once again. Maybe I was more at home in a car driven by my dad than anyplace else.

We were on the Beltway, and then we weren't. The city's false modesty was replaced by a suburb's actual modesty: on either side of a plain avenue stood flat-roofed brick buildings, with shops at street level and awnings that bore the most straightforward of business names. The Lunch Box, Ace Cleaners, Atlantic Appliance. From there we turned onto a street of narrow wooden houses on narrow lots, their clapboard not recently painted, with chain-link fencing around the yards and trash barrels standing sentry.

The sky was dark over the house in question, a house split in half, with two front doors, A and B. The right side of the porch was strewn with random junk, some of which I could identify as, say, children's toys, while much of the rest seemed to be parts of unknown wholes. My thoughts started to overheat. This could be a crack house, a whorehouse. Unlikely but possible.

Dad and I went up to the door on the left side, and simultaneously I was reporting it all to some future listener, Courtney, I suppose. I imagined telling her that we'd knocked, heard a voice say something indistinct, then found the door unlatched. Dad pushed it halfway open, then fully open. I told her that the living room was sorrily lit by an overhead fixture and furnished with a shapeless couch of gray leather substitute and a maroon recliner, both angled toward a large television. A young guy with an earring and a soul patch and a face more consternated than friendly sat on the recliner, changing channels.

"Is Sam around?" I said.

"You his professors or something?"

I said no just as Dad said yes.

"Yes and no, okay. Why're you looking for him?"

"We're actually looking for someone else, someone he knows."

"He's not here."

"Do you know when he'll be back?"

His shoulders bounced, a snort or maybe a hiccup, and he said he didn't.

"Could I leave a message?"

"You could," he said.

In my line of sight was a shelf with books and a small carved pipe and a plastic miniature of some ancient Egyptian deity. I was ready to walk away, but my father stepped into the space between chair and television and then introduced himself.

"Tim Atherton."

"I'm Nando," he said.

"You're what?"

"My name is Nando."

"We're looking for a girl, a young girl named Nina."

"Sam's little friend? She was here."

"They were here together?" I asked.

"Naw, she was looking for him too. But he—"

"What?"

"I don't think he'd like me telling people."

"We really need to find her."

"I guess it's public record, though."

"What is?"

Nando shifted in his chair, and he seemed to listen to something we couldn't hear. He took a breath, fidgeted more, and then began.

"He got arrested like a week ago. It was bullshit. This bitch came over here and said she was supposed to buy from me. I wasn't here, so he told her to come back later. But she was all, I need it now. He knows where my stash is. And he's not a very sophisticated person, he doesn't realize, he never thinks for a second about maybe it's a setup. The narc, she looked maybe twenty years old, that's what he told me. He was just trying to be nice, he brings it out to her. So then he gets arrested."

"And they're still holding him?"

"He's not a citizen or anything. Student visa, man. They're going to send his ass back to Turkey, is what they told him."

"Did you tell all this to Nina?" I asked.

"Not all of it. She was already upset so I didn't say about how they want to deport him."

"Do you know where she went from here?"

"I don't." He stood up and looked through a pile of papers on a side table, then left the room. We could hear him opening drawers. He returned and handed my dad a used envelope with something written on it. "This is the place where he is. It's out toward Frederick. I don't know who you people are, but if you have any way to help him—"

He paused, and I saw that he was worked up. "He's such an innocent guy, you know? I mean, he's from a village. His dad is, like, a fisherman. He didn't have any idea."

Then we were in the car again, headed back to D.C. We wanted to keep looking for Nina but had nowhere to look. It was too late at night to try to go to the jail that Nando had named. I wondered if Nina had tried to go there, wherever it was. I pictured her in some painted-cinder-block lobby, backpack still over her shoulder, pleading with a night guard.

My dad was pissed. "What is wrong with these people?" he was saying, and at first I didn't know who he meant. "They just pick these guys up, I don't know if they have quotas to meet or what, but why they're bothering with some college kid . . ." I wouldn't have expected him to take up so strongly for someone he'd never met, based on a tale told by a dude with a soul patch, but he'd had his own experience with threatened prosecution, I remembered. "If they deport that kid, and he doesn't get his degree and he's on some list of people who can never come back here . . ."

"It's fucked up," I said, though normally I wouldn't have used those words around my dad.

"It is," he said. "Can you think of anywhere else she might've gone?" He didn't want to end the search, and neither did I.

"Not really."

"Her poor father. Remember that night you and Courtney came home so late?"

"Which night was that?" I pretended I didn't know which night he meant.

And then he told me the whole story. Or no, not the whole story, but this much:

"Your mother was on a business trip," he began, "and I was downtown until late, at the lawyer's office. There were weeks when I had to go every night. I would stay for hours in one of the conference rooms, this little conference room with no windows and shelves of law books on all sides. Every night I would go through documents. There were tons of them, boxes and boxes. I hadn't been charged, but I was being investigated, and so I had to try to get ready for anything and everything, whatever they might bring against me. The kitchen sink. There were thousands of pages to be read, and the minicassettes I'd used in my Dictaphone, I listened to all of those, I went over it all. It was—it was tiresome. Awful, really.

"The irony was, about a year, maybe a year and a half earlier, I'd done something very similar at work, at the White House, in terms of looking through documents, looking for something incriminating. A report in the media had made some hay about Oliver North and the Contras, and some members of Congress got mad about it and were wanting to look at all our files. I was asked to review the files ahead of time. I went through stacks of memos, looking for ones that might have reflected badly on what North was up to, and I'd pulled about six of them and handed them over to my boss. I never asked what he planned to do about them, but still, if anything, that was the most—the most iffy thing I'd done, I thought I could get nailed on that. In other words, not for whatever was in the record, but for my part in removing something from the record. Even though I had not personally done anything more than locate and hand over the memos.

"Still, I went on reading through all that material. Night after night. I felt I had to do whatever I could. I was no big shot, but I could've gone to jail. There was that chance. It was a dark time. I would come home and I would peek into each of your bedrooms, yours and Maggie's and Courtney's. I would look at you guys sleeping and—

"Well. In other words it would be late, ten or eleven, by the time I left the law firm. More than once, a few times I think, I drove by Dick's house before I went home. It wasn't on the way, not at all, but sometimes I would just drive for a while, drive and think. I couldn't talk to Dick about what was happening, we weren't supposed to communicate with other people who were potential subjects of investigation. He was living in Bethesda with his wife and his stepson, who I guess you know. It was a big house they bought after he got married to her. A fine house.

"So that one night I turned onto his street and slowed down, and I go by the place, and I'm just speeding up again when I see Dick walking down the street. There's no sidewalk, he's just walking a little ways ahead of me on the left side of the road. I can see his light-colored hair. I pull up beside him and roll down the window, and that spooks him, like it would anybody at that time of night. At first he starts to walk faster. Then I say, can I give you a lift? He turns and blinks and says, As if I didn't have enough people on my tail.

"He was still walking, and I was inching the car forward. He told me that this was the only time he could be out in public without feeling like everyone was watching him. They all think they know, he said. Yes they do, I said.

"Then he stopped and said, let me ask you something. Do you believe that ethics are universal? He asked me that, which was strange. It's not a question that people, the people I know, typically ask each other, much less in the middle of the night, through a car window. And I'd never took Dick to be someone with a strong interest in ethics, but now all of a sudden he's wanting to know did we do anything *unethical.* Congress can go screw themselves, he was saying, but in that case who do we answer to?

"Finally he walks around to the passenger side and gets in the car. I guess that would've been the Pontiac? No, I take that back. It was the VW. I drove us around the block and Dick took a flask out of his coat and offered it to me. I said something like, but don't you think it was worth it? He gives me this look like I'm speaking gibberish and asks me, what are your antecedents? What was worth what?

"The experience, I said. The chance to serve.

"He wasn't having any of that. You don't really believe that, he said, do you? I realized he'd probably been sipping out of that flask for a while. We lost, he said.

"I wasn't inclined to start an argument, and so I asked him how his wife was doing, and he laughed and said she was as good as could be expected. And then he asked about you girls, wanted to know how my three girls were holding up.

"So here we are driving around at about ten miles per hour and flouting the open container law of the state of Maryland, and for a little while we say nothing, and then Dick out and asks me what did I want. I said I wanted it all to be over as soon as possible. No, he says, what *did* I want, what had I wanted, before? In my career, what had I wanted? As long as we'd been friends, that subject had always been off-limits, we never said it directly. I don't know why. I knew Dick was very ambitious, but we'd never said to each other, I ultimately want to be this or I want to be that. That night, though, I realized he'd had it all mapped out for himself. He told me that before the scandal he'd figured that if Bush senior won in '88 then he would've had a good shot at OMB director. And that was one difference between us. I had goals and ambitions, but at that moment, with everything falling apart around us, that was the last thing I thought about—you know, now I'll never get to be director of the Office of Management and Budget? The last thing.

"Then he said he was thinking about moving back to Connecticut. He also said he'd been in touch with a couple of publishers. That was how it was, everyone scrambled to get a lawyer and then right after that everyone ran out and tried to get a book deal. To help pay for the lawyers, if nothing else.

"We said good night and I drove home, and when I got back to our house I looked in on Maggie, and she was asleep, but then I looked for you and your sister, and when I realized you weren't home, I was—I was— You girls were usually pretty responsible about telling us where you were going and about getting back at a reasonable hour, so this was—

"I called your mother, and she got very upset. She screamed at me over the phone. Why hadn't I been home, what was I thinking? It wasn't just because of you and Courtney not being home. It was everything. Up until then she'd kept herself pretty buttoned up, but that night she let me have it.

"Then I called the police, who were not very helpful. They told me that to go looking for every teenager who isn't home at one a.m. would tie up the entire department, and to call again if you guys were still missing the next morning.

"So I sat in the living room and I waited. It felt like hours that I sat there. And finally, finally I heard a car stop outside, I heard a door open, I went to the window and saw two cars. I was so angry. I was ready to rake the both of you over the coals, and then I saw that your sister was with Dick, who I'd just seen earlier in the night. There he was, and she looked—it looked like she'd been crying. She walked up the stairs with him. Before I could say a thing she made a face at me, like I was, I don't know. She was angrier at me than I was at her. You remember how she was then. I didn't know how to—how to get to her, and I should've—I know I wasn't—Well, I didn't know how.

"She went inside, and Dick said to me that she'd called his house because she'd been stranded somewhere and hadn't been able to reach me or your mother. I couldn't quite get my mind around it. Sure, if a friend of one of you girls had called in the middle of the night and I thought she was in trouble, I would've gone to pick her up, and later Courtney explained it, she said she'd been trying to call his stepson, her friend or boyfriend or whatever he was. But when Dick first told me, he just said that she'd called *him*. That was the last time I spoke to Dick, as a matter of fact. The very last conversation we had. I didn't . . ."

He stopped midsentence. He looked out at the road, and for a second I couldn't recall where we were going or what we'd been doing. Who had we been hunting for, really? I told him to take me back to my apartment, since I didn't know where else to go. He didn't want to take me back—he wanted to continue our search—but we had no more leads.

We sat in the car outside my building. Nearby, a long blue Dumpster occupied two parking spaces in front of a town house that had just been sold. The car heater was turned up high, chapping our lips, making me feel feverish. I wasn't ready to go in, because it seemed there might be something else we should do or at least say before giving up. I waited. There was so much he'd never talked about, the old scandal just a small province in that country of the unsaid.

And then did I will it? Dream it? Over the rumble of the engine, the heater, the space between our seats, he went on with what he'd been saying earlier, picked up with it as though he'd never paused.

"Didn't talk to him again. Even later on, after the hearings, we never spoke.

"That spring, as you know, Courtney had her trouble with the police, and I . . . here she's always been a straight-A student, very responsible, and then all of a sudden she's arrested? In jail? My god. And not only that, she'd also just turned eighteen, and I didn't want for this to be public, for her to have to have this thing follow her around the rest of her life. I didn't want it to wind up on the news, and I was scared that it would because of me, you know, daughter of former White House official gets arrested.

"So I called Jodi and asked her, I said here's the situation, Courtney was arrested. How do I keep this out of the news? I wasn't supposed to be talking to her either, to anyone in the press. She told me there wasn't a whole lot she could do. But if she did hear that someone was on the story she would warn me.

"And then she asked me, very casually, it was very much of a since-I've-got-you-on-the-line-I-might-as-well, she asked about an article that one of her colleagues was working on. It was about that Bible, I don't know whether you would remember this, but North and McFarlane took this Bible with them on a trip to Tehran, to give to the Iranians. I always thought that it was odd, but I'll never understand why people made such a fuss about that one thing. At the time it hadn't been reported yet, and from what Jodi told me her colleague had got several facts wrong, and though I suppose I should've just kept out of it, I corrected her. On background, I said that it was this way and not that way. She asked me, is it true that this was all Dick Mitchell's idea? I said I didn't know whose idea it was, probably North's. Dick could've run out and bought the thing, I told her, but it had to be on North's instructions.

"The whole business seemed so minor that I hardly gave it a lot of thought. She'd said she would try to help me, and I tried to help her a little. But I was also scared for Courtney and very tired and in retrospect I would say not careful. Not careful when it came to Dick. I shouldn't have said what I did, because it got out that he was the guy behind the Bible and whatever else they said he was behind. I wonder now what was going through my head. I shouldn't have said even that much."

Dad looked down at his lap. What could I say to him? I wanted to thank him, at least, for telling me what he'd told me.

"Did you read the pages I gave you?" he asked.

I said I thought the memoir was off to a promising start, but I could hear myself, I sounded apologetic. I suggested he write out the story he'd just told me.

"I don't know about that," he said.

"You should."

"I'll think about it."

I thanked him, though I don't think he knew what I was thanking him for—taking me to Wheaton and back, that's what he must've thought. He told me he planned to report the missing car to the police, and he waited for me to enter the building before driving off. Once he was gone, I stepped outside. The sky had a reddish tint, with a few stars like embers. There were lights on at Daniel and Nina's place. I went back in.

An envelope appeared in my mailbox the next day, containing the key to the Camry and an unsigned note explaining where the car was parked. I would've liked to call Nina, but Daniel had ordered me to keep my distance. The car was waiting just where the note said, and straightaway I started for Albemarle Street, forgetting to ask my father to update the police. I hadn't driven it a mile in the direction of his house before I was pulled over. I spent a long time stopped in the right lane of Massachusetts Avenue, trying to convince a skinny but jowly cop that I hadn't stolen Dad's car. We happened to be across the street from an embassy, where a small boy watched from an upstairs window. Finally I drove the rest of the way to the house with a police escort, and that waifish officer walked me up the half flight of concrete stairs and got my father to confirm my story before leaving me alone. I sat in the living room for a while, still rattled by the experience of having come under suspicion, and while my twenty minutes was nothing compared to what had befallen Dad, I still made that comparison, and saw something I hadn't before then.

t had been so reassuring to be ferried around by Dad that I no longer understood what it meant to feel reassured, to feel that I was in exactly the right place, not if a car and D.C. roadways and the sound of his voice sufficed. My apartment was far less comforting than the car, and the next night I balked at it all. The plate of crumbs left on top of my latest to-do list, the pile of professional clothes in the corner, the cheap Cuban coffee maker on the stove, the pans and knives from the supermarket, this shabby parcel where I'd penned myself.

I had intended to go on writing, to record my family's experience of the long investigation, the awful late eighties, when Dad was on the hook. For even after he'd found a new job and otherwise might've gone on with his life, he could hardly go on with his life. The independent counsel was a methodical, moralizing man who proceeded slowly, left everybody hanging. It was 1989, 1990 before the trials started, and by then you had crusty old ex-spooks and ex-somebodies who, worn down by years of waiting, of legal expenses, of whispers behind their backs, of dwelling in the alternate universe of a scandal nobody cared about any longer, broke down in tears on the witness stand. Which was maybe no more than they deserved, maybe less than they deserved—I myself have no clue what they deserved. I only know that during my last two years of high school, Courtney had left and the house was gloomy and quiet. Sometimes I heard my parents arguing in their bedroom. Maggie entered a rigorous training program for dancers that ate up all her afternoons and evenings, and I just found other places to be. I became more social than I'd been before, went to more parties, slept over at other girls' houses. I was the funny one, offering up sarcasm, imitations, whatever I could do for a laugh, ha!

By the time I left for college, Dad had learned that no charges would be brought against him. And still the battle continued: he was informed by the government that in fact he'd never been considered a target of investigation, which not only stripped him of his very struggle, but also put him, put the whole family, in a financial hole. For if you were a "target" against whom charges were ultimately dropped, you were entitled to some reimbursement of your legal fees, but otherwise you were stuck with the entire tab. He had to submit a petition maintaining that while he may not have been a "target," he had qualified as a "subject" under the law. Once, when I was home on vacation, I found a copy of that document: *Mr. Atherton was clearly a 'subject' of the investigation, as defined both by the ordinary usage of the word 'subject' and by Section 9-11.150 of the Department of Justice Manual.* And in another paragraph: *Although the Independent Counsel may have eventually dropped Mr. Atherton to the level of a witness, he was most certainly a subject for a significant period of time.*

Witness or subject? That was one of the questions I'd been trying to sort out for myself, all these years later, but I hadn't found an answer. There was no jewel in the slagheap, and no lifting my father out of that pitiful moment in which he'd had to plead with the court to recognize him as more than a mere bystander. Now, in 2005, it was too late: what good would it have done him to be recognized after so many years, by such a partial and ambivalent judge as myself? Here I had started out writing a cautionary tale about my father, the father whose mistakes I didn't want to repeat, and then somewhere along the way it had become a cautionary tale about myself, or rather about the depreciated model of myself I carried around, the feckless witness I considered myself to be.

Even so, I refused to accept Courtney's idea that this was all a dead end. I wasn't ready to renounce it. I simply came to the not so revelatory conclusion that when you write about your family, it's not for their benefit. And whatever it had done for me, was already done.

I was invaded by a discomfort I can only recapture in part, a furry weed pushing up through cracked ground, a weed that had become too deeply lodged, by the time I saw it was there, to pull out with my hands. Resentment was one piece of it, but I'm talking about that kind of resentment that bangs around looking for a target, or a subject, that dredged up a boss who'd underpaid me some time ago, also a night in 2001 when I'd gone to a party with my then boyfriend and he'd decided (without telling me) to give crack a try, also a comment my mom had once tossed off, starting with a skeptical *Now, if you were ever to get married . . .* And along with all that I felt a more general restlessness, like a person who can't sleep because she's lying in bed thinking furious thoughts, except that I wasn't in bed or trying to sleep.

I stared out the window at the dark street. I had to get out, had to go somewhere, no matter that I had nowhere to go. I thought of "nowhere to go," oh that magic feeling, thought of the summer car trips we had taken in the late seventies and early eighties, the good years of the Pontiac Grand LeMans wagon and "You Never Give Me Your Money" trumpeting quietly from the tape deck, as we passed through Pennsylvania and Ohio, as our dog farted on our suitcases in the way back.

It was drizzling out and warmer than I'd expected it to be, everything damp but also sharp. I walked to the Metro but then saw a taxi and waved it down instead.

When I got out of the cab, the clouds had hidden the sickle of moon, and the drizzle had turned to solid rain. A handful of boisterous men with near-shaved heads huddled together in the door of a restaurant, as someone turned the volume up and down on their jazzy laughs. The street split apart, two lanes descending under an intersection while one lane hugged the storefronts, and the wet cars dove into the dark tunnel, and some part of me knew my own delusion, that is to say I knew I might not be acting in my own best interests, but when did I ever?

I called Rob from under the awning of his building. He didn't answer, but just then a middle-aged couple came out the front entrance, and I slipped inside and into an elevator that opened its doors for me. As I neared his apartment I heard, or thought I heard, his voice. I knocked and nothing. I knocked again. "Hey, open up," I said.

He opened it maybe a third of the way. "What are you doing here?"

"I have to talk to you."

"This is not a great time."

"Could you let me in?" Even as I asked I was pushing my way inside. The place looked different with all the lights on, his jacket over a chair, an open bag of chips on the dining table, along with his laptop and a couple of beer cans. Rob had on a T-shirt and jeans, he was unshaven and annoyed with me, and still he was handsome, the fucker.

"So what is it?" he asked, as he walked over to the computer to read something on the screen.

In the cab I'd rehearsed the middle of the conversation I wanted to have, but not the beginning. "I just have some concerns," I said, and then stalled. I tried to clear my throat, which devolved into spasms of coughing.

"Are you okay?" he asked.

He fetched a glass of water and set it down on the table.

"I just would like to know, what happened with you and my sister?"

Now he stared at me. "I've seen her, like, twice in the past fifteen years."

"What happened in high school?"

"We got together a few times. She was kind of a mess."

"She was not a mess."

"Senior year, she was."

"You can't just blame it all on that," I said. "You guys were a couple."

"Blame what? I'm not blaming."

"But something happened."

"Really, your sister was, like . . . Look, if she hasn't told you herself, then I don't know."

I heard the sound of the toilet flushing. "Is there someone in your bathroom?"

"That's from next door."

He was lying. I walked toward the bathroom and opened the door—and there she was. Nina was barefoot, and her hair was down and wet against her shirt, which didn't seem like *her* shirt. It was a man's striped button-down, too big for her.

"Whoa," she said. Then she laughed. "Oops."

I tried to say something but couldn't. Rob, who'd followed me to the bathroom, was tossing out words I didn't catch. Finally I asked, "Whose shirt is that?"

"Hers was soaking wet," Rob said.

"Have you even been home?" I asked her.

"Sam's in jail. I had to find someone who could help. It's not like my dad's going to. You wouldn't."

"She came here and told me about this guy who's detained," Rob said.

I felt sick, wanting to do and say drastic things, but what were they? "This is so . . . I don't even know what to call it. This is insanity."

"I've been on the phone to some people. We're trying to figure out what system he's in," he said. "It might be the county, or it might be ICE—"

"Where are your shoes?" I asked Nina.

"I'm not leaving."

"It's ten-thirty at night. Get your shoes on. I'm taking you home."

"You can't make me go."

"I will call the police and accuse you of things you don't want to be accused of," I said to Rob.

"Nothing happened?" he said.

I thought about my little gun. It occurred to me that although my father had given it to me to ward off a different kind of threat, in my life to date it was the Robs of the world who'd done more damage than thugs or thieves, and this because I'd failed to defend myself against them. I should've kept it, should've had it with me in my purse, but instead I pulled out my phone.

"I'm calling the police right now. She's underage. You gave her beer. I can call them."

"Yeah, okay. Go right ahead. You're as crazy as your sister," he said.

"Maybe I am. She's not, though. Courtney's not crazy."

"Oh, she is."

"I don't know what the hell you're talking about."

"You really want to know?"

"Lay it on me."

"She was obsessed with my stepfather. She thought she was in love with him. It took me a while to catch on, but eventually I figured it out. She went after me to get to him."

"Please."

"She did."

"Your stepfather. You expect me to believe that."

"I don't care if you do or not. She was obsessed."

"I think you went out with her, you sold her pain pills, you dumped her, and then you were cruel to her after that. That's what I know."

"Man," he said, smiling acidly. "Ask her then. You really should."

Although it had seemed that I might have to drag Nina away by
the hair, she came willingly enough—that is to say, grudgingly,
but of her own accord. By the time we stepped outside, all the estab-
lishments were locking up. Bilgy odors wafted out of the alleys. A
man dashed across the street holding a piece of cardboard over his
head and knocked at a black door. I'd found the girl but lost her. I
got us a cab.

The driver had the radio on, and we'd gone through a light or
two when some pop ballad began to play, one of those songs so
simple I wanted to curl up and live inside of it, to float within the
girl singer's breathy voice.

"Was he hitting on you?" I asked.

"No."

I was at a loss for something to say that might reach her. The bar-
ricades were so high, and I was so tired. I was also wound tight as
could be. I wished that we could smile at each other again, that I
could ease our way into talking, and then I could tell her to stay
away from Rob, even though I knew that the same warning hadn't
worked on me.

Nina called her father and told him we were nearby. Helen's
bringing me, she said, and I could hear his voice getting louder and
faster before she told him *be there soon* and hung up.

He was waiting out front with crossed arms and wet glasses, in
a big nylon jacket bloated by the wind. When we drove up, he
came stumbling down to the street and wrenched her out of the car
and held her until she pushed and he let go. Then he leaned over to
speak to me through the open car door. I still didn't know whether
she'd been gone the whole time, missing since the day before, or
whether she'd come back last night and then vanished again. I had
no idea whether he was going to yell at me again or thank me.
Maybe he himself could not decide, his face was stung with exhaus-
tion, and without saying anything he stood and shut the door.

Because he was blocking my view of Nina, I couldn't so much as wave goodbye to her.

What Rob had said kept coming back to me. I couldn't buy the idea that my sister, when she was in high school, had fallen for someone our dad's age. She wasn't that unconventional. Yet I had never understood why Dick Mitchell had appeared that night outside the Giant, after Anthony and I had gone there to pick her up. I remembered the look on his face, a look that had gone missing from my parents' faces, tender and fraught, and I could imagine that a girl like my sister, who was starved for that look, might wolf it down.

However: Rob was a liar! I wouldn't believe him.

I was all wet around the edges: my hair, my shoes, the cuffs of my jacket. I heard distant sirens. I wanted to talk to Courtney, but it was too late to call. I was stuck on the image of her and Dick Mitchell, and by image I mean a composite of what I remembered from that night outside the Giant and a kind of blurry film still. I tried to shut it down: Rob was a liar. And Courtney was a drama queen. A drama queen, a perfectionist, a bizarre individual—she was all of those, and then again those were labels I'd pasted on her to cut her down to size. Whatever she was, or wasn't, Rob's accusation had reinforced my latent sense that while I wasn't looking she'd gone down to the underworld and back. She'd made a few trips, perhaps. I wanted to ask, why did you go without me? And maybe she would've said that there was no way to bring me, or maybe she would've said, why didn't you come along?

I sent Courtney a short e-mail, having first written a long e-mail and then deleted most of it.

When we were kids, my sisters and I would swim in a lake near our grandmother's house. Setting forth from a tiny smear of beach, we would enter the water, slowly, holding our arms out like featherless wings. We had to divine with each step whether our feet would land on smooth sand or muck or rocks or weeds. I searched for the good sand, wished it could all be good sand. I remember Courtney choosing to walk on the rocks, making a game of it. *Come over here! It's better over here!* I would call to her (*over here, here, here*) and she would reply, *No, you come over here!*

The thing about my sister was, I held on to that ideal bathing-beauty version of our relationship no matter what, no matter how stupidly we behaved, no matter how much we needled each other. I still believed in some sort of transcendent sisterly intimacy. I suspect she did too. I think maybe this ideal caused us to go at each other all the more, because we both had this underlying disappointment in our ongoing failure to realize it. Every once in a while we came close, though. That's how it survived.

In the morning she called me, about the e-mail. "What did he tell you?" she asked.

"It was very weird."

"Like what?"

"I feel weird even saying it," I said. "You were right about him having some issues."

"Do you want to get something to eat?" she asked.

"Right now?"

"I'm hungry. Is there anything good near you?"

Twenty minutes later, she walked into the Hunan Palace and sat down across from me. She looked old, thirty-five going on forty-five. Here she was. We'd played a thousand rounds of card and board games, ridden thousands of miles in cars together, eaten thousands of meals, but my accumulated understanding of her was corroded by moldy judgments. I was only just starting to grasp how people in families, or at least the people in my family, refused to know one another. And it was hard to say which counted for more, all those games and cars and dinners, or the fact that when she'd had a crisis of her own, we'd been distracted—or had we turned away?—and let her down.

Courtney pressed me to tell her what Rob had said, so I did. "He said that you were, like, into his stepfather."

"I never slept with him."

"Rob didn't say that. Only that you had a crush on him."

"Oh."

"Did you?"

Her eyes glazed over. For a second or two the hurt was right there for anybody to see, until she bit her lip and sent it back to its hole. I wanted to hop over the table and sit next to her and tell her I'd seen that, I'd seen her!

"Wow."

"I thought it was love. I was sure we were in love, Richard and I," Courtney said.

It took me a moment before I realized who "Richard" was. By then she'd already plunged in and was saying things I couldn't quite believe about herself, about Rob, about "Richard." How she used to write his name in her notebooks and then scratch over it so no one would see. How she would want to go over to Rob's house in the afternoons just to sit where he sat, to look at this one photo of him. I had some trouble hearing all this. Maybe everything had happened just as she said, and still it seemed so crazy that I wanted to criticize the story on those grounds. And literally too, I could barely hear her. She seemed to be murmuring this tale to herself.

We were the only customers, and instead of the usual waiters a middle-aged man was working, who had told me, when I'd come in, to go ahead and sit anywhere. In the middle of Courtney's story, he brought our food, glancing at me and at her and then back at me. "Sisters?" he asked. Not for the first time, it was as though having a sister had made me more of a person. I said "yes" with inexplicable pride.

"You're the older one," he said to Courtney. Nobody ever got it wrong—they always guessed that she was older. "You look out for her?"

"She looks out for me, actually," Courtney said.

"Is that right?"

"That's right," I said. None of it made sense. We were just talking.

And then he kept going, he told us about himself in far too much detail, as we spooned food onto our plates and—there was no use waiting for him to leave—started eating. Behind the cash register, a small television was tuned to CNN, reporting that there was unrest in Belize, of all places.

It wasn't until after we left, and she drove me the two blocks back to my building, that she went on with the story. She'd had a crush on Dick Mitchell, a.k.a. Richard, ever since she was about twelve, but then came a time when he started looking at her differently, talking to her differently, and that was when she'd really fallen for him. She used the same word that Rob had: *obsessed*. She'd become obsessed, and because that was the first time she'd felt so strongly about someone, she decided it had to be love. True love. My sister the seventeen-year-old athlete had been a covert romantic—then again who isn't a romantic, at that age?

She'd started seeing Rob, but it was the stepfather she thought about constantly, and when she went to their house she would stare at his picture, or, if he was home, she'd linger too long while talking to him. Rob picked up on it soon enough. Worse, he became convinced that the two of them were having a full-on affair, which, Courtney said, they weren't.

Rob broke up with her, which meant that she never saw Richard anymore. It made her miserable. She hardly ate, she dreamed about him. Sometimes she felt she was losing her grip.

"So what happened that night?" I asked.

"What night?"

"The night I came and picked you up," I said. "That night you got stranded at the Giant."

She said she'd been really fucked up that night and didn't remember it clearly. She remembered going to a party where she drank a lot. She remembered that Rob had been there, and she remembered him taunting her, screaming things at her. "He locked me in a room," she said.

"By yourself?"

"No, he was in there too."

"What happened?"

"It was really loud. The party was. I don't think anybody could hear us."

"And he—"

"I don't . . . You know, it's kind of a blur," she said. "At some point I blacked out. The next thing I remember is when I called you from that pay phone."

I thought of how messy and sad she'd looked when we'd found her, and now I saw that same person making a phone call, her clueless younger sister answering, two frightened girls. "How come you never told me about any of this?" I asked.

She was quiet for a while. Then she said, "It's not who I am."

At first I took this to mean that it wouldn't be like her to tell me, or maybe that she wasn't capable of telling anybody. Later that night, though, after she dropped me off and I went to bed, I would wonder whether she'd actually meant that the story itself wasn't her—that what had happened that night hadn't defined her. She wasn't a partier, wasn't a victim, wasn't the person she'd been that night, was no longer the girl she'd been when she was seventeen. She'd disowned that girl.

I guessed that Courtney remembered more than she was saying, and meanwhile that were I to ask Rob about all this, he would tell a different story, but I was tired of trying to be objective. "I'm so sorry," I said.

She stared steadily at the road.

"I wish I'd known. I wish we'd all known."

"Yeah, well," she said. "Our parents knew. I mean, they didn't know about that night, but they should've known a few things. I was taking all those pills, I was fucking up, and as long as I still got to go to Brown they just bailed. Turned a blind eye to it."

"I know. They couldn't deal."

"I mean, thank god I got arrested. After that I had to go to those meetings, which were kind of stupid but they probably saved me. Mom and Dad never even talked to me about it. God."

"I know."

"And it's like, will I ever stop waiting for them to say they're sorry? I feel like I still can't let them off the hook."

"But Dad is sorry. Can't you tell?"

"Yeah. It's just that having him act guilty and not say any-thing—"

"It's not the same."

"And Mom—"

"Mom's a freak," I said.

"Mom is a freak."

"Did you ever see him again?"

"Richard? I did, actually. One day I left school and drove to his house. I think about it now, and I can't believe I did that, like what if his wife had been there? I guess she had some kind of job. Any-way it was—we mostly just talked, and then he kissed me, and that was—it was weird, I mean for both of us. It didn't go past that. That was the last time I saw him. I think I had this idea that, you know, we would be together later, like after I finished college. But then—"

"It sounds like things had always been rough for him. I can't imagine . . ."

Courtney nodded, and then dismissed it all at once, banishing the ghost of Dick Mitchell from the car with an odd jerk of her chin. I wanted to say more but had no more to say. "So. Anyway . . ." she said. "There's something else."

"Yeah?"

She told me, and I made a sound, a squawk.

"It's still early. And I lost the last one, so I'm really nervous."

I pretended I hadn't known about the miscarriage, tried to re-assure her. But oh my gosh this is so great, I said.

I admit that I was not as happy for her as I might've been in that moment, not purely and selflessly happy. I concentrated on breath-ing. I counted my breaths.

"I'm not telling our parents yet. Just you and Maggie."

"Guess you'll have to quit smoking," I said.

"I don't smoke," she said. "I mean, not really."

That denial was so 100 percent my sister that I smiled, and then I noticed that I did feel something other than fear and envy, something warmer: a little yellow feather of feeling that I stuck in my cap.

And then I was disturbed by a different piece of news, for the next day my mom called to tell me that Jodi Dentoff had died. She'd gone to the hospital to have something removed and while there had come down with an infection and then, my mother said, she'd succumbed to it. That was the word Mom used, *succumbed*, and I had to repeat it to myself before I understood what she meant. I said how shocked I was and so on, stringing those phrases around the concave place that the news had made. Tinny as it might've sounded when I said it, I really was shocked. Jodi had always seemed more alive than just about anybody else.

Somewhere in my head there was a picture of everyone I'd ever known, and now another person in it was blacked out. More and more of the people who'd been present for some stage of my life were now gone, and though this would've been true of any adult following time's arrow in the usual direction, it still gave me pause, and made me think about how I'd grown up in a disjointed world of people from other places and how after college I had mostly lived in other places myself and had never come across most of those people again, never heard a thing about their lives and deaths. I'd turned away from that picture of everyone I'd ever known, I'd rarely looked at it, but still it was a part of me, and the darker it became, the more it demanded to be seen.

I asked Mom if she knew how Dad was doing, and she said only that I should talk to him myself. I called, but he didn't pick up. When I finally got him on the phone he wouldn't talk much about it. He agreed that it was a real shame and then changed the subject.

The service was hardly what Jodi deserved. A woman like her should've been remembered at a palace or at least the Kennedy Center; there should've been a choir or a second-line band or tropical birds; but the Jewish and Catholic sides of her family had disagreed on what sort of funeral to hold, and the compromise service took place at an event space on Florida Avenue, low-ceilinged and musty. It was packed. There were reporters and politicos, but also friends from other places and a handful of young women whom Jodi had helped pay for college.

My mother and Maggie had both come to town for the funeral, and we all went together, except for Hugo, who was visiting his family in Mexico. I sat between Mom and Courtney, and then to Courtney's right came Maggie, and then Dad next to her, on the aisle. We'd reassembled the old family unit, which was strange and comforting at the same time. I couldn't have said how many years had gone by since I'd been someplace in public with both my parents, and strange as it was, still it felt like the most regular thing in the world, even the way they were bookending us—they used to do that in church or at the movies, to contain my sisters and me.

Jodi's mother was still alive, a ninety-year-old woman as tiny as Jodi, or maybe tinier, stooped over, shutting her watery eyes as she accepted one hand after another and held it loosely between both of hers. She didn't get up to speak, but a brother and a cousin and a couple of Jodi's colleagues did. They told charming stories into a microphone that had been placed just slightly in front of the first row of chairs, as it might be at a question-and-answer session following a lecture. And then Dad stood up, unexpectedly, hiked his pants, and walked slowly toward the front. He had a handkerchief in one hand and a set of index cards in the other.

Jodi had been wrong about him, I thought. He hadn't been wrecked, not really. His government career had ended early, sure, but that didn't mean wrecked. For here he was, very much intact, as were we. Pressing on was one of my family's strengths. Let it be said about the Athertons: we had okay manners most of the time, and we ate well, and we went on with it. Dad lifted the microphone from its stand and stepped forward, in front of the crowd, and turned to face everybody. I was nervous for him and I guess instead of him. He was calm, gazing above us at some spot toward the back, where maybe he could see Jodi hovering in midair, hands planted on her hips, chin tucked, eyes full of private glee.

"I should've straightened that bow tie for him," my mother whispered to Courtney.

It was a peacock-blue bow tie—askew, yes, but only slightly—that he'd worn with his black suit. He'd combed his hair so that it hugged his head more closely than usual and traded his everyday glasses for tortoiseshell reading glasses. His look was classically Washingtonian, not exactly well-heeled, not exactly professorial, but a cross between the two. He was entirely of the city that had ground him down and then kept him on.

"I first met Jodi when I was at the State Department," he said. "Back then she was a young reporter covering foreign policy for *The Washington Star*. Some of you here are as old as I am and will remember that newspaper. One day our public information guy comes to me and says can you talk to Jodi Dentoff from *The Star*?

"I won't bore you with an explanation of what the interview was about," Dad continued. "Suffice it to say that I was pretty confident, I thought I knew my stuff, and this young woman on the other end of the phone just took me apart. She caught me completely off guard. She knew ten times as much as I did. And it was still one of the more enjoyable conversations I'd ever had with a reporter. She was just somebody you wanted to talk to, even when it wasn't in your own best interest. She was so smart but also so gracious. Always friendly even when she didn't agree with you. We've lost that kind of sensibility in this town and now we've lost her too.

"In those days it wasn't always easy to be a woman in Washington, in that type of job. I gather it still isn't. From *The Star*, as many of you know, she went to the Washington bureau of *The New York Times*, and then *The Post* after that, and wherever she went she did excellent work, but she was always an excellent friend too. She took an interest in everything, and that included my family, my wife, my daughters . . ."

Dad barely looked at his index cards. He seemed at ease and yet he was, I think, mystified to have found himself at Jodi's funeral. The voice that filled the room, I knew it better than my own, I knew every enunciation, every "er . . . um," and as I looked away, at the other heads, the other pairs of ears, I knew what he would say, knew even though I didn't know. Wherever I looked, his voice was all around me. I thought of Jodi entering the next world as if it were some terrific party, standing just inside the entrance and rubbing her hands together. I imagined a Washington afterlife full of gossip and jostling and long, tedious hearings.

Suddenly I saw myself, at seven or eight, pulling small rocks out of the sand at the water's edge and washing them off, piling them up, then taking a fistful to show my father, who was just climbing into his sailboat. His hair brown, his skin tanned. Waving to me as he tacked away in the Sunfish. I remembered days when he'd tried to teach us sports he didn't know how to play himself, kicking a ball in the park with the three of us girls. I thought of the times he'd lit the grill, opened the wine. I heard his voice and saw all my dads, the driver of cars, the in-house lecturer, the reluctant punisher, the dad waiting with his too-complicated camera as we unwrap the Christmas presents, the dad in a patterned shirt with a huge collar, who leans over a baby, me, tucked in a pram. And then as a young man, the college debate champ, and before that, running across a field in Pennsylvania, wearing a red knit cap, and before that, a two-year-old wrapped in his mother's arms.

Then he was in a boat again, only this time it was my present-day dad, and I saw all the unreachable life he'd already lived, now behind him, an anchor that kept moving, pulling him out to sea. Come back, come back! I ached for all the fathers he'd been before now and all the pre-fathers I'd never even met.

But wasn't that very desire our curse or at least our hobble, the ball my whole family refused to unchain? We wanted one another to be the people we used to be, we wanted for Maggie to play games and love cats, for Courtney to achieve whatever was out there to be achieved, for Dad to be powerful and Mom to keep us out of trouble, for them to be married, and for me to remain the go-between and the goof.

His voice broke off, and it was the silence that made me realize I'd stopped listening to his words. He looked down at the index cards. He seemed perplexed, as if everything he'd written on them had disappeared. When he raised his head back up and stared into the room, he blinked like a man coming out of the water, and I wondered how much he could see through those reading glasses.

"*Agape* is a Greek word for love," he said slowly, then paused again. The room itself seemed to grow more still, as we all waited to see whether he could recover his train of thought, if there was in fact a train.

"Selfless love, in the Christian theology. The love of God for man."

He scratched his nose.

"Is he all right?" Mom whispered.

"If we are lucky, we experience many kinds of love in our lifetimes," he said. "Without that, though I speak with the tongues of men or the tongues of angels . . ."

"We should go get him," Mom said to me. I stayed put. I saw (or thought I saw) an intention in his eyes, in the hold he had on the microphone, in the slow, steady breathing that rustled from the speakers.

"Well."

He took off his glasses, and his naked face was serene as he went on thinking his thoughts, unhurriedly, with no trace of the anger that had lately been percolating in him, or shame, or any self-consciousness whatsoever. His uncorrected eyes seemed to locate us, to find Mom specifically.

"I know I was a burden," he said. "It was too much to ask, perhaps."

She whispered, "No."

"I let you down."

There was scattered applause, as though people wanted to assure him that he hadn't let them down. "Thank you," he said, and with that he walked back toward his seat, coming up the center aisle. As he reached our row, he gripped the back of the chair he'd been sitting in earlier.

His trips to the hospital, had they been false alarms or warning bells? The question of how much longer he'd be around wasn't a question I'd even been asking six months earlier, but then his heart had faltered, and now Jodi had left us. She'd been close to his age.

"I feel a bit off," he said.

Mom popped up and nimbly skirted the rest of us, until she was in the aisle, next to Dad. She took him by the arm. "Can you walk?" she asked.

"Of course I can walk."

They started toward the door. Courtney got up too, but Mom waved her back, signaling us that we should stay. We'll be outside, she mouthed while pointing at the exit. The crowd took a minute to settle. The next eulogist was an elderly fellow, now creeping toward the front of the room. Just before he reached the microphone, Courtney stood up again, and Maggie and I followed her out. I feared to find Dad as he'd been after the panel discussion, in pain, refusing an ambulance, but when we made it to the lobby and then to the street there was no sign of our parents. We called both their phones, left messages.

Halfway down the block was a steak restaurant, and we took refuge there, at the bar, and though it was not quite noon Maggie and I ordered cocktails, which we guzzled while waiting for our parents to call us.

At last Mom called, from another restaurant. She said they were having lunch. We paid our tab and slowly made our way to the address she'd given us. At first we couldn't find it. We were giggling and wandering, and we stopped at a convenience store, where we bought cheese-and-peanut-butter crackers and candy bars. We're starving, we told the guy at the register. We can't find our parents. Take care now, he said. We were twelve years old! I could've spent the rest of the day roaming the streets with my sisters.

At last we turned a corner and there was the place. Our parents were finishing up their sandwiches, which, our mom said, had not been very good. But she and Dad seemed to have been enjoying themselves. Maggie swiped a few potato chips off Dad's plate and asked him how he was feeling.

"Feel fine. Sad day. But I feel fine."

My mother checked her watch. "There's a train I could catch if I leave now," she said, and at first I was taken aback—how could she possibly leave? But then I remembered, she's headed home. And Maggie decided to go with her to the station, and we all hugged, and I tried not to feel left behind, now that it was up to Courtney and me to take Dad back to Albemarle Street.

The house was cool. Dad went upstairs to lie down while Courtney and I turned on the lights, turned up the heat, and boiled water in the kettle, trying to liven up the place by some means other than talking to each other. When we did speak it was in hushed tones: What kind of tea do you want? Should we try to make dinner? The rapport of the other day had faded. Instead we were courteous.

My tea tasted strange—smoky and bitter—but I kept sipping at it. I sat in a chair in the living room with my mouth puckered over my mug, and Courtney sat across from me, on the sofa.

I told her I'd quit temping. I was going back to L.A.

"Oh," she said, sounding two notes, higher and then lower.

"What about you, how's the office?"

"The office—" She stood up and bolted to the bathroom. I heard her throwing up. I heard a faucet go on, off, on, off. When she came back, her eyes were wet and she was holding a glass of water.

"So has it been bad?"

She groaned. "I'll be fine for a while and then it's like, boom. Get me a paper bag."

"Oh man. So have you told Dad yet?"

"Not yet."

Our father upstairs, resting. Our old house, stilled. The creases now starting to show on our own faces. Our eyes met: an unexpected, raw shyness. We drank our tea.

'm not great with endings. Neither was Lawrence E. Walsh, who in December of 1986 was appointed independent counsel for the Iran-Contra matter, and who persisted in his efforts for more than six years. A former judge, already in his midseventies when he was summoned to Washington from Oklahoma City, he worked relentlessly at the job. He limited himself almost entirely to his downtown office and the Watergate Hotel, where he took a room. Even his staff considered him aloof: he brooded behind his desk, a tall old man with uneven front teeth. To this city of pragmatists he'd come like a patrician avenger, a ghost of justice past, a righteous perfectionist on a mission to elucidate the murkiest of cases. He sought, in vain, access to the classified documents he needed to press a conspiracy charge. He watched as the joint committees granted immunity to North and Poindexter so that they could testify before Congress, and he later saw those two men's convictions overturned because of it, while others against whom he'd won convictions were granted pardons by President George H. W. Bush. "The path Independent Counsel embarked upon in late 1986," he wrote in his final report, "has been a long and arduous one." Though a jury sided with him in every case he brought to court, Walsh was only able to prosecute the lies and cover-ups, not the weapons sales to Iran or the aid to the Contras or the diversion of funds from one to the other, and when the eighty-one-year-old Walsh finally returned to Oklahoma, many rated him a failure.

But he'd had a long and varied career before then, and afterward went on to write two books, to give speeches, to live for many more years—and that, perhaps, was its own kind of victory.

We're sitting at the kitchen table, Dad and I are. I'm peeling an orange, and he's scanning the newspaper. The phone on the wall rings. He tells me not to get up and speaks to the phone—*hold on, hold on*—while closing in on it.

He says hello and then asks a bunch of questions. "You've talked to him? . . . Pamunkey Regional Jail, where on earth is that? . . . When's the hearing?"

Dad was able to find the court-appointed lawyer representing Samed a.k.a. Sam, and over the last two weeks he's been hounding her about the case, hounding her and helping her too. He was the one who figured out how to locate the kid's parents in Turkey. My father would've made a good reporter—I have no idea how he's tracked these people down. As it is, he's taken his animus against the current administration and funneled it into trying to advocate for this kid. He's also contacted Daniel a couple of times, who has agreed to let Nina attend any court hearings that don't conflict with school. Presumably they'll all conflict with school, but we'll see.

Back at the table after the phone call, he tells me what the lawyer had to say, breaking it all down, the procedures, the time line, how the lawyer thinks there's a chance that Sam will be able to stay in the country, though not an excellent chance. I offer Dad half of the orange and the papers draw us in again. The radio is tuned to the classical station and the smells of toast and orange peel surround us, and I don't even mind the pseudospouse thing that we seem to be doing here. Maybe it goes without saying, but the relationship of adult child and parent has not been an easy or obvious one for us. It keeps on shifting too.

He's calmer these days. We both are. He still listens to melancholy music, but lately I've not heard him go off on the subject of the Bush administration, which is probably for the best.

How glad he'll be when Courtney tells him that she's going to have a baby! I might be happier for him than I am for her. I can picture just how her announcement will light up his face, how his eyes will widen and shimmer even as he makes his stilted reply. ("Very good," he'll say, or maybe "Hurrah." As though he were not allowed to use the word *I*, to say *I am excited for you* or *I am so delighted to hear that*.)

I'm headed back to L.A. next week and in a good mood about it. From a distance the city seems full of possibilities, and though I know that once I'm back there it won't seem quite that way anymore, I'm treating this good mood like a house plant, trying to keep it alive, to do better than I've done with my other house plants. I already have some meetings set up—that is, I have one meeting on the books and some other tentative meetings. The scheduled one is with my manager's ex-wife, who recently joined one of the big talent agencies as a junior rep. I'm going to tell her about some new ideas I've had for Washington comedies.

On the table is a sugar dish that dates to my childhood, a white ceramic bowl that stands on legs, with lion's paws at the base, at least I always thought of them as lion's paws. They are paws of some sort. Two of them are chipped, but amazingly the bowl has never broken, and I consider swiping it—I've been scooping up tokens to take back to California with me, things I'll never need there, but for some reason I think it'd be nice to have this physics textbook, or that unfinished painting I made in tenth grade, or the sugar bowl, or snapshots I'll surely misplace: my sisters on the back deck, me on a hobby horse. I've been eyeing everything in the house. There's a part of me that wants to compress it all and bring it with me, even as there's another part of me that can't wait to escape one more time.

The phone rings again and Dad yells at it again, then picks it up. "Hi, Maggie," he says, and then, "How's New York? Getting much snow up there?" Here, it's one of those days when the atmosphere seems to have arranged itself in distinct thermal strata: slow, fat snow falls out of a cold sky, through layers of warmer air, and melts upon landing.

He returns to his chair with the phone, a strand of hair falling over his forehead, his lips parting to speak, his torso filling and emptying. Here's this body that has lately become a disruptive guest, hinting at an intention to leave before the party ends. His eyes range around the room and I can tell he's waiting for an opening in the conversation, so that he can inform Maggie of some random thing he read in the paper. He'll share that, then offer to hand over the phone to me. He reaches for a section of orange.

I can remember watching my dad like this when I was a kid, looking on as he did his projects around the house. I can remember thinking a thought that had the force of an inner mandate, which was that I would not, could not outlive him. Oh no. That just wasn't going to work.

Better that he be frozen, I felt. And so I tried to freeze him—we tried to freeze one another. As he wipes a bit of juice off his chin and tells Maggie about Sam's case, that same announcement sounds inside my head, as resounding as it is ordinary: I do not want to be here without him. No, no, I do not. I should tell him this, I think. Would it be so hard just to say it? Why can't we say these things to each other? Instead I get up from my chair on the pretext of taking a plate to the sink, and as I pass by him I reach for his shoulder and let my hand rest there. He tenses and then relaxes and then goes on talking.

ACKNOWLEDGMENTS

Thank you to everyone who read drafts of this book and offered advice and encouragement: Kirk Walsh, Dominic Smith, Amy Olsson, Alix Ohlin, Andrew Bujalski, Rebecca Beegle.

Thank you to the MacDowell Colony and the Ucross Foundation. Thank you to Amy Williams.

Thank you to everyone at FSG, most of all Emily Bell, for masterful edits delivered sunny-side up.

And thank you to Alexander and Irene, for coming along in the meantime.